The Hills Remember

The Hills Remember

The Complete Short Stories
of James Still

Edited by
Ted Olson

UNIVERSITY PRESS OF KENTUCKY

Scholarly publisher for the Commonwealth,
serving Bellarmine University, Berea College, Centre College of Kentucky, Eastern
Kentucky University, The Filson Historical Society, Georgetown College, Kentucky
Historical Society, Kentucky State University, Morehead State University, Murray
State University, Northern Kentucky University, Transylvania University, University of
Kentucky, University of Louisville, and Western Kentucky University.
All rights reserved.

Editorial and Sales Offices: The University Press of Kentucky
663 South Limestone Street, Lexington, Kentucky 40508-4008
www.kentuckypress.com

16 15 14 13 12   5 4 3 2 1

The stories "Snail Pie," "Pattern of a Man," "Maybird Upshaw," "The Sharp Tack," "Brother
to Methuselum," "The Scrape," and "Encounter on Keg Branch," from *Pattern of a Man
and Other Stories* by James Still, are reprinted by permission of Gnomon Press. Previously
published stories not included in *Pattern of a Man* are reprinted by permission of Teresa
Perry Reynolds. Previous publication information appears at the end of the book.

Library of Congress Cataloging-in-Publication Data

Still, James, 1906-2001.
    [Short stories]
    The hills remember : the complete short stories of James Still / edited by Ted Olson.
        p. cm.
    Includes bibliographical references.
    ISBN 978-0-8131-3623-3 (hardcover : alk. paper) — ISBN 978-0-8131-3641-7 (ebook)
    I. Olson, Ted. II. Title.
    PS3537.T5377 2012
    813'.52—dc23   2011046134

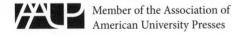

Contents

Introduction

Integrally associated with eastern Kentucky and often considered "the Dean of Appalachian Literature," James Still (born July 16, 1906) was reared in Chambers County, Alabama. He attended Lincoln Memorial University in Harrogate, Tennessee, then Vanderbilt University in Nashville, and finally the University of Illinois in Champaign-Urbana, before moving to eastern Kentucky during the early years of the Great Depression. Still would call the Cumberland Plateau home until his death on April 28, 2001. He lived primarily in Knott County, Kentucky—either at the Hindman Settlement School in Hindman or eleven miles from that town in a log house on Wolfpen Creek.

Despite a lingering public perception that Still was a hermetic figure who spent much of his adulthood living in one rural section of eastern Kentucky, Still was always a citizen of the world. He served three years in Africa and the Middle East with the U.S. Army Air Force during World War II, and he taught at Morehead State University during the 1960s. Later, based in Knott County, he gave frequent readings and talks across Kentucky and Appalachia and often traveled to other states and nations both to conduct research and to experience other places and cultures.

Although Still happened to live in and to write about eastern Kentucky, his literary evocations of a section of the Cumberland Plateau and of the folklife he witnessed therein constitute some of the finest writing about any region in the United States. Still worked in three genres, but while his mastery of poetry and the novel has been frequently lauded, his significant work in the short story form has been overlooked. This is unfortunate because some of Still's short stories are among his strongest literary efforts, and a few of his short stories are as fully realized and memorable as any in the history of American literature.

Publication History

Still's short stories have not been as recognized as his novel *River of Earth* (1940), or his posthumously published novel *Chinaberry* (2011), or his poetry, in part because the short story as a genre has often been overshadowed by other literary genres. One of the goals of this collection is to bring Still's achievement in short fiction into clearer focus for a new generation of readers. As editor, I hope that Still's stories will once again be read often and widely across the United States alongside works of short fiction by the acknowledged masters of the genre. (I say *once again* because in earlier decades Still's short stories were read across the United States, and a number of his stories were featured in major national periodicals and anthologies.) Reflecting a distinctive individual artistic voice and vision—thus bearing obvious thematic and stylistic differences from classic short fiction by such American authors as Poe, Hawthorne, Jewett, Hemingway, Welty, or Cheever—Still's finest stories exhibit the highest standards associated with the short story genre: structural concision; a striking, resonant use of language that approaches poetry; memorable presentation of an intriguing situation; and universality of meaning.

Another reason why Still's short stories have garnered less attention than his novels and his poetry is that Still himself frequently and unabashedly revised previously published stories to provide skeletal support for larger works; indeed, his novels *River of Earth* and *Sporty Creek: A Novel about an Appalachian Boyhood* (1977) were constructed from recycled short stories. Regardless of Still's artistic and economic incentives to reuse his short fiction in new contexts, I hope the readers of *The Hills Remember* will conclude that these stories stand on their own with considerable grace and power.

This book features all twenty-four short stories previously reissued in the three short story collections published during Still's lifetime: *On Troublesome Creek* (1941), *Pattern of a Man* (1976), and *The Run for the Elbertas* (1980). *The Hills Remember* also incorporates the original published versions of the twelve pieces of short fiction that Still grafted into *River of Earth*, as well as the story that first appeared in *Sporty Creek*. The additional sixteen short stories in *The Hills Remember* include six that heretofore have been published only in periodicals ("These Goodly Things," "Horse Doctor," "A Bell on Troublesome Creek," "Lost Brother," "Hit Like to 'a' Killed Me," and "Bare-Bones") and ten that have never been published in any form ("Sweet Asylum," "The Hills Remember," "Incident at Pigeon Roost," "Murder on Possum Trot Mountain," "On Pigeon Roost Creek,"

Introduction

"The Straight," "Sunstroke on Clabber Creek," "The Hay Sufferer," "Chicken Roost," and "From the Morgue").

Virtually all of the short stories that Still incorporated into his novels or that were brought together into book collections initially appeared in prestigious literary periodicals—such as the *Virginia Quarterly Review, Yale Review,* and *Prairie Schooner*—or in general interest periodicals, including some of the major magazines of Still's era (ten stories were published in the *Atlantic* and four in the *Saturday Evening Post*). Other Appalachian authors of his generation (such as Jesse Stuart) similarly placed short stories in national literary and popular periodicals, suggesting that Still's publishing history is not in itself exceptional. Nevertheless, given the number of Still short stories that first appeared in leading periodicals, it is not an exaggeration to say that during Still's early career influential literary figures nationwide were familiar with his work and that countless people nationwide at some point read one or more of his short stories. Beginning during the middle years of the Depression and continuing for a decade, Still possessed a national literary reputation, and his short stories played a major role in that achievement.

The first of the three collections of short stories to appear during Still's lifetime, *On Troublesome Creek* was the third of three books that he published with Viking Press, the other two being his poetry collection *Hounds on the Mountain* (1937) and his novel *River of Earth.* Collectively, the ten stories in *On Troublesome Creek*—and especially such memorable stories as "I Love My Rooster," "Journey to the Settlement" (later renamed "Journey to the Forks"), and "Brother to Methuselum"—marked Still's emergent mastery in the realm of short fiction. Indeed, the fact that *On Troublesome Creek* received considerably less critical attention than *River of Earth* had less to do with any negative response to Still's short fiction and more to do with the fate of most short story collections; even those from leading national publishers and even those featuring stories by major American authors (Hemingway, Fitzgerald, Faulkner, and Steinbeck, for instance) tended to generate fewer sales, and less critical response, than novels. *On Troublesome Creek* no doubt also suffered from the timing of its publication (the year of America's entering a second world war): by 1941, regionalist fiction was falling out of favor, as readers were seeking a literature that articulated overtly internationalist perspectives.

Still enlisted in the U.S. Army Air Force in 1942 and served in northern Africa and the Middle East through the end of the war. Although he was remarkably prolific during the decade before the war, Still's literary output inevitably declined during his stint as a soldier. Nonetheless, while serving overseas he wrote what is arguably his finest—and certainly his most frequently anthologized—short story, "Mrs. Razor."

After the war, Still endured a difficult return to civilian life, and he published comparatively little for several years. In the late 1940s and 1950s, however, he wrote some of his finest stories, including "The Nest," "A Ride on the Short Dog," and "The Run for the Elbertas." National recognition for Still's work in the short story genre followed, as several of his stories from this period were selected for inclusion in two prestigious short fiction anthologies: "Job's Tears," "So Large a Thing as Seven," "Bat Flight," and "The Proud Walkers" in *The O. Henry Memorial Award Prize Stories*, and "Mrs. Razor," "A Master Time," and "A Ride on the Short Dog" in *The Best American Short Stories*.

By the 1960s, Still's work was no longer commanding a national readership, but some individuals among a new generation of eastern Kentuckians began to recognize Still as a compelling figure, part modern-day Thoreauvian hermit, part citizen of the world. By then he was teaching composition and literature classes at Morehead State University and mentoring such younger writers as Wendell Berry and Gurney Norman, and Still was soon recognized regionally as a major pioneering figure from the Appalachian literary renaissance. Crucial to his emergence as a regional literary icon was a 1968 scholarly article published in the *Yale Review*, written by critic Dean Cadle, that article reassessed Still's work and drew wider attention to *River of Earth*. (Cadle's promotion of that novel led to its republication by the University Press of Kentucky in 1978.) Also significant was the 1976 appearance of *Pattern of a Man*, a collection of ten previously published short stories from throughout Still's career, edited by publisher and poet Jonathan Greene and issued by Greene's Gnomon Press. The timing of *Pattern of a Man* was uncanny, coinciding with the 1970s-era launch of Appalachian studies, a multidisciplinary academic field that offered a forum for discussion of Appalachian regional issues from scholarly, activist, and artistic perspectives. To people associated with that regional studies movement, Still's writings were a revelation—direct yet profound narratives reflecting the cultural values of Appalachia.

When Still died at the dawn of the new millennium, at age ninety-four, he had secured a lasting reputation among readers of Appalachian literature based on a relatively small number of literary works. Virtually everything that Still published during his lifetime, regardless of the genre, was set in eastern Kentucky, yet his works were stylistically distinctive and thematically universal, and his oeuvre has long deserved a broader readership beyond the hills and hollows of his adopted, and much beloved, home in eastern Kentucky.

Literary Legacy

In the decade after his death, Still stayed on people's minds, and his works remained in people's hearts. Two book-length collections featuring writings by a host of authors—*James Still: Critical Writings on the Dean of Appalachian Literature* (2007) and *James Still in Interviews, Oral Histories, and Memoirs* (2009)—offered personal and scholarly reflections upon Still's life and work, while scholar Claude Lafie Crum, in his 2007 monograph *River of Words: James Still's Literary Legacy,* contributed a sustained analysis of Still's literary achievement. Revival of interest in Still reached a crescendo in 2011 upon the posthumous publication of his final novel, *Chinaberry*. That novel, edited by author Silas House, is unique in Still's oeuvre for several reasons: *Chinaberry* is not only the major work from Still's later years, but it also stands as Still's lone major work to be situated outside of Appalachia (it is largely set in Texas). And unlike Still's other two novels, *Chinaberry* reflects a self-contained, unified vision rather than having been pieced together out of disparate narratives borrowed from previously published short stories.

As a volume, *The Hills Remember* constitutes the completion of a project I first discussed with James Still in 1999. In conversations that year, we talked about ways to disseminate his life's work to the widest possible readership, and Still gave me his blessing to oversee two book collections. The first book, *From the Mountain, From the Valley: New and Collected Poems,* was published by the University Press of Kentucky in 2001. While Still played a role in realizing that project (though he died just before that book was officially published), I had to complete this short-story collection without his input. I decided to employ the basic approach of *From the Mountain, From the Valley* as a template for this project, and I hope that *The Hills Remember* would make its author proud.

Editorial Matters

I have organized this compilation of Still's short stories chronologically, based either on the date of a story's first publication or, in the case of his never-before-published stories, on my best estimate of the approximate time of composition. Unfortunately, Still's typed short story manuscripts generally lack typed or handwritten information regarding the specific date of composition or revision, but a few of the never-before-published stories possess one clue as to their relative time of composition: Still's current return address typed in the upper left corner of the page—in some cases Alabama and in other cases Kentucky. The task of constructing a chronology of Still's short stories benefitted greatly from the late Terry Cornett's helpful (if incomplete and occasionally inaccurate) James Still bibliography; the publications list I incorporate as an appendix in this book is intended to provide the fullest possible representation of Still's publication history in the short-story genre. While twelve short stories previously published in periodicals were subsequently reworked into *River of Earth*, I include the earlier versions so that readers today can appreciate the narratives in the same way that Still's contemporaries first read them, months or in some cases years before the novel appeared.

Eight of the ten short stories published here for the first time—as well as the story "Bare-Bones," which was first published in 2010 as part of a promotional piece published in *Appalachian Heritage* to announce this collection of Still's short stories and which is essentially a longer, "alternate" version of the published Still story "One Leg Gone to Judgment"—previously existed as manuscripts housed among the James Still Papers held at the University of Kentucky Special Collections. The other two never-before-published Still stories included here, "Chicken Roost" and "From the Morgue," were found by Still's daughter, Teresa Perry Reynolds, in manuscript form among the various Still papers not yet transferred to a formal archive. In transcribing the never-before-published short stories, I made every effort to represent Still's textual intentions. In a few cases, Still wrote notes directly on the manuscripts indicating that he considered them the most complete drafts of the stories, and I used such drafts when transcribing those short stories. Most of the never-before-published stories, though, exist in only one extant draft, obviously necessitating the use of those single sources as definitive texts. Still frequently included both handwritten commentary and textual adjustments on otherwise typed manuscripts, and in a few instances I deduced handwritten words or phrases that were undecipherable on manuscript pages.

My overarching assumption in selecting definitive texts of Still's previously published short stories was that Still himself preferred the last-published version of each story, because he had guided that version of that particular story through multiple editorial processes over the years. (He left no instructions voicing discontent with the last-published versions of any of his short stories.) While a number of Still's short fictional pieces were subsequently incorporated into novels, I included those original pieces in this collection because Still himself endeavored to ensure that they were initially published as short stories. (This seems to be supported by the fact that three of the pieces that were incorporated into *River of Earth*—"Job's Tears," "So Large a Thing as Seven," and "Bat Flight"—had previously been published independently in major literary periodicals as well as reprinted in the prestigious *O. Henry Memorial Award Prize Stories* series.) This collection features versions of two short stories taken directly from the text for Still's *Sporty Creek*—"The Force Put" and "Plank Town"—in part because there were not any previously published periodical versions of those stories ("The Force Put" originally appeared in *River of Earth*) and also because within the emphatically episodic structure of *Sporty Creek* those two story texts worked essentially as stand-alone narratives.

In transcribing the short stories for inclusion in *The Hills Remember*, I let stand Still's many uses of dialectal speech, though I attempted to standardize orthographic representations of certain dialectal words and phrases across this volume when such standardization did not adversely affect a story's aesthetic integrity and rhythmic flow. Readers should note that Still's short stories received often dramatically different editorial treatment from various editors over the years, and absolute standardization of his distinctive literary rendering of Appalachian dialectal speech across such a large body of stories was neither possible nor advisable, given the fact that each of Still's stories was constructed out of a singular blending of formal and informal stylistic elements. I have corrected all obvious spelling or grammatical errors that appeared in the last-published versions of these stories.

And what does the chronological arrangement reveal about Still's trajectory as a crafter of short fiction? The early stories (from the 1930s to 1941) reflect Still's discovery of his primary subject matter—the people and folk culture he encountered in and around his adopted eastern Kentucky home. During this period, Still was experimenting with using Appalachian dialect, and thus his Depression-era short stories (and accordingly *River of Earth*) are infused with his brilliant literary approximation of Appalachian speech. Still's wartime and postwar short stories exhibit a more direct narrative style, employing a sparer approach to language and a more restrained use of dialect. Noteworthy for their acuity of psychological vision, these later stories examine complex characters in tightly structured narratives, and during this latter period Still proved his mastery of writing short fiction from tragic as well as comic perspectives.

Still's short stories constitute the connecting link between his poetry, the genre he investigated earliest and that provided him with a form for experimenting with language, and his novels, which granted him the opportunity to assess the full, contextualized life of a character or a family. His short stories expanded upon the strengths of his poems and ultimately encouraged his imagination to explore the extended narrative novel form. In his haunting and resonant short stories, Still distilled his visions and his values into minimalist landscapes. Indeed, to many readers his short stories seem closer to outpourings from the oral tradition than to conventional, self-consciously composed "literary works." They stand out as evocative and timeless yet remarkably simple tales and legends from the soul of Appalachia.

Please visit *The Hills Remember* book page at www.kentuckypress.com for a glossary of dialectical words and phrases, quotations, photographs, audio clips, and more information about the life and works of James Still.

Sweet Asylum

The blooming of the late Elberta peach trees on the east side of the house and the disappearance of Caesar Middleton's winter growth of beard were simultaneous declarations of spring's triumph over late frost and recurring quinsy—a sign more reliable than the first mockingbird, or the sudden vapid lengthening of Blue Jonny's weather string.

Middleton's customary ritual, the careful grooming of his beard into a masterpiece of tonsorial workmanship, was foregone this April morning. He came downstairs at five-thirty for his usual breakfast, a ration of white meat fried in buttermilk batter, hot biscuit, and coffee. After the third cup of the viscous black liquid from Aunt Sage's coffee pot, he tapped the pewter saltcellar impatiently with his spoon. Aunt Sage hurried in from the kitchen, wiping the sticky remnants of ribbon cane syrup from her purple lips as she came.

"No more coffee in the mustache cup," Middleton commanded. The sharp edge of an early awakening was in his voice. Aunt Sage jerked her head affirmatively, the labyrinthian maze of her braided hair raising for a moment like a mat puffed out by the wind as she bent to take his plate away, and settling again on her head with the orderliness of black honeycomb.

"Take a kettle of hot water upstairs for my shaving," he continued when sufficient time had elapsed for a scrupulous mental recording of his first demand, "and tell Blue Jonny to bridle the bay mare." He slid his chair back noisily over the stained oak floor. Standing beside the table, he occupied himself for a moment with a toothpick, jerking it back and forth between pursed lips in a series of nervous jabs, the edge of his dental plate clicking against the sliver of wood.

He was aware suddenly as he dropped the toothpick into the mustache cup of a poignant aloneness, the emptiness of the three-leaved table, the elegiac air of the paneled room, the smoky-faced clock over the china closet. But this sentimental eruption was only momentary, a throwback to the late nineties when his wife and three sons sat here in this room with him, talking in conversational vagaries. He could not remember one sentence, preserved in its entirety, that was uttered here during all those years. His wife had died, his sons had grown out of his home and influence, and now there remained only the level atmosphere of commonplaceness marked with a cenotaph of chairs and a table. The white lightning of nerves and opinions had not struck in those days.

He found his shaving mug in the cupboard. A vague recollection of some attached sentiment, a birthday or a holiday gift, irritated him. Grasping it by the thick porcelain handle, he marched up the stairs, depositing it with a clatter on the washstand.

A minute examination of his beard awakened him to a dismal reality that the graying strands had hastened a majority over the red since September. Another year and the sneaking frost of his sixty-five years will have left white and chastened the last bright relic of youth: he would be one with the autumnal cotton fields, the white shroud of pear blossoms beside the smokehouse.

As the beard fell away from his face before the measured sweeps of the blue steel razor, his brain fomented rebellion. Old age, impotence, enough! Senility did not fit into the fixed canons of his judgment. Time would come, he saw plainly, when he must make a frank acceptance of nature and its unfathomable ways or be lost in the morass of accumulating years. This stark loneliness that pinched his soul with the increasing years was mastering him of late. He needed someone to pluck him out of it. The new agrarianism, the young generation of planters knocking their heads together for commercial sport, were too clearly pointing out his fogginess and the inescapable fact that he belonged to a past generation of economic recklessness.

In the grosser areas of his thinking there were fresh and unforgettable memories of mortgages, notes, endless duns. During the nine-year transition from forty-cent to seven-cent spot cotton, he had not sold a bale, voluntarily joining the ranks of the land poor. There were ninety-six bales stored in the field barn, held there by the determination to get fifteen cents or let it rot where it was. Many the time during these intervening years his voice had become momentarily husky with pride in his stubbornness; now, as he thought of it, he doubted the common sense of his judgment. His rope of sand was crumbling.

Gentility was no longer a sweet asylum, a wall between himself and crass materialism. Pride seemed rather puny now with debts that were more pressing this spring than he had known before. There were few merchants at Christopher he did not owe, and who were not inspired by the one-cent rise in cotton with a new urgency to collect.

He winced at his thoughts, and at the steady pull of the razor. A drop of blood upon his cheek suddenly cleared his mind for more intent concentration upon his shaving and lent a greater flexibility to his jaws as he twisted them into grotesque shapes so that the razor might pass over an unwrinkled surface.

An hour later Middleton came out into the front yard and waited by the green trellis of Lady Penzance roses until Blue Jonny brought the mare from the lot. The eagerness of new awakening life, the mouse-eared leaves on the water oaks, and the subtle sweetness of plum blossoms stirred him immeasurably. Something as miraculous as the sap that stirs the oak seemed to swell in his blood. He sprang into the saddle, secretly marveling at his unexpected litheness. The pendulum had truly swung backwards!

Shortly before ten o'clock Middleton passed the city limit post of the county seat. Squatty bungalows, salmon-tinted stucco dwellings, architectural mushrooms outside the aristocratic walls of Christopher proper, crowded the red clay banks above the road. When the quiet magnolia-shaded avenues were reached, he allowed the bay mare to fall into a slow walk, arranged his black tie, and tilted his faun-gray hat to a more personable angle.

The home of the late Judge Stroud, sitting obliquely at the corner of Waverly and Tillers avenues, came into view beneath the ancient trees. Middleton could see the copper-colored bricks through the leafless tangle of ivy flowing up to the mansard roof. White voile curtains fluttered out of the windows fronting on the wide veranda.

Mrs. Stroud was not in sight, a fact that sorely disappointed him. There was an air of lifelessness about the place; the ivy on the walls and the crepe myrtle had not yet joined in the green renascence of spring. It seemed that they only waited for her to appear and reanimate them with her benign smile that was more of June, he remembered, than of April. Forty years ago he had known her as Lala Radcliff, and there had been that gentle understanding between them that four decades had failed to thoroughly erase. Her father had favored a lawyer, a man after his own profession and heart rather than a gentleman farmer, and she had not disappointed him. Those were the days of paternal obedience, courage, and self-abnegation.

There on his jogging mare, one of those rare moments of understanding came to him. The white light of decision emerged from some subcutaneous quality of his reasoning, laying his way clear and tearing away the veil of years of less inspired reasoning and opinions. This day he would sell his cotton, whatever the price, lift the first mortgage off the homeplace, and clear up the most irritating debts. In the early afternoon he would visit Lala. Forty years could not have made any great difference; love springs eternal, passion flows as infinitely as rivers to the sea, nothing is irrevocable.

There were other considerations that kept intruding into his thinking quite apart from the satisfactions of refurbished love. Was it his subtle business acumen working after a quarter of a century of decadence? Before his death Judge Stroud held the second mortgage on the Middleton homeplace. That he had not foreclosed prior to his toppling from the judge's rostrum into his grave was due to the faith of the first mortgage holders. The Judge's entire estate had gone to his wife. Lala now held that second mortgage, a scrap of paper so innocent, yet so potent in its barefaced power.

Middleton barely glanced at the Stroud house as he passed, a habit achieved since the second mortgage had gone to rest under its eaves. He knew Lala was there, sewing perhaps; then it occurred to him that he had never seen Lala do anything except smile exquisitely, lean gracefully in doorways and hold her beautiful hands. Forty years ago Lala's chief care had been the protection and nourishment of her flowerlike beauty. All other feminine concerns were vulgar beside this one splendid desire to preserve that which no other young lady in Christopher possessed in such abundance and delicacy.

Forty years had not gone without some withering effect, but time had laid its hand lightly upon her with increasing gentility and mellowness. She had become less willowlike and fastidious in person, more studied and even-tempered in manner. These were observations he had made eight years ago, before Judge Stroud's death; since, she had buried herself behind the brick masonry of her home, no longer attending the social functions or riding out into the country in her tasseled carriage. He heard of her rarely now.

Middleton rode unhurriedly into the square, the fort of his creditors whose half-cloistral business houses faced it on four sides. He noticed with mild surprise that a retrenching county government had desecrated the first floor of the courthouse with the office of a loan company and a barber shop since he had last been there. There was no less dignity in his arrival because the square was practically deserted, as might be expected on a Wednesday, or for reasons of his late indulgence in a mental somersault. He hitched the mare to one of the posts swarming with sparrows on the south side and made his way through dust shoe-mouth deep to the cracked pavement.

Miss Phearing thrust her waspish head out of the door of the Ladies Wear Shoppe and smiled professionally.

"Nice day," she beamed as he came up. Middleton raised his hat solemnly.

"We could do with some rain," he said, stamping his feet to clear the dust from his shoes. With that he passed on. Ordinarily he would have chatted with Miss Phearing for at least a half hour, remembering as she poured out meticulous details about nothing in particular, that her state of perpetual eligibility had gone unchallenged these twenty years. This day more weighty matters claimed his attention.

At the entrance to the house of Rucker S. Winningham, cotton buyers and dealers in tenant necessities, salt, meat, lard and flour, he paused to read the final ginners report for the past season. *Alabama, 930,000 bales. Cotton quotation, April 6th, Spot Cotton 7 cents.* The one-cent gain still held. Turning into the store he was halted by a lusty slap on the back. It was Rogan, the county tax assessor.

"Mighty glad you came into town today," Rogan said.

Middleton looked with sudden contempt at this suspected display of office-holding authority.

"Would have called you on the phone last night," Rogan went on, "but you know there ain't no privacy on the county line."

"Now Mr. Rogan," Middleton began firmly, "if it concerns taxes, I'll be seeing you in your office before I leave town today."

Rogan smiled damply. "It ain't that exactly," he said. "I've got an idea where I can help you."

"Help me?" Middleton was incredulous. "I've almost forgotten about you being up for reelection. That's a standing order with you, Rogan. The tax assessor's office hasn't been out of your family in my memory."

"Let's go where we can talk," Rogan said.

They went inside among the sacks of cottonseed hulls.

"There ain't no getting around me wanting your vote," Rogan began, "but I ain't asking you for nothing. Ain't I always been careful when I assess your property? Live and let live, that's me. But what I specially wanted to tell you was what the Christopher Business Men's Club decided on yesterday. There are fifty-two members and everyone is going to buy from one to ten bales of cotton from the farmers at twelve cents a pound. That's five cents more than market price. Naturally they expect to get most of it back on debts. Still they'll be helping out in a pinch."

"Where do I come in?" Middleton asked impatiently. Rogan rubbed his palms together until they rasped like dry leather.

"I'm going to buy ten bales off you, that is, if you'll come across with a promise to sort of use your influence in the election next August. The idea of the cotton buying was to help the small farmer, the ones that raise just a couple of bales a year and stay hog-tied half the time. You've got all the cotton you've raised in ten years, but I know the traces ain't pulling so easy. You ain't to let anybody know I bought it off'en you, though."

"That sounds like sense to me," Middleton warmed.

"I could manage more than that if you'd sort of strain yourself for me in Beat Four." Rogan spoke in deep earnestness. His face tightened into a mass of threadlike wrinkles.

"Could you rid me of twenty or thirty?" Middleton was smiling cannily.

"Ten is all I can swing on my own hook," Rogan said regretfully, "still I think I can work it around so the other club members will buy some from you. At least forty bales, if you'll promise to carry Beat Four for me."

"How would you work that," Middleton asked pointedly.

Rogan's hands were working with a sort of visionary anticipation.

"I'll ask about a dozen merchants," he said, "the ones you owe. Each one might buy several bales from you. My job does give me a little persuasive influence. They'll buy if I ask them to special. They'll think they are the only ones buying from you. And we'll do it on the quiet."

Middleton leaned back against the sacks of hulls. "I've got ninety-four bales in my field barn," he said. "If you'll sell every bale of it, Beat Four will go ninety percent for you. You know the people are pretty near going to clean out that courthouse this time. Nothing short of a miracle can keep you in office. Beat Four votes would go a long way."

Rogan stumbled to his feet. "Meet me at my office about three o'clock this afternoon," he said, visibly moved. Little quivers of excitement were disturbing the shallow wrinkles on his face. It was powder gray, the color of worn earth.

The courthouse clock had already struck four when Middleton rode out of the square toward Waverly Avenue. The fortuitous deal with Rogan had resulted in particular advantages for both. The whole of his ninety-five bales had been placed among the merchants. They would be paid for on delivery at twelve cents a pound; his debts would be wiped out and the first mortgage on the homeplace taken care of. The second mortgage holder, Lala Stroud, now alone remained to be bargained with, a renewal of affections forty years removed. These years between must be neutralized with the magic chalices of the new season, a new beginning. What afterglow of sentimentality remained must be rekindled into a steady flame.

The bay mare was glad to be moving again. She quivered with expectancy of the alfalfa hay waiting in her stable, shook her head impatiently with her master's unhurried manner, and quickened her pace only to have him tighten the bridle.

Middleton was suddenly aroused from his thoughts by a clatter of hoofs. A moment later a negro came into sight riding furiously down Cusseta Row, his overall jacket flowing behind him. The bay mare whinnied. It was Blue Jonny on Tess. Middleton waited until he came up. Blue Jonny was breathless and could hardly speak.

"Yore barn, Mister Caesar, yore barn done burned to the ground," he blurted.

"Which one?" The words came thickly from Middleton's lips.

"The field barn, Mister Caesar, the one with yore cotton in it. All of it done burned." Blue Jonny was blubbering through his tears and sweat.

Middleton did not move for a moment. A pallor, white as death, swept over his face. Vague noises trumpeted in his temples.

Slowly he gathered up the reins and turned into Waverly Avenue. He felt an impulse to ride swiftly down the road toward the homeplace, but he checked himself. Nothing could be done there now. He left Blue Jonny with the horses in front of the Stroud house and walked up the narrow graveled lane. One thought clung tenaciously in Middleton's mind. Only Lala Stroud could save him from utter ruin. There must be no wavering now; he must marry Lala and with her help salvage his property.

He lifted the knocker mechanically and struck it against the brass receiver. The metallic sound echoed through the house. Presently there was a rustle inside the door, and a young woman wearing a brown duster opened it warily. There was a pinched curiosity in her face.

"Is Mrs. Stroud in?" Middleton wondered at the calmness of his voice. The woman in the duster drew back into the hallway. Middleton almost expected the door to be closed in his face. She sniffed audibly and dabbed the corner of the duster in her eyes.

"Miss Lala passed away two weeks ago," she whispered huskily.

The Hills Remember

"Ole Aus has been shot!"

These strange words poured down into Rangey, the hill-town county seat. Old Aus Hanley was dying on the left bank of Troublesome Creek with a load of buckshot in his back. Men shouted the news hurrying to their stables. The courtroom was suddenly empty of tobacco-chewing spectators, jury, and judge. The dry creek bed became a stampede of men on mules and horses, some riding bareback, threshing their mounts with heel and spur.

Sheriff Byson, his black hat slanted against the wind and the ends of his red mustache curled toward his ears, called to a deputy: "Who done it?" The deputy did not answer, merely slapped his horse furiously with the palm of his right hand. Old Aus Hanley, meanest man on Troublesome—aye on God's green earth—was going to die. Old Aus was going to lay back in his own blood—the man who had a graveyard all his own across Stormspur filled with men he had killed. The fox of the Kentucky hills had met the bullet God molded for him the day he was born.

Aus Hanley lay spraddle-legged upon the powdery sand, his head resting against a saddle-seat. Red stains spread out from a shapeless hat crushed against his side where the charge had come out. His face, swathed in a week's growth of beard, was unwrinkled with any evidence of pain, but his eyes, black and burning, had that look of quizzical surprise seen in the eyes of a startled doe.

In a half hour they were all there; all of Rangey to the last man and child stood in a semicircle about the wounded man; all who lived for a mile up the Left Hand Fork and the Right Hand Fork of Troublesome Creek were there staring in a sort of reverent awe at the man they feared and admired. They had never thought it would come to this: Aus Hanley, with eleven notches in his gun, lying with his back on the ground. Mixed with the crowd were the kin of those he had slain, looking bewildered in the revenge they had not shared.

None of them would have shot Aus Hanley in the back. It would have been like bedding a rabbit, or shooting a fox after it had gnawed a foot off to escape a trap.

Luke Storr had not tried to escape after the shooting. Standing on a jut of rock high above the creek bed, he had fired toward the broad back of Hanley as he passed. When Hanley tumbled to the ground he crept down the embankment and took his six-shooters. Now as he stood beside the sheriff, whose belt curved awkwardly with Hanley's pistols, his trembling hands were trussed in handcuffs, and his thin face pale and twitching. Why he had shot Hanley in such a cowardly manner was not evident in his watery, red eyes. But there was a stink of green sugar-top on his breath.

Aus Hanley was gradually getting weaker. The patch of red spread out into the sand beside his body. He crushed the hat tighter against his side. A faint sallowness was beginning to show beneath his beard and the wind-tan. The sheriff and judge had offered to plug the wound but he waved them back without a word. Old Aus would make no compromise at this late hour with the law and justice. They thought if Old Doc Beardsley was there something might be done, but Doc was off on Pushback with a case of slow fever and might not be in for days. Words had been sent to Hanley's wife and sons. It would be hours before the news could get across Hog Shoulder, down Squabble Creek, and up Laurel Fork and the Hanley family could urge their nags to the Forks of Troublesome.

Hanley stared into the crowd before him, looking into each face, examining it minutely as though he hoped to carry away a deathless impression of it. Presently his burning eyes fell on Luke Storr standing beside the sheriff. His eyes roved from Luke's new brogans to his meal-yellow face, and there they rested, became calm and peaceful. Old Aus Hanley was sizing up the man who had done him to death.

Luke shuffled his feet nervously in the sand and tried to push into the crowd, but the sheriff thrust him back in front. His lips trembled and he bit them furiously. The bolstering courage of the sugar-top was wearing thin. Now he was thinking of Old Aus's sons, Jabe and Pridemore. They would avenge their father, shoot him through the jail window the minute they galloped into

Rangey. Nobody would try to stop them. Nobody ever tried to stop a Hanley from doing anything. The weight of his conviction bore upon him through his addled senses, and his knees felt brittle as dry canes.

Hanley cleared his throat and spat upon the ground. "Brang Luke over hyar, Byson," he said. His husky voice was low and collected.

The sheriff pushed Luke forward to where Hanley lay.

"I didn't figger to be killt by a lousy skunk-cat," Hanley said. There was no emotion in his voice.

Luke began to snivel. "I was drunk. I wasn't aiming to do it. . . ."

Hanley spoke again. "They was some who might have shot me in good rights, but I ain't never had no trouble with you, nor any of yore kin."

Luke was not afraid of Aus Hanley now. He feared only the inevitable revenge that Jabe and Pridemore would deal out before the sun-ball dropped behind the mountains. He fell upon his knees in the sand beside Hanley and began to beg.

"Aus, fer God's sake tell 'em hyar to tell yore folks I didn't mean to do it. I was drunk. I didn't know what I was doing."

Hanley shook his head slowly as if in great pain, drew his hand from the wound and stretched his arms until they were straight and stiff as boards. Anyone could see he couldn't last much longer. Then he relaxed and his lips moved.

"My sons ain't a-goin' to kill you, Luke. I ain't wanting them to follow in their old poppy's way o' life." His voice trailed off thin and wistful. "Aus Hanley ain't never shot no man in the back. I ain't figgering these hyar hills whar I was born and raised is going to forget that."

Suddenly Hanley's left arm shot out with the swiftness of a catamount's paw, caught Luke across the small of the back, and drew him downward. His right arm lunged a single driving stroke toward Luke's breast. The sheriff, caught for a moment off his guard, recovered and jerked Luke backward. Luke's legs threshed about for a moment and were still. The handle of a Barlow knife protruded at an angle from his breast. When the startled crowd thought to look again at old Aus, his eyes were glassy and unseeing.

Incident at Pigeon Roost

Cotton Wallin's face shone like black ivory in the straw-yellow glow of the oil lamp. Perspiration crowded out of the crinkly mat of his graying hair and glistened in oily drops on his forehead. He sat motionless beside his daughter's bed, watching for a sign from her purple lips. Her half-closed eyelids were drawn down like dark scallops. For an hour there had been no recognition of suffering in her face, but as he watched, her left hand lifted from the pillow and began to work over the Pine Bloom quilt, her bloodless fingers pulling at the loose frays of wool. A murmur of voices hummed in the room like the swarming of wild bees.

"She's pickin' at the kivers."

Cotton heard the words as through a mist. His blood-shot eyes ran up the wall plastered with pages from a mail order catalog to the book lying on the mantle. They rested there a moment, then lifted higher to the shotgun hanging on a willow rack.

"If'n Lou Cindy dies, I'll kill Jubal." The words trembled in Cotton's throat. It was Jubal's fault, he knew. Lou Cindy hadn't gone traipsing around with his kind.

A breath of cool night air penetrated the heavy odor of camphor and warm bodies, rippling the cheesecloth curtains at the front window. A dust of ashes sifted along the floor from the cold hearth. Someone had opened the door.

Jubal stood in the open doorway, his head bent slightly beneath the low sill. He strode into the room and stood beside the bed. Cotton lifted his head mechanically. Lou Cindy lay so still it seemed that she no longer lived.

Jubal cleared his throat huskily. "I'm a-goin' ter see she don't want fer nothin'," he said, moved for the moment with a compassion he had not anticipated.

Cotton stared out of the window. A bluebottle fly buzzed on the pane. He watched its wings beat futilely against the foggy glass.

"I'll be doin' the right thang," Jubal continued. "Don't yawl be worryin' none 'bout me."

Cotton made no answer. Jubal glanced resentfully at him and shuffled out of the room, leaving the door open wide behind him.

Jubal felt better outside. A cool wind blew across Pigeon Roost Swamp, rattling the dead burs in the cotton fields. The moon shone clear and white. Darkness lurked only under the chinaberry trees and the water oaks. Out by the barn, two young men were wrestling on a pile of alfalfa hay. Others sat watching on bales of cotton stacked against the lot fence. He heard their amused grunting and easy laughter.

"G'won, Luke, hold 'em whar you got 'em."

"Ketch 'em by his britches, Pike, en throw 'em over yer haid."

Their merriment was like a dash of cold water in Jubal's face, washing the tenseness and poignancy of the sickroom from his mind. He walked eagerly toward them.

The wrestlers broke as he came up.

"I'll rassle anybody here," he said, unbuttoning his shirt and tossing it on the hay. He playfully drew the muscles of his arms and shoulders until they bulged like knots on a towline. No one offered to try him.

"Take on any two of yer," he said. His thick lips curled contemptuously at their cowardice. The men who had been wrestling nudged each other.

"G'won, take 'em on," Luke urged.

"Naw you, you kin do better'n me," Pike said.

Jubal snatched up his shirt in disgust.

"Reckon you could knock down a bale of cotton wid yer shoulder?" Luke asked sarcastically.

"Gimme a lief?" Jubal grinned.

A bale of cotton was dragged from the pile and set on end. Jubal walked away from it a few yards, swung around quickly, and ran back, striking it near the center with his shoulder. The bale toppled over on its side. It was set up again. Only Pike succeeded in upsetting it, as Jubal had done.

"D'yer reckon you could butt it down with yer haid?" Luke asked, angry that he had not done as well as Jubal and Pike.

21

"Mought and I mought'n," Jubal said. "Pike kin have first try."

Pike held his head low and lurched against the bale. It did not budge. Jubal measured off five steps, crouched, and sprang toward it with all his force, striking it higher than he had intended. It rocked unsteadily but did not fall.

Waiting a moment to recover his wind, Jubal measured off ten steps. He started from a half-kneeling position, digging his toes into the ground and gaining momentum with each stride. Nearing the bale he stiffened his neck and pressed his chin against his chest. As he struck the bale there was a sharp snap, as though a splinter had been broken with the head of an axe. The bale tumbled on its side. Jubal lay still upon the ground with his face turned toward the barn. His eyes were glassy and unseeing in the moonlight.

The men crowded about him. "Done went and broke his neck," Luke said. They were dazed with the wonder of it.

Suddenly they were aware of an unusual stirring in Cotton Wallin's house. Moans and loud cries drifted across the lot. One voice rose tremulously above the others. "Oh Lord, she's done gone, she's been tuk away." Someone began singing there and the moaning merged with the hymn.

Lord, Lord, waitin' on the shore,
Waitin' fer the boat ter Gloryland,
Lord, Lord, waitin' at the gate,
Waitin' fer to enter the Gloryland.

The door of the house swung open. Cotton Wallin came down the steps with a shotgun in his hands. He saw the men standing in the moonlight near the lot fence and walked toward them. They faced him as he came up.

"Whar's Jubal at?" he asked hoarsely.

Murder on Possum Trot Mountain

It was pine-blank murder. There was no getting 'round that. And it was about as simple a piece o' business that been done on Caney Creek from the mouth to the head in many a sweet day. But there always something that lets the coon out of the trap. A fellow does a grain o' something that goes agin' him, or draps a careless word that sets the woods afire with deputy sheriffs.

When Clayt Darrow first mentioned it to me, I tells him he's a damn fool right off. If you want to kill a man you better put blinders even on the nag you're riding.

Clayt reminds me of a dog trying to lay down on shuck. He'd been trying to make up his mind to it a long time, but he ain't got the nerve. He knows I ain't been packing no particular brotherly love for Sibo Bonner since my foxhound tuk up with him six months ago. That is, I hear tell my dog is at his place, though I ain't sot eyes on him and I've watched by the hour from the top of the mountain. Anyway my pap didn't like his pap, and my grandpap and his grandpap swapped a couple o' shots at each other way back. I always reckoned Sibo was a rattlesnake.

I knowed Clayt would make up his mind to it sooner or later. Me and Clayt had been running 'round together nigh on ten years, ever since we was little scrappers. We'd done lots o' meanness. Once we got us a hollow log and stretched a strip o' dried bull's hide over it and sawed on it with a bow made out of a hickory limb. You could have heard that noise ten miles on a cold night, and it sounded like a passel o' wildcats screaming and tearing each other's eyeballs out. The cattle all over the country jumped the fences and went flying the other way; the horses and mules kicked the barn doors down and tuk out after them. Well, we done more thangs than I could tell in a full moon, but we never done a thang that we got by with. Clayt always give us away. He got too tickled over something we'd done. He'd look guilty as the devil for a month after we'd pulled a little meanness.

Me and Clayt had done a lot o' thangs together but we ain't never killed a man. We's cut saddles off of horses hitched at the church-house at night just for puore cussedness; we'd tuk boards out o' swinging bridges and watched somebody drop through to the creek. I reckon we done about everything mean thar is to do on this green airth. But you could depend on Clayt letting it out someway. Afore long I stopped running with Clayt. I was gitting sort o' tired rotting out six-months terms in jail because Clayt couldn't keep his face straight and his tongue civil.

When Clayt named it to me about killing Sibo Bonner I laughed plumb in his face. He says I got a yellow streak running down my back wider than a handsaw. Then he names my hound dog to me Sibo had fetched off; then he says he'd be willing to bet me a war pension, if he had one, that Sibo would never let me git in shouting distance o' Ransey. And I knowed my chances o' sparking Ransey was pore as a mare's skeleton when the buzzards got through with it.

Clayt says he'll split that bunch o' money Sibo is packing since he sold that bunch o' timber on Big Branch with me. I kin have my foxhound back, and I'll be setting pretty as a beagle with Ransey.

I tells Clayt he's a damn fool if he thinks I'm a-going to get messed up with him in any sort o' scrape. I ain't never had a mind to kill nobody. It made me kind of woozy down in the stomach when I thought about pinting a gun at a fellow when he ain't expecting it and sending a slug o' lead into his heart. But I knowed Clayt was a-going to do it. He got sort of franzied at first, but with about four or five shots o' rotgut he'd put a case o' dynamite under the courthouse if it entered his mind he wanted to do it.

No amount of talking would have got me into that mess but I listened to how he was a-going to do it. I reckon it was slick because it was so simple. He was going to wade up Caney for a mile, blow his fox horn outside Sibo's house, and when he came out take him between the eyes with his gun. Then he'd wade back down the creek. Clayt had been more careful about his tracks than anything else, saying a fellow couldn't make tracks on a streak o' water, which was right nigh the truth.

We argued about where it would be best to take Sibo. I allowed behind the ear was the best place, just like you would a shoat at hog-killing time, but Clayt thought different. Between the eyes he says is the best place, and I got to reckoning if it was his killing he'd have the right to do it the way he wanted to.

As the night come 'round for Clayt to do his business I got powerful uneasy. I wanted to let Sibo know somehow, but I figured I better keep my mouth out o' Clayt's doings.

Well, Clayt done it just like he said he was a-going to. I heard it first thing the next morning and I tuk out for town. It's a pretty good thing to be 'round and let folks see how clear your conscience is after such doings. And instead o' going the shortcut through the gap I tuk right down Caney way, square by Sibo's homeseat.

When I come in sight thar was a powerful big crowd thar, but somehow I didn't feel any longing to see Sibo in the fix he was in. As I come to the edge of the yard where it tetched the creek, Ransey come running down to stop me. Her eyes were red as beet pickles from crying, but she had her chin up, and I reckon she was prettier then than ever I seed her. I felt plumb sorry for her, and begin to wish I'd tipped her ole man off.

"Pap has a hound dog in the cow stall that somebody says belongs to you. He's had him for nigh three weeks and ain't been able to find out who he belongs to. He's been a-hanging 'round."

I begin to git sorrier than ever. It would tetch a body's soul to see Ransey looking like that. I told her I was powerful sorry to hear about her pa. Then I asks her where he was shot at, in the forehead or behind the ear? I reckon I must have looked funny the minute I said that. I could have bit my tongue square off. She didn't say nothing for a minute; then all of a sudden she screamed. You could have heard her a mile.

These Goodly Things

"It's a sight on this green airth what that woman has done to this hollow," Granny Henderson said, brushing a wisp of gray hair back neatly with a wrinkled hand and lifting her eyes toward the mountains rising before her cabin door. "Ain't nary woman here in these Kentucky hills got the git up and go like Mrs. Keyes. She puore lives her religion."

I drained the glass of spring-cooled buttermilk Granny Henderson had just brought me and placed it upon the window sill. "Is Mrs. Keyes a mountain-bred woman?" I asked.

"Mrs. Keyes is furrin to these parts," she said, settling herself in the willow rocker to tell me the whole story. "She come from somewhar outside the hills to teach a school here on the Left Hand Fork of Troublesome Creek nigh on ten years ago and she tuk right to us people, married her a man here and settled down jist like one o' us. We thought she'd be high falutin' at first but she's the most humblest o' God's creatures. First thing we know she's settin' up waitin' on Lige Jones's wife, Lucy, and nussed her through a case o' typhoid fever and nary another one of the family had it. Mrs. Keyes is always talkin' about something called 'sanitation,' meanin' by that keepin' everything clean and biled out 'round sick folks. When Lucy got well, we knowed straight off the hand o' the Lord was over her heart, and when she started out gittin' everybody 'noculated she didn't meet no argument like she would if she hadn't already worked a cuore.

"Next thing we knowed diphtheria broke out and she had a doctor come and he stuck some needles in all the children and was the last we heard o' the chokin' disease. Seems like thar warn't no stoppin' her though. She gethered up all the children with the eye disease and sont 'um on to the trachoma hospital. She said the govermint looked out after such things.

"We ain't never been much to visit. We've always stayed home and minded our own business, but Mrs. Keyes put a stop to it. She said it warn't sociable, nor Christian. Afore we knowed it we was havin' a sewin' circle every Wednesday and ere we could complain we all liked it so much we jist kept it up.

"She ain't hardly got that started ere she got all the children goin' to the schoolhouse fur Sunday school, and it shorely does a heart good to see them children walkin' in the path o' the Lord, larnin' Bible verses, and sangin' the purtiest songs about Jesus.

"Then it 'pears to me lak she's shorely got her hands full, but there ain't no calculatin' that good woman. She starts gittin' books in from somewhar, books for chaps, stories, and things with big print fur the older folks. I've tuk to readin' a powerful lot this winter on account o' them books, and they've brightened many a lonesome day."

Granny Henderson paused and looked wistfully toward Mrs. Keyes's home on Ivy Point. A thread of blue smoke was wavering from the chimney there upon the late afternoon breeze.

"These people hereabout on Troublesome ought to appreciate Mrs. Keyes," I said, wanting to hear more about her.

"We do think a powerful lot o' her," Granny Henderson said, looking away again and smoothing her starched apron. "I asked her one day why she does all these goodly things fur us pore people and she jist laughs and says she reckons she is jist a selfish person after all because most of all in this world she wants to be happy and the only way she kin do that is to help other people be happy. Mrs. Keyes is puorely a Christian soul if there ever was one on God's green airth."

All Their Ways Are Dark

The mines on Little Carr closed in March. Winter had been mild, the snows scant and frost-thin upon the ground. Robins stayed the season through, and sapsuckers came early to drill the black birch beside our house. Though Father had worked in the mines, we did not live in the camps. He owned the scrap of land our house stood upon, a garden patch, and the black birch that was the only tree on all the barren slope above Blackjack. There were four of us children running barefoot over the puncheon floors, and since the year's beginning Mother carried a fifth balanced on one hip as she worked over the rusty stove in the shed-room. There were seven in the family to cook for. With the closing of the mines, two of Father's cousins came and did not go away.

"It's all we can do to keep bread in the children's mouths," Mother told Father. "Even if they are your blood kin, we can't feed them much longer." Mother knew the strings of "shucky" beans dried in the fall would not last until a new garden could be raised. A half-dozen soup bones and some meat rinds were left in the smokehouse; skippers had got into a pork shoulder during the unnaturally warm December, and it had to be thrown away. Mother ate just enough for the baby, picking at her food and chewing it in little bites. Father ate sparingly, cleaning his plate of every crumb. His face was almost as thin as Mother's. Father's cousins fed well, and grumblingly, upon beans and corn pone. They kicked each other under the table, carrying on a secret joke from day to day, and grimacing at us as they ate. We were pained, and felt foolish because we could not join in their laughter.

"You'll have to ask them to go," Mother told Father. "These lazy louts are taking food out of the baby's mouth. What we have won't last forever." Father did not speak for a long time; then he said simply: "I can't turn my kin out." He would say no more. Mother began to feed us between meals, putting less on the table. Father's cousins would empty the dishes, then look sourly at their

28

plates. They would wink, and thrust their brogans at each other under the table. They would chuckle without saying anything. Sometimes one of them would make a clucking noise in his throat, but none of us laughed, not even Euly. We would look at Father, his chin drooped over his shirt collar, his eyes lowered. And John's face would be as grave as Father's. Only the baby's face would become bird-eyed and bright.

When Uncle Samp, Father's great-uncle, came for a couple of days and stayed on after the weekend was over, Mother spoke sternly to Father. Father became angry and stamped his foot on the floor. "As long as we've got a crust, it'll never be said I turned my folks from my door," he said. We children were frightened. We had never seen Father storm like this, or heard him raise his voice at Mother. Father was so angry he took his rifle-gun and went off into the woods for the day, bringing in four squirrels for supper. He had "barked" them, firing at the tree trunk beside the animal's heads, and bringing them down without a wound.

Uncle Samp was a large man. His skin was soft and white, with small pink veins webbing his cheeks and nose. There were no powder burns on his face and hands, and no coal dust ground into the heavy wrinkles of his neck. He had a thin gray moustache, over a hand-span in length, wrapped like a loose cord around his ears. He vowed it had not been trimmed in thirty years. It put a spell on us all, Father's cousins included. We looked at the moustache and felt an itching uneasiness. That night at the table Father's cousins ate squirrels' breasts and laughed, winking at each other as they brushed up brown gravy on pieces of corn pone. Uncle Samp told us what this good eating put him in mind of, and he bellowed, his laughter coming deep out of him. We laughed, watching his face redden with every gust, watching the moustache hang miraculously over his ears. Suddenly my brother John began to cry over his plate. His shins had been kicked under the table. Mother's face paled, her eyes becoming hard and dark. She gave the baby to Father and took John into another room. We ate quietly during the rest of the meal, Father looking sternly down the table.

After supper Mother and Father took a lamp and went out to the smokehouse. We followed, finding them bent over the meat box. Father dug into the salt with a plough blade, Mother holding the light above him. He uncovered three curled rinds of pork. We stayed in the smokehouse a long time, feeling contented and together. The room was large, and we jumped around like savages and swung head-down from the rafters.

Father crawled around on his hands and knees with the baby on his back. Mother sat on a sack of black walnuts and watched us. "It's the first time we've been alone in two months," she said. "If we lived in here, there wouldn't be room for anybody else. And it would be healthier than that leaky shack we stay in." Father kept crawling with the baby, kicking up his feet like a spoiled nag. John hurt his leg again. He gritted his teeth and showed us the purple spot where he had been kicked. Father rubbed the bruise and made it feel better. "Their hearts are black as Satan," Mother said. "I'd rather live in this smokehouse than stay down there with them. A big house draws kinfolks like a horse draws nit-flies." It was late when we went to the house. The sky was overcast and starless.

During the night, rain came suddenly, draining through the rotten shingles. Father got up in the dark and pushed the beds about. He bumped against a footboard and wakened me. I heard Uncle Samp snoring in the next room; and low and indistinct through the sound of water on the roof came the quiver of laughter. Father's cousins were awake in the next room. They were mightily tickled about something. They laughed in long choking spasms. The sound came to me as though afar off, and I reckon they had their heads under the covers so as not to waken Uncle Samp. I listened and wondered how it was possible to laugh with the dark and rain.

Morning was bright and rain-fresh. The sharp sunlight fell slantwise upon the worn limestone earth of the hills, and our house squatted weathered and dark on the bald slope. Yellow-bellied sapsuckers drilled their oblong holes in the black birch by the house, now leafing from tight-curled buds. John and I had climbed into the tree before breakfast, and when Mother called us in we were hungry for our boiled wheat.

We were alone at the table, Father's cousins having left at daylight for Blackjack. They had left without their breakfast, and this haste seemed strange to Mother. "This is the first meal they've missed," she said.

Uncle Samp slept on in the next room, his head buried under a quilt to keep the light out of his face. Mother fed the baby at her breast, standing by Father at the table. We ate our wheat without sugar, and when we had finished Mother said to Father: "We have enough corn meal for three more pans of bread. If the children eat it by themselves, it might last a week. It won't last us all more than three meals. Your kin will have to go today."

Father put his spoon down with a clatter. "My folks eat when we eat," he said, "and as long as we eat." The corners of his mouth were drawn tight into his face. His eyes burned, but there was no anger in them. "I'll get some meal at the store," he said. Mother leaned against the wall, clutching the baby. Her voice was like ice.

"They won't let you have it on credit," she said. "You've tried before. We've got to live small. We've got to start over again, hand to mouth, the way we began." She laid her hand upon the air, marking the words with nervous fingers. "We've got to tie ourselves up in such a knot nobody else can get in." Father got his hat and stalked to the door. "We've got to do it today," she called. But Father was gone, out of the house and over the hill toward Blackjack.

Mother put the baby in the empty woodbox while she washed dishes. Euly helped her, clearing the table and setting out a bowl of boiled wheat for Uncle Samp. I went outside with John, and we were driving the sapsuckers from the birch when Uncle Samp shouted in the house. His voice crashed through the wall, pouring between the seamy timbers in raw blasts of anger. John was up the tree, holding on to the scaly bark, so I ran ahead of him into the shed-room. Mother stood in the middle of the floor listening. The baby jumped up and down in the woodbox. Euly ran behind the stove.

I ran into the room where Uncle Samp was and saw him stride from the looking glass to the bed. His mouth was slack. A low growl flowed out of him. He stopped when he saw me, drawing himself up in his wrath. Then I saw his face, and I was frightened. I was suddenly paralyzed with fear. His face was fiery, the red web of veins straining in his flesh, and his moustache, which had been cut off within an inch of his lips, sticking out like two small gray horns. He rushed upon me, caught me up in his arms and flung me against the wall. I fell upon the floor, breathless and not uttering a sound. Mother was with me in a moment, her hands weak and palsied as she lifted me.

31

I was only frightened, and not hurt. Mother cried a little, making a dry sniffling sound through her nose; then she got up and walked outside and around the house. Uncle Samp was not in sight. She came back and gave John the key to the smokehouse. "We're going to move up there," she said. "Go unlock the door." I helped Euly carry the baby out of doors in the woodbox. We set him on the shady side of the woodpile. We began to move the furniture out, putting the smaller things in the smokehouse, but leaving the chairs, beds, and tables on the ground halfway between. The stove was heaviest of all, and still hot. The rusty legs broke off on one side, and the other two bent under it. We managed to slide it out into the yard.

After everything had been taken out, we waited in the back yard while Mother went around the house again, looking off the hill. Uncle Samp was nowhere in sight, and neither Father nor Father's cousins could be seen. Then she went inside alone. She stayed a long time. We could hear her moving across the floor. When she came out and closed the door, there was a haze of smoke behind her, blue and smelling of burnt wood.

In a moment we saw the flames through the back window. The rooms were lighted up, and fire ran up the walls, eating into the old timbers. It climbed to the ceiling, burst through the roof, and ate the rotten shingles like leaves. John and I watched the sapsuckers fly in noisy haste from the black birch, and he began to cry hoarsely as the young leaves wilted and hung limp from scorched twigs. The birch trunk steamed in the heat.

When the flames were highest, leaping through the charred rafters, a gun fired repeatedly in the valley. Someone there had noticed the smoke and was arousing the folk along Little Carr Creek. When they arrived the walls had fallen in, and Mother stood there among the scattered furnishings, her face calm and triumphant.

Horse Doctor

Ole Treble Finney's mare was bound to die. I reckon Ole Treble thought more o' that mare than he did his passel o' young 'uns. And a powerful sight more'n he did his woman afore she left his house for him and the devil to lock horns in.

Ole Treble was a mighty hard man to git along with. He'd kilt two men, I'd heered it told. And his wife had stripes on her like black runners where he'd beat her. She'd carry them marks to the grave, I heered it said.

I reckon all o' Treble's sins piled together in a brashpile would look like a haystack o' puore midnight.

My pap and Ole Treble never lost no time callin' each other brethren. Treble never allowed Pap was much of a hoss doctor. Once he had a jinny to die after he'd called Pap too late. He never got over that proper. A jinny's got a time to die jist like a man. But Treble was quare like that. He always did thank more of his creatures than he did folks. Even his own blood kin.

All Ole Treble ever said about Pap never done no harm. Pap kept gittin' his license every year and his docterin' kept him workin' right peart. Oh I reckon they was a lot in the books Pap never larned. No man kin larn squar' to the end o' nothin'.

But my pap knowed somethin' that the doctor books don't larn nobody. Pap had him a way with creatures that was passin' anythang I ever seen or heered tell of. The fightinest dog would jist walk up to Pap and lick his boots. He could git a horse or a cow to lay down quiet for him to work on 'em.

You ever see a baby that's scairt o' men folks? Won't even let its own poppy come nigh? My pap could sort o' go up to a leetle chap and they would stick out their arms and come to him.

Oh my pap was a purty quiet sort o' fellow. He never went along hollerin' to folks like he was runnin' for county judge. He bore no hard feelin's, but he never was a speakin'-out man. He never passed a chap, or a dog, or a horse without callin' out to 'em. But he was liable to pass a man up without a friendly word. Oh you had to know my Pap or you'd git him down wrong.

When I heered Treble Finney's mare had the bloats I was sort o' tickled. I never tuk no joy in that mare sufferin'. Hit was Treble Finney sufferin' that made me feel good sort o' 'round the edge o' my liver. Hit was Treble needin' my pap to doctor his mare, and him too hard-headed to ask him to come. Hit must o' been like pullin' eyeteeth for him to come and git my pap after all he had said. And he was shore slow as Egypt about it.

But he did come. I wouldn't tuk a war pension for seein' Ole Treble come a-sidlin' up to our homeplace and a-callin' out for Pap.

Pap jist sent me out to tell him he'd be there in a minute. Pap jist set there a-readin' in the paper, gittin' all the good out o' Treble bilin' outside.

When Pap went out to see Treble, I got down on the floor and peeped out the cat hole. I couldn't see nothin' but their boots, but I heered some o' what they said. Pap says he can't go for less than twenty-five dollars. He was askin' Ole Treble twenty-five dollars when he never asked a fellow more'n two. And he never turned down a sufferin' creature if he never got a red cent. Ole Treble went to stallin'. I could see his heels workin' up and down in the dirt.

I heered Pap say twenty-five dollars in puore cash. That must o' burnt Ole Treble squar' through his gizzard to pay cash and the craps not nigh out o' the ground. I got up and sot one eye on a crack in the door. I seen Treble retch down in his pocket fur his money. I reckon he had the deepest pocket I ever seen. He went squar' up to the elbow afore he come out with a roll o' bills.

Pap asked Treble what was the matter with his mare. Treble says hit was the bloats and tells him how she is blowed up. Pap says hit takes a hoss doctor to tell what's the matter with stock. He says this knowin' all the time it was bloats. Treble says he reckons he knowed his mare had et up a sack o' sweet feed, and he knowed the bloats when he seen 'em. My pap says he differs. He says he's the onliest one in this country that got the right to say what's wrong with a mare for shore.

That burnt Ole Treble up. I reckon he wished he hadn't come for Pap. Hit was costin' him money and raw pride. I reckon Ole Treble would liked to have shot Pap squar' through. The last man he kilt was for less than Pap had said to him.

Pap tuk his saddlebags and packed his bottles in. I asked him to let me go, knowin' I couldn't cause somebody had to stay home with our mare. Hit was gittin' nigh her time. But I wanted to go purty bad. I'd had my mind sot on bein' a hoss doctor myself and never turned down a chanct o' pickin' up a leetle extra larnin'.

Pap rid off with Treble and I went out to the barn to take a look at our mare Dolly. Afore I got in the lot I heered her blowin' through her nose. And she whinnied right loud two times. I never thought a thang. I was thankin' she wanted to git out for a drank o' water.

When I opened the door it was dusty-dark inside and I didn't see nothin' for a minute. Then I seen Dolly standin' in the corner with her head down, lickin' somethang on the floor. Then I seen the colt.

Well, I was right smart proud o' that colt. Pap had promised it to me when it come. I got down on my hands and knees in the stall to see what kind it was. Hit was a male. I was right tickled. In a minute he got up and stood on his leetle legs, lookin' at me and his mommy. His legs was like broomstraws. They was that thin. And his leetle head put me in mind of a deer. By that time my eyeballs was gittin' use to the dark stable.

When I seen everythang was all right I lit out for the house. Mommy was right tickled too, and says I can go tell Pap. So I struck out to Ole Treble Finney's place.

I found Pap in Treble's barn. Treble was nowhere 'round. His mare was in a puore bad fix a-layin' there on the ground heavin' and wallin' her eyes. She was blowed up nigh fit to bust. I could see by Pap's face he'd come too late.

I told Pap about the colt and he never said a word. I told about him bein' promised to me, and he never said scat. He jist sot about tappin' Treble's mare. He sot the tapper in the right spot and drove her in. Then he screwed the middle out of the tapper and out biled the gas. Pap struck a match to it jist to show me hit would burn. Hit spewed like burnin' tar. He was doin' all he could for Treble's mare but he knowed hit was too late.

We heered Treble comin' to the barn and Pap went outside and shet the door. I heered 'em arguin' though I couldn't hear right good. Pap was sayin' hit wasn't the bloats and Treble was swearin' hit was. I was scairt Pap was goin' to git hisself shot. And Ole Treble was already sore about that twenty-five dollars. I heered him tell Pap he'd better work a cuore. And he said it like he puore meant it. I knowed he meant it. I knowed that mare better not die.

When Pap come back in the stable I seen Pap was sort o' concerned. Then he tells me what to do. I never thought my pap would o' done it. He told me to go home and not come back till after dark. And for me to brang the colt in the wagon.

What Pap told me jist about broke me up inside. But I never crossed my pap in my whole life. Hit would have been the puore rawhide if I did. I jist lit out hurtin' inside, but thankin' hit was the only way. Givin' my colt up after he'd been promised me tetched to the quick.

It was nigh sundown when I got home and I went right ahead and hitched up the wagon. Ole Dolly rared powerful when I tuk the colt and laid him down in the wagon-bed. I give her a sweet turnip but she never even looked at it. She was runnin' up and down the lot whinnyin' a mighty heap when I left.

As I got close to Treble's place I throwed some sacks over the colt. Hit was plumb dark but I wasn't takin' a chance o' bein' seen.

I driv up behind the barn and Pap come out in a hurry and helped me carry the colt in. When we got him in the stable I seed by the lantern light the mare was dead. But she wasn't half so big with all the gas blowed out. We jist put the colt down and left him there.

I asked Pap how long it had been since Treble was in the stable. He says Treble hasn't been in since he come. Well, we sot thar and waited for him to come. Thar was a light burnin' in the house and we knowed he was still up. I reckon we waited thar nigh two hours.

When we seed Treble wasn't comin' out Pap told me to go fotch him. I called right big outside the house and he come a-runnin'. The way his coat stuck out I knowed he had a gun in his hip pocket. I was plumb scairt for my pap.

Pap opened the stable door and told Treble his mare is dead. The quarest look come over Treble's face. Hit kind o' drawed up in a knot like a ripe 'simmon. He stepped in the stable and looked. He looked at the mare, then he looked at what was standin' in the corner.

Well, he jist looked. But he never turned a hair. He jist looked at that mare mighty close. I reckon he seen that hole Pap made to let the gas out. Maybe he didn't. But he never said nothin'.

I seen my colt was gone for good. Treble was thankin' hit was his colt. I got to hurtin' inside. I reckon I was 'bout to cry.

Treble must o' seen my face. He looked at me right hard, then all of a sudden he busts out laughin'. You could o' heered him a mile. Hit must a shuck his insides powerful to laugh and holler like he done.

When he got done laughin' he tells me he ain't in the colt-raisin' business and I can have it if I want it.

My pap didn't know what to say. He jist laughed too. There wasn't nothin' else to do. He stuck his hands in his pockets and pulled out that twenty-five dollars Treble paid him, and he shucked out two bills. He handed the rest back to Treble. He said bein' the mare died hit wasn't worth more'n two dollars.

They laughed some more. Then Treble says he's got a jug up in the hayloft, and him and my pap skinned up that ladder like a squirrel up a scaly bark.

Bare-Bones

It was quiet on that day, and the willows hung limp over Troublesome Creek. The waters rested about the bald stones, scarcely moving. I had walked along the sandy left bank to Jute Dawson's homeseat, and in the soundlessness of the afternoon young Clebe had not heard me enter the yard and climb the puncheon steps.

He sat at the end of the dogtrot with a long-gun sighted into the kitchen, his crutch leaning against one knee. His right eye was closed to a bead, and I waited until he fired. There was a metallic ring of a bullet striking pots and pans. He hopped inside on his one leg, fetching out a fox squirrel by its gray brush. As he came out he saw me and held the quivering body aloft in greeting. There was a purple dent in the furred head, red drops of blood trickling across the glassy eyes, and a twisted whiskered mouth.

Clebe tossed the squirrel into a wooden bucket, hopped the length of the dogtrot, and brought a chair for me.

"Fox squirrels are takin' the place," he said. "We had a pet creature and he drawed the rest out o' the hills."

He laughed, his thin face spreading. "Nothin' puts the lean in yore muscles like pawpaws and squirrel's breasts. Hit's the Lord's truth."

We settled into white-oak splint chairs and looked out on the untended patch before the house, now thick-growing with purple flares of stickwood. Field sparrows were working among the slender stalks, and the dark bonnets shook in the hot, windless air.

"Poppy and Mommy is swappin' work this day," Clebe said. "Baldridge holp us lay-by our crap two days ago, and they're stirrin'-off sorghum 'lasses to pay back. And I reckon Prony will give us a fresh jug o' fresh 'lasses."

Our chairs were leaned against the shriveled log framing and I rested there, thinking of the wooden leg Clebe had ordered. The word had gone up and down Troublesome that he was to get a leg. The weeks had gone by and he had not come into the county seat at horse-swapping court or the last gingerbread election.

"I reckon Prony Baldridge is a purty good man," he said at length, "but Poppy says he's a straddle-pole. Poppy says he's got one foot that's a Democrat and t'other one's a Republican. And he kin skip betwixt them like all git-out. He tuk a trunk full o' gingerbread to the last election and sold it right five times over to the candidates afore he told folks to come and eat till they busted."

The sparrows set up a clatter in the stickweed patch. Their dull chirps were hollow and rasping, and their gray bodies blew dustily through the weeds.

"Even a sparrow-bird's got two wings," Clebe said. "Hit's a pure Lord's pity I ain't got two feet." He drew the palms of his hands tight and bloodless over the post of the chair.

"Poppy ordered me a wooden leg and it's an eternal time a-comin'. A leg drummer come and measured me up careful. I reckon he knowed the wiggle in every toe afore he left, but I'm a mind Poppy's done been beat out o' that fifty dollars.

"Oh that fifty dollars will go hard with Poppy if the leg don't come. He'd had that money tater-holed for a spell."

Clebe drew out a knife and began to whittle the round of his chair.

"Hit's been a sight o' trouble I've given my poppy," he said. "He was agin' me havin' my leg tuk off when I had blood pizen."

He stopped suddenly and pointed the large blade at me. "I figger you never heard about the funeral occasion fur my leg. Hit was buried jist like folks is. My brother Tom fetched it from the doctor's house in a box and tuk it by the schoolhouse afore books was called.

"All the scholars come out to the road and looked at it. Afore Tom left they was bettin' one another to tetch it. They wanted to know what Tom was a-goin' to do with it, and Tom says he's a-goin' to have a rail funeralizin' on the p'int.

"The teacher run Tom off 'cause she couldn't git the scholars in with my leg out thar to look at. When he left, a bunch o' scholars tuk along after him. They dug a hole up on the p'int here. Ross Morris preached a soul-raisin' sermon; then they tuk a last look and piled the dirt in.

"Then Tom remembers about a fellow havin' the rheumatiz all his life if his leg is buried with the toes curlin'. They dug it up agin and pulled them out straight as could be got. I thought a heap o' my brother Tom for doin' that for me. They buried it and piled some flat rocks on it to keep the foxes from scratchin' thar. They kivered the grave with yellowrod.

"Oh hit's a quare feelin' to git one piece of you buried afore the rest o' you dies. I figger a fellow will have a hard time gittin' all together on Resurrection Day."

When the sun-ball had turned over the point to the west, setting the grave-stones and Aunt Shridy's grave-house against the naked sky, we walked out into the apple orchard. The trees were gnarled with age, their sparse-leaved boughs hanging thinly with tight-fleshed fruit. Clebe shot an apple down for each of us.

As we turned into the stickweed patch the sparrows fluttered up from the ground, settling ahead and rising again in sudden dwarfed flights as we neared again. Clebe thrust his crutch ahead to stir them more suddenly. They zoomed up bewildered and brushed us with their clumsy wings. He laughed shrilly at their flight.

On the creek bank we sat down in the willow shade. Clebe shucked off his shoe and wiggled his toes in the water.

"Hit's the Lord's pity I jist got one foot," he said, "to dig crawdads with, but I'm thankin' I had it comin' to me. I've done a heap o' meanness in my fifteen years. I've give my pap a big lot o' trouble.

"Oncet I got me a hollow log and stretched a strip o' dried bull's hide over it, and I got me a hickory limb and sawed on it. You could o' heard that noise a full ten miles. Hit sounded like a passel o' wildcats tearin' each other's eyeballs out. Cattle all over the country jumped the rails and tuk down the hollows. The horses and mules kicked barns down and lit out.

"Oh I done thangs that would take a stretch to tell. Oncet Seefer Harper got to cuttin' up in church and takin' on unbecomin' to the Lord. Hit was dusty dark outside, and I went backside o' the church-house whar he had his mare hitched. I cut his saddle off. That ole mare whinnied powerful but I never got caught.

"Oh I done meanness since I was a leetle child. I tuk boards out o' the swingin' bridges, thankin' somebody would come long and drop through to the water. Oncet down Squabble Creek, me and John Bulan tuk the well-top and sot it back. One fellow fell in and come nigh drownin' afore we pulled him out.

"I done a big lot o' meanness, but it cotched up with me. Now I got to tickle-toe on one foot the rest o' my days."

He drew his leg out of the water and lay back on the sandy bank. Presently he spoke again.

"I got me an idea if my leg don't come," he said. "I been figgerin' I'd get Poppy to buy me a gentle nag 'bout fourteen hands high. A saddle hurts my knee and I'd ruther ride bare-bones anyway. I allus did pleasure myself ridin' bare-bones afore I got hurt."

He began laughing, slowly and free.

"I allus favored ridin' bare-bones to eatin' groundhog gravy," he said. "Sometime I git to figgerin' that I'd rather have me a nag than a wood leg squeakin' like a wagon tongue in August. Five legs would be a sight better than a wood pole with a j'int in it to fetch along after the rail leg I got. But I shore would hate fur Poppy to lose that fifty dollars he's tater-holed for such a spell."

We rested in the grass, our eyes set upon the green ridge. The hills rose up from the creek, their slopes cut with narrow-shelving plateaus of bluegrass, now seeding and knee deep. The cows rested with their legs drawn under them, and they were so still that the clappers in their bells hung soundlessly. And there, close against the ground, was the cool smell of wild mint.

One Leg Gone to Judgment

It was quiet on that day, and the willows hung limp over Troublesome Creek. The waters rested about the bald stones, scarcely moving. I had walked along the sandy left bank to Jute Dawson's homeseat, and in the soundlessness of afternoon young Clebe had not heard me enter the yard and climb the puncheon steps.

He sat at the end of the dogtrot with a rifle-gun sighted into the kitchen, his crutch leaning against a knee. His eyes were closed to a bead. I watched without speaking until he had fired, and the sound of a bullet striking pots and pans rang from the room.

Clebe hopped inside on his one leg, fetching out a fox squirrel by its gray brush. As he came out he saw me and held a quivering body aloft in greeting. There was a purple dent in the furred head, and red drops of blood trickled across the glassy eyes and twisted mouth. Clebe tossed the squirrel into a wooden bucket and hopped the length of the dogtrot for a chair.

"Fox squirrels are taking the place," he said. "We had a pet one and he drawed the rest out of the hills."

He laughed, his thin face spreading. "Nothing puts the lean in your muscles like squirrel gravy. When I spy a bowl of it on the table I have to clap my hand over my mouth to keep from shouting."

We settled into white-oak splint chairs and looked out on the untended patch before the house, now thick-growing with purple bonnets of stickweeds. Field sparrows were working among the slender stalks and the dark blossoms shook in the windless air.

"Poppy and Mommy are swapping work today," Clebe said. "Lukas Baldridge holp us lay-by our crap, and they're helping him stirring-off his sorghum to pay back. And I reckon they'll fetch us back a jug full of molasses."

Our chairs were leaned against the log framing and I sat there thinking of the wooden leg Jute had ordered for Clebe. The word had gone up and down Troublesome and its forks that a store-bought leg was coming for him, but the weeks had gone by and he had not been seen at either the horse swapping court, or the gingerbread election.

"I figure Lukas Baldridge is a clever man," Clebe said, "but Poppy says he's a straddle-pole of the worst kind. Poppy says he's got one foot that's a Democrat and the other one a Republican. And he can skip either direction, depending on who's handing out the money. He tuk a sled full of gingerbread to the last election and sold it near five times over to the candidates before he told folks to come and eat till they busted. He saw to it every candidate paid in."

The sparrows set up a clatter in the field patch. Their dull chirps were hollow and rasping, and their gray bodies blew dustily through the weeds.

"Even a sparrow-bird's got two wings," Clebe said at length, watching them work among the brown stalks. "A pure pity I hain't got two legs." He drew the palms of his hands tight and bloodless over the posts of the chair.

"Poppy ordered me a wood leg and it's an eternal time a-coming. A leg drummer come and measured me up careful. I reckon he counted every toe of mine and measured them before he got done, but I'm of a mind Poppy's been beat out of the fifty dollars he paid him. My opinion, he's tuk off like Snider's hound with Poppy's money.

"Oh that fifty dollars will go hard with my pap if that leg don't come. If'n it don't, Poppy will shoot him till he looks like a rag doll does he ever get up with him. He'd had that money 'tater holed for a spell before he turned it loose."

Clebe drew a knife from his pocket and began to whittle the round of his chair. "Hit's been a heap of trouble I've give my poppy," he said. "He was against the doc cutting off my leg when I had blood pizen but Mommy talked him to it. Aye, I can look up yonder on the point and see a yellow spot where I'd be buried now if they hadn't."

He stopped suddenly and pointed the blade at me. "I figure you never heard about the funeral occasion for my leg. Hit was buried just like folks are. My brother Tom fotched it from the doctor's house in a box and tuk it by the schoolhouse before books were called.

"All the scholars they come out to the road and looked at it. Before Tom left they were daring one another to touch it. They wanted to know what Tom was going to do with my limb, and Tom said he was going to have a real funeralizing on the point.

"The teacher he run Tom off because he couldn't get the scholars inside with my dead leg out there to look at. When he left, a bunch of the scholars tuk right along after him. They aimed to be in on anything that took place. They dug a hole right up yonder on the point. Well, now, Amos Morris preached the sermon and they tell me it was a scorcher. They tell me that if they was any devils around they'd a sneaked off with their forked tails between their legs. Then everybody took a last look and piled the dirt in.

"Then—you know what? Tom recollects that a fellow is liable to have the rheumatiz all the days of his life if his leg is buried with the toes a-curling. So up they dug my leg again and tried to pull the toes straight and they couldn't. What they done was to get rocks and beat the toes till they did straighten out. Tom done that for me. They buried the leg again and piled big flat rocks on the grave place to keep the dogs and varmints from scratching it up.

"Oh hit's a quare feeling to get one piece of you buried and gone to judgment before the rest of you dies. I'm afraid I might have a busted hard time getting myself together on Resurrection Day."

A Bell on Troublesome Creek

Uncle Jabe told me about it during one of those rare intervals when he grew reminiscent. Usually at such times he had a way of looking toward the past as though the future was a shadowed, uninteresting thing to be endured when it arrived.

I began to realize that after all Uncle Jabe had the forward look. We were walking up Troublesome Creek, picking our way carefully over the frozen stones on the left bank. Suddenly a school bell rang silver clear on the frosty air.

Uncle Jabe stopped, lifted the ear-flaps of his woolen cap, and listened. When the mellow peals had echoed and died among the hilltops, we moved on and he told me about the bell.

"I've been a-livin' all shet up in these hills nigh on to seventy years," he said. "I've lived hard and porely at times but the good Lord has purty nigh give me every lastin' thang I needed, 'ceptin' one thang.

"We got us a road in hyar four years ago, though I ain't shore now whether it's a blessin' or a damnation. We got us a chanct to give our young 'uns a grain o' education.

"But every time I hyar that bell a-clangin' down Troublesome Valley I can't help a-thankin' what might o' been, but jist ain't. Still, I'm a-mind it's a-comin'. Shorely one o' these days when the good Lord makes up his mind, and gits good and ready.

"Then I comes to thank, too, that the Lord has done made up his mind, but the people on the outside that can brang the Good Word in haint made up theirs.

"About seven years ago we started us a church up on Left Hand Fork. We all jist throwed in and started workin'. Dug us a foundation and laid it good and strong as would last out the days o' any of us on this green airth.

"And we bought us a bell, a big, gongy one that could be heered clar up and down the valley. A church-house without a bell would be like a preacher with the quinsy.

"Hit was a bell you'd find hard to turn down on Sunday mornin'. And when you heered it, somehow it was sort o' the voice o' the Lord callin' you down to the church-house, spite o' the weather or that coon hunt you'd planned on right big like.

"We had us a preacher that had fotched hissef on. We thought a whole heap o' him. We'd been usin' the Mill Creek school till our church got through buildin'.

"Well, all of a sudden-like, our preacher got called away, and that good foundation jist stayed thar without anything to hold up except the puore air that don't need no support.

"The bell stayed thar and got all rusty. I would liked to 've pulled down on that rope jist oncet. It got around that the school down at the Forks could use a bell and we give it to them and they fotched it along.

"That bell rings every day.

"When I'm in hyarin' distance I thanks to myself that one o' these purty days we'll have us another preacher, build us a church-house and have another bell as clar and sweetenin' as the one we had afore.

"But I don't know when. I reckon one o' these days agin I lay these old bones down fur the last time and take my peace.

"One o' these purty days."

The Scrape

I was walking up Ballard Creek and reckoning to myself that foxes were abroad and sparking on such a night when I happened upon Jiddy Thornwell sprawled in the road at the mouth of Sporty Hollow. Though the moon was low and the ridges in the shadow, there was enough light to yellow the ground along the creek.

On seeing Jiddy I expected to tickle-toe past and go on to the square dance at Enoch Lovern's where I'd headed. I was traveling late on purpose to dodge rowdies of his ilk. A body with the gumption of a gnat wouldn't fool time in his company, for if ever one was routed to burning Torment, he was the jasper. Fractious and easily riled, and as folks say, too mean to live. Then I bethought myself. I couldn't allow any man to get his neck broken by a wheel or brains stepped in by a nag. An unworthy way to perish. Anyhow, being drunk, he'd have a bottle on him, and after borrowing a gill I'd skeedaddle.

I gave Jiddy a poke with my shoe. He moved a speck and cracked his eyelids. He sat up and made to yawn. And I saw there wasn't much if any whiskey in him, and I knew something was afoot, something to nobody's good.

"Jiddy," I chided, "what the hoot are you doing sleeping in the road?"

He laughed, and jumped up. He had been shamming. Without a doubt he had spotted me before I did him. He aimed to test what I'd do.

"You were laying pretty to have your skull cracked," I jabbered, slapping his pockets. I felt no bottle, just a knife and the 32-squeeze-trigger he regularly packed. When sober, Jiddy wasn't too prickly and overbearing. You could horse around with him. "I've seen characters blind drunk acting with more sanity," said I.

Jiddy inquired where I was headed, and I answered, "Where do you reckon?" Except to attend the square dance at Enoch Lovern's what other reason would either of us have to be on the Ballard road of a Saturday night? He was talking to hear his head rattle. I cautioned, "If you're wanting more than a couple of sashays with Posey, you'd better get a hump on. You're already late."

Jiddy had been sparking Woots Houndshell's daughter for near on to a year but lately Cletis Wilhoyt had been cutting in on him. In headstrongness and pride, Cletis and Jiddy were fair matches. Put them both in a poke and shake it, and it would be a question which would pop out first. Well, I'll confess to it. I was soft on Posey Houndshell myself. Yet I'm no witty, no dumb-head. I believed three's a crowd, and especially when it included these two gents.

"I'm waiting on Cletis Wilhoyt," Jiddy said. "We aim to settle some business tonight. Settle it for all time coming, hereinafter and forever. The winner might travel to Houndshell's, be he in shape to. You're our eyewitness, the prover neither of us bushwhacked the other."

"Gosh dog!" I blustered, and then, "Uh-uh. You're not talking to me. I'm a short spell here." The boilers of hell would explode did this pair lock horns. Hard numbers, the both. Stubborn as peavies. Fellows who don't care whether it snows oats or rains tomcats, they're dangerous to be around. The preachers say what's written to happen will come to pass, whether or no. But I didn't count it my duty to stand by and eyeball this showdown. Hell-o, no!

"Everything is fixed," Jiddy said, not listening. "Cletis swore he'd meet me when the moon is up plumb." He cocked his chin and sighted the moon-ball. "She's low, the old sister, but she's climbing." He grinned. "We'll have what the almanac calls 'useful moonlight.'" And he said, "You'll view a fight that will make the records."

"Yeah," chuffed I, "the courthouse records," and I complained, "Are you figuring I'm going to referee a shooting match? I wasn't born on Crazy Creek, recollect. Bullets are like horses' hooves, they don't have eyes."

Jiddy said, "Pistols are for the chickenhearted, and that's not our case. Not mine or Cletis's. We'll manage otherwise."

"Dadburn it, Jid," I ranted, "you're an idjit if you think I'm mixing in your and Cletis's scrapes. Where do I profit? Sheriffs, summonses, roosting in the witness chair, a big rigmaroar. Aye, no. I've been here, and I'm done gone." Yet you didn't leave Jiddy until it suited his notion. Not unless you wanted your hair parted with his 32-squeeze-trigger.

"Let's round us up a drink," smoothed Jiddy. "Shade Muldraugh has an operation on Rope Works, yonside of the ridge. What say we make a raid on him?"

"Shade's likker is the worst in Baldridge County," I faulted. "The sorriest since Adam made apple-jack. Why, he can't even boil water without scorching it." But I might as well have been talking to a mule.

Jiddy declared, "Whatever Shade is distilling, we'll down. Tonight we'll cull nothing. Pass nothing by."

We set off. Legging it up the ridge I juggled plans in my head to shake off Jiddy, and in a fashion which would leave me blameless. We mounted by knee and main strength, climbing ground so steep you'd nearly skin your nose, and emerged in a clearing where moonlight made blossom the hazel bushes. Jiddy told me to stay there, he'd prospect a bit. I heard twigs snapping for a while, then the heavy breathing of the Muldraugh bull in the valley. A fox barked, an answering yap followed. It was a lonesomey place and I longed to hightail it. But I bethought myself: who at the dance would bother to cut eyes at me? All the girls I fancied were spoken for, Posey Houndshell included. Well, I'd get away from Jiddy in due course. Not just yet. It wasn't good sense to.

Presently I heard Jiddy's squeeze-trigger pop and I dropped flat on the ground, and I stayed flat until I heard leaves rattling and Jiddy walked out of the woods.

"What happened?" I choked, picturing Shade Muldraugh with a bullet in his gizzard, his toes curled.

"Ah, I let off my gun to scare him," said Jiddy. "And did he skeedaddle! Aye gonnies, you could of shot dice on his shirttail." And Jiddy said, "Come on. We'll take our pleasure."

We footed along a bench of land some three hundred yards, and of a sudden there it was in a pocket of a cliff. Muldraugh's works were hid as clever as a guinea's nest, and I doubt I could have spotted it at twenty feet even in broad daylight. Although a fire burned under the pot, the steam wasn't yet up. The worm hadn't begun to driddle.

The lack of the finished product didn't faze Jiddy. He leaned over the tub of still-beer and scooped a gourd dipper full. He drained it, my belly retching at the sight. Then he dipped up a second. I never could swallow such stuff myself. It's sour as whigs. Causes a wild head and too many trips to the White House. "Quit guzzling that slop," I grumbled. "Hit would stop a goat."

Unless you "funnel it," the beer hasn't much power, and Jiddy funneled. He took loose the wire the dipper hung by and thrashed his leg with it as if forcing himself. Finally I said, "Hell's bangers, Jid! Lay off and I'll locate some real stuff, pure corn, the old yellow kind." A big-eyed lie on my part. Nobody made such spirits any more. All you could find was who-shot. But it wasn't merely the beer, or my wanting to vomit watching him that made me promise it. I had finally hatched a scheme.

After a sighting of the moon, Jiddy agreed. She was fully an hour from high. First, he peed into the beer, not that you could nasty it worse than it was. We dropped down the ridge to the Ballard road and backtracked a piece to Pawpaw Branch, Jiddy thrashing his leg with the wire, spurring himself it seemed. "Now," says I, "you do the waiting." Epp Clevenger wouldn't have pardoned me for bringing such a character along. What I'd decided to do was to get Jiddy hoot-owl drunk. With the beer already in him, an easy matter according to my calculations. A few gills of real likker would serve. He'd pass out, and I would scoot.

Epp had a run on and when I came up he was acting mighty uncomfortable. My rattling rocks approaching his furnace had near panicked him. After recognizing me he cried, "Son of a dog! Why didn't you holler, say who you was?" He had to sit five minutes to let his heart stop knocking. He sold me a short-quart on credit, fresh-run, hot from the worm. Bad stuff, he would of admitted. Epp wasn't guaranteeing nothing. Though winded by the climb, I started back directly. The moon wasn't slowing, so I couldn't either. I raced her, you might say.

Well, s'r, when I reached Jiddy the beer hadn't touched him. And he had imbibed nigh on to a half-gallon, the least. A few slugs would of put me under for a day, provided it stayed down. But I've heard it claimed, no matter how much you drink, if you don't want to get drunk, you won't. Beginning to get nervous, I handed Jiddy the bottle, and though it wasn't agey or yellow or pure corn as I'd promised, he upped it and didn't grumble. I skipped it myself, for it had a whang of coal oil and lye, and the pig shorts in the mash didn't recommend it. I eyed Jiddy pulling at the bottle. I watched the moon-ball soar.

The moon took off like Lindbergh. The old sister was flying, and if anything, the more Jiddy drank the soberer he became. Never saw the beat. If Epp Clevenger was fidgity, you ought to of seen me. Hardly a fourth of the whiskey was gone when the moon peaked. The valley lit up wholly, the waters of Ballard shimmered. The ridges were lumpy with trees. And there came Cletis Wilhoyt walking.¯

I trotted to meet Cletis, vowing to him none would gain in a ruckus between him and Jiddy. Woots Houndshell's Posey would slam the door on the both of them when she heard. I even made up a rumor she had already dropped Jiddy like a hot nail, and he didn't need to bother. For my trouble I got called a bad name, and told to go drown myself. That was Cletis. Mean as a horsefly.

There I was between hell and a flint stone. Come a thousand years I couldn't have changed their minds. Their heads were as hard as ball-peen hammers. And this was to be no fair fist scrap either, no mere knockdown combat, with the one who hollered "gate post" first the loser. There would be no pausing, no blow counted foul. Win or perish, endure or die. And gosh dog! They weren't even mad. They talked chin to chin, plotting the battle, cool as moss. By now I was in possession of the bottle and I made up for time lost. Coal oil, lye and pig shorts didn't stop me.

Jiddy called me over to them and gave me his 32-squeeze-trigger. Cletis surrendered an old German luger. The luger was as neat a handgun as ever I fingered. I laid the weapons on a rock. Jiddy produced a wire—the wire he'd packed from Muldraugh's works. He had it doubled in his hippocket. He ordered me to tie an end around his left wrist, and the other about Cletis's. A thing they had agreed on. I did what I was bid do. I bound them to their satisfaction, skin-tight. Next I was asked to treat them to a drink. As Cletis tipped the bottle I noted his face was the color of the air. Following him, Jiddy took a long pull. His countenance—aye, I can't describe it. I recollect his eyes flicked like a wren's tail.

Then Jiddy told me to stand clear. I retreated a couple or three yards. "Farther, farther," ordered Jiddy, and I was stumbling backwards crawdabber fashion when I saw them clasp left hands, and fish in pockets for knives with their right. They opened the knives with their teeth. I saw arms raise and metal glint. It was that moony. My heart didn't knock. It plain quit.

Cletis struck first, as I recall, swinging outward, elbow angling, and had there been a wind the blade would have whistled. I heard a rip like an ax cleaving the limb of a tree. I froze, and I couldn't have moved had the hills come toppling. The span of Jiddy's back hindered my view, and I couldn't swear for certain, but I figured Cletis's knife had split him wide. Yet Jiddy only grunted and plunged his blade as if to sever the key-notch of an oak. Cletis rocked and gurgled. Cletis gurgled like water squiggling in the ground during rainy weather. They kept to their feet, backing and filling, breathing as heavily as Muldraugh's bull had, arms rising and striking. And they kept on striking.

I've seen rams butt skulls till it thundered. I've witnessed caged wildcats tear hide. Neither was a scrimption to this. My body grew roots. My legs were posts without joints. I went off the hinges, I reckon. I begged Jiddy and Cletis to quit. I pled, I bellowed. I shouted till I couldn't utter a croak, and then I covered my eyes and fell down bawling. Since my child days I'd shed few tears, and these came rough. They set my eyeballs afire.

After a spell I quieted. I cracked my lids and peeped out. Jiddy and Cletis were laying alongside each other in the road, laying as stiff as logs. At night red is black, and there was black over and around them. They lay in a gore of black. And the next thing I knew I was running up Ballard Creek. I might have run all the way to Enoch Lovern's if the short-quart hadn't slipped from under my belt. I grabbed it up and threw it winding. It bounced along the ruts ahead and never busted. When I got up to the bottle I hoisted it and drained it to the bottom.

I didn't run any more. I walked, and as I walked I calmed. What was done was done. Predestination, church folks call it. I footed along peart, thinking of what Jiddy had said once about wanting to be buried in a chestnut coffin so he would go through hell a-popping, and I thought about something else. I thought about Posey Houndshell. Nobody stood between me and her.

The Quare Day

There had been no rain during the whole of August. At the month's end the winds came and blew through Little Angus valley, drying the creek to a shallow stream, and now it lay without motion like a long thin pond. Under the banks the waters were stained with shedding willow leaves. The wind had settled before the dew dried on the parched grass. Nothing stirred in the cool air pocketed in the damp hollows.

The sun was high above the hills when the sky beyond the ridge took on a yellow cast. There were no clouds other than a scattering of horsetails. At first the yellowness was only in the west, then it advanced, enveloping hilltop after hilltop until the sun-ball shone dully as through a saffron veil. It spread swiftly east, the hue of sulphur. It came without shape or sound bearing the molten glassiness of a sunset. Flaxbirds settled into the thickets. The dark hollow birds that warbled seldom in late summer sang not at all. Chickens went to an early roost in the sycamore trees, the prickly seed-balls hanging on twig-strings about their heads. They settled without sleeping, pale second lids opening and closing.

Shridy Middleton looked down the valley from the porch of her house. She polished her glasses with a fold of her sleeve and watched the yellow sand in the drying creek bed, the gray-yellow limestone shelved above the bank, the yellow-green of the chestnut oaks on the hills. She brushed her hands nervously over her hair, wondering at the color of the day. The mail hack had passed, and the wheels had rutted their tracks in the creek road. Willa Dowe, their neighbor's daughter, had brought a letter as she came to help with the apple drying, and now Shridy drew it out of her bosom, glancing curiously at the envelope without opening it. In a moment she thrust it back, brushed the meal dust from her apron, and stepped into the kitchen where Willa was paring apples.

"Hit's no use trying to dry fruit today," Shridy said. "The sun-ball has a mote in its eye. The slices would mold before they could cure." Willa was the same age as her son, Rein. Rein, the youngest of eleven, the most cherished, was the "'possum baby," as the saying went. Willa and Rein had in infancy been cradled together when the families visited. To Shridy and her husband Jabe, Willa was the daughter they had hoped for but never had. Although related, the kinship was distant.

Willa stuck the knife into an apple as a holder and went to the door. She stood there a moment, rolling the plaits of her flaxen hair into a tight ball. She made a biscuit of it on her head. "As quare weather as ever I've seen," she remarked. "Mommy says fruit has to get direct sunlight or it'll lose sugar." Then, "I'd better get on down to home, for a bunch of things there need doing up." She paused in her leave-taking, recalling the letter. "But first I'll read what I brought from the mailbox. I'll say it to you and you can tell Uncle Jabe what's in it."

"The letter will keep until later," Shridy said, gathering the peelings into a basket for the chickens. "Hit'll endure till I set my mind to hear it."

Shridy watched her hurry along the path. Reaching the willows at the creek's bend, Willa began to run, her gingham dress flowing about her bare legs. When she had disappeared Shridy went around the house and peered up the hill toward the burned-over patch of new-ground on the second bench of the mountain. Jabe was leaning against a stump he had pulled with the help of his mule. He was staring toward the sun, hat in hand, and with no need to shade his eyes. The mule waited, brushing his nose over the charred earth.

Shridy called to him and the shrillness of her own voice rang in her ears. Jabe did not hear, her words being smothered by the redbud thicket between. She brought the fox horn from its nail by the mantel and blew into it with all her strength. Jabe turned and looked down, cupped his hands and blew an acknowledgement. Although it was not yet noon, he loosened the mule and started out of the field.

On coming from the barn Jabe heaped a turn of stovewood in his arms. Shridy met him on the porch. His face was butter-yellow like the air, his eyes the color of rain water drained from an oaken roof. And he noted her face, the sulphur hue of dry clay. Her hands appeared more leather than flesh.

"Hit's a plumb quare day," he said, going into the kitchen. "Must o' been a storm somewhere afar off to the west. My opinion, the wind has picked up dirt from a mighty spindling country where the ground is worn thin. Hain't the healthy kind like the wild dirt in my new-ground." He threw the turn of wood into the box beside the stove and kneeled to thrust splinters to quicken the coals.

"I'm baking an apple stack cake for dinner," she said, as if that were the reason for calling him in from his work.

Jabe arose slowly from his knees. "You're not baking a cake on Wednesday, shorely. We don't follow having Sunday cooking on Wednesday." He was puzzled. "Sort of uncommon, hain't it?"

She poured the stewed apples into a pan, and began to prepare batter for the layers. "Fruit won't dry on such a day," she explained. "Got to do something with the apples we've peeled." The letter was like a stone in her dress bosom.

Standing in the doorway, leaning against the jamb, Jabe viewed the ragweeds marching along the fencerow of the meadow. They seemed yellow as bolted mustard. A golden carpet spread across the pasture which had been lately mowed.

Shridy called to Jabe from the stove, "You ought to put on a clean shirt if we're to have apple stack cake for dinner. Hit's sort of an occasion." Jabe went into the front room, closed the door and pulled the latch-string inside. He lifted the great Bible from the maple highboy. It was weighty and he sat down and opened it upon his lap. The pages turned familiarly under his hard thumb. He squinted along the double columns, leafing slowly through the chapters, pausing to scan the revelations and miracles. Every page knew his finger, every sentence his eye. The Book was the herald of the past, the prophecy of the future. After a spell he put the Book away, washed himself and donned a fresh shirt.

The sun was poised overhead when he returned. Dinner was spread upon the table. The pole beans, the salt pork, the beet pickles and sliced onions were in the new dishes Rein had sent from Ohio in the spring. The cornbread on its flowered platter was as golden as the day itself. The tablecloth had come from Rein's wife whom they had never seen. They stood by the table and studied the dishes, rimmed with laurel buds. The linen tablecloth was stark white, cold and strange; it was as if the plates rested on snow. Unspoken were the words that Willa had read to them from the note pinned to it when it arrived: *To my dear Father and Mother.*

Jabe and Shridy were uneasy about the note which expressed a warmth they did not feel, sent by one they had yet to know. They had weighed the words, looking startled and speechless into each other's eyes. This was Rein's wife, their daughter-in-law, they kept reminding themselves. The spouse of their son's choosing. But she was not their choice. They had chosen Willa, had counted on his return to claim her. But they must acknowledge Rein's woman, accept her, stranger though she be.

Rein's wife had written a letter after their marriage in June; in July there was another in her small, slanted script. There was none of Rein's stubby scrawling on the pages. Willa had read the letters aloud, for Shridy could not read and handwriting confused Jabe. They had listened quietly. After the second letter Shridy had spoken her fear. "Be it Rein doesn't write the next time, hit's a sure sign his wife is going to do all the talking from now till Kingdom Come. He'll be lost to us."

Jabe drew back his chair and sat down. "We oughten to put these dishes away and just use 'em for company," he said. "They won't wear out before we're gone from the world. They're from him, recollect." Shridy's eyes followed the long pattern of the tablecloth as she sank into her chair and folded her hands into a knot in her lap. The letter with the small, slanted script was like a scorpion in her bosom.

In mid-afternoon they sat upon the front porch. The sun had swollen above the hills and now its yellow mask shone dull as hammered metal. The hound's breathing came up through the puncheon floor in moist gasps. There was no movement along the creekbed road. Nothing except the mail hack had passed during the day. The silence and the yellowness swallowed the valley. A jar-fly fiddled in the maple shading the yard and buttery croaks of a frog sounded from the meadow.

"Hit takes a day like this to bresh up the mind and keep us beholden to the Almighty," Jabe said. "Not many of them as gilded as His throne He lets us see in our day and time."

Shridy swung back and forth in her rockingchair, her right hand resting upon her bosom. When it seemed the letter would jump out of itself she drew it forth and held it out to Jabe. "It's from them," she said.

Jabe jerked toward her. "Who writ it?" he asked impatiently.

"Hit's from her," Shridy said. Jabe sank back into his seat in sudden weariness. His hands clenched the chairposts.

The cows began to gather at the pasture gate. They waited without lowing. Jabe rose slowly from his chair and walked toward the barn. The path curved among the hillocks of earth, running before him into the hills. Little Angus Creek was molten gold. Not a wing stirred in the yellow air.

Job's Tears

The fall had been dry and the giant milkweed pods broke early in September. Lean Neck Creek dried to a thread, and all the springs under the moss were damp pockets without a sound of water. Father had sent me over from Little Carr in April to help Grandma with the crop while Uncle Jolly laid out a spell in the county jail for dynamiting a mill dam. I was seven and Grandma was eighty-four, and we patched out two acres of corn. Even with the crows, the crab grass, and the dwarfed stalks we made enough bread to feed us until spring, but when the grass was gone there would be nothing for the mare. The hayloft was empty and the corncrib a nest of shucks.

Uncle Luce sent word from Pigeon Roost that he would come to help gather the crop early in September. Grandma's bones ached with rheumatism and she was not able to go again to the fields. She sat in the cool of the dogtrot, dreading the sun. We waited through the parching days, pricking our ears to every nag's heel against a stone in the valley, to the creak of harness and dry-wheel groan of wagons in the creek bed. Field mice fattened in the patches. Heavy orange cups of the trumpet vine bloomed on the cornstalks, and field larks blew dustily from row to row, feeding well where the mice had scattered their greedy harvesting. We waited impatiently for Uncle Luce, knowing that when he came we should hear from Uncle Jolly, and that Uncle Luce would take the mare home for the winter.

"It's Rilla that's keeping him away," Grandma said. "Luce's woman was always sot agin' him doing for his ol' Mommy. I reckon Luce fotched her off too young. She wasn't nigh sixteen when they married."

We waited for Uncle Luce until the moon was full in October. The leaves ripened, and the air was bloated with the smell of pawpaws where the black fruit lay rotting upon the ground. Possums came to feed there in the night, and two got into a box trap I set above the barn. We ate one, steeped in gravy with sweet potatoes. I shut the other up in a pen, Grandma saying we would eat it when Uncle Jolly got home. She was lonesome for him, and spoke of him through the days. "I reckon he's a grain wild and hard-headed," Grandma said, "but he tuk care of his ol' Mommy."

One morning Grandma said we could wait no longer for Uncle Luce. She took her grapevine walking stick and we went out into the cornfield. We worked two days pulling corn from the small, hoe-tended stalks. When all the runted ears were gathered she measured them out into pokes, pulling her bonnet down over her face to hide the rheumatic pain twisting her face. There were sixteen bushels. "We won't be needing the barn this time," she said. "We'll just sack up the puny nubbins and put them in the shed-room."

With the corn in we waited a few days until Grandma's rheumatism had been doctored with herbs and bitter cherry-bark tea. Then there were the heavy-leaved cabbages, the cushaws and sweet potatoes to be gathered. The potatoes had grown large that year. They were fat and big as squashes. Grandma crawled along the rows on her knees, digging in the baked earth with her hands. It was good to see such fine potatoes. "When Jolly comes home he'll shore eat a bellyful," she said.

I ran along the rows with a willow basket, piling it full and spreading the potatoes in the sun to sweeten. Once I ran into a bull nettle, and it was like fire burning my bare legs. I scratched and whimpered. Grandma took a twist of tobacco out of her apron, chewed a piece for a few minutes, and rubbed the juice on the fiery flesh. "You ain't big as a tick," she said, "but you're a right smart help to your ol' Granny."

The days shortened. There was a hint of frost in the air. The nights were loud with honking geese, and suddenly the leaves were down before gusts of wind. The days were noisy with blowing, and the house filled with the sound of crickets' thighs. There were no birds in the bare orchard, not even the small note of a chewink through the days.

Before frost fell we went to Grandma's flower bed in a corner of the garden and picked the dry seeds before they scattered. We broke off the brown heads of old maids and the smooth buttons of Job's tears hanging on withered stalks. "There's enough tears for a pretty string of beads," Grandma said, "and enough seed left for planting."

Later we pulled and bundled the fodder in the field, stripping the patches for the mare in her dark stall. "If Luce don't come, Poppet is going to starve afore the winter goes out," Grandma said. "It's Rilla hating me that keeps him from coming. Oh she'll larn all her children to grow up hating their ol' Granny."

Uncle Luce came after the first frost. He came whistling up the path from Dry Neck with the icy stones crackling under his feet. Since the gathering, Grandma had been in bed with rheumatism in her back, getting up only to cook. Uncle Luce was filled with excuses. Rilla was sick, and it was getting near her time. His four daughters had had chicken pox. "I'm hoping and praying the next one will be a boy-child," Luce said. "A day's coming when I'll need help with my crap. Girls ain't fittin to grub stumps and hold a plough in the ground."

Grandma noticed Uncle Luce's hands were blackened with resin, and asked if he'd been logging. "I had to scratch up a little something to buy medicine for Rilla," he said. "My crap never done nothing this year. It never got the proper seasoning. I reckon I'll be buying bread afore spring."

"I was reckoning you'd take the mare home for the winter," Grandma said. "I was thinking you could ride her back to Pigeon Roost."

"I hain't got feed for my own mare," Luce said. "I'll be buying corn for my nag afore another month. I reckon Poppet has already eat up more than she's worth. She must be twelve years old. The day's coming you'll need another nag to crap with. It would be right proper to take ol' Poppet out and end her misery."

Grandma raised up in anger. "Luce Baldridge, if you was in reach I'd pop your mouth," she said. Then she lay back and cried a little. Uncle Luce went over and shook her, saying he never meant a word about old Poppet. He wouldn't shoot her for a war pension.

Uncle Luce didn't say a word about Uncle Jolly until Grandma asked him. She waited a long time, giving him a chance to tell her without asking. "You hain't said a word yet about your own brother," Grandma said. "It's about time you told." Then we learned that Uncle Jolly's trial had come up the last of September, and he had been sentenced to the state penitentiary for two years. "I'll get one of the boys to move in with you next March," Uncle Luce said. "Toll would be right glad to come. He's renting land, anyway. And his wife would be a sight o' company."

"No," Grandma said. "We'll make out. My children I've worked and slaved for have thrown their ol' Mommy away. Now that I can't fetch and carry for them, they never give me a grain o' thought. I've been patient and long-suffering. The Lord knows that."

She was crying again now, thinking how Uncle Luce had waited until the crop was gathered to come, thinking how Rilla hadn't come to see her for three years, and how Uncle Jolly was shut up in jail.

"I figure you'd fare better with Toll than Jolly," Luce said. "Toll is solid as rock and never give you a minute's trouble. Jolly is a puore devil. He jumps in and out of trouble like a cricket. I hope the pen will make him pull his horns in a little."

Grandma's voice trembled as she spoke. "Jolly is young," she said. "He just turned grown last year. He ain't mean to the bone, and he's the only one of my boys that looks after their ol' Mommy. I'm afeared I won't live till he gets back. I pray the Lord to keep me breathing till he comes."

Grandma was quiet again when Uncle Luce got ready to go. She brought out a string of Job's tears she had been threading. "It might pleasure Rilla to have them," she said. "It might help with her time coming."

During the short winter days the sun was feeble and pale, shining without heat. Frost lay thick in the mornings, and crusts of hard earth rose in the night on little toadstools of ice. Footsteps upon the ground rang metal-clear, and there was a pattern of furred feet where the rabbits came down out of the barren fields into the yard. My possum rolled himself into a gray ball in his pen, refusing to eat the potatoes I brought him, and then one morning I found him dead. His rusty, hairless tail was frozen as still as a stickweed. The mare grew gaunt in her stall, and there was not a wisp of straw left underfoot. I gleaned the loft of every fodder blade, and the crib of shucks. I filled the manger with cobs, but she did not gnaw upon them, choosing instead to nibble the rotting poplar logs on the wall. I led her down to Lean Neck every day, breaking a hole in the ice near the bank. After a few days she would not drink, and I began to take a bucket of water to the barn. I fed her a little corn—as much as I dared—out of our nubbin pile in the shed-room.

The cold increased and the whole valley was drawn as tight as a drum. The breaking of a bough in the wood shattered the air, the sound dropping like a plummet down the hills, striking against the icy ridges. In the evenings I took an old quilt out to the barn and covered Poppet. I dug frozen chunks of coal out of a pile beside the smokehouse for the fire, and when it seemed there was not going to be enough to last the winter through I went out on the mountain beyond the beech grove and picked up small lumps where the coal bloomed darkly under the ledge. The fire was fed from my pickings until snow fell, covering all trace of the brittle veins.

There were days when Grandma was too sick to get out of bed. I baked potatoes, fried thick slices of side meat, and cooked a corn pone in a skillet on the fire. We used the coffee grounds until there was no strength in them. When the meal gave out I shelled off some corn and ran it through the coffee grinder. It came out coarse and lumpy, but it made good bread.

As Grandma got better she would sit up in bed with a pile of pillows at her back. She slept only at night. During the day she was busy listening and counting. She knew how many knots there were in the ceiling planks. She could look at a knot a long time, and then tell you a man who had a face like it. Most of them were old folks, dead before my time, but there they were. There was one knot that looked like Uncle Jolly. Grandma used to look at it by the hour. "I'm afeared I'll have to piddle my days out looking at this knot," she would say.

One day she counted the stitches in the piece-quilt on her bed. They ran to a count I had never heard. "I learnt to figure," Grandma said, "but I never learnt to read writing. My man could read afore he died, and he done all the reading and I done the figuring. We always worked our learning like a team of horses." We had no calendar, but Grandma worked out the number of days until Uncle Jolly would get out of the penitentiary. "It's nigh on to six hundred and fifty-five," she said when the counting was done. The time had not seemed so long before. Now it stretched along an endless road of days.

There were hours of talk about Uncle Jolly. Grandma said he had held no old grudge against Pate Horn. Grandpa used to log with Pate before he died.

Uncle Toll had married one of Pate's daughters. It had been the dam he built across Troublesome Creek that Uncle Jolly hadn't liked. The fish couldn't jump it, and none could get up into Lean Neck to spawn. He sent Pate word to open up one end of the dam until the spawning season was over. Pate didn't move a peg. Uncle Jolly went down one day and set off two sticks of dynamite under the left bank, blowing out three logs. He went down, with daylight burning, to blow that dam up.

"Jolly ought not to done it," Grandma said. "It looks like the Lord is trying my patience in my last days when I'm weak and porely."

Sometimes she would tell about the things Uncle Jolly had done as a boy. "Once he got a hollow log and tied a strip o' dried bull's hide over it," she said. "Then he got a hickory limb and sawed on it. It sounded like a passel o' wild-cats tearing each other's eyeballs out. Cattle all over the country jumped the rails and tuk down the hollows. The horses and mules kicked barn doors down and lit out. Oh he never meant no harm. It was just boy-mischief."

Near the middle of December the mare stopped eating the nubbins of corn I took her. She would mull her nose in the bucket of water without drinking, and roll her moist eyes at me.

I opened her stall door and let her wander out into the midday sunlight. She did not go far, lifting her leaden hoofs through the snow, and turning from the wind. Presently she went back into the stall and stayed there with her head drooped and her eyes half closed. One morning I went out and found her stretched upon the ground. Her nose was thinly sheeted with ice. She was dead. I latched the stall door and did not go back to the barn again that winter.

January was a bell in Lean Neck Valley. The ring of an axe was a mile wide, and all passage over the spewed-up earth was lifted on the frosty air and sounded against fields of ice. Icicles as large as a man's body hung from limestone cliffs. Grandma listened to the little sounds when her work was done. She was better now. At times when the wind was not so keen she cooked on the stove instead of the fireplace, but it was hard to keep warm in the drafty kitchen.

One Sunday Grandma heard a nag's hoofs on the path to the house. It was Uncle Toll from Troublesome Creek. He brought a letter from Uncle Jolly and he read it to us. His face was dull with worry. Uncle Jolly was coming home. There had been a fire in the prison. "Mommy, do you reckon he broke jail during that fire?" he asked. "He ain't nigh started his spell."

"Jolly is liable to do anything he sets his mind to," Grandma said. "He always had his mind sot on looking after his ol' Mommy. I reckon he'd do anything to get out." And now there was no joy in his coming. There was nothing to do but wait, and those three days before he came seemed longer than any count Grandma ever made.

Suddenly he was there one morning, hollering to us from the yard. There was Uncle Jolly. He had slipped up on us, and even Grandma had not heard him come. He stood there before the door, his eyes bright as a thrush's. He had on a black suit, and a black hat with the crown pinched up sitting at an angle on his head. We sat looking at him, awed and not moving. He jumped into the room and grabbed me up in his arms, pitching me headlong toward the ceiling and bumping my head against the rafters. It hurt a little. He jerked Grandma out of her chair and swung her over the floor. She was laughing and crying together. "For God's sake, Jolly," she said, "don't crack your ol' Mommy's ribs."

Then he was all over the house, prying and looking. He opened up the meat box and sniffed into it. He thumped the pork shoulder we had been saving. "Ripe as a melon," he said. "It smells like kingdom come." He reached elbow-deep into his pocket and drew out a knife. It was a big one. With a single blade open, it was nearly a foot long. There was a blue racer carved on one side with a forked tongue. "I made that in the workshop," he said. "They never knowed I was making it." He swung it through the air, striking toward me. *Plunk* it went into the pork shoulder. Uncle Jolly was devilish like that. Grandma was already sifting out meal, and he cut off a half-dozen slices of meat to fry.

Uncle Jolly found the corn in the shed-room. He picked up one of the runted ears and pinched a grain. "Is this all you raised?" he asked. "We got some mighty pretty cushaws," Grandma said. "The sweet taters done right well, too."

"The mare will starve on this corn," Jolly said. "You know what I'm going to do? I'm going to buy ol' Poppet a sack of sweet feed mixed with molasses and bran. I reckon her teeth is wore down to the gum."

He began to gather up some ears to take to the barn.

"Just you wait, son," Grandma called. "Just you wait till we get dinner over." Grandma looked hard at me. I didn't say a word.

When we sat down to the table, Uncle Jolly began to eat with both hands. "I ain't had a fittin meal since I left Lean Neck," he said. He loaded his plate with shucky beans and a slice of meat, talking as he ate. "I stayed at Luce's house last night," he said. "Luce and Rilla's got another girl-child born three weeks ago."

Grandma laid her fork down and stirred in her chair. "Is Rilla getting along tolerable?" she asked.

"Rilla is up and doing," Uncle Jolly said. "They named the baby after you, Mommy. They named it Lonie."

Grandma blinked and made a little clicking noise with her teeth. "It's good to have grandchildren growing up honoring and respecting their ol' folks," she said.

"Oh Uncle Jolly," I begged, "tell us about the jail fire and how you got out." Uncle Jolly swallowed, the raw lump of his Adam's apple jumping in his throat. "It was the biggest fire ever was," he said. "It caught the woodshop and tool sheds, and it was eating fast. It might o' got the jailhouse if I hadn't stayed there and fit it with a waterspout. Everybody else run around like a chicken with its head pinched off. Then the Governor heard how I fit the fire and never run, and he give me a pardon. He sent me word to go home."

Grandma settled in her chair. "It was dangerous, son," she said. "It might o' burned up the jail. Whoever sot that fire ought to be whipped with oxhide. Some folks is everly destroying and putting nothing back. Who lit that fire, son?"

Uncle Jolly's mouth was too full to answer. He dropped his eyes and swallowed. "I sot it, Mommy," he said. He took another slice of meat, and heaped more beans on his plate. Grandma sat quiet and watching, her blue-veined hands clasped in her lap. Her face was sad, but her eyes were bright with wonder.

"You know what I done coming up Troublesome Creek this morning?" Uncle Jolly asked suddenly. "I pulled another log out of Pate Horn's mill dam. There's a good-sized hole now. The perch will be swarming into Lean Neck this spring."

The Egg Tree

The hail of early June shredded the growing blades of corn, and a windstorm breaking over Little Angus Creek in July flattened the sloping field; but the hardy stalks rose in the hot sun, and the fat ears fruited and ripened. With the mines closed at Blackjack all winter and spring, Father had rented a farm on the hills rising from the mouth of Flaxpatch on Little Angus. We moved there during a March freeze, and the baby died that week of croup. When the sap lifted in sassafras and sourwood, Father sprouted the bush-grown patches, and ploughed deep. With corn breaking through the furrows, and the garden seeded, he left us to tend the crop, going over in Breathitt County to split rock in Brack Hogan's quarry.

There was good seasoning in the ground. Shucks bulged on heavy corn ears. Garden furrows were cracked where potatoes pushed the earth outward in their growing. Weeds plagued the corn, and Mother took us to the fields. We were there at daylight, chopping at horsemint and crab grass with blunt hoes. Sister Euly could trash us all with a corn row. She was a beanpole, thin and quick like Mother. Fletch had grown during the summer, and his face was round as a butterball. He dug too deep, often missing the weeds and cutting the corn. Mother let him take the short rows. He slept during hot afternoons at the field's edge, deep in a patch of tansy with bees worrying the dusty blossoms over his head.

"It's a sight to have such a passel o' victuals after livin' tight as a tow-wad," Mother said. We pickled a barrel of firm corn ears. Tomatoes ripened faster than they could be canned. The old apple trees in the bottom were burdened. We peeled and sulphured three bushels of McIntoshes. Fall beans were strung and hung with peppers and onions on the porch. The cushaws were a wonder to see, bloated with yellow flesh. The crooked-neck gourds on the lot fence grew too large for water dippers. They were just right for martin poles.

"If we stay on here I'm goin' to have me a mess o' martins livin' in them gourds," I told Mother.

"If your Poppy is a-mind to, we'll jist settle down awhile," Mother said. "It's a sight the rations we've got."

With the crops laid by, we cleaned up a patch of ground on the Point around the baby's grave. Mother took up a bucket of white sand from the Flaxpatch sand bar, patting it on the mound with her hands. "We're goin' to have a funeralizin' for the baby in September," she said. "Your Poppy will be agin' it, but we're goin' to, whether or no. I've already spoke for Brother Sim Manley. He's comin' all the way from Troublesome Creek. I reckon we've got plenty to feed everybody."

There was nothing more to do in the garden and the fields, and during this first rest since spring, Mother began to grieve over the baby. Euly told us that she cried in the night, and slept with its gown under her pillow. We spoke quietly, and there was no noise in the house. The jarflies on the windows and the katydids outside sang above our words. With Mother suddenly on edge, and likely to cry at a word, we played all day on the hills. Euly ran the coves like a young fox, coming in before supper with a poke of chestnuts and chinquapins. She often made her dinner of pawpaws, smelling sickly sweet of them. I found her playhouse once in a haw patch. There were eight poppets made from corn-cobs sitting on rock chairs, eating giblets of cress from mud dishes. I skittered away, Euly never knowing I had been there.

Fletch followed me everywhere. Sometimes I hid, wanting to play by myself, and talk things out loud, but he would call until his voice hoarsened and trembled. Then I was ashamed not to answer, and I'd pretend I had just come into hollering distance. He would come running, dodging through the weeds like a puppy. There was no getting away from Fletch.

One day me and Fletch came in from the buckeye patch with our pockets loaded. Mother and Euly were working around a dead willow in the yard, stringing the twigless branches with eggshells Mother had been saving. The eggs had been broken carefully at each end, letting the whites and yolks run out. The little tree was about five feet high, and the lean branches were already nearly covered with shells.

"I allus did want me an egg tree," Mother said. "I hear tell it's healthy to have one growin' in the yard. And I figger it'll be right brightenin' to the house with all the folks that's comin' to the funeralizin'. My dommers ought to lay nigh enough to kiver the last branch afore the time comes. Eggshells hain't a grain o' good except to prettify with."

August lay heavy on the fields when Father came home for three days. Blooming whitetop covered the pasture before the house, and spindling stickweeds shook out their purple bonnets. Father came just before dark, and the pretty-by-nights were open and pert by the doorsill. He trudged into the yard without seeing the egg tree, or the blossoms beside the steps. He walked up on the porch, and we saw his nose was red, and his eyes watery. Mother caught him by the arm.

"It's this damned hay fever," Father said. "Ever' bloom on the face o' the earth is givin' off dust. Sometimes hit nigh chokes me black in the face."

He sniffled, blew his nose, and went inside with Mother. His angry voice suddenly filled the house. Mother brought out an armload of yellowrods, stickweed blooms, and farewell-to-summer that Euly had stuck around in fruit jars.

Father's face darkened when Mother told him about the funeralizing for the baby. "I've already sent on word to Preacher Sim Manley," she said.

Father groaned. "It's onreckonin' what a woman'll think about with her man off tryin' to make a livin'," he said. "Little Green wasn't nigh eight months old, and thar hain't any use of a big funeral."

"We've got plenty to feed everybody," Mother said. "I ain't ashamed o' what we got. We've done right proud this year. I'm jist gittin' one preacher, and it's goin' to be a one-day funeral."

"Thar hain't no use askin' anybody except our kin," Father said. "It'll look like we're tryin' to put on the dog."

"Everybody that's a-mind to come is asked," Mother said. "I hain't tryin' to put a peck measure over the word o' God."

Father got up and lighted the lamp on the mantel. "We'll feed right good down at Blackjack this winter," he said. "I hear tell the mines is goin' to open the middle o' October. I'm goin' back to Brack Hogan's quarry for another two weeks and then I'm quittin'. I'm longin' to git me a pick and stick it in a coal vein. I can't draw a good clean breath o' air outside a mine this time o' year. It's like a horse tryin' to breathe with his nose in a meal poke."

"I was jist reckonin' we'd stay on here another crap," Mother said. "The mines is everly openin' and closin'. The baby is buried here, too. And I never favored bringin' up children in a coal camp. They've got enough meanness in their blood without humorin' it. We done right good crappin' this year. We raised a passel o' victuals."

"Thar's goin' to be good times agin in Blackjack," Father said. "I hear they're goin' to pay nigh fifty cents a ton for coal loadin'. And they're goin' to build some new company houses, and I got my word in for one."

Mother's face was pale in the lamplight. "I reckon it's my egg tree I'm hatin' to leave," she said. "I allus did want me one."

"It's fresh news to me you got one," Father said. "I hain't seed one since afore I married and was traipsin' 'round on Buckhorn Creek. I wisht all the timber was egg trees. They don't give off a grain o' dust. This Little Angus hollow is dusty as a pea threshin'. It nigh makes a fellow sneeze his lungs out."

"I'm a-mind to stay on here," Mother said, her voice chilled and tight. "It's the nighest heaven I've been on this earth."

Fall came in the almanac, and the sourwood bushes were like fire on the mountains. Leaves hung bright and jaundiced on the maples. Red foxes came down the hills, prowling around our chicken house, and the hens squalled in the night. Quin Adams's hounds hunted the ridges, their bellies thin as saw blades. Their voices came bellowing down to us in the dark hours. Once, waking suddenly, I heard a fox bark in defeat somewhere in the cove beyond Flaxpatch.

Mother had set the funeralizing for the last Sunday in September. Father came on the Wednesday before, bringing a headstone he had cut out of Brack Hogan's quarry, chipped from solid limerock. The baby's name was carved on one side with a chisel. We took it up on the Point, standing it at the head of the mound. Father built an arbor there out of split poplar logs. We thatched the roof with branches of linn.

"It's big enough for Preacher Sim to swing his arms in without hittin' anybody," Father said.

Mother came up the hill to see it. "I wisht to God I'd had a picture tuk o' the baby so it could be sot in the arbor durin' the meetin'. I wisht to God I'd had it tuk."

Father cut down some locusts, laying the trunks in front of the arbor for seats, and Mother took a pair of mule shears, cutting the weeds and grass evenly.

Grandma and Uncle Jolly came Thursday morning, Grandma riding sidesaddle on a horse-mule, and Uncle Jolly astraddle a pony not more than a dozen hands high. His feet nearly dragged dirt. He came singing at the top of his voice:

Polish my boots
And set 'em on the bench,
Goin' down to Jellico
To see Jim Shanks.
Holler-ding, baby, holler-ding.

Ole gray goose went to the river.
If'n I'd been a gander
I'd went thar with 'er.
Holler-ding, baby, holler-ding.

When they turned out of the Little Angus sandbar, Uncle Jolly crossed his legs in the saddle, and came riding up the yard path, right onto the porch, and would have gone pony and all into the house if Mother hadn't been standing in the door. Father laughed, saying, "Jolly allus was a damned fool," and Uncle Jolly got so tickled he reeled on the porch, holding his stomach, and he fell off into the pretty-by-night bed.

Grandma hitched the horse-mule at the fence, looking at the egg tree as she crossed the yard. "Hit's a sight," she said, pulling off her bonnet. "I hain't seen one in twenty year."

Aunt Rilla came in time for dinner, walking up from the creek-bed road with Lala, Crilla, Lue, and Foan strung out behind. Uncle Luce and Toll came in the night. Aunt Shridy was there by daylight next morning, and we all set to work getting ready for Sunday. The floors were scrubbed twice over with a shuck mop, and the smoky walls washed down. Jimson weeds were cut out of the backyard, and the woodpile straightened. Mother cut the heads off of fifteen dommers. The stove stayed hot all day Friday, baking and frying. Cushaw pies covered the kitchen table.

"I reckon we got enough shucky beans biled to feed creation," Grandma said. "Lonie, you hain't never been in such a good fix since you tuk a man. You'd be puore foolish movin' to Blackjack agin."

"Since I married I've been driv' from one coal mine to another," Mother said, taking her hands out of bread dough. "And I've lived hard as nails. I've lived at Blue Diamond. I've lived at Chavies, Elkhorn, and Lacky. We moved up to Hardburley twicet, and to Blackjack beyond countin'. I reckon I've lived everwhere on God's green earth. Now I want to set me down and rest. The baby is buried here, and I reckon I've got a breathin' spell comin'. We done right well this crap. We got plenty."

Grandma kept us children shooed out of the kitchen. We hung around Uncle Jolly until he put a lizard up Fletch's britches leg, and threw a bucket of water on the rest of us. "Sometimes I fair think Jolly is a witty," Aunt Rilla said.

Father met Preacher Sim Manley at the mouth of Flaxpatch Saturday morning, taking Uncle Jolly's nag for him to ride on up the creek. But they both came back walking, being ashamed to ride the sorry mount. Father said he didn't know the pony had a saddle boil until he had started with her.

Preacher Sim slept on the feather bed that night. Father took the men out to the barn to sleep on the hay. Grandma and Aunt Lemma took Mother's bed, the rest of us stretching out on pallets spread on the floor.

The moon was full, and big and shiny as a brass pot. It was day-white outside. I couldn't sleep, feeling the strangeness of so many people in the house, and the unfamiliar breathing. Before day I went out to the corncrib and got a nap until the rooster crowed, not minding the mice rustling the shucks in the feed basket.

Mother climbed up to the Point before breakfast to spread a white sheet over the baby's grave. When she came down the Adamses were there, Quin looking pale with his first shave of the fall, and Mrs. Adams flushed and hot, not wanting to sit down and wrinkle her starched dress. Cleve Horn and his family were not far behind.

Before nine o'clock the yard and porch were crowded. Neighbors came up quietly, greeting Mother, and the women held handkerchiefs in their hands, crying a little. Then we knew again that there had been death in our house. All who went inside spoke in whispers, their voices having more words than sound. The clock was stopped, its hands pointing to the hour and minute the baby died; and those who passed through the rooms knew the bed, for it was spread with a white counterpane and a bundle of fall roses rested upon it.

At ten o'clock Brother Sim opened his Bible in the arbor on the Point. "Oh my good brethren," he said. "We was borned in sin, and saved by grace." He spat upon the ground, and lifted his hands towards the withered linn thatching. "We have come together to ask the blessed Saviour one thing pint-blank. Can a leetle child enter the Kingdom of Heaven?"

The leaves came down. October's frost stiffened the brittle grass, and spiderwebs were threads of ice in the morning sun. We gathered our corn during the cool days, sledding it down the snaky trail from field to barn. The pigs came down out of the hills from their mast hunting, and rooted up the bare potatoes with damp snouts. Father went over to Blackjack and stayed a week. When he returned there was coal dust ground into the flesh of his hands. He had worked four days in the mines, and now there was a company house waiting for us.

"I promised to git moved over in three days," Father said. "We got a sealed house with two windows in ever' room waitin' for us."

"I'm a-longin' to stay on here," Mother said. Her voice was small and hoping. "I'll be stayin' here with the children, and you can go along till spring. Movin' hain't nothin' but leavin' things behind."

Father cracked his shoes together in anger. "That's clear foolishness you're sayin'," he said, reddening. "I ain't aimin' to be a widow-man this year."

"I'm sot agin' movin'," Mother said, "but I reckon I'm bound to go where you go."

"We ought to be movin' afore Thursday," Father said.

"Nigh we git our roots planted, we keep pullin' 'em up and plantin' 'em in furrin ground," Mother complained. "Movin' is an abomination. Thar's a sight o' things I hate to leave here. I hate to leave my egg tree I sot so much time and patience on. Reckon it's my egg tree holdin' me."

"I never heered tell of such foolishness," Father said. "Pity thar hain't a seed so hit can be planted agin."

Cold rains came over the Angus hills, softening the roads and deepening the wheel tracks. There could be no moving for a spell, though Father was anxious to be loading the wagon. Mother sat before the fire, making no effort to pack, while the rains fell through the long, slow days.

"Rain hain't never lost a day for a miner," Father said, walking the floor restlessly.

"You ought to be nailin' up a little grave-house for the baby then," Mother said. Father fetched some walnut planks down from the loft and built the grave-house under the barn shed. It was five feet square with a chestnut shingle roof. During the first lull in the weather, we took it up to the Point.

When the rain stopped, fog hung in the coves, and the hills were dark and weather-gray. Cornstalks stood awkwardly unbalanced in the fields. The trees looked sodden and dead, and taller than when in leaf. Father took our stove down one night. The next morning our mare was hitched to the wagon, and the hind gate let down before the back door. Mother gave us a cold baked potato for breakfast, then began to pack the dishes. We were on the road up Flaxpatch by eight o'clock, Mother sitting on the seat beside Father, and looking back towards the Point, where the grave-house stood among the bare locusts.

We reached Blackjack in middle afternoon. The slag pile towering over the camp burned with an acre of oily flames, and a sooty mist hung along the creek bottom. Our house sat close against a bare hill. It was cold and gloomy, smelling sourly of paint, but there were glass windows, and Euly, Fletch, and I ran into every room to look out. Old neighbors came in to shake our hands, but there was no warmth in their words or fingers.

Father started back after the last load as soon as the wagon bed was empty, leaving us to set the beds up. He came back in the night, none of us hearing him drive in the gate.

At daybreak we were up, feeling the nakedness of living in a house with many windows. We went out on the porch and looked up the rutted street. Men went by through the mud with carbide lamps burning on their caps. Mother came out presently into the yard. There was the egg tree. Its roots were buried shallowly in damp earth near the fence corner. Some of the shells were cracked, and others had fallen off, exposing the brown willow branches. Mother turned and went back into the house. "It takes a man-person to be a puore fool," she said.

Lost Brother

I've seen men die.

I reckon I've seen a half-a-dozen drap in their tracks without loosenin' their brogans. I seen Ruf Craig swallow a bullet square in his mouth and go down with his teeth clenched, his lips drawed, and nary a speck o' blood droolin' out.

I seen Brag Thomas soak up a plug o' lead in his heart last gingerbread election. He never batted an eye. Jist sort of sunk down in the mud, his eyes standin' pine-blank open. When they laid him out it tuk five nickels to hold his lids down.

Oh I've seen men head toward eternal torment without a flinch. But men are powerful braggers. They would do this, and they would do that. When it comes to stretchin' out final for the grave-box, no man can say what he'll do.

Death kin come sudden. Here on Squabble Creek it comes that way more'n a leetle. Hit don't tickle-toe up and tell you to lay down and pull the sheet up. And to call yore woman and yore pap and all yore young 'uns.

Hit's like lightnin' strikin' a yaller poplar and skinnin' her all the way down. Hit's like yore heart turnin' square over and givin' you a minute to do all the rest o' yore life's thankin' in. This ole breath kin be mighty puore and sweet when it comes to loosin' it.

I've seen men die. But nary a one that tuk it like a lost brother come home.

Oh nary a one 'cept Ambrose Middleton, who never dodged a chunk o' lead all his days. And never moved a frog-hair to stop the last one. Ole Fiddlin' Ambrose, who never harmed a critter in his life, who made ole Bollen County the best sheriff they ever knowed, and who could fiddle like all git-out.

His fiddle was the sassiest in the hills. He made it hisself out o' best grained cherry. And he drawed and waxed his own catgut. Thar was fourteen rattlesnake rattlers makin' it sound like the one I heered ole Bull had. I heered tell he was the fiddlin'est fool ever lived. I reckon he was favorin' Ambrose. Ruther play than to eat groundhog gravy.

And when ole Fiddlin' Ambrose come to die, I reckon he was tickled and never begrudged a wink o' light that went out o' his eyeballs.

Oh he never put store in livin' like you and me. He wasn't stingy with the calendar. Not since he killt his blood-son Parly nigh goin' on twenty years ago.

He never aimed to do it. Hit was puore accidental, and it was with a shotgun he was unloadin' after he'd come in from a fox hunt. And his belly had been washin' likker for a week afore. He never tetched a drap after that. Not in these twenty years.

Hit's a lot o' tales they tell on ole Ambrose. About him scratchin' up the grave-box with his fingernails the night after the buryin'. About him makin' his bed in the graveyard for three months. I never put a grain o' faith in them tales.

Parly was buried on the ivy p'int yonside the doublins. Never the time did I see Ambrose on that p'int, never the night or day in all my life. Once I seen him standin' in a patch o' moonlight lookin' up thar. I reckon he was lookin' square through that hill at the stars. He stood thar a long time, never movin' or retchin' his eyes down. I streaked off through the thicket and he never knowed I seen him.

I never seen nothin' quare about Ambrose.

There was nothin' quare about him 'less it was the way he sawed the fiddle. He could make yore feet go to beatin' time spite o' wish and damnation.

There was nothin' quare 'less it was the way he stood up to the shootin' and scrappin' when he was the Law. Oh he'd spit death in the face many the time. He never cared after Parly went. With him it was jist hell or no.

After Parly went he was in a puore bad fix. I reckon he jist run for sheriff to give him somethin' to thank about. Well, hit wasn't much runnin' he done. He jist stuck his name on the ticket and said no more about it. Ambrose Middleton ain't asked a livin' soul to vote for him till yet.

Oh he put the cat on the fellows runnin' agin' him. I figger folks voted for Ambrose 'cause he didn't ask 'em to. I figger they voted for him out o' puore respect.

You wouldn't a-knowed Squabble Creek when Ambrose was sheriff. It got to where a fellow could go to a bean strangin' or a log-rollin' without gittin' his skull cracked with a gun-barrel. Or his nose or his ears bit nigh off.

When ole Ambrose was around you'd better keep yore Barlow knife retched out o' sight. Many the time he stepped squar' in where the bullets was a-spewin'. He never got a scratch till his time come at Wage Thompson's squar' dance.

When ole Fiddlin' Ambrose was the Law he jist about opened the jail doors and told all the likker makers to git home. He told them to git to their home-seats and plant a patch o' corn for their women and young 'uns.

But he done one thang he ought never done.

Thar was a boy in jail named Tobe Romer who had jist about growed up yonside the bars. I reckon he'd got more jailhouse victuals than any other kind. His mommy and poppy was dead and he jist run wild on the hills like a fox, a-stealin' and a-preyin'.

Tobe was twenty-one on the record books, but he didn't look more'n seventeen. And he was all the devils in torment rolled in one ball. Oh he'd steal the horns off a billy goat. You had to be good to Tobe Romer or he'd feed pizen to yore hound dogs. Or burn yore house down over yore head. He was a rascal if thar ever was one twixt earth and burnin' hell.

The devil hisself must o' put the idea in Ambrose's head.

He tuk Tobe to his house and treated him like he was his own blood. He give him everythang. Hit was a sight the pettin' Ambrose give that boy. But it didn't make no difference to Tobe. I reckon it come too late.

Hit was like pettin' a wild cat. He jist tuk all Ambrose would give him, then he'd raise more racket than ever. But Ambrose never give up. Tobe always had plenty o' good victuals, and he tuk to more meanness 'cause Ambrose was the Law and he'd never be put in jail agin.

I reckon Ambrose done everythang he could. Everythang that talkin' and beggin' could do. You can't make a saint out o' the puore devil. Tobe jist done what he'd been doin' straight on, and many the knife stayed sharp for his hide. I bet thar was bullets jist achin' for his meat.

I was at Wage Thompson's squar' dance when Ambrose met the bullet that was molded for him the minute he was born. Oh that lead had been a-growin' sixty-two years afore it had a chancet to do its work.

Thar was Ambrose settin' on a splint-wood chair, fiddlin' for puore glory. Oh he could make a fiddle talk sweet talk. He could make it whine like a baby when he had a mind to. He could make it yell and holler, and nigh walk out o' his hands when he put hisself to it.

John Tolbert was callin' the sets and we had danced three, gittin' powerful warm and beginnin' to sweat. He was jist gittin' limbered up good when Tobe come in. He was all lit and his chin was sort of hung over his collar. We looked at Ambrose settin' thar in his chair with his fiddle in his lap. Ambrose jist set thar and never let on.

I went outside with a couple o' fellows to take a drank, and when we come back I see somethin' had happened. Tobe is settin' by hisself in the corner and glarin' at Ambrose pine-blank. Ambrose ain't payin' him no attention.

Somebody tells me Ambrose has told Tobe to leave and stay gone till he sobers up.

But Tobe ain't made a move. And Ambrose ain't sayin' a word. He's jist a-settin' and a-restin' for the next set.

Then, sudden-like, Ambrose gits up and walks over to Tobe. We stood thar froze and wonderin'. He never says nothin', jist stands thar and looks at Tobe. Tobe gits to squirmin'. I reckon his seat was gittin' too hot for him. He gits up and sidles out o' the room.

John Tolbert jumps out in the middle o' the floor and hollers right big, and Ambrose gits to pullin' down hard on his bow agin. First thang we knowed we was shuffling the Squirrel Chase. And the fiddle was nigh talkin'.

Keep yore skillet good and greasy all the time, time, time.

Oh that was a sweet set we was a-dancin'. It must o' been a heap o' noise we was makin' too, draggin' and scrapin' our feet, keepin' time to that music. That music was like a dream you dreamt.

I was swingin' Hebe Fuller's daughter right nigh Ambrose when I heard somethin' crack. You couldn't have hardly heered it with all that noise and everybody laughin' and payin' no attention to nothin' 'cept cuttin' corners proper.

Hit was like somebody had broke a right dry stick in a brashpile. I looked at the window and didn't see nothin'. Then I looked at Ambrose, and I saw the quarest look on his face. But he was still strikin' that catgut with all his might.

Right off I knowed what had happened. I broke loose and started for the door, lookin' back at Ambrose. He shuck his head and I knowed he didn't want me to go out. I didn't say nothin' 'cause there wasn't nothin' to say. If I was actin' quare nobody paid me any mind. I was drankin' right peart.

I jist stands thar starin' at Ambrose. And I seen the happiest look come on his face.

He laughs right out loud and keeps greasin' that skillet with his bow. *Keep yore skillet good and greasy.* Then I knowed he hadn't been hit.

Oh hit would take a charmed bullet to drill ole Fiddlin' Ambrose.

I grabs Hebe Fuller's daughter agin and swangs right swift 'round the corner, feelin' sort o' proud o' ole Ambrose never turnin' a hair.

Oh they'll never forget how he played that set.

When I come back 'round to Ambrose's chair I looks at him agin. He was still laughin' and his fiddle ain't stoppin' a minute. But he looks quare. He was gittin' pale. All the time he's workin' that bow like a cross-cut saw in a walnut log.

Then I takes another look and I see somethin'.

Ambrose is holdin' that fiddle up high but he can't hide it.

I see his shirt and the dancin' jist run clear out o' my feet. It was time to swang, and I swung like my jints was frost-bit. I kept a-goin'. I knowed Ambrose wanted it that way.

We was nigh through that set when the music stopped.

We was caught thar with our feet clear off the floor and no music to put 'em down with.

I heered Ambrose's fiddle hit the floor and one strang twanged.

I never looked. I couldn't look.

I jist drapped down on one knee. My eyeballs was hot as a coal.

Brother to Methuselum

Here on Oak Branch of Ballard Creek we are nearly all kinfolks. We mostly marry amongst ourselves, live and die where we were born, and don't try to run after the rest of the world. Let one of us get twenty or thirty years along, outlast pneumonia fever, typhoid, and grippe, we're apt to inhabit this earth a good long spell. Two or three got to be a hundred or so, so agey they looked liked dried cushaws. But not another who started living square over again after they had passed the century mark as did Uncle Mize Hardburly. He raised a new set of teeth, grew a full head of hair. Not even John Shell, the oldest man in the world, who had his picture in the almanac advertising purgatives, could make this claim. And besides, Uncle Mize's face lost its wrinkles and became as smooth as a June apple.

Uncle Mize was a hundred and three when he began to sprout his hair and teeth. Hair grew back on his noggin as thick as crabgrass in a corn balk. The teeth—they were the real thing. Aye gonnies, it was beyond belief unless you saw them yourself. Gazing into his mouth was akin to peeping into a hollow stump nested with joree eggs. There were the grinders, eyeteeth, and incisors. The full set. And was Uncle Mize tickled! He could stop gumming his tobacco and recommence chewing.

After his rejuvenation, Uncle Mize got to hopping around to beat crickets. He throwed away his specs. Rarely used them anyhow, except to see how finances stood in his snapping pocketbook. He propped his walking stick in a corner, for keeps. Aye, I couldn't remember him without that stick, which was carved to the appearance of a copperhead snake.

Unnatural it was bound to be, Uncle Mize getting young again and the Hardburly burying ground full of people not nigh so ancient. He had outlived two wives. Nine children awaited final judgment in the graveyard. His whole family set had gone to glory, or torment—who can say?—except two sons,

Broadus and Kell. But Uncle Mize took to his rebirth like a sheep to green ivy, gammicking over his farm, beating in a crop, cussing and bossing as in younger days. Broadus and Kell hadn't cleared a new-ground in fifteen seasons. Now, by the hokies! They had to hoist their backsides, whet their shanks, grub and dig. They had to shake hands with a plow handle.

Broadus and Kell were twins, sixty-one years of age, and single. Yet, gosh dog! They couldn't be blamed for not finding dough-beaters when women followed shunning them. They were as alike as churn dashers, homely and tall and stringy, a mite humpbacked, and as common in the face as the Man Above ever shaped and allowed to breathe. As the saying goes, they'd been hit by the ugly stick. How a handsome-looker like Uncle Mize could have sired them beat understanding. Or was there a stranger in the woodpile? Oh there were some people sorry enough to think so.

Maw vowed the brothers put her in mind of granny hatchets burrowing in a rotten log, beetle-eyed and nit-brained. Human craney crows, she called them. Why, I don't suppose even a three-time widow would cut eyes at either. Not along Oak Branch, or the whole of Ballard Creek. Not anywhere in the territory. They were willing all right, willing as ferrets in a rabbit hole, but they got nowhere in the marry market. Kell gave up the hunt at around fifty years of age. Broadus never did.

On account of his years, Maw and the other women on Oak were easier on Uncle Mize than on his sons. Nevertheless Uncle Mize had his rakings. They low-rated him partly because he didn't belong to their congregation, didn't pull his chin long as a mule's collar on Sunday. He would go to church—go *at* church, say. He'd loll in the shade of the gilly tree in the yard, and did a preacher step on somebody's toes too hard in the church-house, they could steal out and talk with Uncle Mize, swell their chest with the fresh air blowing across Oak from the hickory ridge, and forget about eternal damnation. Jawing with Uncle Mize they would presently feel content to wring the pleasures such as they were from this world, and allow the next to rack its own jennies.

I followed hanging after Uncle Mize. You understand how a seventeen-year-old youngster is, big ears and small gumption. Don't know his ankles from a hole in the ground. I relished talk with a speck of seasoning, and Uncle

Mize was the fanciest blackguarder in the mountains, slicking the devil's blessings over his tobacco cud, pouring on the vinegar. He could split frog hairs with words. And Uncle Mize was as generous as weather. He'd let me borrow his pocketknife, and most trees on the meeting-ground have my name carved on their trunk. He kept the knife in his snapping pocketbook and sometimes I found money wedged between the blades. Those days I didn't wink at a dime. Even a penny.

So Uncle Mize shunned the rocking chair and got around more. He visited us sometimes despite Maw's disapproval that he was on top of the earth instead of under it. Once she said in his presence, "Hit's unearthly for a body to become young once they've been old. Hit's contrary to prophecy and the plan of creation."

"Cite me," Uncle Mize challenged. "Quote me scripture on it."

Said Maw, "If it hain't in the Book, it ought to be. Oh I've seen plum thickets bloom pretty in a January thaw and freeze out in February."

"Hazel bushes bust blossoms the first month of the year," Uncle reminded, "and they flourish and endure. It appears the idea of the Almighty for them to flower and beget in winter. And that might sometimes happen in the case of mankind."

Maw had clacked her teeth and hushed. She couldn't outtalk Uncle Mize.

Uncle Mize figured people were jealous. He was reviving, rising again, and they were scared he wasn't mortal. Whether folks will admit to it or not, they want to outlive everybody they know. Especially their enemies. Aye, Uncle Mize didn't account it peculiar, his turning the calendar backwards. "I've aimed to be around a right smart number of years, and I've lived accordingly," he'd say. "I 'stilled my own whiskey, raised my own bread and meat, growed the tobacco I chew, done a mite of everything, and not too much of anything. I split the middle. I've dodged the doctors—the main thing. Oh I've had sicknesses, yes sir. But when herbs of my own brewing wouldn't heal, I let the flesh cure itself. And, by the gods, I believe I'm a brother to Methuselum."

Fellows teased Uncle Mize, yet they made small scrimption off of him. He was as foxy as the next 'un. They'd inquire was he getting youthful all over, or was it in spots.

"Aye, neighbor," Uncle Mize would cackle. "I'm resurrected from alpha to omega, from toe to crown. I'm a match to the apple they call Worldly Wonder. And, hear me, my friends, I'm likely to sire another drove ere there's singing on the point."

"You mean you would wed again?" they would cry.

Uncle Mize would go along with the kidding. "Why, I've married two times in life," he'd banter, "and I might decide to go for twice more—shoe the horse all the way 'round." But Uncle Mize was talking to hear his head rattle. He didn't have any such business in head.

Uncle Mize kept the buck passing, not allowing it to stick on him. Nevertheless, square down, he must of understood he wasn't immortal. Yet he stood in with the best of them, for a while. Now, no, they made nothing off of Uncle Mize. You can't gig a fellow who is laughing harder than you are. It's like spitting into Oak Branch, expecting to hit a fish in the eye. But Bot Shedders, the mail carrier, tried the hardest.

I recollect Uncle Mize got in behind Broadus and Kell and put in a big crop that spring. By hooker-by-crook he planted eleven acres of new-ground corn. Persuading Broadus and Kell to work regular was akin to whooping snakes. Kell was forever hunting a shady spot, Broadus haunting that county seat. Broadus could figure up more reasons for going to town than overalls have pockets. He went to see females riding sidesaddle, though his excuses were otherwise. Though he'd never see sixty again, he wouldn't give up pining after the women. I suppose he was hammered together that way. So it took coaxing and begging and cussing on Uncle Mize's part to get the work done. Toward the end of April he had to hire me.

Broadus and Kell set off one morning for the high swag of the ridge to thin and plow corn. I stayed behind to help plant beans in the sass patch. Me and Uncle Mize finished in less than an hour and then lit out for the swag ourselves, hoes across our shoulders. It was a pull, mounting the slope, but Uncle Mize skinned up it as easily as I. We rested on stumps at the top and gazed below at the corn growing black-green and bonny. The blades rustled, the air smelled of tansy. Two crows flopped overhead.

"Be dom," Uncle Mize chuckled, "crows know a master crop when they spot one."

We dropped into the swag through a redbud thicket and made our way to the edge of the field. Broadus and Kell weren't in view. The mule had dragged the plow across the rows and stood biting tops. Uncle Mize flew mad. What he said would rot teeth. Then he hushed and listened. A belch sounded nearby. He grabbed up a sassafras root and tickle-toed toward the noise.

Broadus and Kell were stretched behind a dead chestnut, a fruit jar between them, drunk as hooty-owls. Kell slept peacefully while his brother dropped anty mars down his collar. Beading an eye on Uncle Mize, Broadus lifted the jar and said, "Come take you a sup, Pap, and loosen up your whistle."

Uncle Mize swung the sassafras. It zizzed, breaking the jar to smithereens. Broadus sprang to his feet, aiming to hightail it, but Uncle Mize brought the root against his skull full force, and it wasn't a pulled lick either. Broadus laid over, cold as clabber. Kell must of dreamt there was a war broke out, for he staggered up, threshed his arms, and when he saw who was there, grumbled, "What you acting so brigetty about, Pap?" Uncle Mize answered with a blow of the root, and Kell could only crouch and fend off the whacks.

On untwisting the mule's harness, Uncle Mize started plowing himself, busting middles, geeing and hawing, and I tried to keep ahead in the row, thinning stalks, but I couldn't. He worked like a twenty-year-old, like a whiteback. And he had the field cultivated by dinnertime. He finished it snorting worse than the mule. I saw Uncle Mize was trembly. I saw the wings of his nose and the tags of his ears were pale. The plowing had hurt him, had set him back considerable. He had overdone.

Uncle Mize took the punies. He moped about the house, satisfied to reclaim his walking stick and rocking chair. He wasn't so branfired feisty thereafter. He would holler to folks going Oak Branch road and invite them to come in and gab with him. He didn't have to beckon Bot Shedders. Bot regularly stopped his mail hack and retailed gossip an hour or so.

Bot was company for Uncle Mize, with me in the fields trying to conquer weeds, and Broadus and Kell piddling. Broadus and Kell! Be there a shady row, it would take them half a day to hoe it. They made friends with the crabgrass, it appeared. They left standing more than they slew.

Well, we'd go in for dinner and find Bot telling some winding yarn that would redden the face of a Frankfort lawyer. I wouldn't believe Bot Shedders on his deathbed.

Bot would stay for dinner usually, and I'll be dadburned if he wasn't a bigger eater than liar. I've seen him down a half-gallon of buttermilk, a bowl of shucky beans, two potato onions, and four breakings of cornbread at a sitting.

One day I heard Bot tell Uncle Mize something offhandedly. He glanced at the old witch of a cousin who did the cooking and said, "Uncle Mizey, you ought to get you a woman to pretty up the house. Be it I was single, and turning back the calendar, it's plime-blank what I'd do."

"Talk sense, old son," Uncle Mize threw back, without smiling. And that was the first I knew he wasn't for joshing any more. It figured. The plowing had undone him.

Bot pulled a dry face. "A man needs a woman to snip the hair out of his ears and keep his toenails trimmed."

"Ruther to own a redbone hound," Uncle Mize said. "When I get easement, I'm apt to take up fox hunting again, the sport that used to pleasure me. I'll spend nights in the hills, listening to the music."

Bot grunted. "It's to be expected a man would lose his courage after he passed the hundred mark. Hit must make a parcel of difference. Even seventy-five might be the cut-off for some, and at eighty the fire is out shorely."

To this Uncle Mize said grumpily, "You have no fashion of knowing until you're there yourself."

"I was a-guessing," Bot said. "Speculating. But I've sort of a notion you've crossed the river. That rocker has captured you for good."

"I have as much man-courage left as airy a person on Oak," Uncle Mize declared. "The fact is, women don't trip themselves up running to marry the oldest feller this side of the Book of Genesis."

"Any day you want to," Bot said, "you can order a woman. If you own property, have a few dollars in pocket, it'll draw 'em like yellow jackets to stir-off."

"I've never heard tell of such," said Uncle Mize. Bot was such a fibber, who could believe him?

"Upon my honor, you can order a woman through a newspaper."

Bot's stomach got to shaking, but he managed to hold his face in check.

"I've no mind to order a woman for myself," Uncle Mize answered, thinking this was another of Bot's big ones, "but, by the hokies, I'd do anything to locate wives for Broadus and Kell."

Following that, Bot Shedders handled affairs to suit his own notion, without even saying "chicken butter" to anybody. He stopped by daily, and when I'd come in he'd be jabbering. And it got to where he would laugh at nothing at all. You might say, "Git," to a dog, or, "The moon'll be full tonight," and he'd double up. He might bust out with nobody saying anything. Yet a month passed before I caught on. One noon when I walked in from the fields, there sat Bot with a mess of letters. I'd never beheld so many to one person—sixteen by count. He reported they were for Uncle Mize, and Uncle Mize was staring at them and hadn't cracked an envelope.

"Who do you figure wrote them?" Uncle Mize inquired.

"Why, Uncle," Bot explained, "these are from women craving a husband. Craving a man the worst way."

Uncle Mize glared at Bot. For once Bot had told the truth. "Where did they get the idee I wanted a wife?"

"I put your name in the papers. Just you looky here." Bot drew a newspaper clipping from his billfold and read aloud: "Oldest Man in Kentucky Seeks Wife."

"Well, well, well," Uncle Mize breathed, and then he said, "Open and read some of their scratching."

Bot ripped the lid off a letter, reading it to himself first. He got to laughing, gagging like a calf with a cob in its throat. He forgot to spit, and ambeer dribbled his chin.

"Reading must be a slow and tickling business," Uncle Mize gibed. "What's the holdup?"

"This one's from Georgia," Bot cackled. "Says she's seventy-two, been a widow forty years, doesn't paint her lips or dye her hair, and keeps a clean house. Says she wants to spend her remaining days of grace with a mate."

"She sounds decent," Uncle Mize allowed, "but she's along in age. Too old for me. A woman ripens quicker'n a man."

"Ah," Bot chuckled, "if it's a pullet you want, maybe she's here somewheres."

He ripped more envelopes, glimpsing at the pages, saying at last, "Here's a girl from Oklahoma who is sixteen. Says her step-paw spanks her for wearing high heels and twigging her hair, and she intends to run away from home. Says she has eternally dreamed of marrying a mountain man, age no hinder. And she signs, "Gobs of kisses, Suzie.""

"Well, coon my dogs!" Uncle Mize blurted. "I hain't going to rob a cradle. No, sir."

Bot wanted to rip more, but Uncle Mize claimed he'd heard all the reading he could abide for one day. Since the plowing he tired easily. "That Suzie," said he, "ought to have the spankings poured on the harder. Was I her pappy, I'd draw blisters with one hand, bust 'em with the other." Then he said, "I don't believe I'll marry, and none of them two now seem fit for Broadus and Kell either. Too elderly, too young, none in betwixt."

"My opinion, Broadus wouldn't be choosy," Bot said. "Anyhow, the letters have barely started coming. You'll have a square pick of the world."

The puny spell hung on. Uncle Mize stayed several days in bed. He was up and down all June and July, drinking cherrybark tea to strengthen his blood, a rag on his chest smeared with groundhog grease for his wind. He wasn't in pain, just weak, sluggish, no account. Bot Shedders stopped by every mail day, keeping peg on Uncle Mize's health, delivering more letters. For Uncle Mize he was right smart company.

Oh, I reckon it was dull for Uncle Mize the days the mail didn't run and with me and Broadus and Kell in the fields. Or me in the fields working by my lone, Kell asleep under a bush, and Broadus at the county seat. Time can hang heavy as a steelyard pea. Flat on his back, I expect a man will do a lot of cogitation. It might have caused Uncle Mize to take a fancy to one of the letters. For days handrunning Uncle Mize would say to Bot, "Bohannon"— that was Bot's real name—"read that there letter again," and Bot would know which one.

"Says her name is Olander Spence," Bot would say. "Says she lives in Perry County, not more'n twenty miles from Oak Branch. Says she's fifty-five November coming, and tuk loving care of her pappy till he died, the reason she never married. Says she can cook to suit any stomach, says she washes clothes so white you'd swear dogwoods bloomed around the house on Mondays. And listen! Says she can trash any man hoeing a row of corn."

The letter pleased Uncle Mize. It livened him more than the cherrybark tea or the greasy rag. A day arrived when he said, "I've settled on the idea I do need a woman fiddling around the house, waiting on me, and hewing out the garden. The hours get teejous counting cracks in the ceiling and listening to the roosters crow. The Perry County woman sounds smart and clever, not afraid to bend her elbows. I've decided to have her fetched."

When Uncle Mize took a notion to do a thing, he was all grit and go. As with the plowing, he got into a fidget, and if he hadn't been plagued by weakness he would have mounted a horse and traveled to Perry County himself. Or if the corn hadn't been overtaken by crabgrass and foxtail, he might have sent me. Broadus and Kell swore and be-damned if they would go. Kell put his number-twelve shoe down flat. "I'm here," he made oath, "and I'm not moving." Kell was too lazy to kill a snake anyhow. Broadus said, "Hain't my wedding nor funeral. I might bring a woman for myself, but I'll do no wife-hauling for another."

Either Broadus or Kell plime-blank had to make tracks. Uncle Mize swore their breeches wouldn't hold shucks if they didn't make up their minds which. When they held out against all argument, he touched on their weakness. They wouldn't shun money. He drew a taw line in the yard and set them playing crack-o-loo. He fished two silver dollars out of his snapping pocketbook for bait. "Farthest from the line goes to Perry County," he decreed, "and both can keep the dollar."

Broadus pitched, coming close to the mark. Kell took a hair sighting, aiming like measuring death, and beat him; he straddled the line with the U.S. eagle. Broadus let in cussing, but he started getting his readies on. Uncle Mize jumped lively for a change, fixing the saddlebags, bridling two horses. Broadus set off, giving the animals their heads, letting them take their sweet time. Being poky was his revenge.

It was a Tuesday that Broadus started for Perry County, and had he returned the following day there would have been a wedding in the middle of the week. Forty miles should have worked out to a day-and-a-half trip. Kell saw to the marriage license. Those years you didn't need your blood "tasted," and you could send for the knot-tieing document. El Caney Rowan, the preacher, came to do the hitching, and along trotted Elihu DeHart. Where you see Elihu you see his fiddle, and him itching to play. Folks within walking distance came. Most everybody on Oak Branch except Maw. Some rode over from Ballard, Snaggy, and Lairds Creek.

But Broadus didn't show up. I hadn't supposed he would make a beeline, being he had gone against his will and want. Broadus's head was as hard as a hicker nut. People waited, the day stretched, and no Broadus. I kept thinking of the crabgrass crowding the corn, the knee high foxtail, and me wasting time. Late afternoon arrived, the cows lowed at the milk gap, the calves bawled. The sun dropped, and folks had to go home frustrated.

I didn't get my natural sleep that night. Uncle Mize sprung a pain in his chest, and I had to sit up with him. I heated a rock to lay to his heart; I boiled coffee strong enough to float wedges; I drew bucket after bucket of fresh well water to cool his brow. He eased about daylight, and before I could sneak a nap for myself, aye gonnies if folks didn't start coming back, only more of them. Overnight the word had spread further still.

People turned from Burnt Ridge and Flat Gap, from Cain Creek, and from as far away as Smacky and Sporty Creek. Oak Branch emptied out totally— even Maw. Maw's curiosity got stronger than her religion. People waded the yard and weeds led a hard life. A pity they couldn't have tramped the balks of Uncle Mize's corn.

Uncle Mize ate common at breakfast: two hoe cakes, butter and molasses, a slice of cob-smoked ham. Then he went onto the porch and people crowded to pump his hand, the men sniggering fit to choke, the women giggling behind handkerchers. Elihu struck up "Old Joe Clark" on his fiddle, and Uncle Mize cut three steps rusty to prove his limberness. I knew Uncle Mize wasn't up to it though. His cheeks were ashen, his ears tallow. After he wrung every hand within reach he told me he aimed to go inside and rest a bit, and for me to rouse him the first knowledge I had of Broadus.

In the neighborhood of eleven o'clock I heard a yelp and glanced toward the bend of the road, and there did come Broadus. You couldn't hear the *clop* of hoofs for the rattle of voices. Folks hung over the fence; they stood tiptoe; they stretched their necks. There came Broadus astride the first horse, leading the second. And nobody rode the second animal. On shading my eyes I discovered the woman sitting behind him, riding sidesaddle.

Bot Shedders cracked, "That other nag must of gone lame, or throwed a shoe. No female ever sot that close to Broadus Hardburly."

I hustled to Uncle Mize's room. The door was shut. I poked a finger through the hole and lifted the latch, calling as I entered. There was no reply. The shade was pulled and the room dusty dark. I waited until my eyes adjusted and then I saw Uncle Mize flat on the bed, his breeches and socks on. I started to shake him, but I didn't. I couldn't. Not a sound came from him. He wasn't breathing. I stood frozen a moment, then I skittered off to bring Kell. Kell reacted as I did, scared and shaky. We took a long solid look at Uncle Mize, and it was the truth. He wasn't with us any more.

"Let's tell Broadus," Kell said. We closed the door, not speaking a word to anybody. Broadus had ridden in at the wagon gate and was helping Olander Spence to the ground. I saw right then Uncle Mize had made a good choice. Olander Spence seemed not too bad a looker, and her hands were big and thick and used to work. Her buckteeth were as white as hens' eggs.

Broadus unbuckled the saddles and flung them onto the woodpile. He said to the Spence woman, "You sit here on the chopblock while I stable and feed the horses."

We walked into the barn, Broadus, Kell and me. They opened the stall doors while I climbed up into the loft for hay, and when I came down Kell had told his brother.

"He blowed out like a candle," Kell explained.

Broadus leaned against the wall, his mouth open.

Kell grumbled, "That brought-on woman has got us into a mess of trouble. A pure picklement. You fetched her here, and you're the one to take her back home."

Broadus shook his bur of a head. He wasn't much for telling his business, but now he had to. "She hain't going nowheres," he said. "Me and her done some marrying yesterday."

Broadus and Kell latched the stall doors and hung up the bridles. They went toward the house, and I just stood there. I didn't want to go back into the room where Uncle Mize was. I felt like cutting down a tree or splitting a cord of wood—anything to brush my mind off of Uncle Mize. I got me a hoe, slipped behind the barn, and on to the farthest field. I slew an acre of crabgrass before sundown.

So Large a Thing as Seven

I was seven on the twelfth of April, and I remember thinking that the hills to the east of Little Carr Creek had also grown and stretched their ridge shoulders, and that the beechwood crowding up their slopes grew down to a living heart. Mother told me I was seven as we ate breakfast. Father looked at me gravely, saying he didn't think I was more than six. Mother said I was seven for sure. Fletch looked down into his bowl of boiled wheat, for he was only five and stubborn. Euly laughed, a pale nervous laughter edged with a taunt. She was going on thirteen and impatient with our childishness.

I knew then it was good to be seven, but I did not know how to think of it. Mother held the baby up and he looked at me, making an odd little cluck with his tongue sucked back in his throat. And I thought that if I could know what the baby was thinking, I would know what a large thing it was to come upon another year.

After breakfast I went out into the young growth of stickweeds beyond the house, believing my whole life was balanced on this day, and how different it must be from any other. I walked on down into the creek bottom. Bloodroot blossomed under the oaks and I sat down on a root knoll, giving no thought to picking the flowers as Euly would have done, knowing they would droop almost at the touch. Sitting there I thought that I would grow up into a man like Grandpaw Baldridge, learning to read and write, and to draw up deeds for land.

Being so full of this thought I could not sit still. I went on around the hill where wild strawberry plants edged into an old pasture no longer used, for we had no stock and the rails were tumbled and rotting. I ran through a budding stubble, feeling the warm tickling on the soles of my feet. Euly and the birds had been in the strawberry patch already. Bare tracks were there on the grassless spots and the fruit was pecked and torn. A few berries were left, half-green and turning. Euly had been there, saying to Mother there might be enough for a pie sweetened with molasses, but she had gobbled them all down.

I sat on the rail fence. Blackbirds called up the hill their hoarse *tchack, tchack, tchack.* Young crickets drummed their legs in the grass—young, I knew, for their sounds were thin and tuneless.

Suddenly there was laughter, long and thin and near. I searched the weed-filled gullies, looking at length into a poplar rising full-bodied and tall at the lower end of the pasture. Euly was swinging in the topmost bough. Fear for her choked me. I called to her to come down, half envious of her courage, but more afraid than anything. She laughed, swinging faster and holding one hand out dangerously.

Fletch was over the hill. He heard us shouting and came up the slope, setting his feet at an angle to climb the steepness with his short legs. His hands were clutched against his pockets.

I ran to meet him, and Euly came down out of the tree to see what Fletch had. He reached one hand into a pocket to show us. It came out filled with partridge eggs, broken and running between his fingers. Euly's face became as white as sycamore bark. She began to cry, knotting her fists and shaking them about. Then she opened one hand swiftly, slapping Fletch on the cheek, and was gone in a moment, running silently as a fox over the hill.

Fletch squalled until he was hoarse, the eggs and tears mixing on his face. I had to find him a pocketful of rabbit pills to get him to stop.

I remember that on the day I was seven Clabe Brannon came for Father. His mare was in labor, and he had come for help, bringing an extra nag for Father to ride. Father was handy with stock and knew a lot of cures. He knew what to do for blind staggers, the studs and bloats. He knew how to help a mare along when her time came.

Fletch and I had just come from the strawberry patch when Clabe rode up. Father came out of the garden where he had been hoeing sweet corn. Clabe was in a hurry and would not get down, but Mother fetched him a pitcher of cool spring water. Father got on the nag and the stirrups were too short. His legs stuck out like broomsticks. Mother laughed at him.

"Biggest load's on top," she said. "You'd better give that nag a resting spell afore long."

"Size don't allus speak for strength," Father grinned. "This here nag could carry me twice over and never sap her nerve."

Father looked down at me, standing there laughing with Mother. "Think I'll fotch this little dirty mouth along for ballast," he said. He reached down, pulling me into the saddle behind him, and I went up over the hind quarters limp with surprise, for Father had never taken me along before. We rode off down the hill, but I did not look back for all my joy, knowing that Fletch's face was shriveled with jealousy, and knowing that I was seven and this thing was as it should be.

We went along up Little Carr Creek, the nag nervous with our unaccustomed weight, her flesh shivering at the touch of Father's heels, and her hips working under me like enormous elbows. Her hind feet bedded in sand and Father clucked. She jumped, almost sliding me off. Clabe took the lead at the creek-turn, reining his mount back and forth across the thin water, keeping on firm ground.

We were soon beyond any place I knew and white bodies of sycamores stood above the willows. The hills were a waste of fallen timbers. Sprouting switches grew from the stumps, and the sweet smell of a bubby bush came down out of the scrub.

"That there is Stob Miller's messing," Father said. "He's got a way o' leaving as much timber as he takes out. A puore fool woulda knowed white oak is wormy growing on the south side o' the hill and mixed up with laurel and ivy."

And we went on. I counted four redbirds flying low in sumac bushes, and there was a wood thrush repeating its alarmed *pit pit* somewhere. Around more turns there were patches of young corn high on the hills in new-grubbed dirt. Chickens cackled up in the hollows. Sometimes I could see a house set back in a cove, and even when I couldn't see for the apple trees and plum thickets, I knew people lived there by the homeplace sounds coming down to the creek. I knew a big rooster walked in the yard, and there were hound dogs under the puncheon floors and stock hanging their heads over the lot fence.

"They's liable to be a colt a-coming over at Clabe's place," Father said. "How would you like to have a leetle side-pacing filly growing up to ride on?"

"If'n I had me one I'd give nigh everthing," I said, "but I'd want it to be a man-colt."

"Clabe might not want to git shet o' him though," Father said. "I reckon he wouldn't want to promise off a colt afore he was weaned."

"Reckon I could git that colt?" I asked, my heart pounding, and knowing suddenly there was nothing I wanted more than this. To have a colt, living and breathing, was more than being seven years old; it was more than anything.

"There ain't no sense trying to see afar off," Father warned. "It's better to keep your eyeballs on things nigh, and let the rest come according to law and prophecy."

We crossed the shallow waters of the creek, back and forth to firm sand-bars. Silver bellied perch fled before the nag's steps, streaking into the shallows under the bank. Father looked down at them, laughing at their hurry.

"Skin your eyes and see the fishes," he said.

Clabe's wife came out on the porch to meet us, her spool legs thrust down in a pair of brogans. Two children hid under the porch, looking out with dirty faces, and an old hen pecked in the yard, bare of feathers behind the wings. Guineas stretched their long necks through the fence palings.

"You was a spell a-coming," Clabe's wife said. "It's a wonder the mare didn't bust afore you got here."

We went around the house to the barn. The hip-roof was broken and sag-ging. Oates, Clabe's boy, waited for us in the lot, watching the mare. He was older than I, taller by a half-foot, and he had buck teeth. Two of them stuck down in the corners of his mouth like tushes. He grinned at us and I thought, looking hard at him, that he had a face pine-blank like a possum.

The mare lay beyond on the ground, her great eyes moist and sorrowful. Clabe had thrown down a basketful of shucks, but she had rolled away into soft dirt where the pigs had rooted. Father walked up to her. She trembled, though not moving in her agony, and a spasm of flesh quivered her flanks. He put his hands on her neck for a moment, then the mare thrust her moist nose into his palms, and let her slobbering tongue hang out between yellow teeth.

The mare began to strain, drawing her muscles down into cords, and I saw two small hoofs. Father stood over her, looping a grass rope around the colt's thin legs. I knew then the pain of flesh coming into life, and I turned and ran with this sight burning before my eyes, and my body cold and goose-pimpled. Standing behind the barn I was ashamed of my fear, though I could not go back until it was over. My humiliation was as loud as the guinea fowls crying in the young grass at the lot gate.

"It's a natural thing," I thought. "It's a natural thing and me running away. It's there and a-going on if'n I see it or not."

I did not go back until Father called me. Oates was watching and hadn't turned a hair. The children were on their knees looking between the fence rails.

The mare was standing now, mouthing the loose shucks on the ground. The foal rested in a pile of wheat straw. His spindling legs were drawn under him and the straws were stuck over his damp body. A horsefly sang around his nose, and he swung his head, having already learned their sting. He looked at us gently and unafraid, then closed his eyes and drooped his head on the ground. I hungered to brush the dark nose, to get near enough to touch the smooth flanks.

"If'n I had me this colt, I'd do a plenty for it," I thought. "When his teeth growed out, I'd pull a mess o' pennyrile and feed him ever day till they wouldn't be a bone showing. I'd take a heap better care o' him than Clabe Brannon, or Oates, or them dirty-faced children. I'd do a puore sight."

Oates walked up to the colt, but the mare drove him away, blowing through her nose, and lifting her heavy lips until her yellow teeth were bared. The colt lay still, its heavy lids closed.

"Colts ain't no good without proper raising," Clabe said, beginning to bargain with Father. "When he's weaned off, I'd be right glad if you take and raise him. He ought to make a fine stud-horse."

"He's looking a leetle puny to me," Father said. "I figger he might o' got hurt a-borning. He ought to be standing up and walking around by now."

"I'd like the finest kind to give you something for helping out," Clabe said. "I shorely would, but they ain't a cent on the place. I ain't doing much crapping this spring. Jist a couple o' acres. We et up a passel o' the seeds afore planting time."

"I ain't charging my neighbors nothing," Father said. "I ain't a regular horse doctor, and got no right to charge. Anyhow, I don't reckon I've got a grain o' use for the colt."

Words were great upon my tongue, but with Clabe and Oates there, I could not speak them. My hope seemed a bloated grain of corn on a diseased ear, large and expectant, yet having no soundness beneath.

"I'd be right glad if you'd take him," Clabe said, knowing Father was stalling.

Father looked at Clabe. "If you're so powerful shore you want to git rid o' him, I'll drap around some fine pretty day and fotch him home. Some far day when he's weaned off and hain't bridle-scared."

Clabe and Father went into the barn. Oates spoke to me, showing his tushes. There was anger in his face, sitting dark as a thunderhead in his eyes. I knew he was angry about the colt, not wanting to give him up. "Paw's got a dram hid in the loft, I reckon," he said. He walked toward the lot gate, turning to look back at me, and I followed, going out by the pen where two razor-backs waded up to their flanks in slop mud. We went out into an old apple orchard, walking side by side. There were mushrooms growing pale and meaty under the trees. Oates kicked them as he walked, shattering the woody flesh of their cups.

"I heered tell mushrooms is good eating," I said, stepping carefully among them. "I'd like to try a mess cooked up in grease."

"They ain't nothing but devil's snuffboxes," Oates said, drawing his lips down sourly. "They're poison as rattlesnake spit."

A wren was nesting somewhere in the orchard. We heard her fussing in the thick leaves, and we heard a cat sharpening her claws on the bark of a tree.

"Looky yonder at that there pieded cat setting in the crotch o' that tree," Oates said, his tushes breaking from his lips. "Paw wouldn't take a war pension for her, but she ain't worth a tick. She wouldn't catch a rat if'n they was a cheese-ball hung around hit's neck. Oncet I took holt of her tail and wrung it right good. Now she has to climb a tree to sit down. You've seed nothing like that, I bet."

"I heered tell of a boy who's got a store-bought leg," I said. "He whittles on it for meanness, and oncet he driv a sprig in with a hammer, and a woman had a spell and fainted."

"That hain't nothing," Oates said, his lips turned accusingly. "I seed a man with one eye natural, and the other hanging down on one side of his face in a meat-sack like a turkey gobbler's snout. Ever time he winked that sack would jump a grain."

"I couldn't stood to look at it," I said. "It would be a pity-sake to have an eyeball growed like that."

Oates stopped under a tree, his eyes hard and his voice nettled. "I heered tell you Baldridges is spotted 'round the liver," he said.

"It's a lie-tale you heered," I said.

"It's a gospel truth," he said. "I seed you run away when the colt was a-borning. And I brung you down here to show you nobody's going to take him, now nor no time coming."

I stood there looking at him, my eyes watering with anger, and for the moment I saw nothing except his tushes sticking out of his mouth, white and hateful, and his hands doubled into a rusty knot. Then he struck me in the face, and I struck back, wildly though with all my strength. We fought, swapping blows silently. Oates's nose began to bleed. He stepped back, his face twisted in fury. He searched the ground around us, picking up a stick of applewood fallen from a tree.

"I'll kill you graveyard dead," he said.

I did not move, and the stick fell swiftly upon my head, shattering in my ears like thunder. My knees doubled under me. Oates spoke, but I could not rise, and his words came as out of a fog, having no meaning at the moment though the words were clear and separate. Later, I knew what he said, looking back and remembering.

"Hain't no yellow-dog coward Baldridge going to git my colt," he said. "That there one's belonging to me, and I'd break its neck afore I'd let him be took off."

After a little time I stood up, feeling the knot on my head. Oates was gone. The wren was worrying among the leaves, chittering and fussing, knowing the cat sat in the tree crotch motionless as a charm. I walked toward the barn, not caring now whether I crushed the mushrooms underfoot.

Father stood with Clabe in the lot, looking at the colt. It was stretched upon the ground, its legs dry and stiff. The mare whinnied, rubbing her nose over the colt's body. I saw its eyes were open and staring. There was no life in them. The colt was dead.

"He musta got hurt a-borning," Clabe said.

Father was ready to go. He looked at my swollen face, though he said nothing, and we set off walking down the creek, keeping to the left bank where the cows had broken out a path in the shape of their bodies.

I walked along bitter with loss, comforted only by the cruel wisdom that the colt had been spared Oates's rusty hands. Being seven on that day, and bruised and sore from fighting, the years rested like an enormous burden on my swollen eyes. We went on, not stopping or speaking until we saw our hill standing apart from all the others.

Mole-Bane

Our house burned in March and we lived that spring in the smokehouse, sleeping in two beds pushed close into the corners, and with strings of peppers and onions hanging from the rafters overhead. We planted our garden early, using the seeds Mother had hoarded, but it was long before the vegetables were ready for eating. Mother cooked under a shed Father built against the house. There was no abundance of food and we ate all that was set before us, with never a crumb left. Father told us the mines were closed in the headwaters of the Kentucky River and there was hunger in the camps. We believed that we fared well and did not complain.

Father's face was thin as a saw blade, and it seemed he had grown taller, towering over us. His muscles were bunched on his arms, blue-veined and not soft-cushioned now with flesh. He went hunting, searching through the sedge coves and swampy hollows, never wasting a shot. We ate squirrel and rabbit, broiled over hot coals, for there was not a smidgin of grease left in the stone jar. The handful of bullets was hoarded in a leather pouch. Never more than three were taken for the rifle-gun, and Father rarely missed.

With spring upon the hills, it was strange now to go out and kill in the new-budded wood. The squirrels moved sluggishly, carrying their young. Rabbits huddled in the sedge clumps, swollen and stupid. Once Father brought a rusty-eared rabbit home, setting Euly to clean it. When she came on four little ones in its warm belly, she cried out in fear of what she had done, flung the bloody knife into the dirt, and ran away into the low pasture. She stayed there all day crying in the stubble and never ate wild meat again.

We had come through to spring, but Mother was the leanest of us all, and the baby cried in the night when there was no milk. Mother ate a little more now than the rest of us, for the baby's sake, eating as though for shame while we were not there to see, fearing that we might not understand, that we might think she was taking more than her share.

The garden grew as by a miracle, and the blackberry winter passed with the early April winds, doing no harm. Beans broke their waxen leaves out of hoe-turned furrows, bearing the husk of the seeds with them. Sweet corn unfurled tight young blades from weed mould, timid to night chill, growing slowly and darkly. Crows hung on blue air, surveying the patch, but the garden was too near the house. Our shouts and swift running through the tended ground kept them frightened and filled with wonder.

Before the garden was ready, Mother and Euly gathered a mess of plantain and speckled jack, and we had salet greens cooked with meat rind. The beans were still young and tender, and the potatoes thin-skinned and small. We watched the beans grow, measuring them day by day with joints of our fingers, and dug under the potato stalks carefully with our hands so as not to bruise the watery roots. We picked off the potato bugs and scraped their egg patches from the leaves. Fletch saved the bugs in a fruit jar, pinching off buds to feed them when we were not looking.

We went out into the garden in the cool of the evening, turning the vines to look for beetles on the underleaves. Father would pull off a bean and break it impatiently between his fingers, looking hungry enough to eat it raw.

"I figger they're fair ready for biling," he would say. "It's time we had a mess."

"They ain't nigh ready," Mother would say. "When a bean snaps like you'd broke a stick, hit's time. They ain't had their full growth."

One morning we found the heaped trail of a mole across the garden, damp with new earth. Father was angry, stamping the ridge of its path with his feet, packing the ground down hard where it went among the bean vines. He whittled two green walnut sprouts, shaved the bark until they were brown with sap, and drove them in the farther ends of the trail.

"That walnut juice ought to git in its eyes and turn it back," Father said, laughing a little savagely and rubbing his hands in the dirt.

Euly begged Father to dig the mole out. "If'n I had me a moleskin, I'd make a powder-rag out o' it," she said. "When I get me some face powder, I'd have a mole-rag to rub it on with."

Father looked darkly at her, and she ran out of the garden, ashamed of her vain-wishing.

On the day the men came from Blackjack, Mother was washing clothes, and Father swung the battling stick for her on a chestnut stump. Euly saw the men first as they climbed the hill from Little Carr Creek, and she ran to tell us. "They's three men a-coming, and they got mine caps setting on their heads, and two of them has got pokes."

We went around the smokehouse and looked down. They were still a quarter off, and their legs were awkward like a hound's against the steep climb. Mother went back to the tubs. Father waited, shading his eyes from the sun-ball, trying to see who they were. And he knew them long before they turned over the last short curl of the path, and he knew why they had come.

"Hit's Fruit Middleton and Ab Stevall and Sid Pindlar," Father said.

The men came into the yard, looking at the gray pile of ashes and the charred ends of rafters where our house had burned.

"We heered about your burning," Fruit said. "Hit's a puore pity with times so hard and all the mines closed up tight as a jug. We'd a come and raised you a house, but we heered you was living in the smokehouse and gitting along peart."

"We're so packed-up inside we do all our setting out here on the ground," Father said. "We got one chair, but it's holding a washtub."

"Aye, God," Fruit said. "We've done so much setting these last eight months it's like pulling eyeteeth climbing that hill."

"Setting and hearing our bellies growl," Sid said, dragging the poke he held back and forth across the ground. "The grace o' God tuk us through the winter. We've come out skin and bone. We would a planted a garden if they'd been any seeds. They was et up, and anyhow there ain't a fittin place to drap seeds in the camp with all the beasts scratching and digging."

The men glanced out across the garden, now thick with growing, and with the furrow-ridges lost among the leaves. Father slouched down, looking worried.

"We was thinking you could spare us a mess o' beans out o' your patch," Fruit said. "Our womenfolks and children are right mealy in the face."

"Begging comes hard for us who's used to working for our bread," Ab said.

"The beans ain't half-growed yet," Father said. "They ain't nigh filled out."

"We hain't asking you to give us nothing," Fruit said, the wrinkles around his eyes drawing tight. "You'll be paid when the mines open. Aye, God, we ain't asking for a handout. Our folks need some green victuals."

"They ain't nigh ready," Father said again, and he trod up and down in his tracks without moving from where he stood. Then he looked off down the hill, saying quietly and sadly: "I got my first hungry folks to turn down. I never yet turned a body down. Go out and see what you can find fittin to eat."

The men walked out toward the garden. Mother was hanging clothes behind the smokehouse and she saw them jump over the split-paling fence, their pokes flaring up in the wind. Father went around to the washtubs, standing there helpless, not knowing what to say. Mother began to cry silently, saying nothing.

"You can't turn down folks that's starving," Father said at last, and he knew his words sounded foolish and with no weight. He began to hang a tubful of clothes on the line, spreading them out clumsily until it sagged, and the shirtsleeves were barely clear of the ground. He tightened the line, drawing the raveled cord with all his strength.

The men came out of the garden after a spell. They came with their pokes bulging at one end. We knew they had picked every bean, that not one was left.

"Our womenfolks will be right proud to taste a mess o' green victuals," Fruit said. "You'll shorely git your pay when the mines open."

Sid held his poke up and laughed. "You got a right fair garden," he said. "I seed a brash o' blossoms on them vines. In a leetle time you'll have all you kin eat."

They had turned to go when Ab suddenly pulled something out of his pocket and threw it upon the grass. It was a dead mole.

"I dug this varmint out o' the garden patch," he said. "I seed where he'd holed up under a pile o' dirt and I scratched him out. They ain't nothing that can tear up a garden like a mole varmint. You ought to plant a leetle dogtick around. Hit's the best mole-bane I ever heered tell of."

Ab hurried down the hill to catch the others, the rocks rattling under his feet. Euly grabbed up the mole and was gone with it before Father could stop her, running swiftly around the house. And Mother ran too, swinging her arms in dismay, for she had heard the clothesline break, and the clean garments now lay miserably in the dirt.

Journey to the Forks

"Hit's a far piece," Lark said. "I'm afraid we won't make it afore dusty dark." We squatted down in the road and rested on the edge of a clay rut. Lark set his poke on the crust of a nag's track, and I lifted the saddlebags off my shoulder. The leather was damp underneath.

"We ought ne'er thought to be scholars," Lark said.

The sun-ball had turned over the hill above Riddle Hargin's farm and it was hot in the valley. Grackles walked the top rail of a fence, breathing with open beaks. They halted and looked at us, their legs wide apart and rusty backs arched.

"I knowed you'd get dolesome ere we reached Troublesome Creek," I said. "I knowed it was a-coming."

Lark drew his thin legs together and rested his chin on his knees. "If'n I was growed up to twelve like you," he said, "I'd go along peart. I'd not mind my hand."

"Writing hain't done with your left hand," I said. "It won't be agin' you larning."

"I oughtn't to tried busting that dinnymite cap," Lark said. "Hit's a hurting sight to see my left hand with two fingers gone."

"Before long it'll seem plumb natural," I said. "In a little spell you'll never give a thought to it."

The grackles called harshly from the rail fence.

"We'd better eat the apples while we're setting," I said. Lark opened the poke holding a Wilburn and a Henry Back. "You take the Wilburn," I told him, for it was the largest. "I choose the Henry Back because it pops when I bite it."

Lark wrapped the damp seeds in a bit of paper torn from the poke. I got up, raising the saddlebag. The grackles flew lazily off the rails, settling into a linn beside the road, their dark wings brushing the leaves like shadows.

"It's nigh on to six miles to the forks," I said.

Lark asked to carry the saddlebag a ways, so I might rest. I told him, "This load would break your bones down." I let him carry my brogans though. He tied the strings into a bow and hung them about his neck.

We walked on, stepping among hardened clumps of mud and wheel-brightened rocks. Cowbells clanked in a redbud thicket on the hills, and a calf bellowed. A bird hissed in a persimmon tree. I couldn't see it, but Lark glimpsed its flicking tail feathers.

"A cherrybird's nigh tame as a pet crow," Lark said. "Once I found one setting her some eggs and she never flew away. She was that trusting."

Lark was tiring now. He stumped his sore big toe twice, crying a mite.

"You'll have to stop dragging yore feet or put on shoes," I said.

"My feet would get raw as beef if'n I wore shoes all the way till dark," Lark complained. "My brogans is full o' pinchers. If'n I had me a drap o' water on my toe, hit would feel a sight better."

Farther on we found a spring drip. Lark held his foot under the cool stream. He wanted to scramble up the bank to find where the water seeped from the ground. "Thar might be a spring lizard sticking hits head out o' the mud," he said. I wouldn't give in to it, so we went on, the sun-ball in our faces and the road curving beyond sight.

"I've heered tell they do quare things at the fork school," Lark said, "yit I've forgot what it was they done."

"They've got a big bell hung square up on some poles," I said, "and they ring it before they get up o' mornings and when they eat. They got a little sheep bell to ring in the schoolhouse before and betwixt books. Dee Finley tuk a month's schooling there, and he told me a passel. Dee says it's a sight on earth the washing and scrubbing and sweeping they do. Says they might nigh take the hide off o' floors a-washing them so much."

"I bet hit's the truth," Lark said.

"I've heard Mommy say it's not healthy keeping dust breshed in the air, and a-damping floors every day," I said. "And Dee says they've got a passel o' cows in a barn. They take and wet a broom and scrub every cow before they milk. Dee reckons they'll soon be brushing them cows' teeth."

"I bet hit's the truth," Lark said.

"All that messing around don't hurt them cows none. They get so much milk everybody has a God's plenty."

The sun-ball dropped behind the beech woods on the ridge. It grew cooler. We rested again in a horsemint patch, Lark spitting on his big toe, easing the pain. Lark said, "I ought ne'er thought to be a scholar."

"They never was a puore scholar amongst all our folks," I recalled. "Never a one went all the way through the books and come out yonside. I've got a notion doing it."

"Hit'd take a right smart spell," Lark said.

We were ready to go on when a sound of hoofs came up the valley. They were far off and dull. We waited, resting a bit longer. A bright-faced nag rounded the creek curve, lifting hoofs carefully along the wheel tracks. Cain Griggs was in the saddle, riding with his feet out of the stirrups, for his legs were too long to fit. He halted beside us, looking down where we sat. We stood up, shifting our feet.

"I reckon yore pappy's sending his young 'uns down to the forks school," Cain guessed. "Going down to stay awhile and git a mess o' fool notions."

"Poppy never sent us," I said. "We made our own minds."

Cain lifted his hat and scratched his head. "I never put much store by all them fotched-on teachings, a-larning quare onnatural things, not a grain o' good on the Lord's creation."

"Hain't nothing wrong with larning to cipher and read writing," I said. "None I ever heard tell of."

"I've heered they teach the earth is round," Cain said, "and that goes agin' Scripture. The Book says plime-blank hit's got four corners. Whoever seed a ball have a corner?"

Cain patted his nag and scowled. His voice rose. "They's a powerful mess o' fancy foolishness they teach a chap these days, a-pouring in till they got no more jedgment than a granny hatchet, a-grinding their brains away with book reading. I allus said, a little larning's a good thing, sharpening the mind like a sawblade, but too much knocks the edge off o' the p'ints and darks a feller's reckoning."

Lark's mouth opened. He shook his head, agreeing.

"Hain't everybody knows what to swallow, and what to spit out," Cain warned. "Now, if I was you, young and tenderminded, I'd play hardhead down at the forks, and let nothing but truth git through my skull. Hit takes a heap o' knocking to git a thing proper anyhow, and the harder hit's beat in, the longer hit's liable to stay. I figure the Lord put our brains in a bone box to sort o' keep the devilment strained out."

Cain clucked his nag. She started off, lifting her long chin as the bits tightened in her mouth. Cain called back to us, but his words were lost under the rattle of hoofs.

"I bet what that feller says is the plime-blank gospel," Lark said, looking after the disappearing nag. "I'm scared I can't tell what is truth and what hain't. If'n I was growed up to twelve like you, I'd know. I'm afeared I'll swallow a lie-tale."

"Cain Griggs don't know square to the end o' everything," I said.

We went on. The sun-ball reddened, mellowing the sky. Lark trudged beside me, holding to a strap of the saddlebag, barely lifting his feet above the ruts. His teeth were set against his lower lip, his eyes downcast.

"I knowed you'd get dolesome," I said.

Martins flew the valley after the sun was gone, fluttering sharp wings, slicing the air. A whip-poor-will called. Shadows thickened in the laurel patches.

We came upon the forks in early evening and looked down upon the school from the ridge. Lights were bright in the windows, though shapes of houses were lost against the hills. We rested, listening. No sound came out of all the strange place where the lights were, unblinking and cold.

I stood up, lifting the saddlebag once more. Lark arose too, hesitating, dreading the last steps.

"I ought ne'er thought to be a scholar," Lark said. His voice was small and tight, and the words trembled on his tongue. He caught hold of my hand, and I felt the blunt edge of his palm where the fingers were gone. We started down the ridge, picking our way through stony dark.

Uncle Jolly

The pawpaws got ripe while Uncle Jolly laid out a two-week spell in the county jail for roughing Les Honeycutt at a box supper on Simms Fork. Father rode over to Hardin on a borrowed mare to see him, taking the word Grandma had sent us. I went along, riding behind Father, carrying three pawpaws in a poke. They were fat ones, black and rotten-ripe, smelling sweeter than a bubby tree. We reached the head of Little Carr Creek when the sun-ball stood overhead, and it made us hungry to smell the poke, mellow in the heat.

"How many paws you got there?" Father asked. I said, "Three," and Father said he reckoned we ought to eat one apiece, saving the greenest for Uncle Jolly. "The greenest will be the keepingest," he said.

I pulled out the smallest, and the tender skin came half off in my hand, the sticky juice oozing out of the yellow flesh. Father popped it in his mouth, blowing the big seeds over the mare's bony head.

"Hain't you eating one?" Father asked.

"I'd be nigh ashamed to take Uncle Jolly just one paw," I said. "One just calls for another. If 'n I got started, it would take a bushel to dull the edge on my tongue. Anyhow, I like 'em better when they've had a touch o' frost."

"Hain't no use taking that sorry Jolly a grain o' nothing," Father said. "I figger he gets along pearter on jail cooking than anything else. He's et a-plenty. Two years he got in the state pen for dinnymiting Pate Horn's mill dam, and after he'd been shet up nine months they give him a parole. Now he's fit and cracked two o' Les Honeycutt's rib bones, and them Honeycutts might make a sight o' trouble. Hit's not beyond thinking they'll fotch him back to Frankfort."

"Uncle Jolly fit him square," I said. "I heard Les cut the saddle off his nag. No man a-living would a took that."

Father drew the reins tight in his hands and we set off faster down the crusty road. "Jolly was sparking Les's sweetheart," Father said, his words louder and a little angry. "I don't lay a blame on Les. They's a lot o' things bigger'n eyes and ears you never seed or heard tell of."

We went on, not speaking until the wheel-deepened road crawled over the ridge into the head of Troublesome Creek. We stopped where the waters drained out of a bog, spring-clear and cold. Father got off the mare and let her drink, and I slid to the ground. The mare drank her fill and Father tied her to the muscled limb of a hornbeam while we scooped up water in our hats.

"You can set in the saddle a spell," Father said, when we were ready to go. He swung me up, pulling himself behind, and we went down the trace of waters into the valley. The mare swung her head nervously, crowding against the ditch growth. Father kept reaching for the reins, jerking her back into the road.

"Hit's a pity you can't hold her out o' the blackberry vines," Father said. "If this keeps up, I won't have a stitch o' britches against we reach Hardin. These here briars are raveling them out, string at a time."

At the creek's fork we turned into Hardin, hitching the mare to a locust post before the courthouse. Uncle Jolly saw us coming and shouted out to us, his face tight between the window bars. Logg Turner opened the jailhouse door. We went into a stone-damp hall, Logg fumbling through his long keys for the one to Uncle Jolly's cell.

"I could nigh open it with my eyeteeth afore you picked the key," Uncle Jolly said, twisting his mouth like Logg's.

We went into the cell, the door catching itself back on rusty hinges. Uncle Jolly grabbed me by the arms, swinging me around twice, scraping my heels on the walls. "Big enough in here to swing a fox by its tail," he said. He dropped me atop a quilt-ball on his cot and shook Father's hand until the knuckles cracked.

"Hain't no use breaking a feller's arm off," Father said.

Logg rattled his keys and grinned at us. Jolly winked at him, making a sly pass at the keys and tipping them with his fingers. Logg jerked the iron ring back, quickly though not uneasily, knowing Uncle Jolly's ways.

"Fotch some chairs for us to set on," Uncle Jolly said. "Hain't you got no manners?"

Logg showed his stumpy teeth. "Fotch 'em yourself," he said. "They's a bench setting just outside the cell." He went up the hall, leaving the door open, and Uncle Jolly dragged the whittled seat in.

"Logg's mighty feisty for election time to be so nigh," Uncle Jolly said.

"Hit's a tall risk not locking that door," Father said.

"I ain't going nowheres," Uncle Jolly said. "Next rusty I cut, it's the pen two years for shore."

"Your ma sent me to say what you've spoke," Father said. "She never reckoned you'd have sense to know."

"This is my pigeon roost," Uncle Jolly said. "I nest right natural in jail, and it's a fact. I get lonesome sometimes, though, nigh enough to start figgering a way out. Reckon I can't trust myself to stay locked up long. Nobody here but me now. The sheriff turned everybody out to pull corn. They won't be finishing their spells till after gethering."

"You just got nine days more," Father said. "Looks to me you could nail yourself down till then, but I wouldn't trust you spitting distance. Two breaks you made out o' this jail times past."

"If I had me somebody to talk to," Uncle Jolly said, "I'd fare well."

"Logg ought to be a heap o' company."

"Ruther hear a bullfrog croaking."

"Nine days haint long—one Sunday and eight weekdays."

"I'm liable to scratch out afore then."

"That's fool talk. They'll salt you down in Frankfort for shore."

"Wouldn't pitch a straw for the differ."

Pawpaw scent lay heavy in the room, pushing down the mullein-rank jail smells. Uncle Jolly looked at the poke in my hand. "If I was a possum," he said, "I wouldn't know better what you got."

I drew out the pawpaws, holding them toward him. "A good frosting would make them a sight better," I said.

"Take just one," Father said to Uncle Jolly. "He ain't et since we left home."

Uncle Jolly picked the least, though I held the fat one closest. He pitched it up to the ceiling and let it fall down into his open mouth. The seeds popped out, shot across the room and between the bars into the yard, touching nothing.

"You couldn't do that if your life and neck was strung on it," he said. I tried with my seeds, blowing them hard, but they fell to the floor. Uncle Jolly kicked them under the bed and went out into the hall, calling to Logg, "Have you got any o' them biled shucks left?"

We spooned up the beans Logg brought, coated with grease, and as good eating as anything on this earth. They were good to bite into, tender and juicy. I could have eaten more, but I did not speak of it, thinking Logg had scraped the pot.

"I ain't got nothing agin' jail victuals," Uncle Jolly said. "They come regular as clock-tick, three times a day."

"If your belly's content, hain't no cause to snake out afore your time is up," Father said. "Your ma sent on word for you to stay."

"If I had me somebody to talk to, hit wouldn't be so branfired eternal," Uncle Jolly said. "All I do is set and set, and then set some more."

The mare whinnied in the yard. Father got up and looked out, getting uneasy and ready to go. "Sun-ball's drapping fast," he said. "Four hours' ride twixt here and home. Ought to be a-going."

"Set yourself down," Uncle Jolly said. "I ain't got my talk out."

Father walked across the room. He looked at me and cocked his head. "Reckon you could stay here nine days?" he asked.

"This ain't no place for a chap," Uncle Jolly said.

"He'd be a sight o' company," Father said. "I figger you'd hang around yourself if he was here."

"Hit's agin' the law for a chap to stay shet up in jail," Uncle Jolly said, "but Logg gets right free when he's needing votes. He could put a cot and chair in the hall, and that wouldn't be in jail nor out."

"Getting late," Father complained. "I'll talk to Logg, and mosey along. I figger Logg'll let me have my way. My vote is as good as the next un."

Logg said I could stay. I wanted to, though I knew first frost would come any morning now, and I would miss my fill of pawpaws. They were best after a killing frost, mushy and sweet, falling apart almost at a touch.

When Father was ready to go, I went out into the yard to see him off. He rode away, the mare walking swiftly toward the forks with her great bones sticking out hard and sharp. Uncle Jolly leaned against the window bars and called down, "First time I ever seed a feller straddling a quilting frame."

With election time near, the county seat was filled with people, their mounts chocking stiff heels in the courthouse yard. Before daylight, horses came sloshing through the creek, setting hoofs carefully into dark waters, feeling out the quicksands.

"Candidates thicker'n groundhogs in a roast-ear patch," Logg told us. "Got where a feller can't go down the road peaceable."

"Bet you argue as many votes as the next un," Uncle Jolly said.

"I don't worry a man's years off."

"You'd vote your ol' nag and jinny if they was registered."

"I get a vote any way can be got, buy or swap, hogback or straddle-pole, but when they're drapped in the ballot box, I allus say, 'Boys, count 'em square and honest.'"

Two days before Uncle Jolly's time was up, Logg came hurrying down from the courthouse. He came with his keys jingling on his belt, and we heard him coming afar off.

"I seen Les Honeycutt talking to Judge Mauldin," Logg said. "I figger he's trying to get you sent back to Frankfort. Les's folks can swing nigh every vote on Jones Fork, and the judge knows it. He can't be reelected with the Honeycutts agin' him."

"I never pushed Les's ribs in fur enough," Uncle Jolly said. "I reckon the judge hain't going to give plumb over. He'll be needing a few Baldridge votes on Little Carr and Defeated Creek."

It was dark inside the jail when Judge Mauldin rattled the iron door, though light held outside. Night chill had settled into the wall stones, and there was a hint of frost in the air. He came in, rubbing his fat hands. Logg opened Uncle Jolly's cell, and I followed, going close behind Logg. Judge Mauldin sat down heavily on the cot, twisting his watch chain around a thick finger. There was a bushtail squirrel carved from a peach seed hanging on the chain's end, real as life.

"Reckon you heard the Honeycutts are trying to hog-tie me into sending you back to Frankfort," the judge said.

"I heard a little sketch," Uncle Jolly said, threading his arms through the bars.

"I can't spare a vote," the judge said.

"You'll lose a mess either way," Uncle Jolly said. "I got no notion o' going back to the pen anyhow. A log team couldn't drag me there agin. Hit's like pulling eyeteeth just to stay in this jailhouse."

Logg brought in a smoky-chimneyed lantern, holding a match to the oily wick.

The judge cracked heavy knuckles against his palms. "I'm not a-going to send you back," he said. "I got it figgered this way. You stay in jail till election time—then it won't matter who rows up. I just want me one more term. Logg'll let you out the minute Honeycutts get voted on Jones Fork."

"That's eight days a-coming," Uncle Jolly said. "Hit'll keep me here plumb till hog-killing time. Like setting on a frog-gig staying, and me knowing I could snake out anytime the notion struck."

"You've gone nowhere yet, as I can see," Logg said.

Uncle Jolly looked at the ring of keys hung on Logg's belt. "Never took a strong idea," he said. "I ain't safe in here long as there's a key walking around. I can't trust myself to stay shet up."

"If you don't stay, I'll be bound to send you back to Frankfort," Judge Mauldin said.

The judge stood to go. I went out behind him, Logg following and locking the door, and hooking the ring on his belt. Uncle Jolly thrust his arms through the bars as Logg turned, lifting the ring with a finger, quick as an eye-bat. I glimpsed it all and waited, holding my breath, fearing for Uncle Jolly. The judge and Logg walked up the hall, not looking back nor knowing. When they had gone, Uncle Jolly took one key off, handing the rest to me. "Go take the others back," he said. "This one won't be missed for a spell."

I went to bed early, for there was no heat in the cold hallway. In the night I waked, thinking someone had spoken. Uncle Jolly had called, speaking my name into pitch-dark. His words were barely louder than the straw ticking rustling in my ears. I stepped out on the stone floor, feeling my way to the cell. Uncle Jolly was there, though I couldn't see him. He reached through the bars and found my hand, putting the stolen key in it.

"You go home at the crack o' day and get a wad o' dirt betwixt us afore Logg misses it," he said. "Give it to your grandma and tell her to keep it eight days, then have your poppy fotch it back—eight days and not a minute yonside. Tell her I said hit." I felt my way along the wall, crawling back into the warm spot in my bed, and slept until the slosh of horses' feet in the creek came up the rise.

Logg opened the jailhouse door for me when light broke. The steps were mouldy-white. The season's first frost lay heavily on the ground. "Hit's a killer," Logg said. "This here one ought to make the shoats squeal." I set off, walking fast over the frosted road, knowing the pawpaws were fat and winter-ripe on the Little Carr ridge.

Bat Flight

The flat fruit of the locust fell, lying like curved blades in the grass. August ripened the sedge clumps, and the days lengthened until Father came home from the mines in middle afternoon, no longer trudging the creek road at the edge of dark, with a carbide lamp burning on his cap. He came now before the guineas settled to roost in the black gum beside the house. We watched the elder thicket at the hill turn and plunged down to meet him as he came in sight. Fern was the swiftest, reaching him first and snatching the dinner bucket Father carried. She hid in the stickweeds to nibble at the crusts in the bucket, scattering the crumbs for the fee larks seeding the grass stalks. Lark waited halfway down the path and Father would swing him to his shoulder, packing him to the house like a poke of meal.

One evening in middle August Father sat on the battling block after supper, whittling a spool-pretty for the baby.

"I saw Jonce Weathers, the Flat Creek schoolteacher today," he said. "He was going along, single stepping, like his bones was about to break at the joints. I caught up with him and he let off a spiel about being tired square to death. He did look a sight tender, and I reckon if he'd been laying flatback picking slate out of a vein like I had all day, he'd been to bury. I asked him how many scholars he had and he says eighty-six, he thinks, but they wiggle so he couldn't count 'em for sure. I said I had two chaps ought to be in school. He says send them along, now he did."

Mother sat on a tub bottom holding the baby, watching Father notch the spool. "It's a long walking piece," Mother said. "Four miles one way. But I always wanted my young 'uns to learn to figure and read writing. I went two winters to school, and I been, ever since, a good hand to learn by heart. I never put my schooling to practice though, and I've nigh forgot how."

"I learned as far as 'baker' in the blue-back speller," Father said. He threaded a wax cord through the spool hole, twisting match stems in the end loops until they pulled tight against his hand. The baby's eyes widened. When the spool was put on the ground it rolled along like a tumblebug.

The baby laughed, holding his hands out for it, and stuck it into his mouth. He bit the spool with milk teeth newly edged on his gums.

"No use putting off another day," Father said. "I told Jonce Weathers to nail up another seat for you chaps."

Fern picked up the baby and ran around the battling block with him, running with joy. Lark squatted down on a broad chip, knowing he was only six, and too young to go. He cried a little, making no more sound than a click bug in tall weeds.

At seven o'clock next morning Fern and I sat on the puncheon steps of Old Hargett church-house. We had gone early, meeting only miners on the creek road with their mud-stiff britches rattling, their cap lamps burning in broad daylight. "Them's the brightest scholars ever was," one of the men said, "a-going to books ere crack of day."

Fern spoke her scorn, though not loud enough to be heard. "Dirt dobbers," she said.

The church-house door was chained and padlocked. We waited, looking across the foot-packed ground to the graveyard hidden behind a stickweed patch. A bushtail squirrel crept down a scalybark to wonder at us with bright eyes. "I bet he's tame as a house cat," I said. "I bet he is." Two bats flew around the eaves, disappearing with dull squeaks, and then we heard the dinner buckets of the scholars cracking together upcreek and down.

The children came into the yard and set their buckets by the steps. The boys crouched on their knees to play fatty hole, the bright marbles spinning from rusty fists into the dirt pockets. Fern went into the graveyard with the girls. I watched the boys, standing a little way apart. The losers held their knuckles to be thumped, clenching them against the pain.

A boy named Leth came up to me and said, "Let's me and you play big ring," and he loaned me two marbles. One to put in the ring, and the other to shoot with. I held them in the cup of my hand, and they were fine to look at—green as a moss pool, with specks like water fleas in the glass. He drew a great circle with the toe of his brogan. We squatted on our heels. I clenched a marble between thumb and forefinger, feeling its perfect roundness, smoother than any acorn.

"Yonder comes the teacher," Leth said, "but there's a spell yet before books. Jonce Weathers has got to clean after the bats. The floor gets ruint every night."

"Where, now, do them bat-birds stay of a day?" I asked.

"Yonside the ceiling, hanging amongst the rafters," Leth said.

We played two games of big ring. Then we stood at the church-house door watching Jonce sweep with a brushy broom.

"Ain't Jonce the littlest teacher you ever saw?" Leth asked. "He's got scholars nigh big as he is. Be a wonder if he don't get run off. Two teachers they got rid of last year, and they'd a-made two of Jonce."

"I bet he's sharp as a shoe sprig," I said. "Size don't count for sense."

"I saw his arm muscle once," Leth said. "It wasn't much larger than a goose bump."

When the bell rang we went inside. I kept close to Leth, finding a place beside him on the bench where the primer children sat. Leth's feet touched the floor, but I could only reach it with my toes. The older boys came in late, the warped floor creaking under their steps. Jonce glared angrily at them. Books were opened, thumbs licked to turn the pages, and bright pictures spun under their hands.

"I've got no book," I said to Leth.

He held his so both of us could see. "We're reading Henny-Penny," he said. "Look at that old dommer hen planting three grains of wheat. Ain't that a peck of foolishness? Fellow who writ this book is a witty."

"I can't read writing," I said, "but I know my letters."

"What's the biggest river ever was?" Jonce stood before the older boys, holding a book square as a dough-board.

"Biggest river I ever saw was the Kentucky, running off to the bluegrass, and somewhere beyond."

"It's a river in South America, far off south, many thousands of miles."

"There's a place called South Americee, over in Lott County. Now it's the truth."

"This river is the Amazon. It's one hundred and sixty-seven miles wide at the mouth."

"I looked that word up in the dictionary and it said Amazon was a fighting woman. River or woman, I don't know which."

Cricket throb, dry and ripe, came through the window, dull against Jonce's words leaping over the room. He leaned from the pulpit, swinging his arms. Scholars stretched to draw numbers on the blackboard. Three classes in arithmetic were going at one time, three threads of voices intent as crickets. My feet hung from the bench, heavy as lead plumbs. "My tongue is dried to a string," I told Leth.

"Hold up one finger and crack the others," he said. Jonce saw me at last and nodded, and I went out into the yard, being no longer thirsty where the air was free of bat smell and wood rot. I sat down on a mossed rock under the scalybark, and the bushtail squirrel came halfway down, head foremost, unafraid. A titmouse whistled overhead, lonesome and questioning.

As I sat on the rock a boy ran out of the church-house, jumping the five doorsteps. His books were caught under his arm as he hurried down the creek road, leaving hat and dinner bucket behind. The squirrel fled up the scalybark; the titmouse hushed. Jonce came out into the yard to look down the road after the boy. I slipped back into the schoolroom before he returned, wondering at the quietness there.

"Jonce put Toll Mauldraugh back in the fifth reader," Leth said, his voice husky with anger. "Toll reared up and Jonce cracked him with a figger book. Reckon Toll ought to be put back a grade, but I don't like to see nobody strike my kin. Uncle Hodge'll give Jonce trouble sure. He thinks the sun riz in that Toll."

Fern and I ate out of a shoebox at noon. We laughed when it was opened, amazed at what was there. Fried guinea thighs and wings, covered with a brown-meal crust. Two yellow tomatoes. A corn pone, and a thumb-sized lump of salt.

"Mommy must of killed the guinea before daylight," I said. "I never heard a peep."

"I hope it wasn't my little ring-tailed one," Fern said. We had turned our backs on the others before looking into the box, but now we were not ashamed of what we had to eat.

"I couldn't stand to know I've eaten my little ring-tail," Fern complained, and gave one of her pieces away.

The children spread their food on the grass. They ate biscuits fist-big, with lean-streaked meat. Leth had milk in his dinner bucket. He crumbled corn bread into it, eating from the bucket with a wooden spoon.

Before the bell rang the girls went into the graveyard. The boys huddled together under the creek-bank willows, burying their feet in damp sand, talking.

"I reckon we don't need to run Jonce off," John Winns said. "Hodge Mauldraugh will be doing that right soon." He sniggered at his own words.

"That Jonce has the quarest walk I ever saw," Eli Phipps said. "I'd give a pretty to see what kind o' run he's got."

The clapper shook in the bell. Leth got up, his marbles rattling in the deep of his pockets. "I like Jonce for a teacher," he said, "but I don't want to see nobody whipping my folks."

I walked across the yard with Leth. The older boys waited until the others were in the house before stalking in, clumping brogans on the floor. Jonce sat quietly in the pulpit, looking into a book that was a full hand thick. Pages flicked from his thumb. I looked up at him and saw his eyes run back and forth like an ant on a leaf. He stood up at last, grinning down at us.

"I've been learning about bats," he said. "They're unhealthy critters, festered with chinch bugs and lice, scattering plagues of diseases. And I learnt a bat's not a bird. It's a mammal, kin to man."

Whispers flowed over the room, protesting. "I'm not kin to a bat," a voice spoke. Leth nudged me with his elbow, frowning.

"We've been living in a bat-house long enough," Jonce said. "Tomorrow I'll bring a poke of sulphur, and we'll give them a dose of fire and brimstone." Leth's eyes rounded. The older boys arose from their seats, grudges buried under the promise. "Four or five of you fellows bring mine lamps. We're going to have a bat-fly in broad daylight."

He came down out of the pulpit with the first reader in his hand, waiting until the scurry of voices died before sitting in front of our bench. Leth held his book before us. Henny-Penny stood on the page, cackling, her comb as red as a beet.

Jonce looked at me, and I was suddenly frightened. "Little man," he asked, "can you read in the primer?"

My tongue balled in my mouth. "I can't read words," I said, "but I know my letters."

"Fried guinea's breast in my dinner bucket," Father said. "I could hardly believe my eyeballs. I loaded two cars of coal extra after I'd et."

We were sitting on the woodpile, between suppertime and dark. Bee martins flew up from the lower ridges where clouds were banked yellow as fall maples. There was still light enough for Mother and Fern to study the third-grade spelling book. They sat high on the poplar logs, out of the baby's reach, for he wanted to pull at the pages.

"This speller's not belongin' to me," Fern had said. "See what it says on the kiver, PROPERTY OF THE STATE OF KENTUCKY."

"You won't be eating fancy victuals in the week middle from now on," Mother said. "I'm going to learn myself to spell the words I've forgot, and a sight of them I've never come across. A body ought to be able to spell things they lay hands to every day, and things going by. Take them martin-birds flying there. I've seen martins all my born days, but I can't say the letters to their name."

"I'm uneasy Jonce Weathers is going to get spelled down before the year is up," Father said. "They run two teachers off from Flat Creek School last year." Fern had told Father about Toll Mauldraugh, proud in knowing I was out of the room when Jonce struck Toll, and that I saw none of it.

"A little devilment is natural amongst chaps," Father said. "I'm not blaming the scholars. It's their folks tearing up the patch, putting fool notions in their heads. I figure a man ought to rack his own jennies, and stop piddling in other fellers' business."

"I always wanted my chaps to read and spell and figger," Mother said. "Always put a lot of store by that. Another rusty cut and they'll close the school sure. As long as we keep living here, Flat Creek School is their only chance earthy."

Night came up the hill, settling into the ridge pockets. The martins melted into the dark. "Time to hit the shucks," Father said, rattling poplar bark under his feet, but he made no move to go inside. The baby clucked where he sat between Father's knees.

I squatted on the chopping block, thinking of Jonce's promise. "If I had me a mine lamp, I could help scare bats tomorrow," I said. "Bats a-hanging by the bushels in the church-house loft, messing up the floor of a night. Jonce is going to smoke them out tomorrow."

"Jonce says a bat ain't a bird," Fern said.

Father grunted. "I always liked a flock of bats nigh," he said. "Mosquitoes and gnats live hard when they're roosting close around. I judge it's bad luck to kill a bat." He got up to go, swinging the baby up on an arm. The baby was so sleepy its head slid down into Father's hand.

We were on the road early next morning, going along with Father to the fork turn. The sun-ball broke out of the timber as we passed the mouth of Dry Creek. I wore an old mine cap with a carbide lamp hung over the bill, the round of the head pinched and fastened with a latch pin.

Miners came down the creek, walking toward Buckstone. They looked at my cap, and bat their eyes at each other. "Aye gonnies, if I don't believe Jonce is teaching them chaps to mine coal," one said. "Three we've passed wearing the gear."

When we reached the church-house most of the scholars were there already. The older boys had mine lamps, and carried snuffboxes filled with carbide lumps in hip pockets. The lamps smelled like burnt wool. Leth had a flambeau made out of a rag stuffed in a bottle of coal oil.

Leth loaned me two marbles again, and they were the same ones—green as a catbird's eggs. I held them in the frog of my hand, clicking them together, watching the flea flecks sparkle.

"Them's the prettiest marbles ever was," I said. We squatted down to play a round of fatty hole.

"If you beat me out," Leth said, "they're belongin' to you." We played three games, and I lost them all. "You can have them anyhow," he said when Jonce rang the bell. "Reckon I've got a peck besides."

I caught the marbles up, trying to feel suddenly that they were mine. In the deep of my pocket they felt strange and cool against my leg, small and precious. "I'm going to fotch you a hatful of chinquapins," I said. "By grabbies, I am."

The big boys went in first, putting their lamps on the water shelf, taking their seats expectantly. Jonce glanced at the door, but there were no stragglers. He counted the scholars, jabbing a finger toward each one. "Not an absent or tardy scholar," he said. "Everybody present like it was the last day of school." He leaned out of the pulpit, elbows anchored on Preacher Claud Sorrel's Bible. The classes began, chalk scratched across the board, walking with giant letters, swelling into words. Numbers, finger-counted, mixed with things spelled. "*R-a-m,* ram, a brute sheep. . . ." "Eleven plus nine comes to . . . twenty, I reckon. . . ." "*E-w-e,* eouw, the one that drops the lambs. I had me a lamb once I thought a sight of. Saved its tracks in clay and got them yet."

We glanced at our mine lamps, thinking of bats hanging under the roof.

Jonce saw Hodge Mauldraugh first. He came into the church-house with Toll, standing there darkening the door, saying no word. We looked back, stretching from our seats. The grass crickets were suddenly loud above the hush. Jonce came down out of the pulpit, walking toward the door with the floorboards squeaking under his odd shuffle. He stood in front of Mauldraugh, his hands slightly lifted, open. Mauldraugh spoke, and his words were filled with cold anger. They poured out of him like sluice water.

"I'm not agin' you reaching my boy back a grade," he said. "What he learns, I want it got proper. But I'm agin' my boy being whipped. I do all the scourging for my house. Nobody's going to beat my chap and keep drawing breath."

"I'm running this place," Jonce said. "Drawing pay to school-keep and whip as I see fittin. When a scholar goes against the rule, I'll not spare the rod."

Mauldraugh spoke as though he had not heard, pushing Toll a little way toward Jonce. "I'm bringing him back to school," he said, "but I'd better never hear of him being touched. I'd better never hear. . . ." He went out of the door, and Toll took a seat beside John Winns, glancing about, hard-eyed and proud.

The classes were doubled so all would be over by noon, and the afternoon free for the bat-fly. I learned to read the first page in the primer. "Henny-Penny found a grain of wheat. . . ." I sat on my legs, for they ached from hanging over the bench without reaching the floor.

"Little man," Jonce said. "I'm going to hammer together a box for you to rest your feet on."

We ate hurriedly at noon. I had a lunch bucket of my own now, and sat with the boys upon the beech roots laid bare by creek flood. There was a baked horse apple in my bucket, oozing sugar from the top, and cushaw blooms, fried in meal batter, tasting like fish. We scattered the crumbs to the minnows working the shallows; we lit up our lamps.

Jonce dragged a ladder from under the church-house floor, setting it against the wall inside, beneath the trapboard. Eli Phipps went up first to slide the board away. We climbed after, grasping the creaking ladder slats, holding our lamps aloft. The floor gave under a step, nails prying loose from rotten wood. "Walk the joists, boys," Jonce said. "Likely to fall square through the ceiling." Below, the girls laughed, and the boys who had no lamps shouted from the ladder's end. Toll Mauldraugh's voice rose above them all, thick with scorn.

The bats hung under the hip of the roof, higher than any of us could reach, wings folded against limp bodies. We held our lamps toward them. The mouse-furred patch gave no living sign. Jonce wedged a dishpan he carried between the joists. He poured a ring of sulphur in the pan, whittled a shingle and started a fire. A smudge of gray smoke rose toward the roof, musty with burnt sulphur. The bats stirred, trembling, waving like old leaves.

The smoke grew until our lamps yellowed through it, and we began to cough. One bat fell, spreading the web of its wings before striking the floor. Suddenly they all came down, weaving drunkenly through the smoke, blowing about our heads. They flew swiftly, escaping at last out of the boxed eaves and through the traphole in the floor. Shouts came from below as the bats rained into the room. The smoke thickened until our eyes smarted, and we hurried down the ladder.

The bats were gone when we got down. We put out the lamps, and wiped watery eyes with our sleeves. The scholars who had stayed behind were knotted around a bench, their backs turned to us, and there was none to see how proudly we came down the ladder. The scholars bent closer to the bench, the joy of the bat-fly gone out of their faces. Jonce threw the hot dishpan into the yard and walked toward them, wondering. They stood aside as he came. Fern sat on the bench, holding a hand to her neck, her face white as beech bark. I was frightened, and the lamp fell from my hand.

"Toll Mauldraugh put a bat on me," Fern said. "It bit my neck."

Jonce's eyes searched the room, lighting on Toll standing against the blackboard, edging toward the door. Jonce sprang toward him, catching his sleeve as he crossed the threshold, and pushed him toward the pulpit. He caught up a willow pointer and struck Toll sharply across the legs, once, twice, and then Toll cried out in pain and anger, jerked loose, and leaped through a window. Jonce stood awkwardly with Toll's torn sleeve in his hand.

"Jonce ought never done that," Leth said to me. "He ought never touched Toll."

"Jonce ain't scared," I said. "Nary a grain, now."

"Uncle Hodge'll be coming," Leth said. "He vowed a fellow ain't going to draw breath who whips Toll."

Jonce folded a handkerchief and wrapped it around Fern's neck. "Everybody can go home now," he said. "Everybody can go."

I went to the water shelf for my bucket, standing on my toes to reach the handle. As I pulled it down I heard a mousy noise. I stood on a bench and looked, and there was a bat in the shelf corner. I opened my bucket and popped it in, closing the lid down tight. I walked out of the church-house with Fern, Leth coming behind us. "It's not more than a quarter mile up to Uncle Hodge's place," Leth said. "He'll be coming soon."

The scholars stood at the graveyard fence, looking up the creek road where Toll had gone. Fern caught hold of my hand, crying a little. "I ought never told," she said. "It's ruint our only chance earthy."

Hodge Mauldraugh came down the cove road, walking slowly, walking with his right hand in his hip pocket, wrist-deep and bulging.

"Uncle Hodge ain't going again his swear word," Leth said, and his speech was anxious, justifying his kin.

I looked at Leth and his eyes were cold and strange, and I saw then that he had Mauldraugh eyes, like Toll's. I stood apart from him, hating him suddenly.

I drew out the two marbles he had given me, dropping them at his feet. They lay on the ground, green as millet juice, but he did not pick them up or look where they had fallen.

Hodge came into the church-house yard, bending a little to search the windows. We heard his feet clump on the front steps, the floorboards rub under his weight, and a pistol shot. I turned and ran down the creek road, sick with loss, running until there was no wind in my body. Fern came swiftly behind, soundlessly as a fox runs.

We climbed the hill to our house in early afternoon, standing breathlessly at the door, looking in at Mother playing with the baby. I pulled the lid off my dinner bucket and the bat soared out, swinging like a leaf in a wind.

"*B-a-t*, bat," Mother said.

Pigeon Pie

"1868 it was," Grandma said, and her words were small against the spring winds bellowing in the chimneytop. She spread her hands close to the oakknot fire, blue-veined like a giant spider's web. "That was the year pigeons came to Flat Creek, might nigh taking the country."

I squatted on the limerock hearth before an ashhill where the bread baked, holding a broomstraw to know when it was done. We had not eaten since morning, and my hunger seemed larger than the ashhill where the bread was buried.

"Them pigeon-birds were worse than a plague writ in the Book," Grandma said. "Hit was our first married year, and Brack and me had grubbed out a home-seat on Little Flat, hoe-planting four acres o' corn. We'd got a garden patch put in, and four bee gums a-working before I turned puny, setting and waiting our firstborn. I'd take a peck measure outside and set me down on it where I could see the garden crap growing, and the bees fotching sweetening. There was a powerful bloom that year, as I remember, and a sight o' seasoning in the ground."

Bread smells thickened in the fireplace, and I stuck the straw into the ashhill. It came out with a sticky lump on the end. My hunger could hardly wait the slow cooking. I turned my head so Grandma couldn't see me eat the raw dough.

"Hit was early of a May morning when the pigeons came," Grandma said. "A roar sot up across the ridge, and Brack came down out o' the field, looking north where the sound was. We waited, dreading a wind tying knots in the young corn, shredding the blades with hits fingers, but nary a cloud we saw. The sound got bigger, and nearer. 'Hi, now, you git inside,' Brack said, and I did, fearing my child would bear a mark if I tuk a sudden fright. I allus followed my man's word when I was puny-like. I looked through the wall-crack and saw the first pigeons come down the swag, the light brightening their wings, gray like rock-moss and green underside. Then they came in a passel, and the sun-ball was clapped out, and hit got nigh dusty dark. Brack, he took a kindling wood stick, knocking at them that flew low, drapping four. After a spell they were gone, and we had breasts o' pigeons for supper, fried in their own grease. Brack allus was a fool for wild meat. 'Hi, now,' he said, a-cracking bones betwixt his teeth, 'I'd give a pretty for a pot-pie cooked out o' these birds.'

"Harl Thomas come up Flat Creek afore dark, saying he'd heard the pigeons had done a sight o' damage to the craps over at the Forks. He had a poke o' sulphur and was going to the doublings three miles yonside the ridge where the roost was. 'A sulphur smudge will bring 'em down,' he said. 'I'm a notion salting a barrelful. My woman feeds nothing but garden stuffs and sallet-greens of a summer. I allus liked a piece o' meat alongside.' Brack wanted to go, but knowing it was near my time, he never spoke of it. 'A pigeon pie would make good eating,' he said. 'I figger on eating me one afore them birds traipse clear off to another country.'

"Harl and Brack went outside, and I heard Harl laughing. He went off a-cackling like a guinea-hen. I got sort o' dizzy and tuk to bed. Pigeon-birds kept a-flying around in my head, thundering their wings. I tuk the big-eye and never slept a wink that night."

Wind drummed in the chimney and a gust caught up the oakknot smoke, blowing it into our eyes. A sift of ashes stirred on the hearth. I tried the bread again, the straw coming out slowly, though clean. I raked a bed of coals closer to the ashhill with the poker.

Grandma balled her hands on her knees, waiting until the smoke thinned and the ashes settled. "Hit was the next day the birds come a-thrashing through the hills proper," she said. "I was setting in my garden, guarding hit agin' the crows, when I heard a mighty noise a-roaring like Troublesome Creek having a tide. Brack was up in the corn patch, so I never went inside, wanting to get a square look at the birds. I never give a thought to me being puny. In a little spell they came over the ridge, flying low down, a-settling and looking for mast. A passel sot down in my garden and begun to eat and scratch. I run up and down hollering, throwing clods and a-crying. Hit was like trying to scare a hailstorm off. The birds worked around me like ants, now. I ran and hollered till I couldn't, then I set me down on the ground, feeling sick to die.

"The next thing I know I was in the house, and thar was a granny woman setting beside the bed with something wrapped up in a kiver. Now I knowed what was in that thar kiver, but I was scared to look. Brack come in laughing and said hit was a boy-child. He brought the little tick over to the bed, and I couldn't wait to look, asking, 'Has hit got a mark?' 'No mark particular,' Brack said. 'His left hand hain't natural though.' The kiver was opened and thar the chap was, hits little face red and pinched up. Brack pulled the left hand out, and on the side was a finger-piece no bigger than a pea, having nary a nail nor jint. I cried, now, looking at hit.

"'Hit won't be thar for long,' Brack said. He got out his razor and 'gin to strap hit hard, putting a hair edge on the blade. When I figgered what he was going to do, I let in hollering and screaming, worse than I did when the birds tuk my garden patch. The granny woman held me in bed, and Brack tuk the baby into the kitchen. I listened, catching for a sound o' the baby, but he never made one. I reckon hit never hurt much. Brack brought him back and thar was a drap o' water in its eyes. The granny woman cooked up a pigeon pie for supper, but I couldn't touch a bite. I've never eat a bird since."

The bread was done. I raked it out on the hearth, blowing ashes from the brown crust. When it was broken, the goodness of it filled my eyes and throat. "A pair o' pigeon legs would go good with this bread," I said.

Grandma looked hard at the hoecake, then broke a piece for me, taking none for herself. She took the poker and shook the oakknot fiercely, raising a blaze of sparks. "I hain't a grain hungry," she said.

Twelve Pears Hanging High

"Hit's me so thin that keeps the baby puny, a-puking up his milk, holding nothing on his stomach," Mother said. "If I got a scratch, I'd bleed dry. I need a tonic, fleshening me up, 'riching my blood."

Nezzie Crouch sat on the meatbox watching Mother string tiny beans, too young to be picked. She had come up from Blackjack to learn about our moving, walking three miles to carry the word back to the camp. The question waited in her eyes. She took a fresh dip of snuff, holding the tin snuffbox in her hand and pushing the lid down tight. Three red tobacco leaves grew on the wrapper, sticking up through the print.

"Well, now," Nezzie said, opening her stained mouth, "there's cures a-plenty for the picking. Ole herb doc down at Blackjack says there's a weed for every ill, if you know what to pick and how to brew proper."

"Picking and brewing, I don't know which, nor how."

"I heered tell a little 'sang is right quickening to the blood."

"Woodsful of 'sang they used to be, but I hain't seen a prong in ten year."

"So scarce hit might nigh swaps for gold."

"Don't reckon they's a sprig left on Carr Creek."

"Well, now, hit ain't all gone. I seen a three-prong coming up from Blackjack a-blooming yellow. I seed that 'sang standing there so feisty, and I says, 'Hain't that a sight, nobody's grubbed him yet,' and I broke a bresh to hide it."

"Standing there belonging to nobody."

"Agin' the road it was; nobody's, so far as I see."

"If I had that there root, I'd try it."

"Belonging to nobody but ground and air. Hit growed from a seed nobody dropped. This chap can go piece-way home with me and fotch it back."

Nezzie brought out a sourwood toothbrush and worked it in her mouth, pushing the snuff back into the pocket of her cheek. "I hear tell you're moving to Blackjack agin," she said. She had named it, looking over my head through the door, putting no weight on the words.

Mother finished stringing the beans and hung the bucket on a peg, bringing out new-dug potatoes to scrape with the dull side of a knife. They were knotty and small. "The mines hain't opened yet," she said. "They keep putting off."

"Tipple's been patched, and they're ready to start. Better chance o' work if you're living in the camp."

"Brack might walk to and from the mine of a day," Mother said.

Nezzie took the toothbrush out of her mouth. "They's a tale going 'round that you folks are about starved out up here. I see you've got a fair garden patch coming along. Not a grain o' faith I put in such talk."

Mother's hands worked busily over a potato, the skin coming off paper-thin, wasting none of the flesh. "We've got plenty," she said, "a God's plenty." Her voice was as sharp as the bright blade of the knife.

The baby caught hold of the bedfoot and pulled himself up, spreading his legs for balance. Nezzie watched, laughing to see him bend his knees. "Look how he tromps his foot and hops up and down like a bird in a bush," she said. She bent over him, touching his pale face. "Hit's little hide is so tender. You ought to make that 'sang tea for shore."

"When it 'gins to blow 'round the north points of a morning," explained Father, "sign hit's going to weather."

"I hope the rain won't scare the guinea-hen off that nest I set this morning," Mother replied. "Twenty-six eggs there was."

"Now you ought to saved a few out to fry," Father said.

Rain set in before noon, the waters falling thick upon the hills. The draws filled, emptying downward. The martins hid in their gourds, swinging in the drenched air. Little Carr rose, swelling through the willows, swallowing the green rushes. Damp winds whipped around the house, smelling of earth and water.

Mother set the pans where the roof leaked. We pushed the beds catty-cornered, away from the drips. Father sat on the trunk, the knots of his knees drawn under his chin. Fletch and I crawled on the floor, turning our faces upward, letting drops of water fall into our mouths. Euly came from behind the stove, leaving the corncob poppets to ask a riddle Mother had whispered to her. Her eyes lit up.

Twelve pears hanging high,
Twelve fellers riding by;
Now Each took a pear
And left eleven hanging there.

Father's face widened for he knew the answer, having told Mother this riddle himself. Fletch looked at me, but I did not know how eleven pears could be left hanging. My head felt hollow.

"Hit was a chap six years old sprung that there riddle on me," Father said. "Taulbee Lovern's boy. Sharp as a sprig, that little feller is. Knows his figgers square to a thousand, and says his a-b-abbs, backwards and forwards. Hain't been school-taught neither. Never darked a schoolhouse door."

"I wisht I had me a pear," I said, still trying to figure the riddle.

Father glanced at Mother, his gray eyes burning in the woolly light. "Taulbee Lovern's boy, it was," he said. Mother looked at the baby sleeping at the bedfoot, never lifting her face toward Father.

"Who, now, is Taulbee Lovern?" Euly asked.

Euly's question hung in the room like the great drops of water growing under the shingle roof, stretching before dropping.

"Who is Taulbee Lovern?"

"A child too knowing is liable to die before they're grown," Mother said.

"As bonny a chap as ever I saw," Father said. "Don't reckon he's drawed a sick breath. Fed and clothed proper since he was born." Father's face got dolesome, and his voice lowered into the sound of rain beating the puncheon walls. He looked into all the corners of the room, at the two beds standing in the middle of the floor, at the empty meatbox, at the ball of clothes piled on the table to keep them dry. He looked at Euly standing by the bedboard. He looked at Fletch and me squatting on the floor listening, our heads cocked to one side. "One chap Taulbee and Doshia had," he said. "Three hundred acres o' land they own, and a passel o' that is bottom flat. Six-room house with two glass windows in every dobbed room. Taulbee's tuk care of his own. They've never gone a-lacking."

Mother's face reddened. "I hain't complaining of the way I'm tuk care of," she said. "We hain't starved dead or gone naked yet. I hain't complaining."

"Twelve pears hanging high," Euly began, but we were not listening. "Who is Taulbee Lovern?"

"He was your ma's first beau," Father said, "the man she might o' chose."

The baby opened its eyes.

"Hush," Mother said.

Euly went back to her poppets behind the stove, speaking doll-talk to the cobs. I crawled between the meatbox and the wall, going there to wonder about Taulbee Lovern's boy and how it would be to know square to the end of everything. I found a sassafras root, and I chewed it, spitting red juice through a crack in the floor. And I wished I had a pear, one as mushy ripe as a frosted pawpaw. I felt I could eat the whole dozen hanging on the riddle-tree.

I licked the flakes of salt off the meatbox with my tongue. An ant marched up and down, feeling along the board, and I saw four grand-daddy spiders. Three were tight in a corner, their pill-bodies hung in a web of legs. A fourth walked alone. I took up a shoe and slapped the proud walker, and he went down, flattened upon the floor. He lay quivering in a puzzle of legs and body. As I watched, he rose up, moving into the corner. I crawled away from the meatbox, not wanting to see again the gray spot where he had bled.

Father held the baby in the flat of his two hands. Little Green stared into his face. "Take me," Father was saying, "I never tuk natural to growing things, a-planting seeds and sticking plows into the ground like Taulbee Lovern. A furrow I run allus did crook like a blacksnake's track. A sight o' farming I've done, but it allus rubbed the grain. But give me a pick, and I'll dig as much coal as the next 'un. Now I figger every riddle ought to have an answer. Them mines won't stay closed forever and aye."

Euly brought a poppet for the baby to hold. He looked at it gravely for a moment, clutching the cob in a tallow-white hand, and then began to cry softly, a tearless smothered cry.

"So puny he's been," Mother sighed. "I'm uneasy."

In middle afternoon the rain slacked for a spell. We went out upon the washed earth, stepping on grass clumps to keep clear of the mud. The swollen tide of the creek flowed high above the rushes, whipping the willow tops. A wet wind blew down into the clouds banked against the hills. The martins came out of their gourds, soaring in blunt flight, coming back to sit on the pole.

"Look at that ole martin-bird picking his teeth with a straw," Fletch said.

The guinea eggs hatched. The speckled fowls were wild as partridges. They were swift as granny-hatches in the pennyrile. We rarely saw them. The grass tops shook where they fed. The metal clink of their voices grew. Once when it rained they roosted noisily under the house. We looked at them through a floor crack. There were fourteen biddies, and we remembered there had been twenty-six eggs.

"That ole guinea hen hain't got a grain o' sense," Mother said. "She's running them little 'uns square to death, a-taking off through the weeds like a ruffed grouse, a-potter-racking and giving them chicks nary a minute to pick their craws full."

"That's their born nature," Father said. "Guineas are hard raising. Bounden to lose some. Hit's the same way with folks. Hain't everybody lives to rattle their bones. Hain't everybody breathes till their veins get blue as dog-tick stalks."

"Next guinea eggs I set are going to be under a chicken hen," Mother said.

I chose a guinea, claiming it for my own, but afterwards I was never sure which one was mine. Euly chose the littlest. Its feathers were covered with pale freckles thick as hops. "Aye, now," Fletch said, sticking out his lips. "They're all belongen to me."

"Just so I get in on the eating," Father laughed. "I bet one would be good battered and fried, tender as snail horns."

"Hain't nigh big enough," Mother said. "Would be wasting meat."

Father lifted his head from the crack. There was hunger in his eyes, a longing for meat that our garden patch could not cure. "If I had some gun shells, I'd go hunting a coon," he said. "I seed some tracks this morning."

"I got a fine mess o' squash cooking for dinner," Mother said.

Father sat down on the meatbox. "Recollect the time we had boiled gourds for dinner?" he asked Mother.

"I do right well. I come across four gourds one day growing behind the barn when we lived on Quicksand Creek. Yeller and pretty they were, looking a sight like summer squash, not having any necks to speak of."

"Oh them beans tasted like a gall pie. Recollect?"

"Chickens wouldn't even touch 'em."

"A fowl's got a taster like folks. You never seed one peck a gourd."

Father got off the meatbox and pushed the lid aside. He plowed his hands through the salt lumps. "Hain't even a pig knuckle here," he said. "This box holds nothing but a hungry smell." He dug deeper, straining the loose grains through his fingers. Something clung to his hand, a thin white stripping, a finger wide. "Looks like a johnny-humpback," he said. It did look like a worm.

"Hell's bangers," Father said. "It's a scrap o' meat." He rubbed the salt off and held it up. "Sowbelly," he said, and it was.

"Wouldn't fill your hollow tooth," Mother scoffed. "It's that little."

Mother washed the meat string. She held it over the pot. It dangled in her hand. We watched. It looked pine-blank like a johnny-humpback.

"Wait," Father said. "It hain't big enough to give a taste to that pile of squash-mush. Bile it up in a little broth for the baby."

The Butterfly Mine loaded its first gon of coal the last week in June. Word came up the river, drifting back into the creek hollows. Scratchback Mine put fifty men hauling fallen jackrock and setting new timbers. The Elkhorn blew its steam whistle one morning at three o'clock. The blast rose out of Boone's Fork, across He Creek and She Creek, lifting into the hills of the upper Kentucky River country. A shift of men was going into the diggings for the first time in eight months. Roosters waked, crowing. Our guinea hen flew noisily out of the black birch.

Father got up and lighted a fire in the stove. The shagged splinters trembled in his hands. He piled in wood until flames roared up the rusty pipe. The top of the stove reddened, the cracks and seams of the cast iron becoming alive, traced like rivers on a map's face. Hoofs clattered along Carr Creek before daylight. Men came down out of the ridges in twos and ones, hats slanted, feet out of the stirrups, riding toward Elkhorn and Scratchback. A pony went by, shoeless, feet whispering on the rocky ground. A man rode bare-bones.

"They're wanting coal up at the big lakes," Father said. "Hit'll be going over the waters to some foreign country land."

After breakfast Father got out his mine lamp, polished the brass with spit and a woolen sleeve. "Hit's been a long dry spell," he said, "but they'll be working at Blackjack soon. Any day now, aye gonnies. Tipple's been fixed. A new spur o' track laid up to the driftmouth. Patched up the camp houses a sight too."

"It's only two miles down to Blackjack," Mother said. "I figger you could walk it of a day. Pity to fotch the baby off into a camp, and it so puny."

"We'll get a house yonside of the slag pile this time, away from the smoke," Father said.

"Smoke blowing and a-blacking, no matter where you set down in Blackjack holler. I recollect the last move we made into the camp. Tobacco cuds stuck in the cracks, snuff dips staining the room corners, and a stink all over. I biled water by the pot and tub, washing and scrubbing, making hit so you could draw a healthy breath."

"Living here, it'll get me home after dusty dark. I reckon we ought to move down."

Father started off toward Blackjack. We watched him move along the creek road, his long restless stride eating dirt, pushing the distance back. The grass birds droned out of the bottom fields as he approached. The fork-turn swallowed him, and we went into the garden to pick bugs. The baby crawled between the bean vines, pulling at the runners. I gave him a wax bean to nibble with his new milk teeth. He gobbled it down, wanting more. I gave him a yellow tomato. He bit it, making a wry face. He sucked the tender pulp cut and then cried because I feared to give him another. Mother came from the far potato rows. She sat down on a crabgrass clump and opened her bosom. The baby jumped in her lap, beating tiny fists in the air.

"He's might nigh starved," I said, scared the bean and tomato were going to colic him.

"When your pap sets to work, I can buy me a tonic," Mother said. "The baby will fatten up then. I been taking 'sang tea, but it does me no good."

I got more worried the baby would get sick. I made a whistle from a young hickory sprout for him. I found a June bug and tied a sewing thread to its legs, letting him hold the thread while the bug flew around and around, wings humming like a dulcimer string. But Green didn't get sick. He ate two bean leaves before I could snatch them away.

Father came home in early afternoon. His arms were full of pokes. We ran to meet him, even Mother going down the path a way. We grabbed the pokes Father carried, running ahead, shouting up to Mother, holding the shuck-brown bags aloft. We emptied them on the table. There was a five-pound bucket of lard, with a shoat drawn on the bucket. Brown sugar in a glass jar. A square of sowbelly, thin and hairy. A white-dusty sack of flour, and on it a picture-piece of a woman holding an armful of wheat straws. And there was a tin box of black pepper and a double handful of coffee beans.

We looked in wonder, not being able to speak, knowing only that a great hunger crawled inside of us, and that our tongues were moistening our lips. The smell of meat and parched coffee hung in the room.

"I start digging tomorrow," Father said, drawing himself tall and straight. The string of red peppers hanging from the rafters tipped his head. "They put my name on the books, and I drawed these victuals out of the commissary on credit."

A lean hand reached toward the table, blue-veined and bony. It was Mother's, touching the sugar jar, the red-haired meat, the flour sack. Suddenly she threw an apron over her head, turning away from us. She made hardly a sound, no more than a tick-beetle.

Euly held the sugar jar over the baby's head, and he reached toward it with both hands. "Twelve pears hanging high," she said.

"We hain't moving down to the camp after all," Father said. "Leastways, not before winter sets in. That Blackjack school won't open up till September, I heered."

Father lighted a fire in the stove. I fetched three buckets of water from the spring, not feeling the weary pull of the hill, not resting between buckets. The nobby heads of the guineas stuck out of the weeds behind the house, potter-racking. The smell of frying meat grew upon the air, growing larger than the thought of ripe pears, or the body of any hunger.

Two Eyes, Two Pennies

"A fair place you've got here," Uncle Lott said. He sat in the kitchen after supper, under the white bloom of the lamp, his chair leaned against the wall. We had moved out of the hills into the coal camp at Houndshell two days before, and he had come to stay a spell with us. His eyes rounded, looking. Three fly-bugs walked stupidly across the ceiling, wings tight against their bodies, drunk with light. Fern peered through the smoky windows into strange dark. Lark crawled around the table, pushing a matchbox, playing it was a coal gon. "Never you lived in such a branfired good house as I've got reckoning of," Uncle Lott said. "Aye gonnies, there's window glasses looking four directions." He tipped the blunt end of his mustache with a thumb. It was a knuckle joint long now, combed out stiff and thin, the hairs as coarse as a boar's whiskers.

"Camp houses setting on three sides and hills blacking the other," Mother said. "Can't see a thing beyond." Her words were dolesome, though not complaining. She glanced at Uncle Lott as she dried the dishpan, and Father looked, too, from where he sat beside the stove. A thready web of veins was bright on Uncle Lott's cheeks. His hands rested on his knees, fat and tender, and they had none of the leathery look of a miner's. I remembered then what Mother had said to Father before supper, whispering in the kitchen while Uncle Lott napped in the far room.

"Fifty years old if he's a day," she said, "and never done a day's work. Man of his years ought to be married, keeping his own. A shame he'll put up on his kin when there's work a-plenty, not lifting a hand. Oh I always wanted to bring up my chaps honest, never taking a thing unbelonging to them, never taking a grain they don't earn. It's folks forever setting bad examples that turns a child wrong."

Father had frowned. "If Lott ever got started digging—" he began, and then turned away, saying no more.

139

Lark was listening behind the stove. "Now, I never tuk a thing unbelonging," he had said.

Father reached into the woodbox for a soft splinter to whittle. Thin slivers curled under the blade of his knife until he held a yellow stalk bright with wooden leaves.

Lark came from under the table to claim the splinter, taking it back for his play. We heard him blowing, shaking the leaves with the wind of his breath.

Father snapped the blade into its case. "It's a sight how good the mining business is getting," he said. "Big need for bunker coal up at the lakes, afar yonder. Jobs laying around loose for them with the notion to work."

Uncle Lott looked frightened. The veins on his cheeks burned full and red.

"Lott, if you want me to speak to Sim Brannon, I will," Father said. "He's foreman at Number Two, and the best man to work for I ever had. I was raised up with Sim, and I figure he'll take on any of my kin if I just say the word."

"I seed Sim Brannon this morning," Lark said under the table. "He's the biggest man ever was."

Uncle Lott settled the front legs of his chair on the floor. He hooked his thumbs together, pulling one knuckle against the other. A muffled cough came out of his throat. He grunted. "I hain't been well lately," he said. "A horn o' Indian Doctor tonic I'm taking after every meal."

"I got Harl and Sid Middleton put on today," Father said. He weighed his words as he spoke. Mother glanced swiftly at him. Her mouth opened in dismay, knowing suddenly that Father's cousins would come to live at our house, too, making us fretful with their dark and stubborn ways.

"They were setting in wait for me at the drift mouth this morning," Father went on. "I spoke to Sim Brannon for them. I said, 'Sim, here's some of my kin. I'd take it as a favor if you'd give them a little mite o' something to do.' And by grabbies if he didn't put them to snagging jack rock."

Lark raised his head above the table, holding the shagged splinter aloft, and looking at Uncle Lott. "Recollect the time Harl and Sid cut yore mustache string off?" he asked.

Uncle Lott's face reddened. He tipped his mustache ends and sat up angrily.

"I thought them two were holed up at Yellow Creek mine for the winter," he grumbled. "I heered somebody say it."

"The Yellow is just a one-horse mine," Father said. "Always a-hiring and a-firing." Then his voice dropped, holding the words low in the small of his throat. He looked guiltily at Mother. "I reckon they'll be boarding here with us. Might be along hunting a bed tonight."

Mother's eyes hollowed. Her hands grew limp about the dishrag. I tried to remember Harl and Sid, wondering why Mother did not want them to board with us. I thought of our four rooms, square and large, believing them enough for us all, and I could not think why Mother would want us to live lonesome and apart. I thought of Harl and Sid and Father sitting before the fire on winter evenings, legs angled back from the blaze, speaking after the way of miners. They would brag a little, drawing back the corners of their mouths. "I loaded four tons today if I shoveled one chunk." . . . "I heard a little creak-creak, and hell's bangers if a rock size of a washpot didn't come down a-front o' me. Hit scared my gizzard, I tell you." . . . "I set me a charge o' dynamite, lit the fuse too short and got knocked flat as a tape." . . . And Uncle Lott would speak from where he sat behind them, scornful of the mines, telling of what he had heard at the storehouse, and the others would listen as though a child had spoken.

Mother's lips began to tremble. She hung a dishrag on a peg and went swiftly out of the room, her clothes rustling above the fry of the lamp wick. Father leaned forward in his chair, and then he strode through the door, following Mother.

Fern turned from the window where her hands had been cupped against the light. "I just saw a woman pass along, a-walking by herself," she said. "I bet she's the fortuneteller, going somewhere in the dark of the night."

Uncle Lott's eyes lighted up. They opened round and wide. "Has she gone beyond sight?" he asked.

"Gone off down the road," Fern said.

"Rilla Todd, it might o' been," Uncle Lott said. "She's a widow woman, fair as a picture piece. She goes a-traipsing all hours, selling broadsides with verses writ on them."

"What do them verses say?" I asked.

"They're writ about her man getting killed in the mines," Uncle Lott said. "I forget how the lines run, but they've got rhymy words on the ends. It's music not set to notes."

"Wish I had me a broadside," I said.

"For any piece o' money, be it a penny or greenback, she'll shuck off one from a little deck she's got," Uncle Lott said.

Fern turned from the window, blinking at the light. "If I had some money, I'd get my fortune told," she said, "a-knowing who I'll marry, dark or fair, and who'll be coming to my wedding."

"I know where they's a mess o' pennies," Lark said, "but you'd better not touch 'em." He held the shaggy splinter high, pointing toward the mantelpiece in the front room. We remembered the four pennies he had found once. They were stacked inside the clock, behind the pendulum. "Was somebody to die, them's the pennies to put on their eyes," Lark said.

Uncle Lott laughed, the web of veins ripening on his face. "Never takes more'n two," he said. "Two eyes, two pennies."

"Hush," Fern said, listening. We pricked our ears, hearing only the lamp wick's clucking for a moment. Then brogans shuffled outside, came nearer, and stopped. There was no sound of feet on the doorsteps. We waited, knowing it was Harl and Sid, wondering how they moved so quietly. Suddenly Fern sprang back from the window, her face paling, fright catching in her throat. Lark dropped the splinter, breaking off the shags. Uncle Lott jumped, too, being as scared as the rest of us. Two faces were pressed against the glass. Eyes looked in through a fog of breath; noses were tight against the pane, looking like wads of dough.

"Them two are born devils," Uncle Lott said.

"Sim Brannon's a dog, if there ever was one," Harl said.

Harl and Sid stood on the porch with Father, kicking heels of mud from their boots, scraping dirt crumbs from hob toes. It was Saturday and they had come home from the mines with silver rattling in their pockets. I heard their feet grinding the floor and I came out from under the porch where I had been hunting doodlebug holes.

"Sim always has been square with me," Father said, rolling the pouch holding dynamite caps into a ball. "Little troubles are bounden to happen." He bent down, carving the mud away with the long blade of his knife.

"He's set us digging a vein not thick as a flitter," Sid said, his mouth full of scorn. "Hit's eighty feet off the main tunnel, mixed up with jack rock, and a feller's got to break his back to wedge in."

"Feller can't make brass, a-digging that vein," Harl said. "For a pretty I'd set a fuse and blow that trap in."

"Stick and dig," Father said. "You're the last fellers tuk on. Sim can't give a pick and choose. I say dig that coal out, and don't start pulling any rusties." He shucked his boots off, taking them under his arm, and went inside in his socks.

I climbed the steps. Harl was shaking his feet like a cat come in out of the dew, his thin lips speaking against Sim Brannon.

"I'll wash your boots for a penny," I said, "and shine them till they'll be nigh like a looking glass."

They cocked their heads, their eyes dark as chinquapins under the bills of mine caps. "What would you buy with such a bag o' money?" Sid asked. They laughed, shaking their pockets, jingling their pay.

"I'd buy me a broadside off the peddle woman," I said. "I would, now."

Sid reached up and caught hold of the porch joist. He was that tall. A grin wrinkled his mouth. "They dropped no pennies in my pay pocket," he said. "Get that Lott to beg you a broadside. He hangs around that Todd woman every chance. This morning I saw him standing in the road middle talking to her, standing there with his brogans hitched with yarn strings."

Harl struck his hands together, laughing. "I nigh broke my neck stumbling over Lott's boots last night," he said. "I tuk me a blade and eased it up through the eel-strings. They cut like butter."

"You oughten to do it," I said, feeling sorry for Uncle Lott. "It's not honest."

"I'd give a pretty to stick him and Sim Brannon in that mine alley and set off a box o' dynamite this side," Sid said. "By grabs, I would."

They scrubbed their boots on the porch a bit more, clapped out the carbide flame on their cap lamps, and went inside. The floor was dark where they stepped, marking their way over the scoured planking.

I pulled off my shoes as Father had done, tipping into the house. I set them on the hearth of the front room and looked at the clock on the mantelpiece. Fat smells of soup beans drifted in from the kitchen, hanging among the beds. I stood on my toes, reaching into the clock, feeling behind the pendulum for the pennies kept there. I pulled them out, cupping them in my hand. There were four, worn and blackened, having no faces to speak of. "If'n I had me a penny—" I said aloud; and then I suddenly put them back, spying about to see no one was looking. I took my shoes and went into the kitchen. Father was warming by the stove. I stood behind his chair and looked over his shoulder, but I couldn't raise the courage to ask him for a penny piece.

Harl and Sid were already at the table. "The beans aren't nigh done yet," Mother warned, but they would not wait. They filled their plates from the boiling pot, whispering together as they ate. We heard Sim Brannon's name spoken. Little wrinkles of anger dented their foreheads. Uncle Lott looked up from the corner where he was making a hickory whistle for Lark, a grain of uneasiness in his eyes.

Lark heard too. He came and stood between Harl and Sid, not being the least afraid. "I seed Sim Brannon one time," he said. "I reckon he's the biggest man ever was."

Father chuckled in the deep of his throat. "The biggest man ever was come from a fork o' Flat Creek," he said, recollecting. "Died more'n thirty years ago, and he tuk a nine-foot coffin. Bates, his name was, kin to the Bateses on Shoal Creek. Stood seven feet six, in his stocking feet."

Uncle Lott leaned against the wall. He was cutting a blow notch in the hickory whistle. "Abraham Lincoln was a big man," he said, "biggest feller I ever saw."

"You never saw Abe Lincoln," Father said.

"I never saw him in the flesh for truth," Uncle Lott said, "but I saw a statue o' him in Louisville once. It stood nine foot, if it stood an inch, and his head was big as a peck measure. Oh he had a basket of a head to carry his brains in."

"That was just a statue, a-made big and stretched out," Father explained. "The man who hacked that rock picture carved him standing out on purpose."

Harl and Sid held spoons in their fists, listening to Father and forgetting to eat. Father never batted an eye telling this tale. It was the bound truth. "This feller Bates, he wasn't just strung out tall," Father said. "He was big according, head to toe. Three hundred and five he weighed, and not a grain o' fat he had. I saw him pick up Podock Jones once, rocking him in his arms like a baby. I liked to died laughing, seeing ole Podock's beard waving up and down, and him looking like a born dwarf."

"By grabbies," Uncle Lott said, "I'm kin to the Bateses on Flat Creek."

Harl's spoon clattered on his plate. "How much kin air you to that queen bee who peddles ballad verses?" he asked. The black bead of his eyes was on Uncle Lott. "I see you two forever swapping talk."

Mother opened the stove door and took out the cornbread. She shook the pan to see if the pones were stuck. "I hear Rilla Todd's a good woman, and sets honor by her dead husband," she said. "Got a homeseat her pure own. That's more'n most folks can brag about."

"Her man's been dead three years," Harl said. "Three years buried and she hain't married another." He looked slyly at Uncle Lott. "I don't figure she'll be taking up with jist any ole drone."

Uncle Lott knicked at the whistle. The vein patches were bright on his cheeks.

"That woman's the best song scribe ever was," I said. "Makes verses up right out of her head."

"Reckon she'd make a rhyme about Sim Brannon if something went bad wrong with him?" Sid said, stretching his neck to swallow.

"Now, looky here," Father warned, "Sim Brannon could break a common man down like he was a shotgun. I'm agin' starting trouble."

"I wouldn't be scared to tip him," Sid said.

"Sim's been fair with me. Anything he'd name I'd stand by."

"Feller can't make shoe leather digging that sorry bone vein. Had my way, the roof o' that tunnel would be setting agin' the ground."

Sid looked suddenly at Harl. He spoke, "If that tunnel was closed—" then bit his words off. They whispered together again. They pushed their plates back and went into the far room, and presently left the house.

Before the beans were full done I tiptoed into the front room and felt inside the clock. I took the rustiest penny—so black it looked like a button. "I'll put one back in its place the first chance," I thought. "I'm just a-borrowing." When I slipped it into Uncle Lott's hand he spied hard, at first not knowing what it was. I whispered in his ear, and he grinned. "I'll be seeing her tonight," he said. "I'll buy you a broadside for shore."

We sat down to eat. Our plates were filled with beans from the pot, the goblets poured full of buttermilk, the bread broken and passed. Uncle Lott ate hurriedly, and set off on the dark road, and we were alone in the house. There was none of Sid's and Harl's tromping in muddy boots, or Uncle Lott's groans after a heavy meal.

"It's good to have a little peace," Mother said. "It's like heaven on earth." The dread went out of her face. She glanced around the table and her eyes grew bright as a bird's. "You've every one got buttermilk mustaches," she said, laughing quietly. We wiped them off with the backs of our hands, and then we played a riddle game. Fern knew a pack.

"Six legs up and two legs down, and that's the way he went to town." . . . "Nothing on God's earth got legs on hits back, now." . . . "Twelve pears hanging high, twelve fellers riding by; now Each tuk a pear, but left eleven hanging there." . . . "By grabbies, that one can't be."

Lark got down from the table and crawled about, blowing the whistle Uncle Lott had made for him. "I'm an engine pulling sixteen coal gons," he said. While Mother washed the dishes we played crack-a-loo, pitching beans at a floor seam. Mother lifted her hands out of the dishpan. They hung like dripping leaves. Her face became grave, her eyes dulled. "Pity it can't be like this every night of the world," she said. "Living apart, having our own."

Lark went to sleep under the table. Father picked him up, taking him to bed in the far room. Suddenly we heard a quick step, and a sharp word Father had spoken to himself. He came to the door between, standing there holding a leather pouch. His face was tight with anger. He pulled the slip string of the pouch and thrust his hand in, unbelieving. "All my dynamite caps have been tuk out o' this pocket," he said. "What sort o' rusty can that pair o' witties be up to now?"

Mother wakened me in the black of the morning, standing over the bed with a lamp. I saw the fright in her eyes, and her trembling hands. The glass chimney shook inside its ring of brass thumbs. She told what had happened to Harl and Sid—the little she knew, all not yet being known. "Living or dead, there's no telling," Mother said. I jumped out of bed, and into my britches. I jumped out thinking of Uncle Lott and the pennies. "Two eyes, two pennies," he had said, and now both Harl and Sid might be stretched out cold, and there would be nothing to hold their eyelids down. I was good scared.

Uncle Lott's bed was empty, the covers thrown back from the trough his heavy body made in the mattress. He and Father had hurried to the mine when the word first came. Harl's and Sid's bed hadn't been slept in, and I thought how they had been buried all these hours, deep underside the earth, with nobody knowing whether they still drew breath. A chill fiercer than the cold of the room crept under my shirt.

Drawing on a pea jacket, I went barefoot into the yard. The road was alive with folk shaken out of Sunday morning's sleep, trudging over frosty ruts toward the mines. Daylight grew on the ridge. A smoky coldness hung in the camp. Men had their hands almost to elbows in britches pockets; women clasped fingers into balls against their breasts. Voices rang in the air, arguing. "Hit's like it was with Floyd Collins. Recollect? Buried in that sandstone cave, yonder in bluegrass country." . . . "What, now, would them fellers be doing in a mine, middle o' the night? I ask you that." . . . "Them Middletons hain't caught in that tunnel. I figger hit's just a general fall, the ground a-settling down of its own accord."

Fern came and stood beside me, watching, sleep still in her face. Three boys ran up the road shouting. "Look," Fern said. "Yonder comes the fortune-telling woman." I looked, picking her from the others. She came hobbling, her uncombed hair tucked beneath a coat collar; and she was old, old, and the seams of her face were like gullied earth. Fern drew back, speaking under her breath. "Now, never do I want my fortune told, a-knowing everything coming, a-knowing when I'm going to die."

Cold ate through the pea jacket. I shook. My teeth struck together. "I wouldn't want a ballad writ about folks gitting killed in the mines neither," I said. "I wouldn't, now."

The sun-ball rose, yellow and heatless. The burning slagheap near the tipple wound its smoke straight as a pole into the sky. The chill drove us indoors, and we looked over the camp from our kitchen window, seeing the chimney pots were cold, the people all gone to the drift mouth. I begged to go. I cried a speck, but Mother wouldn't hear of it. "Wait," she said. "Your Father said he'd send word." And while we waited she brought a cushaw from the back porch, and began to peel off the mellow skin. "Three pies I'm going to make," she said. "Harl and Sid'll be starved when they get back."

Fern's chin quivered. "Never a bite they'll eat," she said mournfully. "Their mouths shut for good, their eyes with pennies atop." She crossed the room, and I knew suddenly where she was going. She went out of the kitchen. I heard the clock door snap. I stood by the window, as quiet as a deer mouse, scarcely drawing breath. She came back looking hard at me, knowing. She whispered to Lark and they both looked, eyes round with accusation.

When the cushaws were boiling Mother got out a bag of cracklings. She crisped a handful of rinds in the stove. "Six pones o' fatty bread I'm going to make," she said. "Lott and your Father and all the other fellers digging will be hungry. Nary a bite they've had this living day." She started a pot of shucky beans cooking; she opened a jar of wild-plum pickles.

A granny woman came down from the drift mouth. We saw her through the window, her breath blowing a woolly fog. We hurried into the yard to stop her at our gate. "What have they learnt?" Mother asked.

The granny woman cleared her throat. "Nothing for shore," she said. Her voice was thin like a fowl's. "There's a chug o' rock fell down, but no sound beyond. Feller says he seed them go in the mine last night. That's all they know—jist a feller says. Oh never'd I trust a man's sight Saturday after dark."

She moved on, grumbling in the crisp air, and we heard a tramp of footsteps on the road. The miners were going home. They came on by our house, blowing into their freezing hands. They huddled together against the cold, speaking hoarsely amongst themselves. "Them two hain't there, and never was." . . . "Aye gonnies, gitting a feller up with a lie-tale in the dead o' Sunday morning. Hit's a sin."

Morning wore away. We no longer looked out of the window, no longer hoping, believing that Harl and Sid were buried beyond finding. The shucky beans got done; the cushaw pies, yellow as janders, were shelved behind the stove. The fatty bread waited in pans to be baked at the last moment. Mother gave Lark a pickled plum and his eating of the vinegary fruit set my teeth on edge. Hunger crawled inside of me, though larger than any hunger, larger than anything, a knot of humiliation grew in my chest. It grew like a branching root. "If only I never tuk that penny piece," I kept saying to myself, dreading the time when Mother would know of it, being sure Lark would tell, for he was only six and could not keep a secret. "If only I hadn't borrowed—" And I looked up. We all looked, startled. There was Sim Brannon standing in the kitchen door, filling the space with huge shoulders and the greatness of his body. His head stuck inside the room, for the door was not tall enough.

"We've come on that pair o' rascals," he said, his words and laughter sudden as a thunderclap. "They dinnymited the tunnel betwixt them and the opening, closing up that thin-vein holler where I try out my new diggers. They set the charge wrong and trapped themselves proper."

"Are they hurt?" Mother asked anxiously.

"Not a scratch, and hollering to git out," Sim said. "Everybody give up and left except Lott and your man. They scrabbled and they dug, and now they's only a foot o' rock betwixt. Any minute they'll dig through. Oh I tell you, that Lott is a man-mole. I hired him square on the spot." He glanced at the bean pot, the pies, the pickled plums. His lips slackened with hunger.

"When the digging's over," Mother said, "all of you come and eat here. They'll be plenty for all."

"We will, now," Sim said gratefully. "I hain't et since last night. We would o' pretty nigh caved in if Rilla Todd hadn't set a bucket o' coffee biling for us at the drift mouth."

"Ask Rilla Todd to come too," Mother said. "Say she's welcome."

Sim turned to go, stooping under the door top. He paused suddenly, his great head bent, listening. Boots tromped on the back porch; blunt steps passed into the far room, walking, walking. We waited. After a while two heads stuck through the kitchen door. Harl and Sid stood there with clothes bundled under their arms, their mining gear hung over their shoulders. They looked at the table, then fearfully at Sim, and drew back. Mother opened her mouth, but no words came out. The door slammed, and they were gone.

"Looks to me you've lost two boarders and me two miners," Sim said, grinning.

Uncle Lott told us as we were sitting at the table. Rilla Todd sat beside him, weaving her willowy fingers in her lap. "We're marrying next Sunday for shore," he said. His face reddened, the thread veins quickening on his cheeks.

"A feller getting a job, house and a dough-beater at one time is square in luck," Sim said, his words booming with laughter.

"Nothing sorry as a bachelor feller," Father said, teasing. "A woman helps a man hang on to his money, and keeps him honest."

Fern and Lark looked queerly at me. Lark's chin was barely above the table. "Thar's one o' my pennies a-missing out of the clock," he said. "That hain't honest, now."

I felt shriveled and old. All I had eaten seemed a great knot inside of me. My spoon clattered to the floor.

Uncle Lott grinned. The ends of his blunt mustache pointed out like fingers. His cheeks burned. He shoved a hand into a pocket and drew something out. It was a rusty penny. He spun it on the table. "I borrowed it to get a little chew o' tobacco," he said, "and I plumb forgot to spend it."

The bread was broken, the shucky beans passed, the pickle bowl lifted hand to hand. Mother glanced at Father and Lott and Sim. She looked at Lark and me. Her eyes grew bright as a wren's. "All of you fellers have buttermilk mustaches," she said.

On Quicksand Creek

Aaron Splicer drove a bunch of yearlings into our yard on a March evening. Heifers bawled and young bullies made raw cries. We hurried out into the cold dark of the porch. Aaron rode up to the doorsteps, and Father called to him, not knowing at first who he was. "Hello?" Father spoke, and when he knew it was Aaron, called heartily, "'Light and shake the weather."

Aaron opened his fleeced collar, rustling new leather. His breath curled a fog. "If this Shoal Creek mud gets any deeper," he called, "it'll be beyond traveling. A horse bogs to the knees." He slid to the ground, limbering his legs.

Father led Aaron's horse into the mare's stall. He brought a brass-trimmed saddle onto the porch. Aaron shook his boots, loosening mud balls, letting them fall on the steps. His tracks smudged the floors. Mother prepared a meal for him, our supper having long been eaten; and Lark and Zard and Fern pried at Aaron with their eyes. I studied his leather clothes: ox-yellow coat, belt wide as a grist mill's, fancy boots. I'd never seen boots matching the ones he wore. Father had a costly pair, a pair worth eighteen dollars, yet they weren't lengthy, or pin-pointed, or hid-stitched like Aaron Splicer's.

Aaron shucked off his coat. A foam of sheep's wool lined the underside. "Thar's not a cent in yearlings," he said. "Hit's jist swapping copper for brass. Beef steers are what puts sugar in the gourd, and nary a one I've found betwixt here and the head of Left Hand Fork."

"Crate Thompson cleaned the steers out o' all the creeks forking Troublesome," Father said. "I've heard a sketch about him being on Quicksand now. I reckon they's a sight o' beef in the neighborhood o' Decoy and Handshoe."

Mother brought a plate of creaseback beans, buttered cushaw, and a soursweet nubbin of pickled corn. Fern raked coals upon the hearth for the coffeepot. While Aaron ate, Father had me and Lark brighten Aaron's boots. We scraped the caked mud away, rubbed on tallow, and spat on the leather. We polished them with linsey rags until they shone.

"I never saw boots have such sharpening toes," Father said. "You could nigh pick a splinter out o' yore finger with them." He thrust his own boots forth to show the bluntness of the shoecaps. "But cattlemen allus crave leather with trimmings."

Our cats leapt upon my knees. They watched Aaron, twitching their whiskers, tensing their spines; they held crafty oblong eyes upon him. I thought, "I'm liable to be a cattleman when I'm grown up, and go traveling far. Yet it'd take a spell to get used to thorny boots. I'd be ashamed to wear 'em."

Aaron finished eating, wiped his chin with the hairy back of a hand, and walked his chair nearer the fire. Father offered him a twist of home-raised tobacco. He bit a chew, stretching the poles of his legs to the hearth, saying, "I'd take a shortcut to Quicksand if I didn't have these yearlings on my neck. Maybe I'd get thar before Crate Thompson buys every last steer." He rubbed his chin stubble; he frowned till his face wadded to wrinkles. "Reckon your eldest boy could round them calves to Mayho town for me? A whole day would be saved."

I raised off my chair, hoping. I was nine years old, old enough to go traipsing, to look abroad upon the world.

"Ho, ho," Father chuckled, big to tease, "you wouldn't call that turkey track of a forked road a town. Now, Hazard or Jackson—" he hesitated, seeing Mother's eyes upon him. The posts of his chair sunk level with the floor. "That's a good-sized piece for a boy to walk alone. Thirteen miles, roundy 'bout."

"I'll pay a dollar," Aaron said. "A whole silver dollar. Silas McJunkins's boy will be at my house with the money when they're penned. Silas's boy is driving two cows down from Augland in the morning."

"I saw Mayho on a post-office map once," Father said. "Hit looked to me like a place where three roads butt heads. But if this town soaks hits elbows in Troublesome Creek, hit's bound to be a good 'un."

Mother sent Fern, Zard, and Lark to bed. Before going herself she brought in a washpan and a ball of soap. Father poured hot water from the kettle, and Aaron washed his face and hands, then pulled off his boots and soaked his feet. His feet were blue veined and white, and his heels bore no sign of rust.

"You've got townfolks' feet, all right," Father said. He picked up Aaron's boots, matching them with his own. "They're the difference betwixt a razor and a froe." He grunted in awe. "Man! These boots are bound to make a pinch-knot out o' the frog o' yore foot."

Aaron champed his tobacco cud. "They're right good wearing," he said.

"When I thresh my oats," Father spoke, grinning, "I'm a-liable to buy me a pair."

I set off behind the yearlings with daylight breaking, and before the sun-ball rose I had reached the mouth of Shoal Creek and turned down Troublesome. The yearlings pitted the mud banks with their hoofs, and I sank to the tongues of my brogans. My coffee-sack leggings were splattered; my feet got stone cold. A wintry draft blew, smelling of sap.

The sun-ball rolled up a hill, warming the air, loosening the mud. The yearlings nearly ran my leg bones off. I cut switches keen to whistling; I hollered and hollered, and I stung their behinds. I herded the day long, knowing then how it was to be a cattleman.

Chimney sweeps were funneling the sky when I rounded the yearlings into Aaron Splicer's barn lot. Dark crept into Mayho by three roads, coming to sit among the sixteen homeseats crowding the creek or hanging off the hillsides. I saw Ark, Silas McJunkins's boy, atop a fence post, eating a straw. Though a boy, he was man-tall. His hair shagged over his collar and hid his ears. And he was as muddy as I.

Ark helped pen the calves, and I got a whole look at Mayho town before night blacked everything. A clever place I found it, with Easter flowers blooming on leafless stems in yards, and bare trees growing in rows. One house stood yellow as capping corn, and new-painted. "If I lived in a town," I told Ark, "I'd choose here."

"Mayho's a wart on a hog's nose," Ark said.

"Trees yonder lined up a-purpose. Easter flowers a-blooming the winter."

"I choose woods God planted," Ark said. He raised his arm. "Hit's growing spring. Thar's chimley sweeps raising spit to glue their nests."

We beat on Splicer's kitchen door. Aaron's woman opened it a crack, but we didn't cross the sill, for she saw our muddy clothes and told us to sleep in the barn. She handed us a plate of cold hand-pies, and a rag bag of a quilt. We ate the pies in the barn-loft; we burrowed into the hay, leaving only our heads sticking out.

"A mouse wouldn't raise young 'uns in that trampy quilt," Ark said.

I wondered about my silver dollar. Before going to sleep I asked Ark for it.

Ark swore, "Aaron Splicer never give me a bit o' money. He aims for us to drive steers on Quicksand, and said we're to catch a wagon going that way tomorrow. Claimed he'd pay then, and pay double. Two dollars apiece."

"My poppy'd be scared, me not coming straight home," I complained. "I hain't never been on Quicksand. I oughtn't to go." I felt a grain hurt. "Aaron said he'd send me a dollar. A silver dollar."

"He's not paid me neither," Ark said. "He's got us in a bull hole. I've heered he'd shuck a flea for hits hide and tallow, but he'll bile owl grease ere he pinches a nickel off me."

"I ought to be lighting a rag home," I said.

We came on Aaron Splicer a quarter-mile up Quicksand at Tom Zeek Duffey's place. He was waiting for us, and had already rounded four prime steers into Tom Zeek's lot.

"I hain't located Crate Thompson," Aaron said, "but I've diskivered thar's big beef on this creek, head to the mouth. I'm aiming to get it bought and driv to the railroad siding at Jackson in four days. A four-day round up." And Aaron lifted a foot, pointing at his steers. He kicked the board fence, trying the lot's tightness. "I figure I've put the cat on Crate. These brutes guarantee grease in my skillet." He walked the lot, admiring his cattle.

We looked at Aaron's boots. Tom Zeek and Ark laughed a little. Ark said, "Was he to fall down, he's a-liable to stick one o' them toe p'ints in himself. I'd a'soon wear pitchforks."

"I allow they're tighter than a doorjamb," Tom Zeek chuckled.

"Hain't tighter'n the drawstrings on his money bag," Ark said. "I know that for a fact."

"Dude's his nickname," Tom Zeek told us, "and hit's earnt."

Tom Zeek's woman called us to supper. Not a bite we'd had since the day before, except for a robbing of chestnuts from a squirrel's nest. The table held fourteen kinds of victuals, and Ark and I ate a sight. We drank buttermilk a duck couldn't have paddled, so thick and good it was. We stayed the night, sleeping deep in a feather tick.

The next morning Aaron rousted us before daylight. Tom Zeek Duffey's woman fed us slabs of ham, scrambled guinea eggs, and flour biscuits the size of saucers. We set off, with Aaron ahead. Though willows were reddening and sugar trees swollen with sap, a frozen skim lay on Quicksand Creek and rock ledges were bearded with ice. The sun-ball lifted its great yellow eye, warming and thawing, and by midday a living look had come upon the hills where neither bud nor leaf grew. Icicles plunged from the cliffs. Redbirds whistled for mates.

Aaron bargained and bought the day long. We slept on the puncheon floor of a sawmill near Handshoe that night. For supper and breakfast we ate little fishes out of flat cans Aaron got at a storehouse. We started downcreek again, and where it had taken one day to go up, we spent two gathering the cattle and herding them to Tom Zeek's place. We ran hollering and whooping in the spring air.

We rounded eighteen steers and seven heifers into Tom Zeek Duffey's lot. Tom Zeek told us Crate Thompson had come into Quicksand country and was putting up at John Adair's, a mile over the ridge. "Hit might' nigh cankered his liver when he heard Aaron had beat him to the taw," Tom Zeek said. "Oh I reckon he started soon enough, but he hain't got a pair o' seven-mile boots like Aaron's." He winked dryly at me and Ark.

Tom Zeek Duffey's lot was packed with steers and heifers, being littler than most folks' lots. Aaron drove extra nails in the board fence; he stretched a barbed wire along the posttops; and he sent for Tom Zeek's son-in-law to come and help him drive the herd into Jackson the next morning. "I wouldn't trust this pen more'n one night," Aaron said. "Hit's too small and rimwrecked."

"Why'n't you take these boys on to Jackson?" Tom Zeek asked. "They'll want to spend the money they've earnt."

I said, "They's something I'm half a-mind to buy." Yet I knew two dollars wouldn't be enough; and I knew I ought to be heading home.

"The Devil, no," Aaron grumbled. "I don't trust fences nor chaps. These boys'd scare worse'n muleycows at the sight o' a train engine. Why, if Ark walked the Jackson streets with that shaggy head, they'd muzzle him for a shep dog."

"I jist like to see boys right-treated," Tom Zeek said.

Ark said, "My hair hain't so long yit you kin step on it with them finicky boots. Anyhow, I reckon hit's pay-time. You promised two dollars apiece."

"I'm a bit short on change," Aaron said, embarrassed for having to speak his stinginess before Tom Zeek. "Cash on the line had to be paid for them cattle."

"I'm a-drawing me a line. Lay them two dollars down."

"I'm broke tee-total," Aaron said. "Won't have money for settling till them steers are sold. Why, boys, I figgered you'd be tickled and satisfied with a small heifer for pay. I'll pick you one—one betwixt the two of you."

"You'd pick a runt. Anyhow, a heifer wouldn't rattle in my pocket."

"Hit's yearlings or nary a thing."

"God-dog!" Ark swore angrily. "I hope yore whole gang dies o' the holler tail."

Tom Zeek said, "I allus like to see boys right-treated."

Ark walked sullenly behind the barn, and I tagged along. We sat among dead jimson weeds. Ark chewed a tobacco leaf and spat black on the dry stalks. "I'm one feller Aaron Splicer hain't going to skin. I'm a hicker-nut hard to crack. Some witties he might fleece, but not Old Silas McJunkins's boy Arkles."

"He put the cat on Crate Thompson," I said. "He'll brag now he's sicked one on us."

Ark brightened, opening his mouth. The tobacco wad lay dark on his tongue.

"Now, I'm a-mind to go talk to Crate. I bet he could trap Aaron. Hit's said Crate Thompson's a sharp 'un." He grinned, blowing the wad against the barn wall hard enough to make it stick; he strode into the barn and fetched out a pair of mule shears.

I cut Ark's hair. I cut the hairs bunched on his neck, the thick brush hiding his ears, the nest of growth on top of his head; I clipped and gaped and banged his head over.

"I feel most nigh naked," Ark said when I'd finished. "Wisht I had me a looking-glass to see."

We went to the spring behind Tom Zeek's house. Ark stared at himself in the water between the butter jars and churns. "Looks to me my fodder's been gathered," he said. He lifted a demijohn of buttermilk and drank it down. I raked a tad of butter from a bowl with my thumb and ate it.

After night fell we climbed the ridge to John Adair's homeplace. John and his woman were gone, late-feeding their stock. Crate Thompson sat before a shovel of fire, driving sprigs into a shoe sole. The shoe was a common old any-body's shoe, and not a cattleman's boot. And Crate was hefty as any of Aaron's steers.

"Draw up a chair and squat," Crate said, speaking with tight lips so as not to swallow the sprigs in his mouth. His eyes were intent on Ark's cropped head. Ark sat down, but I remained standing, awkward and restive.

Ark told Crate our trouble. Crate dropped the shoe, listening with a stub finger sunk into the bag of his chin.

"Where's Dude Aaron got them cattle penned?" Crate asked, his words whistling between the sprigs.

"In Tom Zeek Duffey's lot."

Crate spat the sprigs into his hand. Through his gray eyes a body could almost see ideas working in his head. "Well, now," he said slowly, "I can't think o' nothing but a dumb-bull to cuore Dude Aaron."

"Dumb-bull!" Ark cried in awe.

Crate's great chin quivered merrily. "Strip o' cowhide and a holler log and a rosined string's all it takes. But I'll have no hand in it."

"I'll play my own bull-fiddle," Ark bragged happily. "I know how they're made."

"Hit's agin' the law," Crate warned.

"Boodle zack!"

"They's fellers roosting in jailhouses for less."

"I'm not aiming to be skint."

"Ah!" Crate sighed, eying Ark's head. "A rare scalping you've had already." Ark grinned.

157

"Ah, well," Crate said, breathing satisfaction, "John ought to have an old hide strip hereabouts." He shuffled away to find one.

"I'm scared to do it," I told Ark. "I'm scared to tick-tack."

"We'll have Dude Aaron calling on his Maker," Ark promised.

"I ought to be a-going home," I said.

We searched the pitch dark on the ridge above Tom Zeek Duffey's barn. Ark tapped fallen trees with a stick until he found a hollow log, a log empty as an old goods box, and with a narrow crack in its upper side. A winged thing fluttered out, beating the cold air, lifting. It complained overhead, asking, "*Ou? Ou?*"

"Scritch owl," Ark named.

Ark set to work on the dumb-bull. He drove twentypenny nails at the ends of the crack in the log; he cut notch-holes in the tips of the hide string and stretched it taut over the nailheads. He worked by feel, dark being mighty thick under the roof of tree limbs. Ark had me resin the hide string while he fashioned a bow of a hickory sprout and a twine cord. The dumb-bull was finished.

We perched on the log, waiting for the cattle to settle. We could hear them moving restlessly in the packed lot, though all were swallowed in blackness. We only knew the direction of the house and barn by the noise of the steers.

Ark said, "Aaron's dropped his boots ere now, and I bet the toes stuck up in the floor like jackknives."

A bird chirped sleepily near us.

"I'm getting chilly," I said. Anxiety burnt cold inside me, cold as foxfire. "We ought to light a smudge."

"No," Ark said. "They'd spot a blaze. I'm jist waiting till them brutes halt their tromp. Hit's best to catch 'em in a nap."

I made talk, hungry for speech. I asked, "What are them towns o' Jackson and Hazard like?" My teeth chattered.

Ark chewed a pinch of bark. "Folks thar a-wearing Sunday breeches on weeky days," he explained. "Folks living so close together they kin shake hands out o' windows if they're of a mind. Humans a-running up and down like anty mars."

"I aim to see them towns some day," I said. "I aim to. Now, I've lived in

Houndshell mine camp, yit it wasn't a town for sartin, just houses pitched in a holler."

"I've traveled a sight," Ark bragged. "I reckon I've been nigh to the earth's end. I been to Whitesburg and Campton and Pikeville. I been to Wheelwright and Hyden. Once I went to Glamorgan, in Old Virginia. Hain't that going some'ere?"

I nodded in the dark, thinking of Mayho, thinking of chimney sweeps riding the sky. I thought, "I've already seen Mayho, and I've been on Quicksand Creek. That's far-away traveling." Then we were quiet a long time. I dozed.

A rooster crowed midnight. Ark jumped to his feet. "Hit's time to witch them steers," he said, awaking me. I trembled with dread and cold. I longed to be at home. Ark dragged the hickory bow lightly across the dumb-bull's string, and the sound jumped me full awake. It was like a wildcat's scream, long and blood-clotting and deafening. But that wasn't a circumstance to when Ark bore down. Then it wasn't one lonesome critter; it was a woodsful, tearing each others' eyeballs out. I reckon that squall hustled three miles.

Ark paused. The timber was alive with varmints. A squirrel tore through the trees squacking. Wings flapped and paws rattled brush heaps. Below, in the lot, the steers bellowed. We could hear them charging the board fence, crazy with fear. They butted their heads in anguish, and the ground rang with the thud of hoofs. Yearlings bawled like lost chaps.

"We're not right-treating Tom Zeek Duffey," I said. "We oughtn't to destroy his fence. Now, his woman fed us good."

"A favor we're doing Tom Zeek," Ark said. "He's needed that old rotten-posted lot cleared. He needs a new 'un." And he sawed the hide string again, cutting it rusty. Goose bumps raised on me. A scream came from that log like something fleeing Torment. We heard the fence give way, the boards trampled, posts broken off. The steers lit out, bellowing and running, upcreek and down, awaking the country.

Lamplight sprang into the windows of Tom Zeek Duffey's house, and a door swung wide and the shape of a man bearing a rifle-gun printed the light. The gun was lifted, steadied, and a spurt of flame leapt thundering. Birdshot rattled winter leaves far below us, spent with distance.

"Aaron Splicer'll shoot a lead mine ere he hits me," Ark said, and he dropped the bow and ran. He melted into the dark.

I ran too, trying to follow; I ran plumb into a tree, and fell stunned upon the ground. My head rang, and sparks leapt before my eyes like lightning bugs. When I got up at last, Ark was out of hearing, and there was no sound anywhere. I crept on my hands and knees for a spell. I walked to the ridgetop, skirting around Tom Zeek Duffey's place, coming down to the creek on the lower side. I crept and walked for hours.

Daylight broke as I reached the creek road. Spring birds were cutting up jack, and the hills were the color of greenback money. And there in the road I found a fat heifer. She made a glad moo and trotted after me. I let her get ahead; I drove her Shoal Creek way. She looked to be sugar in my gourd, and a pair of thorn-toed boots on my feet, just like Aaron's.

The Ploughing

I ran into the fields one April morning, thinking to climb to the benchland where Uncle Jolly was breaking new ground. The sky was as blue as a bottle. A rash of green covered the sheltered fence edges, though beech and leatherwood were browner and barer still for the sunlight washing their branches. I began to climb, hands on knees, the way being steep. I went up through a redbud thicket swollen with unopened bloom and leaf, coming at last to where Uncle Jolly was ploughing. The bench spread back to a swag, level as creek land, set up against air and sky and nothing. Uncle Jolly had already broken a half acre of furrows in the rooty earth with the horse-mule Uncle Luce had loaned him.

"Whoa-ho," Uncle Jolly said when he saw me. He drew rein and leaned against the plough handles, blowing. He whistled a long redbird whistle. His forehead was moist, his shirt stuck to his back. He'd been hustling the mule, and was glad of the rest. "Hain't you got a sup o' water?" he asked.

"I never thought to bring water," I said. "I've come up to learn to plough."

A drop of sweat hung and stretched on Uncle Jolly's chin. "Hell's bangers!" he said. "This fence rail of a beast would pull you clear over the plough handles."

"Now, no," I said. "I'm a mind to learn."

He grinned, scratching into the thick of his hair. "A chap never larnt too young," he said. "Just you fotch a jug o' spring water, and I'll try you a furrow." He hung the reins about his neck and leveled the plough. He dug a brogan toe into the black dirt. "Aye, God, this land'll make," he said. "Hit's rich as sin."

I brought the jug of water. Uncle Jolly crooked a finger in its ear, swinging it up on his shoulder. He drank loud swallows. Water ran down his neck; it drained thread streams under his collar.

He lowered the jug and stuck his tongue out. "Seems a bull frog's swum here," he said. "Hit's sort o' wild." He took another drink. I reckon he drank a quart. "I allus liked a wild taste—the wilder, the better," he said.

"What's this mule's name?" I asked.

Uncle Jolly sat the jug by. "Banged if I know," he vowed. "Luce told me, but I can't recollect. Ought to be named Simon Brawl, he's so feisty."

A flock of goldfinches circled the new ground, their cries sowing the air. *Per-chic-o-ree, per-chic-o-ree, per-chic-o-ree.* They settled at the field's edge and it was as if the dry stickweeds had suddenly burst yellow blossoms. They pecked at seed heads; they rattled empty pods of milkweed stalks.

Uncle Jolly glanced over the ploughed land. His furrows were straight as a measure, running end to end without a bobble. "Hain't many folks know how to tend dirt proper," he said. "A mighty piddling few. Land a-wasting and a-washing. Up and down Troublesome Creek, it's the same. Timber cut off and rain eating the hills away. Hit's alike all over—Boone's Fork, Little Carr, Quicksand, Beaver Creek, Big Leatherwood."

"I want to learn proper," I said.

"What's folks going to live on when these hills wear down to a nub?" Uncle Jolly complained. He lifted the plough, setting the point into the ground. I stood there, not knowing what to do. "Best you walk betwixt the handles to get the lay," he said. I got between, holding the crosspiece. Uncle Jolly grasped the handle ends and clucked. The mule didn't move. He whistled and shouted, but the mule paid no mind. Uncle Jolly grinned. "This fool beast won't move less'n you call his name, and that I can't remember."

He tried a string of names. "Git along, Jack! Pete! Leadfoot! John!" He reached down and caught up a handful of dirt, throwing it on the mule's back. The mule started, skin shivers quivering his flanks.

"It's like that every time I stop," Uncle Jolly said. "A horse-mule stubs pineblank like a man."

The earth parted; it fell back from the shovel plough; it boiled over the share. I walked the fresh furrow, and balls of dirt welled between my toes. There was a smell of old mosses, of bruised sassafras roots, of ground newturned. We broke out three furrows. Then Uncle Jolly stood aside and let me hold the handles. The mule looked back, but he kept going. The share rustled like drifted leaves. It spoke up through the handles. I felt the earth flowing, steady as time.

The Ploughing

I turned the plough at the end of the third row. "This land's so rooty," Uncle Jolly said, "I'm going to let you work over what I've already broken. You can try busting furrow middles. Strike center, giving left nor right, and go straight as a die."

I grasped the reins and handles. "Get along," I called, big as life. The mule didn't budge. He lifted his plugged ears and looked at me, sly and stubborn.

"He's a regular Simon Brawl, all right, with steelyard peas for hoofs," Uncle Jolly said.

The mule started after I threw dirt on him. He went down the first row peart enough, ears standing ends-up, for Uncle Jolly began singing at the top of his voice:

Oh I had a little gray mule,
His name was Simon Brawl,
He could kick a chew terbacker out o' yore mouth
And never touch yore jowl.

I ploughed three furrows, and pride swelled in me as sap blows a willow bud. It was like being master where till now I'd only stood in awe; it was finding strength I'd no knowing of. When I doubled back on the fourth row I saw Uncle Jolly sitting on the ground, leaning against a chestnut stump amidst the stickweeds, his eyes closed to the sun. The mule saw Uncle Jolly too, and his ears drooped. He began to walk faster. The harness rattled on his bony body. The furrow crooked a bit, and I got uneasy.

"Hold back thar!" I shouted, but he didn't mend his way.

At the fifth row's end I looked anxiously at Uncle Jolly, hoping he would take over. One glance and I saw he had gone to sleep. I was ashamed to call. The mule hastened the furrow, the plough jiggling, scooping dirt, running crooked as a blacksnake's track. I jerked the lines. I shouted all the mule names I'd ever heard. The share hooked a root and the reins pulled from my hands. The plough jumped a furrow, rising alive-like. And then I called Uncle Jolly, being at last more frightened than ashamed. Uncle Jolly slept on.

We no longer bore north and south. The mule cut northwest, southeast, back and forth, catty-cornered. My feet flew over the ground. We ploughed a big S. We made a long T, crossing it on the way back. I reckon we made all the book letters. We struck into the unbroken tract, gouging a great furrow, around and around, curling inward, tight like a watch spring. I couldn't shout or raise a sound. There was no wind left in me.

A voice sprang across the bench. "Hold thar, Bully!" The mule stopped in his tracks, and I went spinning over the plough. I got up, unhurt. A bellow came from the stickweed patch; it was a laugh near too big for a throat to utter.

I looked in time to see Uncle Jolly rise to his feet, then crumple to the ground. He threshed among the weeds, his arms beating air, laughing in agony. He jerked; he whooped and hollered. He got up twice, falling back slack-jointed and weak. A squall of joy flowed out of him.

And when Uncle Jolly got his laugh out, he came across the field, weaving drunkenly. The mule watched him come, lowering his head, acting a grain nervous.

Uncle Jolly sniggered when he reached us, and I saw a fresh throe boiling inside of him, ready to burst. The mule raised his head suddenly. He licked his yellow tongue square across Uncle Jolly's mouth.

"I bet that-there's a wild enough taste," I said, scornfully.

The Force Put

"Fetch the lamp," Pap said. "I can't see by the light of this blinky lantern."

Saul Hignight's calf had a cob in its throat, and he had brought it to our place on Sporty Creek in the bed of a wagon. He lifted it in his arms, letting it down onto a poke spread upon the ground. It was a heifer, three weeks old, with teat buds barely showing.

I went after the lamp, but Mother feared to let me hold it. She put the baby in the empty woodbox and gave him a spool to play with. She lit the lamp and took it outside, standing over the heifer so that the light fell squarely where Pap wanted it.

The heifer breathed heavily. Her mouth gathered a fleece of slobber. She looked at us out of stricken eyes.

"I'd have brought her before dark," Saul Hignight said, "but I never knowed myself till after milking time. I kept hearing something gagging and gasping under the crib. Figured at first it was a pig snuffing."

"Had you got to the calf sooner, the cob wouldn't have worked down so far," Pap said. He rolled his right sleeve above the elbow. Saul wrenched the calf's mouth open, and Pap stuck his hand inside, up to the wrist. He wriggled his arm, reaching thumb and forefinger into the calf's gullet.

Saul said, "I fished for that cob till my fingers cramped."

We crowded around, looking over Pap's shoulder. Slobber bubbled on Pap's arm. He caught the calf's throat with the left hand and tried to work the cob into the grasp of his right.

"The cob is slick as owl grease," Pap said. "An eel couldn't be slicker or harder to get hold of."

The calf bellowed, a thing stifled bellow through her nose. Her legs threshed, her split hooves spreading. She breathed in agony. Her fearful eyes walled and set.

Saul Hignight glanced suddenly at me. "Here, boy," he called, "help hold the critter." I moved slowly, fumbling. "Help hold!" Dan sprang forward and caught the calf's hind legs, not flinching a mite. Saul glanced back sourly. I turned aside, though not being able to turn my eyes away.

Pap pulled his hand from the calf's throat. "I can't reach the cob, for a fact," he said. "My fist is three times too big. Three times. Maybe a young 'un's hand—"

"Here, boy." Saul cranked his head toward me. "Stick your hand down to that cob and snatch it out."

I shook my head. Saul grunted and spat upon the ground. "The critter'll die while you're diddling," he said, his voice edged with anger. "Try it. I don't want to lose this one. A bully-calf, I wouldn't mind. But a heifer—"

"Me, now," Dan said. He squatted on his knees. He worked his hand into the calf's mouth and into its throat, nearly to the elbow. He grasped the cob and pulled with all his might. It wouldn't budge. The calf fell back upon the poke, gasping for breath. Her belly quaked.

Saul Hignight stood up. "Hain't a grain of use to try anymore," he said. "She's bound to die. Born during the wrong signs of the moon, I figure." He clapped the dirt from his hands and rubbed them on his breeches. "She would of made a fine little cow. Her mother was a three-galloner. Three full gallons a day, not a gill less. She's of good stock."

There seemed nothing more to do. Saul whistled to his mules and turned the wagon around, ready to start. "I can load the critter and drop her off somewhere down the road," he said. "She's as good as dead. The buzzards will be looking for her tomorrow."

"Let her be," Pap said. "I might be able to dislodge that cob yet."

Saul climbed into his wagon. He clucked and jerked the lines. The mules set off into the dark. "She's yours," he called, "skin and hide and tallow."

"Oh could we save her," Mother anguished, "there would be milk for us when the cow goes dry. Milk for the baby." The lamp trembled in her hand.

"There's one sure way to get to the cob," Pap said. He weighed the chance in his mind. "One way sure as weather, but the calf might bleed to death." Mother and Pap glanced at each other. Their eyes burned. "Bleed or choke," Pap said finally, "what's the difference?"

"Let me try first," Mother said. She handed the lamp to Pap, warning him to hold it steady. She poked a hand into the calf's mouth, pushing the tongue aside, forcing the locked jaws apart. She worked feverishly. But she couldn't dislodge the cob. She had Holly try. Then she nodded to me. I knelt before the calf, looking into the cavern of its mouth, dreading to put my hand in.

"Hit's no use," Pap said. "Fetch the hone rock, a needle, and thread. And wax the thread."

Mother ran for them, knowing just where the hone was stored and where the needle and thread were kept. She came back in a moment, took the lamp, and handed the hone to Pap. She sent Holly into the house to stay with the baby. "He's fretted with being alone," Mother said. "Find something to amuse him."

Holly returned almost as quickly as Mother had. "I gave him a hen-fooler to play with," she explained, "and tore a page from the wish-book for him to rattle. I left him crowing."

Pap drew a Barlow knife from his pocket and snapped it open. He spat upon the hone and began to sharpen the blade with a circular motion, swiftly and with precision. The calf was weakening, being hardly able now to suck breath enough for life. Her eyes were glazed. She picked at the air listlessly with her feet.

The calf was turned to its right side, the head lifted back. Mother reached the lamp to me, telling me how to hold it—close and yet away from knocking elbows. "Both hands under the bowl," she said.

She caught the calf's head between her hands while Pap dug fingers into the calf's throat, feeling for the proper spot. He hunted for a place free of large veins. "This is a force put," he said.

The blade flashed in the lamplight. It slid under the hide, making a three-inch cut. Mother looked away when the blood gushed. It splattered on her hands, reddening them to the wrists. Holly began to cry, softly and then angrily, begging Pap to stop. "Stand back, and hush," Pap said. "You make a fellow nervous."

The blade worked deeper, deeper. The horror of it ran through my limbs. The lamp teetered in my hands. Water ran from my eyes and dripped from my chin. I couldn't wipe it away for holding the lamp bowl.

Pap opened a space between the muscles of the calf's neck, steering clear of bone and artery. The calf made no sound. Only its hind legs jerked and its hide quivered. Dan held to the legs, watching all that was being done and not turning a hair.

At last Pap laid the knife aside. He eased thumb and forefinger into the opening and jerked. The cob came out, red and drenched. It spun into the dark. The calf fell back weakly, though beginning to breathe again—a long, strangling breathing.

"Needle and thread!" Pap demanded quickly. Mother reached it to him. Pap folded the inner flesh and sewed it together and then stitched the outer cut. And having done all, he looked at Dan and grinned. "Here's a fellow who would make a good doctor," he praised. "A cool helper. Not one to panic. I'm saying he can call the calf his own."

I handed the lamp to Mother so I could wipe away the shameful tears. I didn't want the calf. I'd been promised a colt.

On Pigeon Roost Creek

I remember the day the court woman came up Pigeon Roost Creek. It was around the first of October when there's a frost pinch in the air and the moon comes up rotten-ripe and full in broad daylight. I was sixteen then, and I'd been in the hills barking squirrels, carrying a rifle-gun near heavy enough to crack my shoulderbone. A day-burning moon always was lucky for me. I'd got two bushtail squirrels and was coming down a woodsy swag to the county road when I saw a little side-pacing filly trotting over the ruts. A woman came riding straddleback, and she wore a quare hat-piece, red as a rooster's comb. I leant my rifle-gun against a stump and stood gaping. Womenfolks up Pigeon Roost made their hats out of dyed shucks, or they took a throw of homespun and stitched a bonnet. Even if they sold enough eggs for a store-bought hat, it never popped your eyes out to look at it. And no woman on all the forks and traces of the Little Tennessee rode straddleback, shameless, like a man rides.

Well now, I waded sawbriars to the road, snatching threads out of my britches, hardly believing my sight. The woman drew rein when she came up to me, and the filly swung her head nervouslike, not knowing what to think either. I knew right off it was Holt Simms's nag, knowing by the bright spot betwixt the eyes. She must have put a spell on Holt to borrow that nag, I thought, Holt being stingy as a dried gourd.

She sat there laughing, fluttering like a pouter pigeon trying to light. I got a square look at her. My eyes got big as a barn owl's. Her face was more like a poppet-doll's than real folks', pretty as a calendar picture. I'd never seen the beat. It's bad luck for a woman to ride a fellow's nag, but I couldn't blame Holt, not a grain.

Now I know what looks fair to me. I've got my own notions. Hulda Miller, up Crofts Knob, always did suit my idea to a fare-you-well—suited me so fine I was stone-blind jealous of Harl Burke taking her to Fifth Sunday meetings,

169

buying her basket at box suppers, and courting at her house on Saturday nights. I liked Harl a sight, though. As good a fellow as I ever hunted with, willing to go the whole rope, free as toll-corn pouring out of the hopper. And he had one of the keenest little hounds ever rubbed a nose on a fox track, called Ring. Ring's ears were big as mullein leaves, and he had a sad human look in his eyes. I know a good dog when I see one, know when they're built to fly off the face of the earth. I was raised up having two or three snoring under the bed at night, and one to put my feet on under the table. Never ate a piece of meat in my life but what a hound got the rind.

I stood looking at the stranger, saying to myself, by juckers, if the girls on Pigeon Roost won't turn grasshopper green when they see her traipsing into Harding, dressed fittin for a wedding.

She laughed down at me, and I tell you I felt like a groundhog dressed the way I was. Well, now I was just seventeen, and I reckoned it didn't matter if my britches were a nest of patches and wouldn't hardly hold shucks. Dirt on me was wood's dirt, clean and pure. She looked augur holes at my ragged shirt. I could have told her I had me three new-sewn ones at home, with nary a patch, but you can't tell a stranger things like that when they don't ask. It wouldn't sound proper.

When Ellafronia Saul got through looking—that's what her name turned out to be—she said, "Good day," low and sweet like a turtledove afar off. I said howdy just like this—"Howdy-do!" Then I didn't know what else to say. My tongue got sticky as a ball of resin in my mouth. Now, I could have said it was the best fox-hunting time ever was with the leaves rattling underfoot and hounds lean as shikepokes, but she didn't look to me like she'd know a hound from a fiest. I writ that down in my head against her. I just stood there like a branfired fool, wishing I'd been born with a tongue sharp as a spread adder's and sense to grease it with.

"I'm traveling to the county seat," she said. "I'd like to know the distance."

"How it runs to a count, I don't know," I said. "Never heard it told. Must be nigh on to four miles by crow-fly, and six by the creek road."

"I'm not thinking of flying," she said, laughing again, and setting her briar-toed shoes in the stirrups.

I saw her teeth were white as ladybean seeds and even-set as corn grains on a nubbin. They never got that way rubbing them with a redbud stick either. I didn't wonder Holt Simms loaned that nag to her, in spite of him being so stingy he'd eat salt to save sugar. If she had asked for my rifle-gun, reckon I'd have given over, much as I think of my old lead-pusher. But Grandma always said it's bad luck to let a woman mount a horse broke to ride men.

She used to put a lot of store by signs and folk-say. "Set my clock by the almanac," she'd say. "That there's God's time." And Grandma used to vow an almanac had more sense in it than all the statute books in Hardin Courthouse put together. I learnt a peck of signs from her. Never let a woman look down a new-dug well. Drop a hook in a waterhole where a woman's been fishing and you'll grow roots in the ground before you catch a bite. A woman can be bad luck, and she can be good, depending on whether the moon is lean or fat, a-waxing or a-thinning. And signs run to truth for reasons unbeknownst.

Well, that woman sat there looking at me, making no least move to go. My curiosity got to rubbing like a cuckerburr in my shoe, and I finally got my mouth to open to speak again.

"Have you got blood kin up at Sawyers?" I asked, acting like I didn't already know pine-blank.

She laughed out, her voice sounding like a little bell swinging on a ewe-sheep's neck.

"None I ever heard of," she said. "I'm the court secretary for the new session."

"Are you the short writer?" I asked.

"I take testimony in shorthand and transcribe it into the records," she said. She gathered up the reins. Holt Simm's nag looked around at me sort of hacked, shin-shivers trembling her flanks.

"Have you got a case coming up in this court?" she asked, idle-mouthed and teasing.

"Now, no," I said. "Never had a grain of law trouble in all my born days."

"I didn't think you had," she said. "You probably keep too busy sewing patches on that shirt to have time for breaking the law."

She jerked the reins and started off, grinning back at me. I stood there sort of lightning-struck for a minute. Then I got so mad I kicked a mud rut and mighty nigh broke my big toe. I jerked that shirt off, never even unhooking the buttons, and threw it into a haw bush. It hung there scarecrowlike and I don't reckon a cowbird lit in sight of that bush all year.

I set out for home, not knowing whether to be mad or tickled. The sun-ball got to pinching my bare back, and sawbriars clawed raw meat. Yonside Painters Ridge I cooled off in a beech swag, setting me down on a moss rock, and then I remembered it was Thursday, my luck day, the day I was born on. I hollered right big, feeling good all of a sudden. My hounds set up a howl down at the homeplace, a full mile away. I went off down the swag, walking spry as a fellow who has seen a redbird on a spring morning.

Harl Burke came down Mole Creek Friday night, rousting me out of bed about the time I got settled into the feather tick. I'd been wrestling corn shocks since daybreak in the high field, and was so dog-tired seemed like there was lead in my bones. I heard Harl calling by the shed-room window, calling low in his throat so Grandma wouldn't wake. I went outside in my shirttail, squinting my eyes in the moonlight. It was that bright. There was Harl and four young hounds hitched to a traceline. Ole Ring was sitting on the top step, looking broody-eyed. When I cracked the door open he shagged up to me, licking the flat of my hand. I thought so much of that hound I didn't even wipe the dog-spit off.

"You must o' beat the guineas to the roost," Harl said. He pulled his case watch out and clicked the lid open. "Hain't more'n eight o'clock by my bug-hull."

"Hell's bangers!" I said. "Where've you started with that litter o' pups?"

"Figgered I'd take the young 'uns up the ridge a piece and let ole Ring learn 'em a few tricks," Harl said. "Fotch your two pups and we'll learn 'em what a fox track smells like."

"Ought to bring ole Trigger along," I said. "She'll throw a pure fit if she's left behind."

"I want my pups started proper," Harl said. I reckon he hadn't forgot the time she'd lost track and treed a coon. But I always treated my dogs square, young or old, letting them have a little run when they felt like it. Ole Trigger'd been a good one in her day. Bet every dog on Pigeon Roost was kin to her, one way or t'other. Trace it back straight, and Ring himself might o' had the same blood. She'd got old though. Twelve, I reckon, rusty jointed and slow as Egypt. Been gumming her food for years.

"Now, no," Harl said. "Leave that fleabag behind. This hain't no granny frolic."

The pups whined, anxious to be off. Ole Trigger came from under the house, shaking doodlebug dust off her hide. She set up a racket when I hitched a cord around her neck, tying her to a blackgum stump. I tried to quiet her and the pups, but you can't choke five dogs with two hands. Grandma waked, sticking her head through the door crack. She had her store-bought teeth out, and her mouth was wrinkled as a mare's nose. "Begone," she said. "Can't get a grain o' sleep with them dogs yowling around." And then she saw Harl standing beside the bubby bush. "Is that you Harly?" she asked, the words dropping sleepily from the hollow of her mouth.

"Hain't my ghost nor shadow," Harl said, teasing. He thought a lot of Grandma, though he wasn't no kin.

Grandma squinted into the yard. "Harley-son, hain't this a Friday?" she asked. Harl grunted, looping the leather strings around his wrist, drawing the pups short.

"Nigh broke your chine-bone hunting on this day going on three years ago," Grandma reminded. "Fell over a cliff-rock."

"One night or t'other, makes no differ" Harl said. "I figger I don't see right good of a nighttime."

"I figger there's a sign writ agin' you on Fridays," Grandma said. "I figger there is."

I fetched my two pups out of the pen, and hung a horn-bugle around my neck. We took up the ridge, tromping through ivy thickets, coming out into a patch of moonlight on top. Yonside, the hills stretched their backbones as far as eyeballs could look. The creek hollows below were day-white, withouten a thimbleful of fog. Lex Tomlinson's Creek. Heel Creek. Turkeyfoot Trace. I could see them head to mouth, every creek and crosshatch.

Harl straddled the log, catching the line over a limb-knot. "Grandma Shackett's got more quare notions than a frog's got wart bumps," he said.

"They work out for a fact sometimes," I said. "They pine-blank do."

"I hain't going agin' prophecy," Harl said. "No fox hunting I've done Friday nights in three years." He pulled a slab of rotten bark off the log, crushing it in his hands—hands big nigh as a slab of bacon. "Hit was a sight, me running off that clift. Not a drap I'd drunk either, not a smidgin." He handed the leather string to me. "Set the dogs doing. Ring'll pick up a track, and the pups can follow. I'm having nary a thing to do with this pup-run. And when you get back, I'll tell why I fotched you out o'bed."

I took the lead lines, breaking through a sourwood thicket along the ridge hip, proud down in my bones to see ole Ring tracking in front, and me making a fancy he was my own. He came on a warm scent after a quarter of a mile and struck down the ridge like a ball of lightning. The pups got so excited they dragged me amongst a thorn bush before I could get the leather knot untied. I listened to their barking for a spell. Ole Ring sounded like a fiddle played down low on the G-string. The pups kept letting out shrill yips of joy, but they were too slow to get a glimpse of a foxtail.

Well, now, I just set me down on a fern clump and looked out across the hills, mellow as ripe cushaws in the moonlight. There was Crofts Knob, and yonside, though I couldn't see that far, was Todd Miller's homeplace. And I got to thinking about Hulda sleeping there with her pretty face on a goose feather pillow, and this same moonlight shining through the window. She'd gone to bed early, I figgered, being Harl never turned up around dusty dark, and maybe she cried a speck when he didn't come or send word. Oh that Harl was the luckiest fellow ever drew breath. The cleverest foxhound in Tennessee River country he had, and Hulda Miller setting company with him two nights a week. That'd come pretty nigh being heaven on earth, it seemed to me then, and I haven't laid-by that notion since.

Oh it fair gave me the mulligrubs to think about it. But there was Ellafronia Saul, a lady stepped square out of a wish-book, and court opening Monday coming. Aye gonnies, I'd be on the spot, first bench behind the jury. Then I got to wondering why Harl fotched me out of bed, and on a Friday night too. My mind gamicked around till it hit on the short-writing woman again. Maybe he'd seen her down at Sawyers. The idea jumped me clear off that fern clump. I plumb forgot about the hounds. I went back along the ridge to where Harl waited, and it was the truth. He'd seen Ellafronia Saul. Stot Howard, a one-horse lawyer from Longfield, had been squiring her around the courthouse, making her acquainted with the folks. Stot had asked Harl to get some guitar and fiddle players for a square dance at ole Judge Middleton's place Friday night. "He's figuring on your mouth-harp," Harl said.

Now, I'm right clever on the mouth-harp. Dolesome ballads pleasure me a lot. "Rowan County Tragedy." "William Bluet." "Ole Talt Hall." I do a passel of jig-songs and ditties too. If it comes to a pinch I can play for running sets. When I've got my druthers, though, I like to do a little foot-scraping myself.

We sat on that beech log, Harl still pulling bark, crumbling it into dust. He told me square how it was with him. It'd been love the first look. By juckers, it's quare how a two-hundred-pounder, tough as whang leather, could tip over so sudden-quick. It seemed a pity about Hulda. "You've been sparking two years," I said. "Hulda's set nobody else down in her parlor-room all that time. She'd make a man the finest dough-beater ever was. Washes clothes so white, looks like dogwoods blooming around her house on Tuesdays. Good to weave and to mix at the dye pot." Oh it must of seemed quare, me talking up Hulda so bonny when Harl knew pine-blank I'd been green-snake jealous of him. "I bet this bluegrass woman never done a thing but set up in a courthouse and diddle jackleg lawyers," I said.

"I've got me an idea o' settling in pennyrile country," Harl said. "Land stretching there flat as your hand. . . ." And then he cocked his head to one side, listening for the dogs. Ole Ring was having it all by himself down on Heel Creek, and the pups were lost at the forks, working the brush in a circle.

Finally Harl slid off the log, shaking himself. I was getting mighty sleepy myself. "Reckon you'd better blow on the horn-bugle," he said.

I blew three blasts, nigh loud enough to wake the dead. Ole Ring heard and came up the ridge after a spell, but the pups took their everlasting time. When they plugged into the clearing Harl hitched his four together, making ready to go. "I'm thinking if hit's handy, you could fotch Hulda down the dance Friday night," he said. "I'll be sort o' busy rousting the music and meal-ing the floor."

Harl started off, ole Ring at heel. I laid me down on a leaf pile, my mind filled with a peck of things to thresh over. The pups wandered into the brush. I kept thinking I'd call them and strike down the ridge. The moon set behind Crofts Knob, and it got chilly. I slept, and the next thing I knew it was crack-ing day, and there was ole Trigger licking me smack-ker-dab in the mouth, and rattling the chain it had taken her all night to pull free of the blackgum stump.

I reckon a dozen almanacs have hung by the mantelpiece since that square dance at ole Judge Middleton's. But it's as green in mind as the rashes grow-ing here on Pigeon Roost Creek. It was the last one the ole Judge had in his house. Longer than I can recollect, he'd held one first week of fall court, even after his daughters married bluegrass lawyers. Fellers came sober to his place, and put on their manners. You couldn't clop brogans down careless on floors, and them shining like a looking glass. Things went proper. It's a pity the judge got riled over what happened that night. Nine times worse it might o' been any other place, by grabbies.

I had in head going up Crofts Creek, telling Hulda I'd be there along nigh the shank o' Friday evening to fetch her down to the dance. I had my mouth full of a lie-tale about why Harl couldn't come. Then I got skittish and sent Riggins with the word, promising him a pup out of Trigger's next batch. Rig-gins came back pretty soon, swearing Hulda had struck at him with the bald-headed end of a broom. "She was that het up," he said. "She knows about you and Harl hanging around Ellafronia Saul."

Now, I'd gone to court three times; been going anyhow since I was a chap. I went wearing a branfired new shirt, with nary a patch. Holt Simms was there too, big as life, on the front bench. Harl wandered in and out, restless as a she-fox. I could see he had the mulligrubs. Stote Hyden sat beside Ellafronia at the lawyer's table, whispering behind the pan of his hands. He'd open that pock-etbook mouth of his, and she'd smile as if she owned creation. Once I met her at the stairtop of the courthouse, but she acted like she didn't know me from Adam's ox.

Well, I went to that square dance all by my lonesome. Rode a little pieded nag down to Sawyers, with my mouth-harp deep in my hip pocket, bright as new money. And I had something else tucked under my hatband. Grandma always said if a fellow wants a passel o' luck in one batch, just carry a feather off a hoot owl's head. I hitched my nag in Judge Middleton's yard, seeing I was a grain early, for only three horses were tethered there.

I was easing the saddle a bit when a yip came out of the dark, and there was ole Trigger. She'd trailed me all the way, bless her mangy hide! I ran her under the porch so she wouldn't go tracking right into the house.

"Hickory Shin" Bates was sitting in a corner of the parlor-room, rosining his bow. Darb Suttles had his mail-order banjo, and John Cotter and Mell Sorrels held guitars on their laps. A piano box sat in the corner, but not a soul on Pigeon Roost knew how to play it. Ole Judge Middleton's daughters used to make it sound like a cage o' mockingbirds, I've heard it said. We got in key, and by that time the folks started coming, traipsing down the hall in twos and ones, the fellows slapping each other on the back, the girls edging along on their toes, hardly letting their heels touch the floor, rustling new dresses; and the Judge, and the ole Miss Middleton, stood under a great lamp swung from the ceiling, bowing and creaking stiff backs, and the top of the Judge's bald head shone like the moon-ball itself.

"Blow a song-piece on the mouth-harp," somebody said, and I played "The Merry Golden Tree," a ballad of a foreign country land, and Darb Suttles sang the words low in his throat, sad as a turtledove's call.

There was a little ship and it sailed upon the sea,
And it went by the name of Merry Golden Tree
As it sailed upon the low and lonesome low,
As it sailed upon the lonesome sea.

And while Darb sang, Hulda passed into the hall with her brother John, and I glimpsed her wish-book dress, white as tuliptree blooms and scattered with rosebud prints, real as life. I looked at her pretty face, and my mouth got dry, the harp tightening on my lips. I knew again what a fool Harl was, and the witty I'd been. And suddenly there was a hush. Darb's words petered out, and my breath thinned into the harp. Ellafronia Saul came down the hall on the arm of Stote Hyden. She tripled along, a little smidgin of a woman, rising not a grain taller than Stote's top vest button, and the dress she wore rippled like shoal-water in moonlight. By grabbies, it seemed I was looking at her for the first time. Her neck wasn't much bigger than my wrist, and her poppet-doll face was as pale and brittle as Grandma's hen-and-biddy dish.

I looked the parlor-room over and found Harl sitting yonside the piano box. He'd tickle-toed in, unbeknownst to me, and he sat there glaring into blue air, the mulligrubs eating him up alive. Ellafronia had turned him down for Stote, I knew pine-blank. I spied at her again. I couldn't think of her cooking fatty-bread and washing Harl's britches, to save my life. She was a woman tender as a snail's horns.

About that time, Crat Lovens jumped-hopped to the floor middle and hollered right big, and when Crat hollers, the rafters shake.

Come on folks, come ye one and all,
Grab yore partners, we're ready for the haul.

We struck up "Hook and Line." I bore down on my harp to keep "Hickory Shin" from drowning me out. Darb Suttles fretted the banjo like a spider hustling a web, and John Cotter and Mell Sorrels flicked their metal-tipped playing fingers over guitar strings lightning-fast.

The dance began, slap-clop, crow-hop—Crat Jones calling the sets out of the cave of his mouth. "Find yore partners, hain't no sin; promenade, and gone agin." Hulda was paired with her babe-brother John, Stote Hyden swung Ellafronia Saul. Fifteen couples moved over the mealed floor—"Left, to right, and ocean wave. . . ."

Harl sat through the first set, leant against the piano box, and when it had ended and the couples rested for second wind, he came out upon the floor, his face a little skinned-looking from a new shave, and his gray eyes burning. Hulda caught hold of her brother's arm, afraid Harl was coming to her, and maybe a grain afraid he wasn't. Harl stepped up to Ellafronia, gentle as a ewe-sheep, as if Stote hadn't been within forty miles. I got scared, I tell you. It looked like bad trouble. A flick of scorn ran over Ellafronia's face. She turned her proud head toward Stote and winked—batting one eye, foxy as ever I saw. Stote gave over, though his face was tight with anger. The second set began. Rusty jints had got warmed up, and this time we played "Ole Joe Clark" to a fare-you-well. Oh that there "Hickory Shin" Bates purely sawed catgut.

I kept an eye green on Stote, and before long he called Felt Wayland, whispering a bug in his ear. Felt edged outside, coming back in five minutes though, and it had me fuddled. Stote got in fair humor, beginning to clap to the music, beating time with a briar-toed shoe.

When the second set ended, Stote walked toward Ellafronia. Folks turned and looked, moving a little way apart. Harl stood in front of Ellafronia, heading Stote off. Stote's face got grim as a skull. He plunged his right hand into a pocket, and when it came out, swinging through the air, a pair of brass knuckles shone on his fist. They caught Harl square on the chin, but he didn't go down. He just stood there shaking his head, unbelieving. In a minute, ole Judge Middleton was standing betwixt them, mad as a wet turkey. Harl lit for the door, waiting on the porch for Stote, and Stote had to follow, settling what he'd started.

We crowded onto the porch, hush-mouthed and nervous. Harl unhitched his mare, and the saddle fell off. I knew then pine-blank what Felt had been up to. He'd whittled that saddle-seat with a knife. I looked for Felt, but he had skeedaddled, and it might o' been a good thing. Harl and Stote galloped off, Harl riding bare-bones, and we could see them for a half mile, the moon being that bright.

Well, now, I was standing there, and aye gonnies if Hulda didn't come up to me, coming so nigh it made me have goose bumps. Then I figured that hoot-owl feather under my hatband was beginning to work after all. She leant her head over and said, wee down in her throat, "Go after them." And I went. I whistled up Trigger and lit a shuck down the road, Trigger running ahead to smell out the tracks.

Harl and Stote had gone lickety-split down Pigeon Roost, then turned up the ridge, plumb to the tiptop. Hadn't been for my hound, I'd missed them sure. I plugged up to where they were standing ten yards apart in a clearing, above the cliff-rocks, and holding pistols in their hands. I didn't know what they'd said to each other. I know Stote's face was white as dough-bread. I got behind a tree, spying around it. Sudden-quick, Stote leveled his pistol-gun and fired. He missed, and Harl didn't move. Being closest to Stote, I got a glimpse of his gun, and if I hadn't been so scared and out o' wind I'd a-busted laughing. He'd borrowed a little pearly handled squeeze-trigger off Felt Wayland. I'd swapped that gun to Felt myself for a set o' mink traps, and knowing Felt wasn't safe with gunpowder, I'd crooked the sight-piece a grain.

It looked bad for Stote, I tell you. Harl never was what you'd call a sharp-shooter—I reckon because his eyesight wasn't good as most fellers'—but he wouldn't have to shoot a lead mine to hit a chunk big as Stote. Well, it was Harl's time to shoot, but aye gonnies if Stote didn't lose his nerve and shoot three bullets, one jamb after another, missing every dabbed time. Harl stood there, cool as mint. He brought his gun level and took a step or two forward, squinting in the moonlight. I couldn't bear to look. I just tucked my head behind the tree and waited. Well, now, I waited a spell, and nothing happened. Not a sound I heard. Then I spied out, and there was Stote running off the ridge in a mighty hurry. And nary a sign o' Harl could I see.

I got up to the place where Harl had been standing fast as two legs could fetch me, and by juckers if he hadn't stepped square off the cliff before he could shoot. I remember then it was Friday, his bad-luck day, and I knew pine-blank this thing had happened.

Black as Egypt it was below, seventy-five feet down into pitch dark. I hollered and squalled, getting no answer. I figured then he must o' broken his neck, and I climbed down, risking my bones, snagging and scratching to the bottom. There was a thicket of sumac at the foot of the pocket, and a steep bed of limerock dropping to a bench level. Even Trigger couldn't climb down into the pocket, and he couldn't reach the bench from below. I lit a pine-knot, but nary a sight or sign I found of Harl. Aye gonnies, I searched till crack o' day. The only way I could ever figure he got out was to edge around the cliff, walking like a fly-bug on a wall, and I don't reckon he could o' made it then unless-en the devil was holding him up by the seat of his britches.

Well, now, Stote Hyden got his walking papers from ole Judge Middleton for starting a racket in his house, and Stote had to go back to Longfield to practice. Ellafronia Saul traipsed to where she'd come from, marrying a bluegrass lawyer, I've heard it said, but you can't nail much truth in what you hear this day and time. Nigh on to six years ago, a medicine drummer came through swearing he'd seen Harl up in pennyrile country, a land so flat you can see five miles withouten your eyes hitting against anything. I had the drummer up to my place to eat a new robbing of poplar-bloom honey and to talk a spell. He said Harl was wearing glass specs, and he like not to have known him; and he was in the dog business, raising and selling foxhounds. After Harl skipped the country ole Ring sort o' took up with me, and I've still got a batch of dogs he sired by Trigger. I wouldn't take a war pension for a one of my fourteen foxhounds, but if Harl ever comes back to the hills, he can take his choose and pick.

And while that drummer talked, Hulda sat afar in the corner, like a wife ought to sit when there's a strange man in the house, and she never said a word. I always did figure I got the sweetest little woman ever beat dough.

The Straight

I shall call him Abner Stegall, which was not his name. When I moved to Mule Creek country, it was he who declared to B. J. Claymore and the storehouse crowd, "My opinion, the feller's been rode out of Linemark School on a rail, else he'd not o' left a good job." And later, when this notion proved false, he told them, "There must be an enemy after his hide. The ground got hot over there and he tuk off. For what other cause earthly would a man come backside of the county and endure a fox's life? The next time I go to Linemark I'll learn the truth on that feller, what he's running from."

Abner, a sometimes miner, lived temporarily on Ivy Branch, a valley opening into Lower Mule below the Foot, in a home called the old Malahide homeseat. He left the mine camps "for good and forever" every two or three years and had lived in various abandoned homeseats along Mule; he stood six feet six bare-heeled, too tall for mine labor, he claimed. This was his second period of residence on Ivy. A lumber company held legal title to the valley and Abner was a squatter. Ivy had been one of my ways home until Abner grumbled to Claymore, "Might's well live on a highroad, so much passing lately. My old woman's mad, says got to hang shades to the windows to stop the spying in."

My occasional journeying up Ivy had been to pass through the beech forest above the valley head where flying squirrels might be seen. But I had already decided to shun the place. On approaching Abner's house the previous week I had heard a shout. Two small children playing in the yard ran under the floor, the front door slammed, the window holes were covered, and I caught a glimpse of Abner at a corner of the house furtively watching me.

When I arrived at the Foot for my mail the following week, B. J. Claymore drew me aside and told of Abner's further complaints. A patch of 'sang he had expected to harvest in the valley head had disappeared, and a bee tree that bore his ax-mark claim had been robbed. Claymore quoted Abner, "That newcomer's the guilty devil." Abner had kicked the horseshoe keg in apparent wrath and swore, "God dog! A body can't have a thing nowadays." Claymore's advice to me had been, "Steer clear of Ivy, and the head of the valley, and the mountain beyond. There's a reason, but I don't want to speak it."

I grunted disinterestedly.

Claymore reddened. "I didn't want you to find out the hard way," he said.

"I regret not getting a taste of the wild honey," I said. "And if I'd found the 'sang, I'd have dug it likely. Sells fifteen dollars to the pound, I hear. Already I'm feeling out of pocket."

Claymore grinned weakly, and our talk ended. We had been in the rear of the storehouse, and I joined Jace Malahide, Hask Wycherly, and Tilford Cleveland at the front. Jace held his guitar on his knee. Hask said, "According to Ab Stegall you're a bear for honey." He was trying to get a rise out of me.

I used Hask's own favorite expression to reply, which was about the only way you could break even with Hask. "Right as a rabbit's foot," I said. And knowing Hask's penchant for teasing, I asked, "How do you and Abner Stegall hit it off?"

Hask's face soured, his countenance bespeaking his reply. Hask and his fellow prankers at the Foot spared Abner as he was obviously slow of wit and reputedly sharp of temper. A tale is told that once in emptying a pocket on a counter in search of money to purchase tobacco Abner brought forth a handful of bullets. A bystander had observed, "Ab, you've got more lead than silver," and Abner had nodded dully. Minutes later, the tobacco bought, a cud pouched in his jaw, Abner suddenly repeated, "More lead than silver," and threw his head back and gagged. And then, unaccountably, he got angry, his eyes fired, and he stalked out of the storehouse.

Hask said to me, "You and Old Ab will make cronies yet. He's spitting in your tracks right now, but you wait. He'll mellow up."

"I want to know one thing," Jace Malahide addressed me. "Ab's got a daughter, sixteen or eighteen, and have you seen her in passing along Ivy?" He strummed the guitar idly. "She's fair as a dove on a limb, and suits my notion to a hair, but I'd die single ere I'd call Old Ab Stegall pappy."

"Hell's bangers!" Hask blurted. "Who named Ab Stegall in the first place? I say we switch the subject."

My knowledge of Abner and his family remained limited, and I did not try to improve it by inquiry. I knew him on sight and met him along the creek now and then. We spoke our greetings heartily enough and passed on. He was thin and bony, all hasps and hinges, as the saying goes, and had the sticklike walk of the gaunt and tall. I used to come on Abner's teenage sons fishing along Lower Mule. During dog days, a season of low water, they fished with sledge-hammers, wading upcreek and striking exposed boulders. Perch and bass in the vicinity of the boulders were momentarily numbed by the sound and easily gained. I suspected the Stegall boys of dumping the walnut hulls I found in pools near the mouth of Ivy, drowning the fish. Abner himself, reportedly, had dynamited the creek more than once, and perhaps in this fashion obtained the only eel ever caught in Mule Creek. I never saw Abner's wife or the daughter living at home. Two married daughters and a son lived in mine camps.

One day Claymore drew me into the storehouse yard under the pretext of pointing out his choice of a route for the county road through the Foot. I had once chagrinned him by remarking I wished the roads kept at their present distance. He had chuffed, "You and Old Wick Jarrett hold the same notion. Man-o! This is the twentieth century. Wake up." But the morning we stepped outside the storehouse, there had been no preliminary discussion of highways.

Under the hitching-post willows Claymore said, "Just wanted to cut you out of the crowd so we can talk freely. Yesterday Ab Stegall asked if you'd come down lately and said, 'I'm itching to question him, ask the straight on two, three happenings.' Tom Bud Cranch and Til Cleveland and a couple more were settling in, and we all asked what happenings, and Ab wouldn't tell right off, and we picked at him, and he said, 'Killings.' Everybody hollered, 'Ah?' and he said, 'I got the facts at Linemark, teeth to teeth, no hearsay.'"

I also breathed, "Ah," and I noticed Claymore's eyes sharpen.

"We'd heard the wind slew before," Claymore assured. "Til and Tom Bud took your part. Til said, 'Ab, you've strifed that feller right along. Whyn't you two make fair weather?' And Tom Bud threw in, 'What's the purpose of fresh-ening old troubles?' Ab got meeky, and he allowed, 'No harm to burn off the waters, see what's in under.' And Tom Bud said, 'You neighbor that feller, hear me? If he suffered a wrong the law'd clap you in jail first thing, guilty or no.' Ab said, 'You reckon?' and 'I've got ought against him.' The hurries was eating him up. He left right shortly."

"My trespassing on Ivy Branch upset Stegall uncommonly," I observed.

"Ab sees a booger behind every tree. His nature."

I said, "An occupational disease, I figure."

Claymore glanced narrowly at me. "Hmmn."

Claymore consulted his great silver watch, momentarily expecting Hod Burchell with the mail pouches. With eyes yet fast upon the timepiece he declared, "You've never mixed in a killing," and paused, watch in hand, apparently awaiting my concurrence. I gained a moment to think by spitting out the willow leaves I chewed. How much of an explanation was practicable? I decided on the minimum. When I did not reply immediately, Claymore held the watch to an ear, appeared dissatisfied with its performance, hammered the edge against the base of a thumb, and listened again.

"Now, no," I said.

I happened upon Wace Pottsfield, John Rennett, and Abner Stegall at the sand-bar mouth of Harls Branch on Laurel. I had gone downcreek to the sugar orchard an hour or so before. It was Sunday, a few weeks after my talk with B. J. Claymore. They sat on a pile of beech logs, idly grooving the trunks with pocketknives. The three spoke, "Howdy," and Wace Pottsfield added, "Join up." Then Abner invited, "Climb and help whittle."

"Whose log heap?" I inquired, making talk.

"John's," Wace said, "but don't mind the ownership. Climb and roost."

"I'll go along," I said indecisively.

John reminded, "Sunday's a rest day."

"Come around," Abner insisted, and suddenly lifted an arm. We shook hands. I saw Wace and John cut their eyes at each other, probably as surprised as I, and as Abner had shaken hands, they offered theirs.

I climbed onto the logs and opened my Barlow. The logs had endured a year's weather on the ground, and the bark was soft and wood-thieves scurried underneath. I grooved and sliced, and I noticed Abner stared long at my knife. It was a two-bladed Barlow jack B. J. Claymore sold for seventy-five cents.

John said, "These logs are going into mine props. Won't hurt to scar 'em."

"Sorry timber, beech is," Wace commented.

Abner said, "Can't beat it for barrel staves."

"All right for patching timber," said I.

The subject played out.

Abner asked me, "How've you been standing the times?"

"Common," I answered. "How have you?"

"Common."

The talk lapsed.

After a studied pause Abner inquired, "Your kin—you hear from them, I reckon. They're well?"

"Common. Your family, they're in good health?"

"Common."

To get out of the conversational rut I said, "I hear you caught an eel in Lower Mule several years ago."

"Upper Mule," Abner corrected.

"What did you do with it?"

"The hide made shoestrings."

We spoke no more of the eel. We dug steadily into the wood. The sun beat upon the unshaded logs and heat danced the sandbar. We began to sweat. We scraped water beads from our brows with the dull side of the blades. Presently Abner said to me, "Let's have a look at the weapon you're handling."

We exchanged knives. Abner tested my jack's edges with a finger, plucking them as a guitar string is plucked. He mumbled, "This trick wouldn't cut butter. The metal's dead." I examined his knife. It was a cattle, with clip, spay, heavy duty, and sheepsfoot blades. The edge of the heavy duty had a razor's sharpness. Abner handed back my knife, and I returned his. I said, "Yours is the boss."

"Is that all the body protection you pack?" Abner inquired.

"Yep."

"A danger to leave home with that plug. Must have got it off a punchboard."

"Hmmn."

"You ever see a knife fight?"

I nodded.

Wace and John ceased whittling and cocked their chins attentively. And it occurred to me that neither our meeting at the mouth of Harls Branch nor the present subject of conversation had been chance. Abner probably saw me go downcreek, fetched Wace and John as witnesses, and had awaited my return. Abner drawled, "Let's hear about the scrape."

I made brief, "Two boys began whacking at each other and were dragged apart before serious damage was done."

"Gee-o," John commented, "that battle was over ere it begun, to hear you tell it."

Abner raised his cattle knife dirk-fashion and stabbed the log and left it sticking. "A feller ought to spend money on a knife. Don't expect to buy a suiting one under three dollars."

Wace tempered Abner's instructions. "Ah, now, he might have the finest make of gun at his house."

"Pistol or rifle?" Abner asked, accepting Wace's theory, his voice hard and imperative.

Both John and Wace appeared suddenly embarrassed by Abner's abruptness, and Wace made a delaying statement, "'Lysses Jarrett's the one owns the weapons. I was at his house and he lifted a mattress and there lay three shotguns and a rifle, and he ope's a trunk and shows two pistols, and he says there's some old-timers in the closet, not worth looking at."

Abner reiterated, "Pistol or rifle?"

"A hog-rifle," I reported, "with a bullet lodged in the barrel."

John related offhandedly, "Recollect Crock Wills renting up my creek? The house burning? The house burnt of a night and he lost everything. Wiped out. Saved just the shirttails and gowns they slept in, and them scorched. Did Crock grunt over lost furniture and his naked family? Now, no. Says to me, 'I'm sick to my heart for losing my guns. I had five.'"

Abner said, "A body never knows when they'll meet a killer, by day or by night."

"I have no known enemies," I said.

Abner thumped the handle of his knife, causing it to vibrate. "Didn't you mix-up in a killing over at Linemark a few years back?"

"I witnessed a shooting."

"I mean you spoke up when you could o' kept sort of quiet, not helped stir a mess."

"The Grand Jury summonsed me, and later I was summonsed to testify at the trial."

"You tuk sides, I hear."

"I knew neither the slayer nor the slain."

John said, "The way you tell it I can't make heads or tails of the shooting."

"John," I said, "you've reminded me of my turn on the witness stand. The commonwealth's attorney was questioning me when a lawyer for the defense jumped to his feet and appealed to the judge, 'The witness is using such big words the jury can't understand what he's saying.'"

Abner insisted, "I've heard it two or three ways. What's the straight?"

"The straight is this," I said, making a show of patience. "I saw a person lift a gun and fire, and I saw another fall to the ground."

"That trouble the reason you moved over here, backside of the county?"

"I lived on at Linemark for five years."

Though my explanation obviously didn't satisfy Abner, he moved on to further inquiry. "I heard a sketch about this chap at Linemark Schoolhouse, and there was a ruckus, and you in the middle of it.

"A fellow tried to break up a school program. It was just a question of who would put on the show, the Linemark School chaps or a fun-box in the audience."

Wace mumbled, "How'd it end?"

"The fun-box won."

Abner hastened his investigation. "Last winter, down in Leckett County, there happened a bad killing. And where was you? Right on the spot, big as life."

"An accidental witness."

Abner pulled his cattle knife from the log and snapped the blade into its case. "After all the scrapes you've horned in on, you oughten to live without body protection." His voice grew earnest. "Knock the stuck bullet out of the hog-rifle. Buy a strong knife."

I folded my Barlow. "This plug has served my purposes pretty well."

Abner arose. He sighted the time of day by the sun; he shifted his feet, ready to leave. Then he turned and lifted an arm toward me. We shook hands again. He declared solemnly, "All I've spoken today is in your behalf. Just wanted the straight of the truth. And I say guard yourself. Who knows when a rascal will be met?"

"Who knows?" I said.

When the stream lowered in the fall, Abner bought an old truck and drove it up Mule to the mouth of Ivy. The stone-locked bed of the branch proved impassable and the truck was left at the mouth. In early December he and his family sledded their household goods down the branch, loaded the truck, and drove away.

A few days after Abner moved, I walked into the storehouse at the Foot and B. J. Claymore greeted me, "Good-bye, Abner Stegall." Claymore sat in the post-office corner, writing in a ledger, and he eyed me to see how I took the news. After a moment of silence he added, "Moved, pulled stakes, gone the road."

"Ah," I said.

While Claymore worked, I drew a chair to the stove. I recruited the fire and set the iron seams winking. One of my feet had slipped into a hole of water coming down, and I rested it upon the iron apron. The door of the storehouse, ajar for light, let in a steady flow of cold air along with the grayness of middle afternoon, and I alternately shivered and baked. By the time my shoe began to steam, Claymore banged together the halves of the ledger and joined me at the stove.

"Zizzards," Claymore chuffed. "Tonight will freeze clappers in cowbells." He filled a coffeepot and placed it on the stove. He reached into a sack and pulled forth a yellow apple. "Eat it," he said. "That's a Golden Delicious, out of my own orchard."

189

I ate the apple, and I asked, "Where's everybody?"

Claymore shrugged. "Gone home."

The coffee boiled. Claymore fetched cups, blew the dust out, handed one to me, saying, "I reckon hardly a dozen have drunk from it since the last washing." We stirred lumps of brown sugar into the coffee with splinters off the kindling pile; we talked, and mostly about Abner. Claymore believed the Stegalls had moved either to Bug Dust or to the new mine in Old Virginia we had lately heard much about. The new mine had a fourteen-foot vein, and a body could work standing up, and it was said coal flowed through the driftmouth like a stream in tide. But Claymore decided, "I can't picture Ab in a mechanical mine. Beyond a doubt he moved to Bug Dust."

While we drank the coffee, Claymore told of Abner's changed attitude toward me. "He was set pine-blank against you till the showdown on Harls Branch. That day you made a bud out of him." He grinned, "Next shipment o' good knives I get, I'll sell you one for cost." And Claymore mentioned his settlement with Abner. "He came in here last week and asked, 'How much do I owe?' and says, 'Here 'tis.'" Claymore seemed impressed by Abner's unexpected bounty. "Well, he paid his debts, settled with the ledger. That speaks good for him."

"How did Abner make a living?" I inquired. "He raised a small garden patch, nothing else. And I understand he never hired out for wages."

Claymore looked wry, his eyes sharpened. "The same question exactly he asked about you once." He didn't comment further.

We finished the coffee. My foot got dry.

I bought a two-pound poke of salt and five pounds of sugar. I received no mail, so Claymore gave me an old newspaper. As I lifted the pokes to depart, Claymore said, "Now you can travel up Ivy Branch any time the notion strikes."

"That's the long way around," I reminded, though I felt tempted to go that day, despite weather and distance.

The wind blew full in my face as I started upcreek, and I walked along slowly, half of a mind to visit Ivy Branch. At the first turn of the valley, where the mountain broke the wind's force, I paused. The afternoon was perishing, and it was turning colder, but I bethought myself I could spend the night in the old Malahide house, and go home on the morrow. I crossed Mule, passed the Foot on the farther side of the creek, and trod a carpet of willow leaves to the mouth of Ivy.

On the banks of Mule, trenched sand mapped the backings and turnings of Abner's truck. The white sand bore dark stains as if a wounded beast had crawled there and bled. Along Ivy I found the tracks of sled runners and calculated four round-trips had been necessary to haul Abner's goods. The waters of the branch were low and shone with a golden cast, due to a seepage of natural petroleum. I was once told that during a spell of extreme drought the branch had dried to oily pools of such richness they could be lighted by a match, and Abner's children had played at burning off the waters. I passed the sawmill site where lay the giant flywheel of a steam engine. I hurried on. Higher, along the ridgetops, the wind soughed, but the valley floor held a breathless, unmoving chill.

A mile and a quarter along I reached the old Malahide place. The doors hung wide. Dry weed stalks in the yard were plumed with feathers from a rent bed-tick. A hen clucked among the bluing weeds, and I wondered that she had escaped the foxes. In the yard knelt a kitchen stove, one front leg bent underneath, the other buckling. A girl-child's slippers, too new for casting away, sat forgotten on the top doorstep.

I walked around, through the house, barn, and cellar, and along paths to the spring and garden. I wondered at the number of fruit jars lined by the cellar wall and under the kitchen floor. Blue slivers of broken jars were scattered about, which must have made perilous the steps of barefoot children. The house and grounds bespoke careless living and hasty departure, but the woodyard was in good order. A master woodchopper had labored there, and expertly chopped sticks for stove and fireplace were evenly sized and stacked, and the chips heaped neatly into piles.

With a bush top I swept the planking of the big room, and I brought in wood and built a fire. The chimney drew smoke lazily, I recall. There seemed a clog in the chimney. I closed the door and the draft mended. After warming, I dug in the garden, unearthing a hatful of Irish potatoes and a few onions; I found a stalk of red peppers shining in the dead grass. I fetched springwater in a lard pail. And when the ball of the sun dropped behind the ridge, I played fox. I caught the hen as she wended to roost.

By nightfall the hen simmered in a battered aluminum pot, and I cooked her slowly and long, adding potatoes, onions, and a red pepper. I wished Abner might have had a taste, for once in his presence Hask Wycherly had remarked that at mealtime I took a handful of salt into the vegetable patch and dined like a rabbit; and Abner, fully believing, had asked, "What, now, does he eat of a winter?" Hask had replied, "Lives on salt, I reckon." The stew turned out satisfactorily, even if a bit stringy. I ate the last mouthful.

I read the newspaper Claymore had given me, then spread it before the hearth and lay upon it. I watched the dying fire, and I remember the dark moss of soot waving along the chimney's back. Had I drawn my head closer to the fire and glanced up, I might have seen a coil of metal in the throat of the chimney. Abner's brass distillery worm was found there the next spring by one of Hod Parson's boys.

Sunstroke on Clabber Creek

The last food jars had been given out at the relief center on Dry Creek when Sebe Hammers pushed through the crowd. "I shore want you to git over to my homeseat this day," he said. "You hain't never been thar. The other govermint visitor was scairt of my woman. I reckon she is a grain crazy, but she wouldn't harm a hair."

Sebe was a short man, firm and heavy, and built close to the ground. He stood there wiping his raw eyes with a handkerchief, a small print square of cloth you could have pitched broomstraws through. It hardly covered his horny palm. The crowd looked at him and at the handkerchief. He held it up, and the red print flowers were bright in the sun. It was a woman's handkerchief. "I want you to see how rail pore folks live," he said.

Sebe was afoot. My horse-mule, Sugartop, had a saddle-boil and we couldn't ride double. I set out walking with Sebe, leaving the nag behind in Sol Jefferson's stall. We took up Trace Hollow and over the ridge with the sun-ball beating down on our backs. A scope of clouds lay flush with the hills toward Angus Creek, but there was nothing overhead to break the heat.

We stopped under the half-shade of a clump of haws going down yonside of the ridge. Blades of heat strained through the leaves, burning like points of light under a sunglass. "Hit's shore a hot day," Sebe said. "I reckon it's the hottest day ever was." I wiped the salt sweat from my eyes with my shirttail and lay back upon the steamy ground, resting. Sebe saw I had no handkerchief. He held the damp ball of cloth toward me but I shook my head. He wiped the red rims of his eyelids and spread the scrap of cloth in the sun to dry.

"Reckon you've got trachoma?" I asked.

"Hit's jist a leetle sore-eye I got," he said. "And I jedge hit catchin'."

Leaber Flint was waiting at the ridge-foot for us. He had heard our brogans rattling the rocky trail. "We hain't got a dustin' o' meal in the house," he said.

"Me and my woman and chaps is livin' hard as nails. They hain't enough grease in the bucket to fry a strip o' sowbelly. I figger the govermint is bound to do somethin.'"

He led us through a huckleberry thicket to his puncheon slab house set under the hill. An old hen pecked in the yard, and there were three small naked children looking at us through a paling fence. Leaber's wife came to the door with a baby at her breast. "Them children's got a dress apiece," she said, "but hit's been so hot I let 'em pull 'em off. I heard tell hit does them good to git their hides tanned."

It was cool in the house, and dark after the bright sunlight. The air was musty and rank. There was one bedstead covered with dirty quilts and a rotting shuck-mattress. The stove was propped on two stacks of flat rocks. Beside it a pile of ashes rose from the floor almost as high as the stove itself. They had been wet down to keep them from scattering. The meal barrel was empty, smelling like a rat's nest. The grease bucket had a fistful of lard in it.

Leaber followed me through the house, brushing his hands over his scrubby beard. When we went outside again I sat down on the steps, writing a few words in a notebook. I had got overheated. My eyes burned as I followed the lines, and a dull ache, black as a thunderhead, lay behind them.

Leaber talked on as I wrote. "I'm patchin' me two acres o' corn but that won't nigh feed my woman and chaps. I hain't got no garden. Hit's been dry as bones. Anyway we et up the seeds in March. Now if I had me some seeds hit's still too hot. Plants is mighty timid a-comin' on right now."

When we had cooled off we walked on down Clabber Creek, staying close under the thin willow shade. My face and hands burned with the prickly heat, the sweat poured from my forehead, and my hair was sobby under the hot vacuum of my hat. A sharp thorn of pain struck backward from my eyes into my brain.

Lim Conners called us in for a drink of springwater. The windowless rooms of his house were clean and the floors yellow-white from scrubbings with a shuck mop. The rope-strung beds were billowing white with ticks filled with chicken feathers. But there were flies swarming about us in the dogtrot. They bit us and we kept busy slapping at them.

Another mile down the creek, John Stoll's widow called to us to come in and eat a bite. Sebe hollered back that I was going to have a meal with him. As we walked on he told me about the nit-brained child at the Stoll place. "John Stoll ought to a-killed one man afore he died," Sebe said. "Big Coll Tolbert come to his house drunk while his wife was a fur piece along and scairt her so the girl-child was marked when hit was borned. John was a-layin' off to spike Big Coll, but he got hisself sawed up at a stave mill afore he got a chanct."

My head ached fiercely as we walked, the pain wavering before my eyes like the pulsing heat over the stones ahead. My face was no longer wet. It was hot and dry, the heat seeming to boil inside me without being able to get out. Clabber Creek stretched endlessly before us. The water was thick and glassy and seemed not to move at all. As the sun-ball turned overhead we came to the mouth of Short Fork, and to Sebe Hammer's house. It sat back in an old apple orchard, and we walked up to it through rows of bean poles.

"Don't you mind my ole woman none," Sebe said. "She's puore crazy."

Two mangy hounds challenged us from the puncheon steps and dived headlong under the house when Sebe threw a chunk at them. Lulu, Sebe's wife, stood on the porch. She looked at me out of nervous eyes, brown as peach-stones between raw lids, and reached out a moist hand. "Yore furrin to Short Fork," she said. "We hain't never seed you afore, but yore a welcome body if you kin put up with pore folks' ways." She went back into the dark shade of the house. As we cooled on the porch we could hear her working over the stove, and the hoarse clucking of her voice singing an Old Regular hymn. "My woman is right quietlike this day," Sebe said.

My head was feeling like a water bucket by now—large, hot, and hollow. In the shade the heat still danced before my eyes. I had come near a sunstroke, I thought. I wanted to sit still, and not to move at all, but presently Sebe took me around the house to the barn. The hip roof had its back broken. The logs were rotten and worm-eaten. There were only shucks and knotty corncobs in the crib. He had no cow. There was a razorback pig with a belly flat as a flitter in a pen. "Hit won't be meat till first frost," Sebe said. "I hain't got a grain o' nothin' to feed hit on. I jist pull weeds and feed hit, but they hain't got enough fleshnin' to put an aidge on his teeth."

195

I asked about his plow-mule. Sebe twisted his face up and laughed. "Thar ain't a nag on this Short Fork," he said. "We've got a porely lot o' folks on this creek. We all jist knock out our craps with a hoe. And hit's pritty hard on the rheumatiz in my jints."

We sat down under the thick shade of an apple tree and Sebe told me about the folks on Short Fork. "We hain't right healthy on this fork," he said. "We air all kinfolks one way or 'nother. I'm squar' kin to myself and back agin. We don't git out much, and nobody comes in here. All the land is tuk up. Hit might do right good crappin' if hit wasn't standin' on one end.

"My woman is the only one thet's crazy, but she hain't got the breast complaint like some o' the women. Sometimes I reckon I'm glad hit's her brains thet's weak and not her lungs thet's bein' et up with consumption. Oh we hain't a healthy lot here on this fork. I reckon hit's the fogs, and the damp hollers, and the sun not a-shinin' in nigh more'n half the day."

Lulu called and we went in to eat. A table in the shed-room was set for us with two bucket-lid plates. There was a knife beside each plate but no fork or spoon. We scooped the shucky beans up with the broadside of the knife, fighting the flies off with one hand. They could sting like a bee if they lit.

I was sick, and not hungry, but I ate a little and drank three cups of black coffee. The food fell into my stomach like lead. Lulu stood over us, watching every mouthful we ate, and I saw that she had Sebe's handkerchief. She brushed her face with it, and held it up to see the red print flowers.

After eating we sat on the porch again. "I'll be puore thankful if the govermint kin do somethin' for us folks on Short Fork," Sebe said. "We're 'bout to piddle out." His words came as though through a fog. I was dull, and suddenly very sick. My dinner churned uncertainly in my stomach. I told Sebe I had to go, but I sat on with my chair leaned against the wall, and presently I slept.

Lulu's laughter wakened me. It was shrill and raucous. Sebe was holding her, calm and unmoved as one might hold an angry child, and she struck at him with her bony hands. She was mad, but she laughed. I jumped out of my chair. The floor seemed to swing under my feet.

"I've got to go," I said, and Sebe kept saying, "Hain't no use to be scairt. She's jist havin' a spell. She won't harm a hair."

I ran down the path through the beanstalks to the creek bank. I fell down in the hot sand, and my dinner came up in choking gusts. I couldn't stop to get my breath, but when there was no more I got up and walked on, wavering along the path as it curled through the hot sun. My skin was dry as leather, parched as old poplar leaves.

I thought about my horse-mule in Sol Jefferson's stall six miles away and wondered if I'd ever make it. From there it was fourteen miles home.

I walked a long time. The earth under my feet seemed to move and flow behind me. Then I was out of the valley and on the mountain, knowing that I had strayed, that I was lost. I knew I'd had a sunstroke, and that I'd have to keep going. To lie down was to die. There on the mountain the buzzards would pick my bones. It might be days before anyone came along this trail. I had to keep going.

When I could walk no longer, I lay down in the middle of the path. If someone came along they would be sure to see me. They could not fail unless it was dark, and then a horse might step in my face. I reached into my pocket and found a handkerchief to wipe my mouth. Brushing it across my lips, I saw red print flowers bright upon the cloth. It was Sebe's handkerchief. Lulu had put it in my pocket. I threw it down and rolled over to the edge of the path. There a mule or horse coming along the trail might not step on me, might shy away before they reached me. Then I drifted away in unconsciousness, not caring any more about buzzards or the feet of any animal.

The Hay Sufferer

He was eating radishes in my garden, a spider of a man no more than five feet in height, arms and legs bony, the skin of his face as weathered as the leather cap he wore. I had been at table eating a noon meal when I heard something sneeze and had come outside to investigate. "Hello?" I spoke into the yard. "Howdy," a voice replied, and I discovered him squatting by the radish bed. He sneezed twice, in the manner of a cat. He reached a hand into a canvas budget beside him and got a handkerchief to brush his nose and dab at his moist eyes. "I'm a hay sufferer," he said.

"There are victuals on the table," I invited, "and you're welcome to eat."

"I've got my belly full now," he declined. He popped a radish into his mouth, cheeks pouching like a squirrel's, chewing with relish. It was late spring, the radishes fibrous at the heart and the tops ready to seed. "I'm here to clean out your well," he said when the pulp was swallowed. "I got the word to come."

To my knowledge I hadn't set eyes on him before and had sent no message; but my well needed drawing clear, the mud dished up and walls freed of web and root. Spiders had matted the stones inside the well-box, their silks glassy with trapped moisture; a honeyvine circled the well-box half around and runners pierced the crevices. The bucket snatched leaves with its ears in passing up and down. The water tasted swampy. And yet I asked, "The word? From whom did you get it?"

"My business is well cleaning," he said, muffling a sneeze, "and your neighbors below begged, 'Stop at the place of the lone-living man on Mule Creek. When you come within a throw you'll hear a typing box going like starving woodpeckers. Go, for he'll never know to have his well freshened, snakes and lizards a-falling down, creating disease.' I heard no typing box, but I thinks to myself, 'They ought to be a house yonder, up them side-waters. I want to see that typing box.'"

"I'm proud to get my well cleaned," I said. In truth it hadn't been done properly since I had come to live at the place, and I'd had to be content drawing the water off after rainy spells and fishing the bottom with frog gig and grabhooks. The well-top was a single slab of rock, with a bucket-hole chiseled in the middle, and only the smallest-boned of men could pass through. Here was one fitted by nature for the undertaking.

He began to unlace his shoes. He rid chest and bladed shoulders of the shirt he wore. From the budget he drew work breeches, and he went behind the well-box to change. The breeches were wet, and I judged he had worked in a well downcreek. He called, "'Gin to raise the sour water."

While I drew off the water and threw it on the ground, the well digger rested in the shade of the honeyvines, his head thrown back against the stiff vines on a latch of arms, sneezing and talking. As the sweep had lately begun to guide to one side, striking the bucket against the far wall, I knotted a rope to a pail and raised the water by hand. Swift drawing was necessary to keep ahead of the seeping well-spring.

"Climbing down wells is a blessing to a hay sufferer," the fellow said. "Cool, dampy, no dust to the air. I'd be happy to live below when the weeds are spitting powder. All a man can do who's poor to his pocket is to work in mines or dig wells, and both I've done. They struck me out of the mines on age. Now, the rich, I hear, go to live upon the oceans, shunning the rag blossom. Oh I've cried and snorted my life through."

He paused now and then to sniffle and sneeze and to wipe his eyes and nose. He told me a bit about himself. "Born in West Virginia, raised in Tennessee, come on a purpose to Kentucky. I'm a three-state citizen. Where mountains rise, I'm at home." He'd had two wives and lost both by death. "Two women have waited on me," he said. He had daughters living here and yon, Tennessee mostly, and a son in the north, he didn't know where.

And when he mentioned his son his words rang as if spoken into a churn. "We raised him sigoggling opposite to the right way. After four daughters we were tickled to have a man-child. We pampered and petted. Upon my word and honor he took to whiskey while a chap, went nigh direct from tit to bottle. I hided him scandalous, beat him till he got too big to handle. In jail and out he was for fifteen years, and me tomfool bailing him out. I'd not bail him now if he was frying in torment, for a lesson. Last year he got into bad trouble and headed north, and before he left he says, 'Pap, I've taken my last drink, my final-last,' and I was so sick to my heart over his sorry life I says, 'The last is what the shoemaker killed his daddy with.' He couldn't stay sober and out of jail handcuffed to a preacher."

I drew the well as empty as could be got, and when the bucket began to rise with scarcely a cup of water he made ready to go down. He tied the rope to the sweep standard and raised tiptoe on child-sized feet upon the well cover to secure the knot. He swung his weight to test it. Tears fell from his eyes as incidentally as rain. He grasped the rope and spun into the well. The step-holes having long since fallen out, he descended hand over hand, his almost-prehensile feet clasping the rope. The mud on the bottom reached to the caps of his knees.

He scooped mud into the bucket with his hands, and I drew it to the surface and heaped it aside to daub the cracks between the logs of the house. The mud smelled of flag-swamps, of ancient fern bogs, and I suspect of the fragrance of the earth on the first day of creation. To get such clay I would have had to go a distance up Laurel where high waters had uncovered a deposit. The clay is yellow while damp, drying to chalky white—a mortar and a paint costing only the elbow grease required to dig and transport, good to plug smoke leaks in a chimney, daub walls, and whiten fireplaces and hearths, and, I've been told, an excellent physic when pills of it are swallowed.

I searched the watery mud, dribbling it up in the heap, discovering the pink joint of a crawdabber's leg, a sodden handle of a drinking gourd, the lip and neck of a pitcher, willow leaves, and a house-cricket with hind legs drawn as for leaping and with antennae unbroken. When the last of the mud had been removed, the well cleaner hand-walked the rope to strip away the honeyvines, and he used a finger as a spindle upon which to wind the spiders' webs. He jerked at the vines as if to remove them forever; he wrought a brief stay against the nature of the well. A season's growth would replace the vine whips, the mud attain its accustomed depth after the first rainy spell, the spiders spread a new cloth overnight. He descended to the bottom again, calling up to me to lower a handful of table salt in the bucket, and when he had got it scattered it about. He stood below with clear water rising slowly about his ankles.

I called down to him: "Are you ready to come out?"

His chin pointed upward. "I'm giving my lungs a vacation," he said.

He climbed out presently, eyes clear and dry, face screwed into a grin. "A wonder all that gom didn't give you a disease," he blurted. He glanced darkly at the pile of mud. "Ought to haul that gom away before it driddles back into the well. It's onhealthy."

I told of finding a host of clay figures at the white mud deposit on Laurel. Children had created images of man and beast and left them to dry in the sun. The figures had great ears and hollow eye sockets, nostrils flared and mouths open. One example of statuary was uncommonly imaginative: six grotesque heads were stacked head on head, totem-fashion. And though I didn't relate it to Mr. Maggers, I had glimpsed the statuette of a woman lying on a Rapps Creek doorstep, formed with startling anatomical precision. It lay fresh-made, damp and yellow. The man of the house had come out to quiet the dogs as I entered the yard and also discovered the mud figure. His jaws had flushed. He flung his hat over it, mumbling angrily, "I'll wring that young 'uns neck." Mr. Maggers grunted. "Not a wonder chaps get wormy, playing in filth." He went behind the well-box. He returned wearing dry clothes, the wet garments wrung and folded, pondering my revelation. I could see a sermon rising in him, the way his hands lifted, palms open, the folded breeches raised in hand like the Book. As Letch Jackson once said of a certain commonwealth's attorney, you could see the worms of thought behind his eyes. "In old times," Mr. Maggers preached, "they was a heathen, and his name was Aaron, and he set him up some images." His arms fell, his voice lowered. "And he come on evil days."

The customary well-cleaning fee was one dollar. Mr. Maggers accompanied me into the house to get his pay, and to see the typewriter. He clenched the bill into a fist, the green ends sticking out, and did not pocket it. He watched the machine uncovered, the paper rolled onto the platen, the specimen lines typed—"The sly brown fox jumped over the slippery log." His gaze was as intent as the sow-cat's when she fancied to leap upon the table and sit beside the clicking mechanism, bowing her head when the carriage passed over, whiskers flicking at the bell's tap, and thrusting a paw at a key as if to snag a mouse.

"I've seen typewriters in plenty," Mr. Maggers explained, "but they were ever sitting aside, like a play-pretty." He recalled the first, thirty-odd years past in a lawyer's office at Stone Eagle, Old Virginia. It had rested under a glass bell. "I thought to myself, that trick must be tender, kept beneath glass like a pound of butter."

I typed his name, the letters in capitals, underscored, trailed by an asterisk:

MR. THOMAS LANCE MAGGERS*

"That's me," he beamed. He hummed enviously. "If I could work a trick like that I'd write a sight of letters—I'd write letters to the nation. Bet you've blacked many a page." Yet when I urged him to write his own name he shook his head. "Ah, no," he said, "I might sprain the box." He questioned, "Ever do a job of writing for other people?" And he lifted his fist, holding up the money I had paid him. "I've got a dollar's worth of letters I want wrote."

"This will make us square and even on the well-cleaning," I said. "You keep the dollar."

He pocketed the bill. His face sobered and his eyes cut back against the wall. He said, "I want letters writ to the head policeman of every city of north United States."

I typed his message to the police chief of New York City, he dictating at my elbow: "I want to know if my boy, Jasper Maggers, is in your jailhouse, and if he is I want to know. I don't aim to try bailing him out, for I wouldn't bail him out of hell if his shirttail was on fire. I just want to know where he is, and I'll be mightily obliged if you'll write to me and say if you've got him. I'm his daddy, asking." I made copies of the message and directed them to the chiefs-of-police of Boston, Philadelphia, and Chicago.

His voice had husked as he spoke. Tears welled in his eyes and beaded his cheeks. He dabbed at them angrily. "The plagued hay fever," he said. "I'm hay suffering."

I Love My Rooster

We lived in Houndshell mine camp the year of the coal boom, and I remember the mines worked three shifts a day. The conveyors barely ceased their rusty groaning for five months. I recollect the plenty there was, and the silver dollars rattling wherever men walked; and I recollect the goldfinches stayed that winter through, their yellow breasts turning mole-gray.

We were eating supper on a November evening when Sim Brannon, the foreman, came to tell Father of the boom. Word came that sudden. Father talked alone with Sim in the front room, coming back to the kitchen after a spell. A chuckle of joy broke in his throat as he sat down at the table again, swinging the baby off the floor onto his knee. He reached for the bowl of shucky beans, shaping a hill of them on his plate with a spoon. Never had he let us play with victuals. "They've tuk the peg off o' coal," he said. "Government's pulled the price tag. Coal will be selling hand over fist."

The baby stuck a finger into the bean mound. Father didn't scold. Mother lifted the coffeepot, shaking the spout clear of grounds. "I never heard tell it had a peg," she said.

Fern and Lark and I looked at Father, wondering what a coal peg was. The baby's face was bright and wise, as if he knew.

Father thumped the table, marking his words. "I say it's ontelling what a ton o' coal will sell for. They's a lack afar north at the big lakes and in countries across the waters. I figure the price will double or treble." He lifted a hand over the baby's head. "Yon blue sky might be the limit."

Our heads turned toward the window. We saw only the night sky, dark as gob smoke.

Mother set the coffeepot down, for it began to tremble in her hand. She thrust a stick of wood into the stove, though supper was done and the room warm. "Will there be plenty in the camps?" she asked, uncertain.

Father laughed, spoon in air. "Best times ever hit this country," he said, jarring the table. "Why, I'm a-liable to draw twice the pay I get now." He paused, staring at us. We sat as under a charm, listening. "We're going to feed these chaps till they're fat as mud," he went on. "Going to put proper clothes on their backs and buy them a few pretties. We'll live like folks were born to live. This hardscrabble skimping I'm tired of. We're going to fare well."

The baby made a cluck with his tongue, trying to talk. He squeezed a handful of beans until they popped between his fingers.

"For one thing," Father said, "I'm going to buy me a pair o' high-top boots. These clodhoppers I'm wearing have wore a half acre o' bark off my heels."

The cracked lids of the stove began to wink. Heat grew in the room.

"I want me a fact'ry dress," Fern spoke.

"I need me a shirt," I said. "A boughten shirt. And I want a game rooster. One that'll stand on my shoulder and crow."

Father glanced at me, suddenly angry.

"Me," Lark began, "I want—" But he could not think what he wanted most of all.

"A game rooster!" Father exclaimed. "They's too many gamble cocks in this camp already. Why, I'd a' soon buy you a pair o' dice and a card deck. I'd a' soon."

"A pet rooster wouldn't harm a hair," I said, the words small and stubborn in my throat. And I thought of one-eyed Fedder Mott, who oft played mumbly-peg with me, and who went to the rooster matches at the Hack. Fedder would tell of the fights, his eye patch shaking, and I would wonder what there was behind the patch. I'd always longed to spy.

"No harm, as I see, in a pet chicken," Mother said.

"I want me a banty," Lark said.

Father grinned, his anger gone. He batted an eye at Mother. "We hain't going into the fowl business," he said. "That's for shore." He gave the baby a spoonful of beans. "While ago I smelled fish on Sim Brannon—fried salt fish he'd just et for supper. I'm a-mind to buy a whole wooden kit o' mackerel. We'll be able."

Mother raised the window a grain, yet it seemed no less hot. She sat down at the foot of the table. The baby jumped on Father's knee, reaching arms toward her. His lips rounded, quivering to speak. A bird sound came out of his mouth.

"I bet he wants a pretty-piece bought for him," Fern said.

"By juckers," Father said, "if they was a trinket would larn him to talk, I'd buy it." He balanced the baby in the palm of a hand and held him straight out, showing his strength. Then he keened his eyes at Mother. "You hain't said what you want. All's had their say except you."

Mother stared into her plate. She studied the wedge print there. She did not lift her eyes.

"Come riddle, come riddle," Father said impatiently.

"The thing I want hain't a sudden idea," Mother said quietly. Her voice seemed to come from a long way off. "My notion has followed me through all the coal camps we've lived in, a season here, a span there, forever moving. Allus I've aimed to have a house built on the acres we heired on Shoal Creek o' Troublesome. Fifteen square acres we'd have to raise our chaps proper. Garden patches to grow victuals. Elbowroom a-plenty. Fair times and bad, we'd have a roof-tree. Now, could we save half you make, we'd have enough money in time."

"Half?" Father questioned. "Why, we're going to start living like folks. Fittin clothes on our backs, food a body can enjoy." He shucked his coat, for he sat nearest the stove. He wiped sweat beads off his forehead.

"I need me a shirt," I said. "A store-bought shirt." More than a game rooster, more than anything, I wanted a shirt made like a man's. Being eight years old, I was ashamed to wear the ones Mother sewed without tails to stuff inside my breeches.

"No use living bare-bones in the midst o' plenty," Father said. "Half is too much."

Mother rose from the table and leaned over the stove. She looked inside to see if anything had been left to burn. She tilted the coffeepot, making sure it hadn't boiled dry. "Where there's a boom one place," she said, "there's bound to be a famine in another. Coal gone high, and folks not able to pay." Her lips trembled. "Fires gone out. Chaps chill and sick the world over withouten a roof above their heads." She picked up the poker, lifted a stove cap, and shook the embers. Drops of water began to fry on the stove. She was crying.

"Be-grabbies!" Father said. "Stop poking that fire! This room's already hot as a ginger mill."

On a Saturday afternoon Father brought his two-week pay pocket home, the first since the boom. He came into the kitchen, holding it aloft, unopened. Mother was cooking a skillet of meal mush and the air was heavy with the good smell. I was in haste to eat and go, having promised Fedder Mott to meet him at the schoolhouse gate. Fedder and I planned to climb the mine tipple.

"Corn in the hopper and meal in the sack," Father said, rattling the pocket.

He let Fern and Lark push fingers against it, feeling the greenbacks inside; and he gave it to the baby to play with upon the floor, watching out of the tail of his eye. Mother was uneasy with Father's carelessness. The baby opened his mouth, clucking, churring. He made a sound like a wren setting a nest of eggs.

"Money, money," Fern said, trying to teach him.

He twisted his lips, his tongue straining. But he could not speak a word.

"I'd give every red cent to hear him say one thing," Father said.

The pay pocket was opened, the greenbacks spread upon the table. We had never seen such a bounty. Father began to figure slowly with fingers and lips. Fern counted swiftly. She could count nearly as fast as the Houndshell schoolteacher.

Father paused, watching Fern. "This chap can out-count a check-weigh-man," he bragged.

"Sixty-two dollars and thirty cents," Fern announced, and it was right, for Mother had counted too. "Wisht I had me a fact'ry dress," Fern said.

"I want a shirt hain't allus a-gaping at the top o' my breeches," I said.

Father wrinkled his forehead. "These chaps need clothes, I reckon. And I've got my fancy set on a pair o' boots. They's no use going about like raggle-taggle gypsies with money in hand. We're able to live decent."

"Socks and stockings I've knit," Mother said, "and shirts and dress garments I've sewed a-plenty for winter. They hain't made by store pattern, but they'll wear and keep a body warm. Now, I'm willing to do without and live hard to build a homeplace."

"Oh I'm willing, too," Father complained, "but a man likes to get his grunt and groan in." He gathered the greenbacks, handing them to Mother. He stacked the three dimes. "Now, if I wasn't allus seeing the money, I could save without hurt. Once hit touches my sight and pocket, I'm afire. I burn to spend."

Mother rolled the bills. She thrust them into an empty draw sack, stowing all in her bosom. "One thing you could do," she told Father, "but it's not for me to say do or not do. If you was a-mind, you could bring the pay pockets home unopened. We'd not think to save just half. I'd save all we could bear, spend what was needed. You'd not see the spark of a dime till we got enough for a house. I say this boom can't last eternal."

Father pulled his eyebrows, deciding. The baby watched. How like a bird he cocked his head. "Oh I'm a-mind," Father said at last, "but the children ought to have a few coins to pleasure themselves with. A nickel a week."

"I want mine broke in pennies," Lark called.

Fern counted swiftly, speaking in dismay, "It would take me nigh a year to save enough for an ordered dress."

"We'll not lack comfort nor pleasure," Mother promised. "Nor will we waste. The chaps can have the nickel. You get a pair o' boots—a pair not too costy. And we'll buy a kit o' fish."

She stirred butter into the meal mush, and it was done. Fern hurried dishes upon the table.

"The pair my head was set on cost eighteen dollars. Got toes so sharp you could kick a blacksnake's eye out. Reckon I'll just make these clodbusters I got on do."

"Them boots must o' been sprigged with gold tacks."

A buttery steam rose from our plates. We dipped up spoonfuls of mush; we scraped our dishes, pushing them back for more.

"Hit's good to see no biled leather breeches on the table for once," Father said. He blew on a spoon of mush to cool it for the baby. "Right today I'll buy that kit o' fish."

"They're liable to draw every cat in Houndshell Holler. Better you plug the cat hole in the back door first."

I slid from the table bench, pulling my hat off a peg.

"Where are you traipsing to?" Father asked.

"Going to play with Fedder Mott. He's yonder in the schoolyard."

"I know Fedder Mott," Lark spoke, gulping much. "He's a boy jist got one eyeball."

I ran the Houndshell road. A banjo twanged among the houses. A hundred smokes stirred in chimney pots, rising, threading chilly air. I reached the schoolhouse, breathing hard, and Fedder Mott was swinging on the gate. He jumped down.

"I'd nigh give you out," he said, his blue eye wide.

I said, "If my pap knowed about the tipple, I'd not got to come."

Fedder leaned against the fence. He was a full head taller than I, a year older. He drew a whack of tobacco from a hind pocket, bit a squirrely bite, and offered the cut to me.

I shook my head.

He puckered his lips, speaking around the wad in his jaw. "They hain't nothing worth seeing in that tipple tower. I done climbed thar." He waited, champing teeth into the wad, making juice to spit. "I'd figured we'd go to the rooster fight. Now you've come too late."

"Was I to go," I said, "my pap would tear up stakes."

Two children ran by, playing tag-o. A man came walking the road. Fedder spat into a rut. The black patch trembled on his face. It was like a great dark eye, dwarfing the blue one. I looked at it curiously.

"Afore long, fellers will be coming down from the Hack," Fedder said. "We'll larn which roosters whooped."

I studied the eye patch. It was the size of a silver dollar, hanging by a string looped around his head. What lay behind it? Was there a hole square into his skull? I was almost ashamed to ask, almost afraid. I drew a circle on the ground with my shoe toe, measuring the words: "I'll go to the rooster fight sometime, if one thing—"

"If'n what?"

"If you'll let me see your eye pocket."

Fedder blew the tobacco cud across the road. He pushed the long tails of his shirt inside his breeches. "You'll spy and won't go."

"'F'ad die."

We saw a man walking the path off the ridge, coming toward us from the Hack. He came fast, though he was still too distant to be named. We watched him wind the crooked path and be lost among the houses.

"Ag'in' we go to the cockpit," Fedder said, "I'll let you look."

"I choose now."

Fedder stood firm. "Ag'in' that time, I will." He hushed a moment, listening for the man who came from the ridge. "Afore long I'll not be wearing this patch," he said. "I've heered o' glass eyeballs. Hit's truth. They say even a hound dog wears one in Anvers camp. Five round dollars they cost, and could I grab a holt on that much, I'd git the schoolteacher to mail an order."

"Won't your pap buy you a glass 'un?"

"If'n I was a flycatcher, he wouldn't feed me gnats."

"I'm going to save money, come every week. I've got me something in my head to buy."

"Hit reads in a magazine where a feller kin sell garden seeds and make a profit. A hundred packages o' squash and dill and turnip sold, and I'd have me enough."

We saw the man afar off on the road. He was heading our way, walking a hippety-hop on short legs.

"Bulger Hyden," Fedder said.

Fedder hailed him as he reached the schoolhouse gate, and he stopped. He shed his coat, being warm from haste, and he wore a green-dotted shirt.

"Who whooped?" Fedder asked.

Bulger Hyden's face grew wrinkled as a doty mushroom; he swung his arms emptily, glancing at the sky's promise of weather. There was a hint of snow. Goldfinches blew over us like leaves, piping their dry winter song above the conveyor's ceaseless rattle.

"Steph Harben's Red Pyle rimwrecked my Duckwing," Bulger grumbled. "Steph fotched that bird from West Virginia and scratches in all the money.

I say it hain't fair pitting a furrin cock." He folded his coat, balancing it on an elbow crotch, making ready to go. "I thought a sight o' my little Duckwing." His voice hoarsened. "I cherished that rooster." And he went on, and I looked after him, thinking a green-speckled shirt was the choicest garment ever a fellow could wear.

Winter came before I could go to the Hack. Snow fell late in November and scarcely left the ground for two months. The rooster fights were halted until spring. I recollect the living river of wind pouring down Houndshell Hollow. For bird and varmint, and, I hear, for folk beyond the camps, it was a lean time. But miners fared well. I recollect the warm linsey coats, the red woolen gloves, the high-top boots; I recollect full pokes of food going into houses, and the smell of cooking victuals. Children wore store clothes. They bought spin-tops and pretties at the commissary. Boys' pockets clinked money. Only Fedder Mott and I had to wind our own balls and whittle our tops. I hoarded the nickels Mother gave me, telling Fedder I might buy a shirt when enough had been saved. Fedder never had a penny. He spoke bitterly of it. "My pap wouldn't plait me shucks if'n I was a chair bottom." And he said, "I hear tell hit's might' nigh the same with yore pap. Hit's told the eagle squalls when he looses a dollar."

Mother spent little. We hardly dared complain, having already more than we had known before. Once, in January, Father tried to figure the amount of money Mother had stored in the draw sack. He marked with a stub pencil, and Mother watched. At last he let the baby have the pencil. "My wage has riz three times," he said hopelessly, "though I don't know how much. Why, fellers tell me they're getting twelve and fifteen dollars a day. Deat Sheldon claims he made twenty dollars, four days handrunning, but he works a fold in the gravy tunnel and can load standing up."

"I've no idea o' the sum we've got," Mother said. "I opened one pay pocket and we're living out of it. The rest I've kept sealed."

"How's a body to know when a plenty's been saved? I hain't in a notion yet setting aside for tombstone and coffin box. Fellers in the mines 'gin to say the buffalo bellows when I spend a nickel."

"If you long for a thing enough, you'll give up for it. You'll sacrifice. The coal famine is bound to end some day. Come that time, we'll fit the house to the money."

Father began to tease. "What say we count the greenbacks? My curiosity is being et raw."

"Now, no. Hit would be a temptation to spend."

The baby sat up, threshing the air, puckering his lips. We looked, and he had bitten the rubber tip off the pencil.

"Hain't he old enough to be saying words?" Father asked.

"He talked to a cat once," Lark said. "I heered him."

"Ah, now," Mother chided. "Just a sound he made. Cats follow stealing in since we bought salt fish. Can't keep the cat hole plugged."

"He said 'kigid.'"

"That hain't a word," Fern said.

Father poked a finger at the baby. "By gollyard, if he'd just speak one word!"

The baby lifted his arms, mouth wide, neck stretched. He crowed.

"Thar's your rooster," Father chuckled, setting his eyes on me.

"I aim to own a real gamer," I bragged, irked by Father's teasing. "I aim to." I spoke without hope, not knowing that by spring it would come true.

"A good thing to have this double zero weather," Father drawled. "Hit driv the poker players and fowl gamblers indoors. But fellers claim that when the weather mends they'll be rooster fights in the Hack three days a week. Hit's high-low-jack, and them fools lose every button cent."

Mother searched the baby's mouth for the pencil tip. "I call this boom a gamble," she said. "It's bound to end." She didn't find the rubber tip, for the baby had swallowed it down.

I told Fedder of Mother's prophecy as we sat by a fire on the creek bank. We had fishhooks in an ice hole.

"Be-hopes the boom lasts till I git me a glass eye," he said. "My mind's set on it. I'd better have a batch o' garden seeds ordered and start selling."

"You couldn't stick a pickax in the ground, it's so froze," I told him. "Folks haven't a notion to buy seeds now."

Fedder rubbed his hands over the blaze, blowing a foggy breath. "I say winter hain't going to last forever neither."

I recollect thinking the long cold spell would never end. January diddled, and February crawled. March warmed a bit, thawing. The breasts of goldfinches turned yellow as rubbed gold again. Fedder got his seeds, though when he should have been peddling them he'd climb the ridge to the rooster fights. Oft when a rooster was killed they'd let him bring the dead fowl home. Father forbade my going to the Hack; he put his foot down. But next to seeing was Fedder's telling. I came to know the names of the bravest cocks. I knew their markings, and the way they fought.

Fedder whistled for me one Thursday evening at the edge of dark. I heard and went outside, knowing his Kentucky redbird call. He stood beyond the fence with a coffee sack bundled in his arms; and he seemed fearful and anxious, and yet proud. His blue eye was wide, and the black patch had a living look. Packages of seeds rattled in his pockets.

"How much money have you mized?" he asked. "How much?" His voice was a husky whisper.

I guessed what the bundle held, scarcely daring to believe. I grew feverish with wonder.

"Eleven nickels," I said. "I couldn't save all."

The coffee sack moved; something threshed inside. A fowl's wings struck its thighs.

"I'm a-mind to sell you half ownership in my rooster," he said. "I will for yore eleven nickels, and if you'll keep him till I find a place. My pap would wring hits neck if I tuk him home."

I touched the bundle. My hand trembled. I shook with joy. "I been saving to buy a shirt," I said. "I want me a boughten shirt."

"You couldn't save enough by Kingdom Come. Eleven nickels, and jist you pen him. We'll halvers."

"Who'd he belong to?"

"Fotch the money. All's got to be helt a secret."

I brought my tobacco-sack bank and Father's mine lamp. We stole under the house, penning the rooster in a hen-coop. Father's voice droned over us in the kitchen. Fedder lit the lamp to count the money. The rooster stood blinking, red-eyed, alert. His shoulders were white, redding at the wing bows. Blood beads tipped his hackle feathers. His spurs were trimmed to fit gaffs. It was Steph Harben's Red Pyle.

"How'd you come by him?" I insisted.

"He fit Ebo, the black Cuban, and got stumped. He keeled down. They was a cut on his throat and you'd a-thought him knob dead. Steph give him to me, and ere I reached the camp, he come alive. That thar cut was jist a scratch."

We crawled from beneath the house. Fedder smothered the light. "Don't breathe this to a soul," he warned. "Steph would auger to git him back, and my pap would throw duck fits. Now, you bring him to the schoolhouse ag'in' two o'clock tomorrow."

He moved toward the gate, the nickels ringing in his pocket. I went into the house and sat quietly behind the stove, feeling lost without my money, though recompensed by the rooster.

Father spoke, trotting the baby to Burnham Bright on a foot. "Warm weather's come," he mused. "Seems to me the Houndshell company ought to pare down on mining. Two days ago they hired four new miners, fellers from away yander."

"I know a boy come from Alabamy," Lark said. "I bet he's from yonside the waters."

"It's United States, America," Fern said.

"Sim Brannon believes something's bound to crack before long," Father went on. "Says hit's liable to come sudden. I'm in hopes my job don't split off."

"Come that time," Mother said, "maybe we'll have plenty saved for a house."

Father reached the baby to Mother. "I'm going to bed early," he yawned. "Last night I never got sixty winkles o' sleep. I reckon every tomcat in this camp was miaowing on the back porch."

"The fish draws 'em."

"A tinker man tapped on the door yesterday," Fern said, "and a big nanny cat ran in betwixt his legs."

"Hit's the one baby talked a word to," Lark said.

Father stretched sleepily. "I'm afeared the baby's a mute," he said. He set his chair aside. "The only thing that'd keep me awake this night would be counting the money we've got stacked away."

I waited at the schoolhouse gate, holding the rooster by the shanks. He snuggled against my jump jacket, pecking at the buttons. He stuck his head in my jacket pocket to see what was there. After a spell Fedder came, his eye patch trembling and the garden seeds as noisy upon him as grass crickets.

"Why'n't you kiver him?" he asked crossly. "He might a-been seen."

"He flopped the coffee sack off," I said. "Anyhow, he's been seen already. Crowed this morning before blue daylight and woke my pap. If I hadn't cried like gall, he'd been killed. Now it's your turn to keep."

Fedder bit a chew of tobacco, bit it with long front teeth as a squirrel bites. He spat into the road and looked up and down. "If I tuk him to my house, he'd be in the skillet by dinner." He closed his eye to think, and there was only the black patch staring. "I figure Steph Harben will buy him back. He's yonside the commissary, playing draughts. Air you of a notion?"

The cock lifted his head, poising it left and right. I loosed my hold about his legs and stroked his bright saddle. He sat on my arm.

"This rooster's a pet," I said. "When I tuk him out o' the coop, he jumped square onto my shoulder and crowed. I'm taking a liking to him."

"I jist lack selling fourteen seed papers gitting my eyeball. Never could I sell dills and rutabagas. If Steph will buy the rest, I'll rid my part. We got nowheres earthy to store a chicken."

"I hain't a-mind to sell."

Fedder packed the ground where he stood. The seeds rattled. The rooster pricked his head.

"You stay here till I git Steph," Fedder said. He swung around. "You stay."

He went in haste, and suddenly a great silence fell in the camp. The coal conveyor at the mines had stopped. Men stood at the drift mouth and looked down upon the rooftops. It was so still I could hear the far *per-chic-o-ree* of finches. I held the rooster at arm's length, wishing him free as a bird. I half hoped he would fly away. I set him on the fence, but he hopped to my shoulder and shook his wattles.

Back along the road came Fedder. Steph Harben hastened with him, wearing a shirt like striped candy, and never a man wore a finer one. The shirt was thinny—so thin that when he stood before me I could see the paddles of his collarbones.

Fedder said, "I've sold my part. Hit's you two trading."

Steph said, "Name yore price. Name."

I gathered the fowl in my arms. "I hain't a-mind to sell," I said.

We turned to stare at miners passing, going home long before quitting time, their cap lamps burning in broad day.

Steph was anxious. "Why hain't you willing?" he asked. "Name."

I dug my toe into the ground, scuffing dirt. "I love my rooster," I said. But I looked at Steph's shirt. It was very beautiful.

"If'n you'll sell," Fedder promised, "I'll let you spy at my eye pocket. Now, while it's thar, you kin look. Afore long I'll have a glass 'un."

I kicked a clod into the road. "I'll swap my part o' the rooster for that striped shirt. It can be cut down to fit."

"Shuck it off," Fedder told Steph.

Steph unbuttoned the shirt, slipped it over the blades of his shoulders, and handed it to me in a wad. He snatched the rooster, lighting out for home, and miners along the road glared at his bare back.

Fedder brushed his hat aside, catching the eye patch between forefinger and thumb. I was suddenly afraid, suddenly having no wish to see.

The patch was lifted. I looked, stepping back, squeezing the shirt into a ball. I turned running, running with this sight burnt upon my mind.

I ran all the way home, going into the kitchen door as Father went, not staying the sow-cat that stole in between my legs. Mother sat at the table, a pile of greenbacks before her, the empty pay pockets crumpled.

"Hell's bangers!" Father gasped, dropping heavily upon a chair and lifting the baby to his knee; and when he could speak above his wonder, "The boom's busted. I've got no job." But he laughed, and Mother smiled.

"I've heard already," Mother said. She laid a hand upon the money bills, flicking them under a thumb like a deck of gamble cards. "There's enough here to build a house, a house with windows looking out o' every room. And a grain left for a pair o' costy boots, a boughten shirt, a fact'ry dress, a few pretties."

The baby opened his mouth, curling his lips, pointing a stub finger. He pointed at the old nanny smelling the fish kit.

"Cat!" he said, big as life.

Snail Pie

Though Maw's face was pale with anger, she didn't speak until Grandpaw Splicer and Leaf and I pushed back our plates. Grandpaw went to the barn to light his pipe, and Leaf followed to ask about the rattlesnake steak Grandpaw claimed he once ate. I crawled under the house, squatting beneath the kitchen floor, listening. I had a mind to learn whether Pap was going to tell of catching me chewing a wad of Old Nine. Maw was as set as a wedge against tobacco. She wouldn't spare the limber-jim. I heard her heel strike the floor impatiently; I heard the rounds of Pap's chair groan in the peg holes.

"Your step-paw has to hush his lie-tales at the table," Maw said, her voice pitching high in her nose. "Since he's come a meal hasn't rested easy in my stomach. We ought to send him back to the county farm."

"Forty years a drummer," Pap said, "forty years of drumming the mountain counties. He's too old to change his ways." The leather of Pap's shoes creaked. "Without a line of big-eyed lies he couldn't have sold gnat balls and devil's snuff boxes. That's what he vows peddling. He's always been a big hand to tease, and means no harm."

"Every time he sticks his feet under the table he talks of pickled ants or fried snails. His idee of being funny. The name of snails I never could stand, much less than the sight of them. Why, my innards turn at the word. And that pipe, foul as a pig pen. I told him straight off a whiff of tobacco smoke sickens me. I warned him to keep it outside of the house."

"Paw's a right smart company for the boys," Pap reminded. In my head I could see him saucering his coffee and blowing across it. "Keeps them occupied, and from under foot. Before he came I couldn't go bird-hunting without them whining to be along." Bird-hunting was Pap's delight. Maw called it his foolishness.

Maw's voice dropped from anger to dull complaint, "Doty and childish,

216

worse than a child. My opinion, his mind is slipping. Why, he might even teach the boys to smoke. I can't get Todd to say what he talks about to them, but Leaf once did. He told an awful thing about a mole."

"Aye, I figure Pap keeps a good eye on the boys. You'd not know they were wormy if he hadn't found out. And he offered to locate some boneset to purge them."

"I'm no witch to start brewing herb tea," Maw said. "A bottle of vermifuge from the store will do the job."

"Come spring," Pap said, "Paw can hoe the garden. Nothing and nobody will fight weeds like an old man. I'll pay him a little to keep him in heart."

"We promised to try him for a month," Maw said. "A single month and not a day beyond." Her words were cold and level. "For three weeks he's been here, and he brings up the subject of moles, slugs, or fish bait every meal. I say you've got to speak to him. He'll quieten or go back to the county farm. The next time he mentions snails—"

Pap clapped his empty saucer against the tabletop. "You oughtn't be so finicky," he declared. He shoved back his chair and got up. I heard dishes clink fit to break. "I hate like rip to call the old man down. I hate to." And then, anger rising, he blurted, "Putting one's kin in the poorhouse is a lately-happening business. A scandal shame! For all time past the agey have been cared for at home, pampered in their last days, indulged and cherished."

"If you'd heard what he told Leaf," Maw countered, her voice shrill. Pap's hand was surely twisting the doorknob. "If you'd heard—"

Pap slammed the door so fiercely the skillets rattled behind the stove.

I hurried from under the house and ran to the barn. Leaf stalked the calf lot on johnny-walkers Grandpaw Splicer had made for him. Grandpaw sat in the crib whittling a cob, smoking and chewing. He was shaping a new pipe bowl with his Barlow knife.

"Grandpaw," I said, "you never did tell me about that mole."

Grandpaw Splicer's eyes rounded, questioning. "Mole?" he made strange.

"You told Leaf," I reminded, acting slighted.

"Ah, yes," Grandpaw said, "what some fellers done with a mole varmint."

He blew a tobacco cud onto a shuck. He knocked pipe ashes into a crack.

Then he opened his mouth suddenly, stuck out his tongue, and drew it back in, exploring. "By the gods!" he said, "I've lost another tooth." He spied into the shuck, and there it was. He pulled out his false plate to inspect the gap in it. "I need me a new set of teeth, but I've no money. It would take many a frog skin. Before long I'll have to gum my food and tobacco."

"I heard Pap say he was aiming to pay you a wage," I said. "I did, now."

"Ho!" Grandpaw breathed. The blue flecks in his watery eyes shone. "Ah!" He looked almost happy. He pitched the tooth into a poke of seed corn and said, "There's one grain that will never sprout." And he began to whack at the nub of the cob in earnest. A kink of smoke twisted from his pipe and the crib filled with the mellow smell of tobacco, ripe and sweet and pungent.

I watched the shaping of the cob, drawing in deep breaths of burning tobacco. "Grandpaw," I said, "I wish you were making that 'un for me."

Grandpaw grunted, clicking his dental plates. "I knowed of a baby once was learnt to smoke in the cradle. Rather to draw on a pipe than his mammy's tit. Gee-o, if that little 'un didn't grow up to be six feet and weighed two hundred pounds. Tobacco was good for his constitution."

"I've been smoking a spell," I confessed.

Grandpaw chuckled. "I figured it was you who slobbered on my pipe stem yesterday. That's why I'm whittling a new one."

"Be the old 'un for me?" I questioned, hoping.

"Now, no," Grandpaw said, "your mommy hates tobacco like the Devil hates Sunday. She'd hustle me back to the county farm before sundown did I give it to you. But if there comes a day you're bound to smoke, just steal this 'un I'm making. I never relished anybody using my regular pipe. People oughten to smoke after each other. Onhealthy."

The bowl of the pipe was nearly finished. Only the marrow of the cob lacked scraping.

"Grandpaw," I said, "I'm scared you're a-going to be sent back. I heard Mommy talking."

"Hear!" Grandpaw chuffed. He put the Barlow down slowly and the pipe bowl fell from his hand. He dipped into the seed corn, filling the pan of his hand with grains, lifting, pouring. His lower lip stuck out blue and swollen, the gray bag of his chin quivered. "Todd," he spoke, "you tell me exactly what your mommy said and I'll chop you out a pair of johnny-walkers like your brother's."

"I choose that pipe," I bargained.

"I'd rather to die than go back," Grandpaw moaned. "Folks there perished already, just won't give up and lay down. Coffin boxes waiting in the wood-shop. A pure death house. Aye, it's cruel. Cruel like what fellers done with a mole once." His eyes dampened, his hands shook, scattering corn. "You know what some jaspers done? They started a mole in the rear end of a bull yearling. That bully ran a mile, taking on terrible, and fell stone down dead."

"I'll keep that pipe tater-holed," I assured. "Nary an eye shall touch it."

"I long to stay on here."

I peeped through the cracks to see that no one was about. Leaf tramped the far side of the lot on his walkers. I told Grandpaw what Mommy had said and he listened, an arm elbow-deep in the corn sack. "Never tell Leaf nary a noth-ing," I warned. "He's bad to repeat. Just six years old, and he doesn't know any better. And don't mention snails."

"I'll play quiet-Bob," Grandpaw said. "By jacks, I will."

We heard Leaf coming *crockety-crock* on his johnny-walkers. He stuck his head in through the door. "Grandpaw," he yelled, his mouth curling with mis-chief, "did you ever eat a horse apple?"

On Saturday Pap went bird-hunting, and there were quails' breasts for dinner, and gravy brown as cured burley. We sat at the table watching Maw cut the breasts in half. She served her plate and passed the dish. Leaf and I had been starved for two days, having taken the vermifuge Thursday and forbidden to eat a bite since. We could hardly wait longer. Our stomachs were about grown together.

Pap grinned at the dish. The breasts were no larger than a child's fist. His jaws set with pride. He had brought down three birds with one of his shots, bagged nine all together; and he had prepared them as well, for Maw would never clean a fowl. He glanced at Grandpaw, seeking a good word for his prow-ess. "Three with one shot," Pap boasted. "You hear me? Three!"

Grandpaw's teeth clicked. His lower lip puckered, and I knew he had thought of something to tell. He raised grizzly eyebrows, wondering if he dared.

"One blast, three bobs," Pap crowed. "And that's no fish tale." His mouth smacked. "Ever see such mud-fat ones?"

"Hit was quare how I killed a bobwhite once," Grandpaw related. He spoke slowly, picking his words, being careful. "Years ago when I lived in the head of Jump Up Hollow I went a-fishing on Shikepoke Creek. I caught so plagued many I had no place to put 'em. I just shucked off my breeches, tied knots in the leg-ends, and filled 'em with the prettiest redeyes and bigmouth bass ever was. So many fish I had to pack that a button popped off. And dadburn if that button didn't fly off and kill a bobwhite."

"Sounds like the truth to me," Pap laughed. "I believe ever word." He winked at Maw. She had stopped eating, uncertain. Then she took another bite. Maw did mortally relish partridge.

Leaf spoke, his mouth full. "Grandpaw, where is Jump Up Hollow? I be to go there."

"Ah," Grandpaw said, poking a lip out. "Why, hit's so far backside of nowhere folks have to use 'possums for yard dogs and owls for roosters."

"I bet that hain't the truth," Leaf said.

"Swear to my thumb to my dum," Grandpaw said.

"I know me a tale and it shore happened," Leaf said. His eyes lit. He glanced at me and Grandpaw. I got a grain fidgety, for Leaf was bad to tittle-tattle.

"Truth?" Maw asked doubtfully. "I say keep it for another occasion. Truth won't spoil." And she served her plate again.

"Hear me," Grandpaw said, thinking back into his skull for another yarn. "It wasn't always good times in Jump Up Hollow. Once a hard winter come. Ninety days snowfall, ninety days hovering zero. Well, s'r, I gave out of bread and I gave out of meat. Not a lick of sweetening was left in the 'lassy barrel. Not a speck of nothing to eat the size of the chine-bone of a gnat."

Maw laid her fork down, waiting. Her mouth was full, but she didn't swallow. I tried to catch Grandpaw's eyes but he was carried away in his telling. He paid me no mind. He lifted a hand, laying off the story-piece. I tried to poke him with a foot under the table but my leg wasn't long enough.

"Well, now," Grandpaw went on, "I got my old hog-rifle and searched the woods. Not a sight or sound of beast or varmint could I see or hear. But hell-o! In the sky there was a buzzard flying. I took hair aim and fetched him down with a single crack, and I 'gin to rip the feathers."

Pap opened his mouth to laugh, but Maw stared angrily at him. She had paled; her lips were tight against her teeth. Pap gulped, undecided. I slid low in my chair and kicked Grandpaw's knee. He grunted. He glanced at me in a fashion to let me understand he wasn't getting carried away.

"Did you cook that there buzzard?" Leaf asked. "Now, no," Grandpaw replied. "I gathered the hungry smell in the meat box, mixed it with frost bite, and fried it with a smidgen of axle grease. Hit made good eating."

Maw swallowed at last. She stared at the victuals in her plate. I felt relieved, though I wished Grandpaw had played quiet-Bob as he had promised.

"I know me a tale," Leaf said, "and hit's the truth. I be to tell it."

"The truth?" Maw asked sharply.

"Gourd-head and tell," Pap joked. I could see he was glad Grandpaw hadn't eaten the buzzard.

"Be certain it is the truth," Maw warned, her voice pitching high and thin. "We could do with some honest speaking."

Grandpaw lifted his chin. He was a whet anxious.

"It was this morning," Leaf began. "That there worm medicine was pinching my stomach."

Maw grasped the tabletop. Her knuckle whitened; her face blanched the color of dough.

"I went in behind the barn," Leaf went on, "and there was Grandpaw and Todd a-smoking. Todd smoking a cob pipe Grandpaw made for him, a-blowing smoke big as Ike Pike. I be to have me a pipe too."

Grandpaw's chin quivered. His shoulders sagged, and he leaned forward and his eyes overflowed. Tears coursed the wrinkles of his cheeks, and he seemed old, old.

Leaf stared and hushed. He couldn't think why Grandpaw Splicer wept. His lips trembled. "Grandpaw," he said, trying to patch the hurt, "did you ever eat a snail pie?"

The Moving

We stood by the loaded wagon while Father nailed the windows down and spat into the keyholes to make the locks turn. We waited, restless as the harnessed mare, anxious to hasten beyond staring eyes. Hardstay mine was closed for all time and idle men had gathered to watch us leave. They hung over the fence; they crowded where last year's dogtick stalks clutched their brown leaf-hands into fists.

I saw the boys glance at our windowpanes, their pockets bulging with rocks. I spied into their faces and homesickness grew large inside of me. I hungered for a word, a nod of farewell. But only a witty was sad at my going, only a child of a man who valued strings and tobacco tags, a chap in a man's clothes who was bound forever to speak things backwards. Hig Sommers stood beg-eyed, and fellows were picking at him. One knelt and jerked loose the eel-strings of his brogans.

Though women watched from their porches only a widow-woman came to say a good-bye to Mother. Sula Basham came walking, tall as a butterweed, and with a yellow locket swinging from her neck like a clockweight.

Loss Tramble spoke, grinning, "If I had a woman that tall, I'd string her with gourds and use her for a martin pole. I would, now." A dry chuckle rattled in the crowd. Loss stepped back, knowing the muscle frogs of her arms were the size of any man's.

Sula towered over Mother. The locket dropped like a plum. Mother was barely five feet tall and she had to look upward as into the sky; and her eyes set on the locket, for never had she owned a grain of gold, never a locket, or a ring, or bighead pin. Sula spoke loudly to Mother, glancing at the men with scorn: "You ought to be proud that your man's not satisfied to rot in Hardstay camp, a-setting on his chine-bone. Before long all's got to move, all's got to roust or starve. This mine hain't opening agin. Hit's too nigh dug out."

The Moving

The men stirred uneasily. Sill Lovelock lifted his arms, spreading them like a preacher's. "These folks air moving to nowheres," he said. "Thar's no camps along the Kentucky River a-taking on hands; they's no work anywheres. Hit's mortal sin to make gypsies of a family. I say as long's a body has got a rooftree, let him roost under it."

Men grunted, doddering their heads, and the boys lifted their rock-heavy pockets and sidled toward the wagon. Cece Goodloe snatched Hig Sommers's hat as he passed, clapping it onto his own head. The hat rested upon his ears. The boys placed their hands on the wagon wheels; they fingered the mare's harness; they raised the lid of the toolbox to see what was in it. Cece crawled under the wagon, back hound to front hound, shaking the swingletree. I watched out of the tail of my eye, thinking a rusty might be pulled.

Father came into the yard with the key, and now the house was shut against our turning back. I looked at the empty hull of our dwelling; I looked at the lost town, yearning to stay in this place where I was born, among the people I knew. Father lifted the key on a finger. "If a body here would drap this key by the commissary," he said, "I'd be obliged."

Hig Sommers lumbered toward Father, his shirttail flying. Someone had shagged his shirt out. "I'll fotch it," Hig cried, stretching both hands for the key as a babe would reach.

"I'm not a-wanting it fotched," Father said. He'd not trust the key to a fellow who wasn't bright. "You've got it back'ards, Hig. I'm wanting it tuk."

Sill Lovelock stepped forward, though he didn't offer to carry the key. "They's Scripture agin' a feller hauling off the innocent," he vowed gravely. "I say, stay where there's a floor underfoot and joists overhead."

Father said testily, "There ought to be a statute telling a feller to salt his own steers. Ruther to drown o' sweat hunting for work than die o' dry rot in Hardstay."

Loss Tramble edged near Father, his eyes burning and the corners of his mouth curled. He nodded his head toward Sula Basham. "I'll deliver that key willing if you'll take this beanpole widow-woman along some'eres and git her a man. She's wore the black bonnet long enough."

Laughter sprang forth, gulping in throats, wheezing noses. Sula whirled, her face lit with anger. "If I was a-mind to marry," she said, grudging her words, "it's certain I'd have to go where there's a man fittin. I'd be bound—"

Sill Lovelock broke in, thinking Sula's talk of no account. He asked Father, "What air you to use for bread along the way? There's no manna falling from Heaven this day and time."

Father was grinning at Sula. He saw the muscle knots clench on her arms, and he saw Loss inch away. He turned toward Sill in good humor. "Why, there's a gum o' honey dew on the leaves of a morning. We kin wake early and eat it off."

"The Devil take 'em," Mother said, calming Sula. "Menfolks are heathens. Let them crawl their own dirt." She was studying the locket, studying it to remember, to take away in her mind. I thought of Mother's unpierced ear lobes where never a bob had hung, the worn stems of her fingers never circled by gold, her plain bosom no pin-pretty had ever hooked. She was looking at the locket, not covetously, but in wonder.

"I'll take the key," Sula told Father. "Nobody else seems anxious to neighbor you."

Loss opened his hands, his face as grave as Sill Lovelock's, mocking. He pointed an arm at Sula, the other appealing to the crowd. "I allus did pity a widow-woman," he said. He spanned Sula's height with his eyes. "In this gethering there ought to be one single man willing to marry the Way Up Yonder Woman."

Sula's mouth hardened. "I want none o' your pity pie," she blurted. She took a step toward Loss, the sinews of her long arms quickening. When Loss retreated she turned to Mother, who had just climbed onto the wagon. Sula and Mother were now at an eye level. "You were a help when my chaps died," Sula said. "You were a comfort when my man lay in his box. I hain't forgetting. Wish I had a keepsake to give you, showing I'll allus remember."

"I'll keep you in my head," Mother assured.

"I'll be proud to know it."

We were ready to go. "Climb on, Son," Father called. I swung up from the hindgate to the top of the load. Over the heads of the men I could see the whole of the camp, the shotgun houses in the flat, the smoke rising above the burning gob heaps. The pain of leaving rose in my chest. Father clucked his tongue, and the mare started off. She walked clear out of the wagon shafts. Loose trace chains swung free and pole-ends of the shafts bounded to the ground.

"Whoa ho!" Father shouted, jumping down. A squall of joy sounded behind us. Cece Goodloe had pulled this rusty; he'd done the unfastening. Father smiled while adjusting the harness. Oh he didn't mind a clever trick. And he sprang back onto the wagon again.

Loss Tramble spooled his hands, calling through them, "If you don't aim to take this widow along, we'll have to marry her to a born fool. We'll have to match her with Hig Sommers."

We drove away, the wheels taking the groove of ruts, the load swaying; we drove away with Sill Lovelock's last warning ringing our ears. "You're making your bed in Hell!" he had shouted. Then it was I saw the gold locket about Mother's neck, beating her bosom like a heart.

I looked back, seeing the first rocks thrown, hearing our windows shatter; I looked back upon the camp as upon the face of the dead. I saw the crowd fall back from Sula Basham, tripping over each other. She had struck Loss Tramble with her fist, and he knelt before her, fearing to rise. And only Hig Sommers was watching us move away. He stood holding up his breeches, for someone had cut his galluses with a knife. He thrust one arm into the air, crying, "Hello, hello!"

The Proud Walkers

We moved out of Houndshell mine camp in May to the homeplace Father had built on Shoal Creek, and I recollect foxgrapes were blooming and there was a spring chill in the air. Fern and Lark and I ran ahead of the wagon, frightening water thrushes, shouting back at the poky mare. We broke cowcumber branches to wave at the baby, wanting to call to him, but he did not then have a name.

Only Mother forbore stretching eyes to see afar. She held the baby atop a shuck tick, her face pale with dread to look upon the house. A mort of things she had told Father before he had gone to raise the dwelling. "Ere a board is rived," she'd said, "dig a cellar. There'll be no more pokes o' victuals coming from the commissary." She had told him the pattern for the chimney, roof, and walls; she told him more than a body could keep in his head, saying at last, "Could I lend a hand, 'twould be a satisfaction."

Father had grinned. "A nail you drove would turn corkscrew. A blow-sarpent couldn't quile to your saw marks. Hit's man's work. A man's got to wear the breeches." Oh Father nearly had a laughing spell listening to Mother's talk. Mother had said, "A house proper to raise chaps in, a cellar for laying by food, and lasty neighbors. Now, that hain't asking for the moon-ball."

I recollect bull-bats soared overhead when we reached Shoal Creek in the late afternoon; I recollect Mother looked at the house, and all she had feared was true. The building stood windowless, board ends of walls were unsawn, and the chimney pot barely cleared the hip-roof. But Fern and Lark and I were awed. We could not think why Mother dabbed her eyes with baby's dress tail.

"Hit's not finished to a square T," Father said uneasily. "After planting they'll be time in plenty. A late start I've got. Why, field corn and a garden ought to be breaking ground. Just taste a grain o' patience."

Mother glanced into the sky where bull-bats hawked. She was heartsick with the mulligrubs. Her voice sounded tight and strange. "A man's notions are ontelling," she said, "but if this creek's a fittin place to bring up chaps, if good neighbors live nigh, reckon I've got no right to complain."

"The Crownover family lives yonside the ridge," Father said. "Only folks in handy walking distance. I hear they're the earth's salt. No needcessity o' lock or key on Shoal Creek."

The wagon was unloaded by dusk dark. Father lighted the lamp on coming from stabling the mare, and we hovered to a smidgen of fire. We trembled in the night chill, for it was foxgrape winter. Mother feared to heap wood on the blaze, the chimney pot being low enough to set sparks to the roof. She knelt by the hearth, frying a skillet of hominy, cooking it mortal slow.

Father saddled the baby on a knee. "Well, now," he said, buttoning his jump jacket and peeping to see what the skillet held, "reckon I've caught a glimpse o' neighbors already. I heard footsteps yonside the barn in a brushy draw, though I couldn't see for blackness till they'd topped the ridge. There walked two fellers, with heads size o' washpots."

Lark crept nearer Mother. Fern and I glanced behind us. Nailheads shone on the walls as bright as the eyes of beasts.

"I figure it to be men carrying churns or jugs on their shoulders," Mother spoke coldly.

"I saw a water-head baby in the camps once," Fern said. "I did."

"Hit might a-been Old Bloody Tom and some 'un," Lark said.

"Odd they'd go by our place," Father mused, "traveling no path." He joggled the baby on his knee, making him squeal. "But it's said them Crownovers can be trusted to Jordan River and back ag'in. I'm wanting to get acquainted the first chance."

"A man's fancy to take shortcuts," Mother replied, nodding her head at the boxed room. "They're men cutting across from one place to another, taking the lazy trail."

Fern's teeth chattered. She was ever the scary one.

"I hain't a chip afraid," I bragged, rashy with curiosity. "Be they boys amongst them Crownovers? I'm a-mind to play with one."

"Gee-o," Father chuckled, "a whole bee swarm o' chaps. Stair-steppers, creepers, and climbers, biddy ones to nigh growns. Fourteen, by honest count.

A sawyer at Beddo Tillett's mill says they all can whoop weeds out of a crop in one day."

"I be not to play with water-heads," Lark said.

"That sawyer says every one o' Izard Crownover's young 'uns have rhymy names," Father went on. "He spun me a few, many as he could think of. Bard, Nard, Dard, Guard, Shard—names so slick yore tongue trips up."

"Are there girls too?" Fern asked.

"Beulah, Dulah, Eulah. A string like that."

Mother stirred the hominy. "Clever neighbors I've allus wanted," she said, her voice gloomy, "and allus I've longed for a house fittin to make them welcome."

"Be-jibs!" Father spoke impatiently. "A fair homeseat we'll have once the crop's planted, and they's a spare minute. Why, I raised this place off the ground in twelve days, elbow for axle. I didn't have half the proper tools; I had no help-hands. I hauled lumber twelve miles from Beddo Tillett's sawmill." He grunted, untangling baby's fingers from his watch chain. "Anyhow, hit might take them Crownovers a year's thawing to visit. Hain't like the camps where folks stick noses in, the first thing. I say let time get in its lick."

We were quieted by the thought of enduring a lonesome year, of nobody coming to put his feet under our table, nobody to borrow, or heave and set and calculate weather. Oh the camps had spoiled us with their slew of chaps and rattling coal conveyors and people's talky-talk. Dwelling there, you couldn't stretch your elbows without hitting people.

I said, sticking my lips out, "I hain't waiting till I'm crook-back ere I play with some 'un."

Fern batted her eyes, trying to cry. "Ruther to live on a gob heap than where no girls are."

The skillet jiggled in Mother's hand. She spoke, complaining of the house, though now it was small in her mind compared with this new anxiety. "Nary a window cut," she said. "A house blind as a mole varmint."

"Jonah's whale!" Father exclaimed angrily. His ears reddened. He galloped his knee. "A feller can't whittle windowframes with a pocket knife. I reckon nothing will do but I hie at daybreak to Tillett's and 'gin making them. Two days it'll take; two I ought to be rattling clods. Why, a week's grubbing to be done before a furrow's lined. Crops won't mature planted so late." He swallowed a great breath. "Had we the finest cellar in Amerikee, a particle o' nothing there'd be for winter storing."

"I reckon I've set my bonnet too high," Mother admitted. "The cellar's got to be filled with canning, turnips, cabbages, and pickling, if we're to eat the year through. Now, windows can be put off, but the chimley's bound to have a taller stacking."

The blood hasted from Father's ears. Never could he stay angry long. He coaxed baby to latch hands on his lifted arm and swing. "Ought to fill the new barn loft so full o' corn and fodder hits tongue will hang out," he said. He taught the baby to skin a cat, come-Andy-over, head foremost. "One thing besides frames I'm fotching, and that's a name for this tadwhacker. Long enough he's gone without."

"Hain't going to call him Beddo," Fern said. "That's the ugliest name-word ever was."

"Not to be Tillett neither," Lark said.

The hominy browned. We held plates in our laps. The yellow kernels steamed a mellow smell. It was hard not to gobble them down like an old craney crow.

Mother ate a bit, then sat watching Father. "I had a house pattern in my head," she said, "and I ached to help build, to try my hand making it according. And I'd wished for good neighbors. But house and neighbors hain't a circumstance to getting a crop and the garden planted. Hit's back to the mines for us if we don't make victuals. Them windowframes can wait."

"I can't follow a woman's notions," Father said. "For peace o' mind I'd better gamble two days and get the windows in." He chuckled, his mouth crammed. "I'd give a Tennessee pearl to see you atop a twenty-foot ladder potting nails." His chuckle grew to laughter; it caught like a wind in his chest, blowing out in gusts, shaking him. He began to cough. A kernel had got in his windpipe. His jaws turned beety; he sneezed a great sneeze. We struck our doubled fists against his back, and presently the grain was dislodged. "Ah, ho," he said, swallowing, "had I a-died, 'twould been in good cause."

Mother lightened. "I'm no witty with a hammer and saw," she said, "and if that cellar's not dug to my fancy, I can spade."

Father sobered. He got as restless in his chair as a caged bird. Of a sudden he turned his head to the door, listening. "Hush-o!" he said. We pricked our ears. "Hush!"

We waited, unbreathing, hearing the harsh *peent* of bull-bats.

"I heard nothing onnatural," Mother said.

Fern shivered. Lark searched under the beds. He knew boogers were abroad at night.

Father reached the baby to Mother, and got up. So sleepy baby was, his head rolled like a dropped gourd. "The mare's restless," Father decided. "She might o' heard Crownover's stally bray yonside the mountain. I'll see that she's latched in tight." He went outside.

"Let's play Old Bloody Tom," Lark said. "I be Tom, a-rambling, smoking my pipe. You all be sheeps."

"Now, no," Fern snuffed. "It'd make me scared."

We children were abed when Father returned. He shucked off his boots and dabbed tallow on them; he breathed on the leather and rubbed it fiercely with a linsey rag. He spoke, faltering, hunting words, "I've been aiming to tell about the cellar."

Mother fitted a skillet's eye to a peg. She paused.

"After I'd shingled the roof," Father said, "I put in to dig. Got three feet down and struck bottom. This house is setting on living rock. I've larnt they hain't a cellar on Shoal Creek. This vein runs under all."

And later, when the light was blown, I heard Father speak from his pillow. "I saw more fellers on the ridge a while ago, walking with heads so square I figured they hefted boxes on their shoulders. I'm a-mind to stop by the Crownovers' tomorrow, asking a hinting question. Hit's quare folks would go a dark way no road treads."

The sun-ball was eating creek fog when Mother waked me. The door stood wide upon morning. "Your father's gone to Tillett's already," she said, "and against my will and beg. He hurried off afoot, saying he'd let the mare rest, saying he'd get the windowframes hauled somehow." She gazed dolesomely upon the fields where blackgum, sassafras, and redbud grew as in a young forest. "I argued, I plead, yet he would to go. Oh man-judgment's like weather. Hit's onknowing."

My breeches were on in a wink. I'd thought to go feed the mare, then hie to the brushy draw to quest for signs of walkers. I went before eating, being more curious than hungry. I fed the mare ten ears of corn; I stole beyond the barn. The draw was a moggy place. Wahoos grew thick against a limerock wall, and a sprangle of water ran out. I found a nest of brogan tracks set in the mud; I saw where they printed the ridge. "If I was growed up," I spoke aloud, "I'd follow them steps, be they go to the world's end." Then I ran to the house; I ran so fast a bluesnake racer couldn't have caught me.

Mother was putting dough-bread and rashers on the table when I hurried indoors. Her face was gaunt with worry. She circled the table where Fern and Lark ate. Baby threshed in his tall chair, sucking a meat rind. "It would take Adam's grands and greats to rid that ground in time for planting," she said. "I tried grubbing a pawpaw, but its roots sunk to Chiney. I'm afeared we might have to backtrack to the mines. We'll be bound to, if the crops don't bear."

"I've seen a quare thing," I said.

Mother paid me no mind. "Two days your father will be gone, and no satisfaction I'll see till he returns. Yet he can't grub by his lone. He'd not get through in time." She halted, staring at the walls, searching in her head for what to do.

"Never was a mine shack darker," she said at last, having decided. She rolled her sleeves above her elbows, like a man's. "I can't grub fittin. I can't dig a cellar through puore rock. But window holes I can saw—holes three feet by five." She fetched a hatchet and a handsaw; she marked a window by tape.

"I'd be scared of a night, with holes cut," Fern complained. "Robber men might come."

"I saw tracks," I blurted. My words were drowned under Mother's chopping. She hewed a crevice to give the sawblade lee.

"It's Father's work," Fern whined. She squeezed her eyelids, trying to cry.

I recollect Mother worked that day through, cutting four windows, true as a sawyer's. The hours crawled turkle-slow. Fern and Lark and I longed for shouting children; we longed for the busy noises of the camps. We could only mope and look at the empty road. Nobody passed upcreek or down, nobody we glimpsed from daybreak to dusk dark. Oft when Mother took a little rest she'd glance the hills over. Oh she was lost as anyone. Loneliness swelled large as mast-balls inside of us.

When night came we heard the first lorn cry of a chuckwill's-widow. The evening chill was sharp. We ate supper huddled to a mite of fire. "One spark against a shingle," Mother explained, "and we'd have to roust a fox from his cave house. That chimley begs fixing."

The dishes were washed and put away. We sat quietly, our faces yellow in the lamplight. The *peent* of bull-bats came through the window holes. Spring lizards prayed for rain in the bottoms.

Mother saw how our eyes kept stealing to the window. The darkness there was black as corpse cloth. "Sing a ballad or play a game," she urged. "Then hap baby will go to sleep."

"Play Bloody Tom," Lark called. "I be Tom, coming for a coal to tetch my pipe. You be sheeps or chaps."

"Now, no," Fern said, "that 'un's scary."

"Let's do a talking song," I chose. "Let's sing 'Old Rachel,' and me do the talking."

We sang "Old Rachel"; Old Rachel nobody could do a thing with; Old Rachel going to the Bad Place with her toenails dragging and a bucket on her arm, saying, "Good morning, Mister Devil, hit's getting mighty warm"; and I spoke, after every verse, "Now, listen, Little Rachel, please be kind o' quiet."

We hushed suddenly. Beast sounds rang the hills. Crownover's stallion had trumpeted afar, and our mare had whinnied.

"Sing ahead," Mother coaxed, "the mare's stall is latched. I saw to it. Sing what the Devil done with Rachel when he couldn't handle her."

We had no heart to sing more. "I propped the stall door," I said. Fern's eyes were beaded upon the black window. "Wisht it was allus day," she said.

"Ah, now," Mother chided, trying to comfort us. "A body gets their growth of a night. I'd not want the baby a dwarf."

"I saw a low-standing man in the camps once," Fern recalled, "not nigh tall as me."

"I saw tracks in the draw—" I began, and hushed. They grew in my mind.

They seemed to have been made by the largest foot a man ever had. The thought held my breath. "Wisht Poppy was here," I said.

The baby sat up, round-eyed, blinking.

Mother spoke, making talk. "I wonder what name your father's going to bring this chap. I promised him the naming."

"He'll fotch a sour 'un," Fern grudged. "Ooge, Boll, Zee. One like smut-face little 'uns wear at the mines."

"I told your father, 'Name him for an upstanding man. A man clever, with heart and pride.'"

"Hope it's a rhymer," I said. "Whoever named them fourteen Crownovers was clever. Hit tuk a head full o' sense to figure all o' them."

"Once I knew a man who had a passel o' children," Mother related. "He married two times and pappied twenty-three. After there come sixteen, he ran out o' names. Just called them numbers, according to order. Seventeen, eighteen, nineteen, twenty—" She paused, watching baby. He slept, leant upon nothing, like a beast sleeps.

"If Poppy was here," Fern yawned, "I bet he'd laugh."

"You'll all be dozing on foot before long," Mother told us. "Time to pinch the wick."

The lamp was smothered; we crawled between covers. Once the light died the window hole turned gray. You could see the shoulders of hills through it. Fern and Lark hushed and slept. I lay quiet, listening, and my ears were large with dark, catching midges of sound. The shuck mattress ticked, ticked, ticked. A rooster crowed. Night wore.

In my sleep I heard the mare thresh in her stall, pawing the ground with a forefoot. I raised on an elbow. From behind the barn came an owly cough, and a voice saying, "Hold!" Someone stood inside the window, tall, white-gowned. It was Mother. I sprang beside her, looking. Fellows topped the ridge as ants march, up and over. Their heads were like folks' heads, but their backs were humpty.

"Six walkers with pokes," Mother said, "carrying only God knows what."

I recollect walking with the sun in my face; I recollect thinking Father would come home that day, bringing the frames to set against robbers and bloom winters. Lark was asleep beside me, and Fern and the baby lay in Mother's bed with their heads on a duck pillow. I recollect glancing through the window and seeing Mother run out of the fields.

I stood in my shirttail as Mother swung the door. Her hair fell wild about her shoulders. For a moment she had no breath to speak. "The mare's gone!" she gasped. "Gone."

Fern roused, meany for being awakened with a start. Lark's eyes opened, damp and large.

"I propped the stall door," I vowed. "Hit was latched and propped too."

"Had Poppy been at home," Fern quarreled, "stealers wouldn't a-come."

"I'd have figured she broke the latch of her own free will," Mother said, "hadn't it been for where the tracks led. I followed."

"Was they brogan prints alongside?" I asked. They grew immense in my mind. "Bigger'n anything?"

"Just bare mare tracks. I followed within sight o' the Crownovers."

Of a sudden I scorned the Crownovers. I could hear blood drum my ears. I said, "If I met one o' them chaps, I'd not know him from dirt. I'd not speak a howdy."

Fern twisted into her garments. "I bet them girl-chaps wear old flour-sack dresses, and you kin read print front and back." She wrinkled her nose, making to cry. "I'm wanting to move to Houndshell." She flicked her eyelids, but not a tear would come. She got angry, angry as I. "Ruther be dust in a grave-box than have to do with them folks. Be my name theirs, I couldn't hold up my head for shame."

"Don't lay blame for shore," Mother warned. "The mare's tracks went straight, yet they might o' veered a bit this side. There's nothing we can settle till your father's here, and he aimed to stop by Crownovers' anyhow."

Fern stamped her feet against the floor. "I wisht this house would burn to ashes. We'd be bound to live at the mines where they's girls to play with, and hain't no robbers."

"Ramshack house, a-setting on a rock," I mocked.

Mother turned hurt eyes upon us. She stood before the cold fireplace and began to lay off with hands like the Houndshell schoolteacher. "Fifteen years we lived under a rented roof, fifteen years o' eating out o' paper pokes. We were beholden to the mines, robbed o' fresh breathing air, robbed o' green victuals. Now, cellar nor neighbors we've got here, but there's clean air and ground and home. I say this house hain't going to burn. That chimley's to rise higher."

"Poppy ought to be a-coming," Lark sniffled.

"The land not grubbed," Mother lamented, "no seeds planted, the mare stolen. Oh it's Houndshell for us another winter." She turned away, her shoulders drawn and small.

We children ate breakfast alone, one of us forever peering through the window hole toward the way Father would come. Fern held the baby, giving him tastes of mush. We scraped the pot; we sopped our plates, for Mother had gone into the far room. But she came as we pushed the chairs aside. We stared. She wore Father's breeches. The legs were rolled at the bottom. "I can't climb a ladder or straddle a roof in a dress," she said. "Allus I've wanted to take a hand with this house. Here's my chance, before your father's back. He'd tear up the patch if he knew."

"It's man's work," Fern said grumpily.

Rocks were gathered, clay batter stirred, a ladder leaned against the roof. Up Mother went with a bucket of mud. I climbed, lifting the rocks in a coffee sack, reaching the poke's neck to her on gaining the tiptop. Mother edged along the hip-roof, balancing the sack and bucket. Her face went dead white. Traveling the steep of a roof was not as simple as spoken.

Fern began to whimper, and the baby cried a spasm. "Come down!" Fern called. "Come down!"

Mother buttered two rocks with clay, placing them on the chimney. They rolled off, falling inside. She was slapping mud to a third when a voice roared beside the house. A man stood agape. A stranger had come unbeknownst. Mother jerked, and the bucket slipped, and the coffee sack emptied in a clatter across the shingles. The fellow had to jump limber dodging that rock fall. He roared, laughing, "Come down, woman, afore you break yore neck!" Mother obeyed, red-faced, ashamed of the breeches she wore.

We studied the man. He was older than Father, smaller, and two hands shorter. His eyes were bright as new ten-pennies. An empty pipe stuck out of his mouth, the bowl a tiny piggin carved from an oak boss. "When a woman undertakes man's gin-work," he spoke, "their fingers all turn to thumbs." He didn't stand back. He hauled rocks and a new batch of clay up the ladder; he fashioned that chimney to a fare-you-well.

Lark and Fern and I whispered together.

Fern asked, "Who be this feller?"

Lark ventured, "Hit might be Old Bloody Tom, come for a coal o' fire."

I mouthed words in their ears. "I'd vow he's not a Crownover. His feet hain't big enough."

"We're obliged," Mother said when the stranger descended. She wore a dress now, though she was still abashed.

The man bowed his arms, tipped the pipe, discounting. "A high perch I've needed to search about. A horse o' mine broke stable last night. I'm looking for him."

Lark raised on his toes, straining to tell of our mare. Mother hushed him with a glance.

"Animals are apt to go traipsing with another nigh," the man continued, eying the barn, "but they usually come home by feeding time. Like as not, they'll bring in a furrin critter, and it's a puzzle to whom they're belongin. I allus said, men and beast air cut from the same ham." He bent his knees to glance under the house, and grunted knowingly. He shuffled to go. "Yonder atop the roof I beheld you've got a sight o' grubbing to do. Hit'd take Methuselum's begats to ready that ground for seed." He started off, speaking over his shoulder, "If you had fittin neighbors, they'd not fail to help." He went downhill and upcreek, and we watched him out of sight.

We set a steady lookout for Father. As the hours crept into afternoon Mother complained, her voice at the rag edge of patience, "Your father ought to come while daylight's burning."

But Father arrived when the bull-bats were flying and night darkened the hollows, and he came alone and empty-handed. No windowframes he brought. I recollect he smiled on seeing our glum faces in the light of the great fire Mother had built. Even baby sulled a mite.

"What bush did you get them pouts off of?" he asked.

Mother lifted her hands in defeat. "I'm a-mind we'll have to endure the camps a spell longer."

"Hark!" Father exclaimed. How strangely he looked at Mother, at us all. The mulligrubs were writ deep upon our faces.

"The mare stolen, no chance for a crop. Oh the sorriest of folks we've moved nigh."

"Hark-o!"

"Them Crownovers hain't fittin neighbors," Fern scoffed. "A man come a-saying it."

I spoke with scorn, "They've got rhymy chaps. Their names sound like an old raincrow hollering '*cu cu cu, cucucu.*'"

"A man come a-saying—"

"Even if the garden and crop were planted," Mother despaired, "there'd be no place earthy to store winter food."

Father grinned. "Why, we've got a cellar dug by the Man Above. Old Izard Crownover says it's yonder in that brushy draw—a cave hole in solid limerock that'll keep stuff till Glory. Now he ought to know."

Our mouths fell open. We could scarcely believe.

"Ah, ho," Father chortled, swinging the baby onto his shoulder. "They's another thing we've got for sartin, and that's a name for this little tadwhacker. He's to be named for a feller proud as ever walked. I'm going to call him Zard, after Old Izard."

"A man come a-saying—"

"Old Izard himself," Father said. "Why, them Crownovers are so proud they dreaded telling us o' using our cave for a cellar. They called hit trespassing. Walked their stuff out in the black o' night."

"The mare might o' broke the latch," Mother admitted, "but her tracks went straight as a measure."

"Come morning," Father chuckled, "you kin look up Shoal Creek, and there'll be the mare and Crownover's stally hauling windowframes in a wagon. And there'll be Old Izard and his woman and all his rhymers a-walking, coming to help grub, plow, and seed. Such an ant bed o' folks you'll swear hit's Coxey's Army."

Father halted, remembering what Izard had told him. He eyed Mother and began to laugh. Laughter boiled inside of him. He could barely make words, so balled his tongue was. "From now on," he gulped, "thar's one thing for shore." He threshed the air, his face fiery with joy. "I'm the one wearing the breeches." He struggled for breath. He choked.

Mother struck the flat of her hands against his back. "The nature of a man is a quare thing," she said.

The Stir-Off

"Come Friday for the sorghum making," Jimp Buckheart sent word to me by Father. "Come to the stir-off party, and take a night."

Father chuckled as he told, knowing I had never stayed away from home. Father said, "Hit's time you larnt other folks' ways. Now, Old Gid Buckheart's family lives fat as horse traders. He's got five boys, tough as whang leather, though nary a one's a match to Gid himself; and he's the pappy o' four girls who're picture-pieces." He teased as he whittled a molassy spoon for me. "Mind you're not captured by one o' Gid's daughters. They're all pretty, short or tall, every rung o' the ladder." He teased enough to rag his tongue. I grunted scornfully, but I was tickled to go. I'd heard Jimp had a flying-jinny and kept a ferret.

Jimp met me before noon at their land boundary. Since last I'd seen him he had grown; and he jerked his knees walking and cocked his head birdwise, imping his father. He was Old Gid Buckheart over again. He didn't stand stranger. "Kin you keep secrets?" he asked. "Hold things and not let out?" I nodded. Jimp said, "My pap's going to die death hearing Plumey's marrying Rant Branders tonight at the stir-off. Pap'll never give up to her picking such a weaky-looking feller." His face brightened with pride. "I'm the only one knows. Rant aims to hammer me a pair o' brass knuckles if I play hushmouth, a pair my size. He swore to it."

"Hit's not honest to fight with knucks unless a feller's bigger'n you," I said.

"I'm laying for my brother Bailus," Jimp explained. "He's older'n me, and allus tricking, and trying to borrow or steal my ferret. I'd give my beastie to git him ducked in the sorghum hole."

"I long to see your ferret," I said. "I'm bound to ride the fly-jinny."

"Bailus wants to sic my ferret into rabbit nests," Jimp complained. "Hit's a ferret's nature to skin alive. Ere I'd let Bailus borrow, I'd crack its neck. Ruther to see it dead."

We walked a spell. Roosters crowed midday. We topped a knob and afar in a hollow stood the Buckhearts' great log house, and beyond under gilly trees was the sorghum gin.

Jimp pointed. "Peep Eye's minding hornets off the juice barrel, and I reckon everybody else's eating. We've made two runs o' sirup already, dipped enough green skims to nigh fill the sorghum hole, and cane's milled for the last."

Hounds raced to meet us. We halted a moment by the beegums. On bowed heads of sunflowers redbirds were cracking seeds. Jimp gazed curiously at me, cocking his chin. "You and me's never fit," he said. "Fellers don't make good buddies till they prove which can out-do."

We waded the hounds to the kitchen, spying through the door. Jimp's father and brothers were eating and his mother and three of his sisters passed serving dishes; and in the company chair sat Squire Letcher, making balls of his bread, and cutting eyes at the girls. Jimp told me their names. The squire I knew already; I knew he was the Law, and a widow-man. "Hardhead at the end o' the bench is Bailus," Jimp said. "Plumey's standing behind Pap—the one's got a beauty spot." Plumey was fairest of the three girls, fair as a queeny blossom. Her cheek bore a mole speck, like a spider with tucked legs; and a born mole it was, not one stuck on for pretty's sake. Jimp told me all of the names, then said, "I wonder what that law-square's a-doing here?"

We clumped inside. Old Gid spoke a loud howdy-do, asking after my folks, and Mrs. Buckheart tipped the cowlick on my head. A chair was drawn for me, and victuals brought to heap my plate. Bailus leaned to block Jimp's way to his seat on the bench, so Jimp had to crawl under the table. He stuck his head up, mad-faced, gritting his teeth. "Ho, Big Ears," Bailus said. The older brothers sat with eyes cold upon Squire Letcher. The squire was a magistrate and bound to put a damper on the stir-off party.

Gid pushed back his chair and spiked his elbows, watching the foxy glances of Squire Letcher. "We're old-timey people," he told the squire, his words querulous. "We may live rough, but we're lacking nothing. For them with muscle and backbone, Troublesome Creek country is the land o' plenty." He swept an arm toward gourds of lard, strings of lazy-wife beans, and shelves of preserves; he snapped his fingers at cushaws hanging by vine tails. "We raise our own living, and once the house and barns are full we make friends with the earth. We swear not to hit it another lick till spring."

Squire Letcher popped three bread balls into his mouth, swallowed, and was done with his meal. He crossed his knife and fork in a mannerly fashion. "Don't skip the main harvest," he sighed in his fullness. "Nine in this family, and none married yet." He smirked, looking sideways at the girls. "But you can't hide blushy daughters in the head of a hollow for long. Single men will be wearing your doorsteps down."

Gid's voice lifted peevishly. "A beanstalk of a feller has made tracks here already, a shikepoke I've never met, a stranger tee-total."

Plumey's cheeks burnt. The mole on her cheek seemed to inch a grain.

Gid went on, "Why a girl o' mine would choose a man so puny is beyond reckoning. I'd vow he's not got the strength to raise a proper living."

Mrs. Buckheart spoke up, taking Plumey's part. "An old hornbeam's muscles show through the bark, but ne'er a growing oak's. And I say you'll ne'er meet a feller with your head allus turned."

The squire flushed merrily. "Gideon, thar's few longing to shake your hand. You'd put a man to his knees or break bones. Recollect I've yet to clap your paw? Oh you're the fistiest old man running free."

The shag of Gid's brows raised, uncovering eyes blue as mill-pond water. "One thing I do recollect," Gid said, "a thing going years past when we were young scrappers." He cocked his head. "I recall we battled like rams once. We wore the ground out, tuggety-pull. But it was a draw."

The squire caught the Buckheart boys' hard gaze. He sobered, shifting uneasily, ready to leave the table. Law papers rustled in his pockets. "Gid," he insisted, rising, "you're of an older set. We never ran together, never wrestled as I remember. I'd swear before a Grand Jury."

"I hain't so old I whistle when I talk," Gid crowed. "Hain't so old but what I'd crack skulls with anybody. Jist any sweet time I kin grab a churn dasher and make butter o' airy one o' my sons." A grin twisted his mouth as he got up. "Now, Square, we shore fit. We did." And Squire Letcher and Gid went off arguing into the midst of the house.

"Who invited that walking courthouse?" Cirius blurted.

"Old jury hawk," U. Z. said.

"He might have come for a good purpose." Mrs. Buckheart chided. "Eat your victuals."

Before we left the table Gid came back. "I've voted the square into going bird-hunting," he said. "Atter his dinner settles one o' you boys hustle him o'er the hills and bring him back so dog-tired he'll start home afore dark."

"I'll go," Bailus volunteered, puffing his jaws, mocking the squire. "I'll wade thorns and walk cliff faces. I'll wear his soles off."

"Travel the starch out o' him," Gid said. "I've a notion he oughten to stay on."

"Who asked that magistrate here anyhow?" John asked, his face sour as whey. "They's more warrants in his pockets than a buzzard's got feathers."

Leander said, "He'll plague the stir-off. Fellers will think he's come a-summonsing. And I've heard a mighty crowd's coming across the ridge tonight."

"We've only invited neighbors and a couple o' fiddlers," Gid spoke fractiously, "but a rambling widower is apt to come unbid any place. Yet I'm more concerned about a tender sprig of a feller who's shore to be here, one I'd ruther see going than coming, ruther to see the span o' his back than his face."

Plumey paled whiter than a hen-and-biddy dish. The boys grunted.

Old Gid began to lay down the law. "Girls!" he said. "You're not to throw necks tonight staring at the boys. Sons! We're going to mark the sorghum hole. We're making puore molasses, and no candy jacks. Keep a watch on the kettle."

"I choose pull-candy to sirup," Jimp said.

I thought in my head, "I bet candy jacks would be good."

U. Z. groaned, "Pap's bounden to dry up the party."

Old Gid's face softened. He chuckled at me and Jimp gobbling pie. "You tad whackers better save a big little spot for the molassy foam."

"Pappy," Jimp asked, "did you and the square sheep-fight once, a-butting heads?"

Old Gid raised his brows and grinned. He stepped to the door and called Peep Eye to dinner.

"I aim to see your ferret," I reminded Jimp. "I want to ride the fly-jinny."

We crept into the smokehouse where the ferret was kept hidden. "A feller can't take a step withouten Peep Eye's watching," Jimp complained, latching the door. In that darksome place I saw giant pumpkins squatting on hard earth, and fat squashes crooking yellow necks. I saw a bin of Amburgey apples, a mort of victuals in kegs and jars; I set eyes on three barrels of molasses. I said, "Them many sirups will turn strong as bull beef ere they can be et."

Jimp whistled a sketch. A furry head lifted above a sack of capping corn. I jumped in fright, and the varmint started, jerking its head down, burrowing into the sack. The ferret wouldn't come out then for all our begging and poking cobs. I didn't get to see the whole of him.

"He's scared," I said.

"My beastie's got nerve spite o' playing timid," Jimp defended. "He'll tackle critters double his size, jist like fisty people. Cagey ones don't show their nerve till they come to a pinch." And Jimp made a wry face, laughing suddenly. He popped his hands together. "I'd give my ferret to see Pap and the square lock horns."

"I'd ruther to see your father shake hands with Rant Branders," I said, knowing by looks that Squire Letcher was snail-weak. "Rant might be tough as whang leather."

"My pap could make Rant eat straw."

"A man's backbone don't print through his clothes."

We listened a bit, our ears against the door; we stole outside, looking sharp. "Yonder's Bailus coming," Jimp whispered, and began to run. I ran after him, though it wasn't Bailus I'd seen. I had glimpsed a girl-child staring around a corner, and she was a Buckheart, for she bore their presence. She had jerked her head away quicker than any ferret.

We ran till the wind burnt out of us; we stopped to rest in a weed patch where noggin sticks grew tall and brittle. "I saw a girl yonside the smokehouse," I said when I could speak. "I bet she heard a plenty."

"Peep Eye," Jimp said. "You can't say 'gizzard' withouten her hearing."

"Reckon she's larnt about Plumey and Rant?"

"Now, no. Hit's the first time ever I did know a thing afore her." Jimp thought a moment. "Was it Peep Eye growed up and marrying off, I'd be tickled. Me, I hain't ne'er going to marry."

"I'm not aiming to be a widow-man," I said, anxious to go to the flying-jinny. I gathered a dozen noggin sticks, snapping them at the root. Their woody knots were like small fists. Jimp picked a bunch too, saying, "Let's crack each other's skulls and see who hollers first."

I winced, dreading the pain, but I wouldn't be outdone. "You hit first," I said.

"No, you."

"I hain't mad. I can't hit cold."

"I'll rile you," Jimp said. He furrowed his brows and spoke a lie-tale. "Yore pappy steals money off dead men's eyeballs, and yore folks feeds on carr'n crows."

I struck, breaking the weed. Jimp cracked one across my noggin. We broke five sticks apiece, and felt for goose eggs on our heads. Then we went on to the flying-jinny at the pasture gap, and there stood Bailus, waiting.

Bailus's face was grave. You could tell he had come begging. "Big Ears," he began, "you ought to lend a hand gitting rid o' the magistrate, else the stir-off will be a reg'lar funeral."

Jimp poked his lips. "Jist a trick to borrow my ferret. You got no use for him bird-hunting."

"The square wants to hole a rabbit or two."

"Hain't fair to skin varmints alive. I'm not loaning, and that's the God's truth."

I studied the flying-jinny, noting its pattern in my head. I felt bound to have Father make one. A long hickory pole it was, pegged in the middle to a sour-wood stump. I straddled the limber end of the pole, hungry to ride.

Bailus's eyes narrowed. "I've heard a bee-swarm o' folks are coming to-night, a drove o' people we've not invited. They's something fotching 'em here. Now, loan yore ferret and I'll tell what." He sniffled, but I saw it was make-like. "Creek water hain't dull as a stir-off with a magistrate keeping tab."

Jimp scoffed. He turned toward me. "I'll give you the first ride."

"Fellers!" Bailus spoke quickly. "Both o' you hop on and I'll push."

Though Jimp's face grew long with doubt he straddled the jinny. We latched our legs about the hickory pole. Bailus began to push, slowly at first, digging his toes into the ground. As the pole swung clear he pushed faster, faster, around and around. We sped. We traveled swifter than a live jinny. A wind caught in my shirt, jerking the tails. I hunkered against the log; I held on for bare life. The earth whirled, trees went walking, and tiptops of the mountains swayed and rail fences climbed straight into the sky. My hands numbed, and my chest seemed near to bursting. My fingers loosened, and I was tossed into the air.

I lay on the ground, stupid with dizziness, and Jimp wove drunkenly, trying to stand. Bailus was nowhere in sight. Then I saw three bright faces, three girl-chaps melting together. My lids went blinkety-blink-blink. When my head cleared I saw it was Peep Eye, alone. She was the spit image of Plumey, though she had no mole on her cheek; she was the prettiest human being ever I did see.

"Air you been dranking john corn?" Peep Eye teased.

"I been ding-donged enough," Jimp blurted. "I'd swap them knucks I'm promised to even up with Bailus."

"He's hasted to steal your ferret," Peep Eye said. "He'll have it and gone ere you kin catch him."

Jimp kicked the ground in anger. "I wish that critter was dead and dust. I do."

Peep Eye stood pretty as a bunty bird. Jimp and I leaned giddily against the jinny pole. Peep Eye said, "I know something you fellers don't. Plumey's marrying Rant Branders tonight."

"Be-doggies," Jimp swore. "Rant promised I was the only one to know. Secrets nor varmints nobody can keep."

"One secret I've kept," Peep Eye bragged. "I've larnt why the square's here. A scanty few knows that."

We pleaded with her to tell, but she wouldn't. She would only talk of the wedding. "When I grow as tall and fair as Plumey," she said, "I'm going to pick me a man who can jounce air one o' my brothers, one strong as Pappy, and able to take his part."

"By doomsday you won't be fair as Plumey," Jimp said contrarily.

Peep Eye frowned. Her mouth puckered.

"You're the born image of Plumey," I said, "except for a beauty spot. Now, I choose a mole on a woman's cheek."

"I kin make me one out o' a soot pill," Peep Eye said.

"Be-doggies," Jimp grumbled. "I hain't ever aiming to marry."

I sat on the pole and swung my legs. "I'll not be a bachelor or a widow-man," I spoke.

Peep Eye looked strangely at me. She raised her arms and pushed me backward, and fled. I stood on my head yonside the jinny.

Jimp said, "Girls allus let a feller know when they like him a mite."

Under the sirup kettle fire blazed so lively the darkness was eaten away, and pale glimmers of lanterns swallowed, and far tops of the gilly trees lit. I sat on a heap of milled sorghum stalks, my molassy spoon ready, anxious to taste the foam. Jimp crouched beside me, grinding his teeth in anger. He'd heard his ferret was dead, and he stared auger holes at Bailus and Squire Letcher. Oh Bailus hadn't got rid of the squire. The squire rested on an empty keg, sighing wearily and clapping a hand to his mouth.

I had Jimp point Rant Branders out. Rant appeared bare-bones, yet in height he stood taller than the Buckhearts. He was long armed and long legged, and a grain awkward. I said, "I bet he's a cagey one. He's a green grasshopper of a man." And I began counting the people who had come to the stir-off. I named my fingers five times and over. I saw Plumey whispering to a bunch of girls, and Old Gid moseying around wondering at the crowd, and Peep Eye flitting here and yon like a silk butterfly. I kept gazing at Peep Eye.

"My beastie's stone dead," Jimp glummed. "That law-square and Bailus's to blame. Had I a chip o' money I'd hire fellers to trick them into the sorghum hole. Be-dogs, I would."

"Fellers'd be scared of a magistrate," I said. "Anyhow, your ferret wasn't shot a-purpose. Hit was mistook for a rabbit."

"My pap hain't afeared o' the Law. He could scare that square in without tipping him."

I caught Peep Eye watching me, and I wanted to leave the sorghum heap. I saw her face was pouty and cold. I thought inside my head, "Hit's not like what Jimp said. I bet she hates my gizzard," but I said aloud to Jimp, "I'm bound to eat molassy foam when it's first done. Hain't but one thing better, and that's pull-candy."

Jimp harped his troubles. "Rant's broke his swear-word. He promised me knucks to fit and then made 'em shooting big. They'd fit U. Z." He fetched them from a pocket and the finger places were the size of quarter-dollars. "I've struck an idee I don't want that fence rail for a brother-in-law. Oh my pap could jounce him with one arm tied."

"Rant hain't grown yit," I said. "He might grow thick. Already he's a high tall feller."

We went to stand by the sirup kettle, breathing the mellow steam hungrily, watching the golden foam rise. Leander chunked the fire and U. Z. ladled green skimmings into the sorghum hole. The hole was waist-deep and marked by a butterweed stalk. U. Z. joked us, "Dive in, boys, and you kin stand yore breeches in a corner tonight." We stepped warily.

Old Gid came with Mrs. Buckheart to test the sirup, spinning drops off of chips, tasting. Gid said, "Stir till it 'gins making sheep's eyes, and mind not to over-bile." He stared unbelievingly at the crowd. "Only a funeral occasion or a marrying would draw such a swarm, and I've heard o' nobody dying. Yet, for a host o' folks, they're terrible quiet."

"Bury some 'un in the sorghum hole," U. Z. laughed, "and they'll liven up."

"I long to see the Law eat a few skims," Leander said, and Peep Eye was hiding behind him, hearing every word.

U. Z. said, "I'm for giving the oninvited something to recollect this stir-off by."

"Amen," Leander said.

Mrs. Buckheart spoke nervously. "We ought to o' saved a couple gallons o' juice for candy, to please the chaps. We've got more sirup now than can be sopped till Jedgment."

"Invited or not," Gid said, "I want folks to pleasure themselves. What's become o' the fiddlers?"

Leander shrugged. "Ever hear of a fiddler loving the Law? They high-tailed."

Old Gid cocked his chin and spoke low. "The size o' this crowd is onnatural. Something's drawed folks."

Jimp's mouth opened, but he'd no chance to get a word in edgeways. Gid latched his thumbs on his galluses and spiked his elbows. "I'm not a born fool," he said. "Why, I know the magistrate come to speak a ceremony. Everybody knows. Even Peep Eye's got the fact writ on her face." He glanced defiantly at Mrs. Buckheart. "Woman! That spindling Branders stranger couldn't make a hum-bird a living."

Mrs. Buckheart's neck reddened. "Stranger to nobody but you. You've ne'er tested his grit, to my knowing."

"Why a daughter o' mine would choose a shikepoke to live with is ontelling."

Peep Eye emerged from behind Leander. "Plumey worships the dirt betwixt Rant Branders's toes," she said. She threw her neck like a hen; she flicked a spiteful glance at me.

My hunger fled. I thought, "I'll not eat a bite o' Buckheart foam," and I tossed the molassy spoon into the fire. I turned away and saw Jimp whispering to U. Z.; I saw Jimp thrust the brass knuckles into U. Z.'s hand.

Old Gid snapped, "Tell that young jake to git his growth."

"Speak to his face," Mrs. Buckheart challenged. "Come, I'll acquaint you."

"Sic him, Pap," Jimp crowed happily.

Gid's brows raised. "Ah," he said. His woman had him cornered. "Ah," he mumbled, "I don't mind shaking Rant Branders's glass hand, but first let me blow a spark o' life into the gathering." And just then Jimp raised on tiptoe, calling, "Looky yonder. They's two fellers rooster-fighting." Two fellows had their feet on marks, their arms doubled. They smote each other.

"Be-dog," Jimp cried, "wisht I was rooster-fighting with some 'un my size." We hustled to see, crawling between folks' legs, getting inside of the circle.

The rooster-fighters halted and the gathering made a roar of joy for Old Gid stepped into the ring, walked past Rant, and leveled a finger at Squire Letcher. Gid's voice rose good-naturedly. "Me and the square have a bone to pick. Allus ago we fit, and nary a one could whoop."

A flat smile withered on the squire's cheeks. He'd not the chance of a rabbit scrapping a ferret.

Gid said, "Let's move nigher the fire for light."

The crowd moved, leading the squire; it pushed and spread until the sorghum hole lay inside the ring. The butterweed stalk vanished. I saw Old Gid's boys bunching behind the crowd, their faces bright and tricky. U. Z. had left the kettle, edging close to Bailus; and both Leander and Bailus grinned oddly at me and Jimp.

But Gid didn't tip the squire. The magistrate stepped off the marked line, giving up ere he'd begun. He didn't even box his arms. He walked backward, keeping Gid at arm's length; he sidled and crawdabbed until he had sorghum-holed himself. He came out green as a mossed turkle. And then it was Old Gid's boys began pushing, and fellows shoved and fought to keep clear of the hole. Jimp and I were in the midst of the battle. Gid's boys soused a plenty; they soused folk invited or not, and they ducked one another too. U. Z. grabbed Bailus, rolling him in headforemost; and Leander caught me, and Bailus snagged Jimp. They dipped us.

I wiped the green skims off my face. I saw old Gid walk up to Rant Branders, saying, "Hit's time we're acquainted," and stuck out his arm. They clapped hands. Gid's jaws clenched as he gripped, his neck corded. Yet Rant didn't give down, didn't bat an eye or bend a knee. He stood prime up to Old Gid and wouldn't be conquered.

Old Gid dropped his hand. He cut a glance about, chuckling. "Roust the square if they's to be a wedding," he said. "Night's a-burning."

Jimp and I hid behind the cane pile, being too hang-headed and shy to watch a marrying. Under the gilly trees Jimp said, "Me and you hain't never fit. Fighting makes good buddies." He clenched his fists.

I knew Peep Eye spied upon us. "You hit first," I said, acting cagey, taking my part.

"Say a thing to rile me."

I said, "Yore pappy's a bully-man, and I'm glad Rant Branders locked his horns."

We fought. We fought with bare fists, and it was tuggety-pull, and neither of us could out-do. And of a sudden Peep Eye stood between us. Her cheek bore a soot mole, and she was fairer than any finch of a bird, fairer even than Plumey. She raised a hand, striking me across the mouth, and ran. Jimp said, "Jist a love lick." The blow hurt, but I was proud. And then we heard Old Gid's voice ring like a bell and saw him waving his arms by the forgotten molasses kettle. "Land o' Gravy!" he shouted. "We've made seventeen gallons o' candy jacks."

Locust Summer

I recollect the June the medicine drummer and his woman came down Shoal Creek and camped three days in our mill. That was the summer of Mother's long puny spell after the girl-baby was born; it was the time seventeen-year locusts cried "*Pharaoh*" upon the hills, and branches of oak and hickory perished where their waxy pins of eggs were laid. Wild fruit dried to seeds, and scarcely would birds peck them, so full their crops were with nymphs. Mulberries in the tree behind our house ripened untouched. Lark and I dared not taste, fearing to swallow a grub. Fern vowed not to eat, though I remember her tongue stayed purple till dog days.

"A rattlesnake's less pizenous than berries in a locust season," Mother kept warning. She knew our hunger; she knew how sorry Father's cooking was. "A body darst eat off o' vine or tree."

"A reg'lar varmint and critter year," Father told Mother. "Aye gonnies, if they hain't nigh as many polecats in the barn as they's locust amongst trees. Yet nothing runs as wild as these chaps. Clothes a puore tear-patch, hands rusty as hinges. Hit'll be a satisfaction when you're able to take them back under your thumb. I'd a' soon tend a nest o' foxes."

"I figure to strengthen when the locusts hush," Mother said. "A few more days o' roaring and they'll be gone." And she glanced at Fern, being most worried about her. "Still, I can't make a child take pride if they're not born with it. Fern's hair is matty as a brush heap. It's eating her eyes out."

"Humph," Fern said. She didn't care a mite.

Lark and I would look scornfully at the baby nestled in the crook of Mother's arm. We'd poke our lips, blaming it for our having to eat Father's victuals. Oft Zard would crawl under the bed to sniffle, and Mother had to coax him out with morsels from her plate. He was two years old, and jealous of the baby. Fern never complained. She fetched milk and crusts to her hidden playhouse, eating little at the table. So it was Lark and I who stubbed at meals. A pone Father baked was a jander of soda. Vegetables were underdone or burnt. We would quarrel, saying spiteful things of the baby, though above our voices rose the screams of the locusts, "*Phar-rrr-a-oh! Pha-rrr-a-oh!*" The air was sick with their crying.

Father would blink at Mother. He'd hold his jaws, trying to keep a straight face. "No sense raising a baby nobody wants," he'd speak. "Wish I could swap her to a new set o' varmint traps. Or could I find a gypsy, I'd plumb give her away."

"I'd ruther to have a colt than a basketful o' baby chaps," I'd say. "I allus did want me one." I would think of our mare, and the promise Father once made. Long past he'd made it, longer than hope could live. He'd said, "Some fine pretty day thar might be a foal. Hit's on the books." But never would he say just when, never say it was a sure fact.

I recollect that on the morning the medicine drummer and his woman came down Shoal Creek I had gone into the bottom to hunt Fern's playhouse. She had bragged of it, nettling me with her talk. "A witch couldn't unkiver my den," she'd said. "I got something there that'd skin yore eyes."

I was searching the berry thicket when a dingle-dangle sounded afar. A spring wagon rattled the stony creek bed, pulled by a nag so small I could hardly believe it, and a man and woman rode the jolt seat. It passed the mill, climbing the steep road to our house. I watched it go, and hurried after; I ran, hoping it came unbeknownst to Fern.

But Fern was there before me, staring. Mother came onto the porch, taking her first steps in weeks. She held the baby, squinting in the light, her face pale as candlewax. Zard peeped around her skirts.

The drummer jumped to the ground, his hat crimped in a hand. He was oldy, and round-jawed as a cushaw is round, and not a hair grew on the pan of his head; he was old and his woman seemed young enough to be a daughter. He bowed to Mother, brushing his hat against the dirt. He spoke above the thresh of locusts, eyeing as if taking a size and measure. "Lady," he said, "could we bide a couple o' nights in your millhouse, we'd be grateful. My pony needs rest." The woman gazed. Her hair hung in plaits. She watched the baby in its bundle of clothes.

Mother sat down on the water bench. She couldn't stay afoot longer. "You're welcome to use," she replied. "A pity hit's full o' webs and meal dust. My man's off plowing, else he'd clean the brash out."

I couldn't hold my eyes off the nag, off the tossy mane that was curried and combed. She looked almost as pretty as a colt.

Fern edged nearer, anxious. "Lizards in that mill have got razor throats. You're liable to get cut at."

"We can pay," the drummer said to Mother.

"Not a pency-piece we'd take," Mother assured.

Fern became angry, and I marveled at her. She doubled fists behind her back. "Spiders beyond count in the mill. Spiders a-carrying nit bags and stingers."

"Lady," the drummer said, speaking to Mother and paying Fern no attention, "I've traveled a far piece in my life." He stacked his hands cakewise. "A host of sicknesses I've seen. Now, when a body needs a tonic, when their nerves stretch, I can tell on sight. I've seen women's flesh fall away like a snow melt. I've seen—"

"Doc Trawler!"

The woman had called from the wagon, calling a bit shrill and quick, tossing her plaits uneasily. She had seen Mother's face grow whiter than puccoon blossoms.

"Ask about the berries."

"Ah, yes," the drummer said irritably, dropping his hands. "My wife's a fool for berry cobbler. She's bound to eat though one seed can cause side-complaint. My special purge has saved her being stricken long ago."

"Ask may we pick berries in the bottom!" The woman's words cracked like broken sticks.

The drummer waited.

Mother stirred uncertainly. "Wild fruit's pizen as strickynine when locusts swarm," she cautioned. "Allus I've heard that."

The drummer's face lit, grinning. He swept his hat onto his head and climbed on the wagon. The woman smiled too, but it was the baby she smiled at.

"That mill's a puore varmint den," Fern spoke hatefully.

The pony wheeled, and they set off for the mill. The drummer's woman looked back, her eyes hard upon the baby.

That night we children sat at the table with empty plates. Grease frizzled the dove Father was cooking for Mother. "They hain't a finickier set o' chaps in Kentucky," Father groaned. "I bile stuff by the pot, I bake and I fry, still these young 'uns will hardly eat a mouthful. By jukes, if I don't believe they could live on blue air."

I wrinkled my nose. A musky smell came from somewhere. I spied at the bowl of potatoes, at the bud eyes staring. "I hain't hungry," I said, but I was. Hunger stalked inside of me.

The musk grew. Lark and Zard pinched their noses and grunted. Yet Fern didn't seem to mind. She spread her hands flat upon her plate, and they were pieded with candle-drip warts.

I grew envious of the warts. I bragged, "I've got a spool will blow soap bubbles the size o' yore head."

"Baby's got the world beat for bubbles," Father said. "Blows 'em with her mouth."

"A varmint's nigh," Mother said, covering the baby's face. She rocked her chair by the stove to fan the smell. "Traps ought to be set under the house."

Father poked a fork into the dove. "I met a skunk in the barn loft," he chuckled. "Stirred the shucks and out she come, tail high. I reckon it's my pea jacket by the door riching the wind."

"Polecats have got the prettiest tails of any critter," Fern defended. "Hain't allus a-miaowing like nannies."

"Their tails are not bonny as the drummer-pony's mane," I said.

"Haste that garment to the woodpile," Mother told me.

I snatched the jacket and went into the yard, leaving it on the chopblock. I looked about. The mulberry tree stood black-ripe with dark. Below, in the bottom, the mill cracks shone. I planned, "Come morning, I'll get a close view o' that nag. I'll say to the drummer, 'Was Poppy of a notion, would you swap to our mare?'" I spat, thinking of our beast.

Father was talking when I got back. "I've set traps the place o'er, but every day they're sprung, bait gone, and nothing snared. I say hit's a question. The only thing I've caught's an old she in the millhouse, and I figure little ones were weaned."

"Once I seed two varmints walking," Lark said. "I run, I did."

Fern stuck her chin out, vengeful and knowing. "I told them folks that mill was a puore den."

Mother saddened. "I've never heard a child talk so brashy to olders. I was ashamed."

Fern raised her hands, tick-tacking fingers. "Humph," she said willfully.

The thought came into my head that Fern's playhouse might be close to the mill. I stung to go and see.

"One thing's gospel," Father laughed, not wanting Mother to begin worrying. "Chaps nor varmints won't tetch my bait. I load the traps and table, for nothing. They're independent as hogs on ice."

"These chaps are slipping out o' hand," Mother said, her lips trembling. "Fern, in partic'lar. Eleven years old and not a sign o' womanly pride. I can't recollect the last time she combed her hair."

"Might's well buy her breeches and call her a boy," Father teased, "yet I'm a-mind she'll break over. Girls allus get prissy by the time they're twelve. Hit's on the books." He eyed Lark and me. "I know two titmice hain't combed their topknots lately."

"You ought to make Fern wear plaits," I spoke. "The drummer's woman wears 'em."

"I hain't going to weave myself to ropes," Fern said. She walked fingers around her plate, skippety-hop. "Hair tails hanging. Humph! Ruther to be baldy."

"Ah, ho," Father laughed. "I come by the mill before dark and talked to Doc Trawler. I saw him with his hat off. Now, his woman don't need a looking-glass. She kin just say, 'Drap yore head down, old man. I aim to comb my lockets.'"

"Once I seed a horse go by with a wove tail," Lark said.

The dove browned, and was lifted to a plate. Father handed it to Mother. The bird was small, hard-fried, and briny it was bound to taste. Father always seasoned with a heavy hand. I thought, "It would take a covey o' doves to satisfy me." I felt that empty. I thought of berries wasting in the bottom; I thought of the mulberry tree. I spooned a half-cooked potato from the bowl, speaking under my breath, "That baby's to blame. She hain't nothing but a locust-bug."

Mother fiddled with the bird. Zard slid off the bench to get a morsel. Presently Mother gave it all to him, saying, "I can't stir an appetite. I can't force it down."

Father groaned. "Be-dabs, if the whole gin-works hain't got the punies. Even the mare tuk a spell today. She wouldn't eat corn nor shuck."

"What ails the mare?" Mother asked quietly. The baby had whimpered in her nap.

I didn't pity the beast, being contemptuous of her. I scoffed, "Bet they's folks would say hit's writ in a book. Now, they's no book got everything printed already."

Father answered neither Mother nor me, but his eyes were sharp and bright. He said, "I forgot the drummer sent a bottle o' tonic. Swore it'd red the blood and quick the appetite. Hit's yonder in my pea jacket. One o' you fellers fotch it."

"I be to go," Lark said. He brought in a tall bottle of yellow medicine.

Father held the bottle aloft, jesting, "If this would arouse hunger, I'd dose chaps, traps, and the mare. Allus been said, when the sick take to eating, they're nigh well. A shore promise." He set the bottle on a high shelf and chuckled. "I wonder from what creek Doc Trawler dipped that yaller water."

"Is that mare's sickness natural?" Mother insisted.

"I heard a gander honk last fall," Father said, "but hit's no sign we've got a goose nest."

Lark said. "I bet she up and et berries."

"Old plug mare," I mumbled. I spoke aloud, "That drummer's got a healthy nag. Hain't much bigger'n a colt. Was she mine, I'd not swap for gold."

"I glimpsed that play-pretty of a nag," Father said. "She's old as Methuselum's grandpappy's uncle. Teeth wore to the gum. Thar she was eating out o' a plate, like two-legged folks. If a woman hain't got chaps to spile, she'll pamper a critter to death. The way with women."

The baby waked suddenly, crying. Father leaned over Mother's shoulder. He clucked. "See her ope her eyes?"

I said, "Ruther to hear a bullfrog croaker."

Lark scowled. "Wust I come on a little 'un nested in a stump, I'd run far and not go back."

Fern twickled her warty fingers at me and Lark; she made a hop-frog of her hands. She knew how to rile us.

"Woe, woe," Father moaned. "I reckon we might's well give this child to the drummer-woman and be done. She's got nothing to pet on but that nag and bald-head man."

I looked squarely at Fern. "I've a fair notion where your playhouse is," I said. "I'm going a-searching."

"Humph," Fern said, but she became uneasy. She rubbed her hands together, flaking the tallow warts. "Unkiver my play-nest and I'll get level with you. I'll pay back double."

Mother sighed, "If a pot o' soup could be made tomorrow, I believe I could eat. Soup with a light seasoning." She rocked her chair impatiently as Fern and I kept quarreling. "I long to tame these chaps," she said.

"You'd have to do what Old Daniel Tucker done in his song," Father said. "Comb their heads with a wagon wheel."

The mulberries were ripe. They hung like caterpillars, ready to fall at a touch. I sat high in the tree crotch among zizzing locusts, longing to taste the berries, and watching Fern. I saw Fern crawl under the house; I saw her skitter up the barn-loft ladder. She went here and yon, and was gone, and never could a body tell where.

I hurried toward the mill. The cow tunnels winding through high growth in the bottom were empty. I listened. A beetle-bug snapped and a bird made clinky sounds. I heard digging. A thing went *rutch rutch* in dirt. I tip-toed; I craned my neck. There amid tall briers the drummer knelt, digging herb roots. The pan of his head was glassy in the sun.

"Did some 'un go this way?" I asked.

The drummer rested. Sweat drops beaded his forehead. "While ago a skunk come in smelling distance. I had to stopple my nose." He sorted the roots, pressing them between his thumbs until sap oozed; he frowned and the meat of his jaws tautened. "It's the contrary season to gather herbs, yit a kettle o' tonic's got to be brewed ere I set off tomorry." He plucked a weed sprig from his grab pocket. "Only could I find more o' this ratsbane."

"I know where they's a passel," I said.

His face slackened. "Help me gather some and I'll be obliged. I can pay."

I cut my eyes about, ashamed to say the thing I'd planned. The words pricked my tongue. I took note that blackberries grew large as a toe in the bottom, and both hunger and the pony grew in my mind. "Would you be in a notion swapping your nag to our mare?" I ventured at last. "I allus did want me a little beast."

"Fifteen years we've fed that pony," the drummer said. He arose, stretching his legs. "She's nigh a family member, and my wife thinks more o' that nag than she does her victuals. She'd skulp me, was I to trade."

How bitter I felt toward our mare. "Our critter'll never have a colt like it was promised," I grumbled.

The drummer stacked his hands. He looked wise as a county judge. "She needs a special medicine," he advised. "I mix a tonic that cures any ill, fixes up and straightens out man or beast—the biggest medicine ever wrapped in glass." He patty-caked his palms. "Now, there's one trade I do fancy. Show me where the ratsbane grows and I'll make you a present of a bottle. One's all I've got left."

I spoke, "Bet was a feller to eat wild fruit, a dram o' that tonic would cuore the pizen. I bet."

A woman's voice called from the mill. "Doc Trawler! Oh Doc!"

The drummer started off. "You stay till I see what my wife's after," he said. I waited, and soon heard him returning, and the cow tunnels were filled with his laughter. He came back shaking with merriment. "That devil of a pony!" he said. "Oh hit's a good thing we're leaving tomorry."

We went to grabble ratsbane and the drummer chuckled all day. He was a fool about that nag. We dug till my back sprung; we dug till the sun-ball stooped in the sky.

Late in the afternoon we stood by the mill with a poke crammed full of roots. I breathed in the smell of cooking victuals and fairly starved. The drummer slapped the poke; he treated it like a human being. "I'll get your pay," he said, and fetched a bottle out of the mill, a bottle no taller than my uncle-finger. "Hit's strong as Samson," he said. "And wait. My wife's fixing something for your mother."

"Is this medicine bound to work?" I asked, sliding the bottle inside of a pocket.

"Hit'll fix that mare right up, shore as Sunday-come-Monday."

The nag walked around the millhouse. She stuck her head in the door, and drew back crunching an apple. The drummer smiled. "See that thar. Didn't I say this hardtail's nigh one o' the family?"

"My colt's going to have folk sense," I bragged.

"This pony's bound to stick her noggin into places," the drummer said. His face wrinkled happily. The crown of his head shone. "Now, what do you reckon she found this morning? A chap's playhouse. Leave it to a long-nose beast to sniff things out. Me and my wife looked, and what we saw we couldn't believe, but thar it was to prove."

"I'd give a pretty to know," I pleaded. "I've got to larn."

The drummer frowned. "For a good reason I don't want that place disturbed till we leave." He scratched his headtop, undecided whether to tell. "Swear you won't take a look till we're on the road and gone?"

"'Pon my word and deed."

"Hit's yonder then," he said, pointing to the lower side of the millhouse where the floor rested on high pillars. "I can't blame your sister for trying to scare us with talk o' spiders and lizards. Oh she's a wild 'un."

The drummer's woman brought a bowl capped with a lid. The plaits of her hair tipped her shoulders, and her eyes were sad as a ewe's. "Reckon we could steal a child off these folks?" she joked her man. "Five in their house. One wouldn't be missed." She handed the bowl to me. "Take this cobbler to your mother. Tell her every berry's been split; tell it's safe to eat."

I ran home, and my heart pounded as I went.

Mother sat alone with the baby. Father stirred soup in the kitchen, and I heard Lark and Zard quarreling there. I uncovered the cobbler, reaching it to Mother. The sweety smell rose in my face. My mouth watered. I spoke loudly, for Mother had plugs of wool in her ears to dim the cry of locusts; I said what the drummer's woman told me to say. The baby leaned to see. Then we heard Father coming, and Lark and Zard following. Mother whispered quickly, "I'm grateful, and hit's a pity to waste, yet we can't trust eating berries. Haste the cobble-pie to the pig pen, and don't name to the others." But time was only left to shove the bowl under the bed.

"All the locusts in Egypt couldn't make a racket equaling these two," Father told Mother. "Fussing o'er nothing but who could blow the largest spool bubble. I mixed hope with that soup you'd soon be up and at these young 'uns. I biled enough to last two days."

"I'll mend once the plague's ended," Mother said. "Any day now the locusts will hush. I long to give these chaps a taste o' soap and water."

"Fern come into the kitchen," Father said, "and it tuk a minute to tell be she varmint or vixen. Hit'd worry the mare's currycomb to thrash the burrs."

Zard peeked at the baby and sulled. He was green jealous. He dropped to his knees and crawled toward the bed. He scampered under.

"Another sight I glimpsed today," Father went on, "and hit was that drummer's woman combing a nag's mane. I never stayed to see if she bowed it with ribbons." He turned upon me, keeping his face sober. "And I've looked up our mare in the books. One more page-leaf to turn before knowing when."

"Only would Fern take a lesson," Mother said uneasily, making a sign. I snatched the bowl, and neither Lark nor Father noticed, for Mother raised the baby's head. Father chuckled, "See the bubble she's pucked with her mouth. Beats any you fellers can blow."

"No bigger'n a pea," Lark discounted.

Father snapped a thumb and forefinger. "Be-jibs, if we hain't got to get rid o' this little 'un. Not a kind word's allowed her."

I stole away to the pig pen, uncovered the bowl, and found the berry cobbler half eaten. Zard had gobbled it. I was fearful, believing him poisoned, thinking he might die. I remembered the bottle of medicine. Could I persuade him to swallow a dose? A thought sprung in my head. I'd dose all—the mare, Mother, and Zard. The drummer had vowed it would straighten out man or beast. They'd take medicine, and not know.

I hastened to the barn, pouring a knuckle's depth of the medicine into a scoop of oats. The mare poked her great yellow tongue into the grain; she ground her teeth. She ate the last bit, and licked the trough. She was mighty fat, I recollect.

On I hied to the house. I tipped inside the kitchen. There was the soup pot boiling on the stove, and I emptied nearly all of the medicine into it. All but one draft went into the soup.

Suddenly a *tick tick* sounded behind the stove. I thrust the bottle pocket-deep and looked. It was Fern, hidden with a comb in her hand.

"Humph," Fern said, hiding the comb. I could scarcely see her eyes through a brush of hair. She spoke threateningly, "I saw that baldy drummer show you where my playhouse is. If you go there, they's something will scare yore gizzard."

"Humph," I said, mocking.

The next morning the locusts had hushed. Cast skins clung to trunks and boughs, and it was as quiet as the first day of the world. Ere dew dried I waited in the bottom for the drummer folk to go. So great the stillness was, my breath seemed a thunder in my chest. I saw the drummer and his woman climb into their wagon and drive uphill to our house; I saw Father shake the drummer's hand in farewell. Fern, Lark, and Zard were staring.

I crept to the lower side of the mill where the floor stood high. I craw-dabbed under. Nothing I saw in Fern's playhouse, nothing save four stone pillars growing up, and an empty pan sitting. "Humph," I thought.

I heard footsteps. I sprang behind a pillar. Fern came underneath the floor bringing a cup of milk and meat crumbs; she brought the bait from Father's traps. Her hair was combed slick and two plaits tipped her shoulders, woven like the drummer-woman's. My mouth fell open.

The milk was poured into the pan. Fern squatted beside it, calling, "Biddy, biddy, biddy," and four little polecats came walking to lap the milk, and three big varmints began to nibble the meat. I blinked, shivering with fright, and of a sudden the critters knew I was there, and Fern knew. The polecats vanished like weasel smoke.

I recollect Fern's anger. She didn't cry. She sat pale as any blossom, narrowing her eyes at me. But not a mad or meany word she spoke. The thing she said came measured and cold between tight lips.

"You hain't heard the baby's been tuk," she said. "Poppy give it to the drummer."

I stood frozen, more frightened than any varmint scare. When I could move I ran toward the house, running with loss aching inside of me.

I thrust my head in at the door. Father was carving spool pipes for Lark and Zard. Mother ate soup out of a bowl, and her lap and arms were empty. Mother was saying, "Now this is the best soup ever I did eat. Hit's seasoned just right."

Father grinned. "You can allus tell when a body's getting well. They'll eat a feller out o' house and home." He saw me standing breathlessly in the door; he laughed, not trying to keep his face grave. "Well, well," he said, "I've closed the books on that mare. A colt's due tomorrow or the next day. That's a shore fact."

"The baby!" I choked. "She's been tuk!"

"Baby?" Father asked, puzzled. "Why, thar she kicks on the bed, a-blowing bubbles and growing bigger'n the government."

I turned, running away in shame and joy. I ran out to the mulberry tree. The fruit had fallen and the ground was like a great pie. I drew the medicine bottle from my pocket; I swallowed the last dose. I ate a bellyful of mulberries.

Hit Like to 'a' Killed Me

Some fellers don't never git growed up. They git killed down.

One time I like to 'a' got killed down. I was a leetle boy, and I tried to go a steepy place and thought I'd take a shortcut. They was an ol' path right side by the hill, and they was a big lot o' bushes thar. I fell amongst the bresh, went a-rolling down that hill, and my leg got hung in a fence at the bottom, and like to 'a' broke hit.

But that hain't all. That's a beginning. Once Grandpaw he tuk me up to the hills a-logging. I climbed a leetle bud bush and 'gin to swang 'round in it, a-having me a time, and they was a big log above me, and hit was propped. Grandpaw he got to pushing the log, and hit come loose and rolled toward me. I seed hit a-coming. I was so scared I was afraid to jump. I nigh froze. Jist as I see the log got close to my bush I swung back, a-scrouging away far as I could git, buddy, and that ar log didn't miss me a hair. Boy, I was scart!

Now, they was another time. I liked to got drowned. I was jist a tadwhacker, six years old, and Grandmaw she tuk me down to Redbird River to wash me with a ball o' soap and rag. They was a "tide" on Redbird, but I aimed to wade me some anyhow. I was naked, and I waded a leetle. Grandmaw she hollered me out. Well, I caught her a-looking some'eres else, and I jumped in agin. Water was so swift hit washed me down to the deep part, in a whirly hole. I 'gin to go 'round and 'round. I was too scared to holler, and too 'shamed to holler. Dee Critch happened to be a-passing in a wagon and seed me, and pulled me out.

But that hain't the only time I liked to got drowned. One time Mam tuk me up Goose Creek above Grandpaw's to pick beans, and I got to playing in the creek mud. Mam told me to git out o' that mud, or I'd stick something in my foot. I thought she'd whoop me so I come out. I come out 'cause I thought she'd whoop me, and I got in my head to slip down to Grandpaw's, so I went down-creek and tuk up by Grandpaw's orchard. Now, Mam didn't know where I was at. She got worried to see I was a-missing. She ast my brother where I'd gone to, and he was scared to tell, thinking I'd git a whooping. Mam she saw my foot tracks where I'd went to the edge o' the creek, and thought I was drowned. She fotched Uncle John in a hurry. He got an ol' long pole and went a-punching 'round next to the bank, and struck a log and thought hit was me. Then he said, "Luley, here he is," and tears 'gin to roll down his cheeks. They went out to Grandpaw's house. Quick as Grandmaw saw 'em she knowed they was something wrong. Grandmaw ast 'em what was wrong. And they told her I'd got drowned shore, and they wanted to borry some hooks to scratch me out. Grandmaw she jist laughed. She knowed I was alive.

Well, once Grandpaw told me he'd take me and my brother 'possum hunting. We got axes and a lantern ready. We walked up Sprang Branch, and we'se going up 'round a ridge, me behind, and I hurt my leg. They went on, paying me no mind, and they went on 'round the ridge. I heered a dog a-barking. I made to go to it. I 'gin to run. I run, and I heered a big noise right behind me. I run to the house nigh dead. Grandmaw ast me what was the matter, and I told her and said they was something up thar like to got me. Grandmaw said hit was jist a big hoot owl. I'd ruther be killed than scart to death.

You want me to tell 'bout slang-shot fighting? One time I went over on Redbird. I met a boy over thar and he told me o' slang-shot fighting. He said they was the best fun in it ever was. When I come back home I told Mace Nevell, and Mace was my buddy, and Mace said we'd git ready to have a battle with some fellers we knowed. We went and had a leetle cabin in the hills. We piled a lot o' logs 'round it, and packed a lot o' gravels up from the creek and got us ready. We'd told them fellers we knowed, and give 'em to the top o' the hill, safe. Me and Mace had two good slang-shots in that ar cabin, and we had us a hole to shoot through and a lid over for kiver. We shot and shot. We shot a pile of rocks. Then Mace forgot and left the kiver off that hole and a rock come through and hit me on the head. Hit like to 'a' killed me.

I don't know how fellers git growed.

Mrs. Razor

"We'll have to do something about that child," Father said. We sat in the kitchen eating our supper, though day still held and the chickens had not yet gone to roost in the gilly trees. Elvy was crying behind the stove, and her throat was raw with sobbing. Morg and I paused, bread in hand, and glanced over our shoulders. The firebox of the Cincinnati stove winked, the iron flowers of the oven throbbed with heat. Mother tipped a finger to her lips, motioning Father to hush. Father's voice lifted: "I figure a small thrashing would make her leave off this foolish notion."

Elvy was six years old. She was married, to hear her tell it, and had three children and a lazy shuck of a husband who cared not a mite for his own and left his family to live upon her kin. The thought had grown into truth in her mind. I could play at being Brother Hemp Leckett, climb onto a chopblock and preach to the fowls; or I could be Round George Parks, riding the creeks, killing all who crossed my path; I could be any man body. Morg couldn't make-believe; he was just Morg. But Elvy had imagined herself old and thrown away by a husband, and she kept believing.

"A day will come," Elvy told us, "when my man's going to get killed down dead, the way he's living." She spoke hard of her husband and was a shrew of a wife who thought only of her children; she was as busy with her young as a hen with diddles. It was a dog's life she led, washing rags of clothes, sewing with a straw for needle, singing by the half hour to cradled arms, and keeping an eye sharp for gypsies. She jerked at loose garments and fastened and pinned, as Mother did to us.

Once we spied her in the grape arbor making to put a jacket on a baby that wouldn't hold still. She slapped the air, saying, "Hold up, young 'un!" Morg stared, half believing. Later she claimed her children were stolen. It wasn't by the dark people. Her husband had taken them—she didn't know where. For days she sat pale and small, minced her victuals, and fretted in her sleep. She had wept, "My man's the meanest critter ever was. Old Scratch is bound to get him."

And now Elvy's husband was dead. She had run to Mother to tell this thing, the news having come in an unknown way. She waited dry-eyed and shocked until Father rode in from the fields in middle afternoon and she met him at the barn gate to choke out her loss.

"We've got to haste to Biggety Creek and fetch my young 'uns ere the gypsies come," she grieved. "They're left alone."

"Is he doornail dead?" Father had asked. And he smiled to hear Biggety Creek named, the Nowhere Place he had told us of once at table. Biggety Creek where heads are the size of water buckets, where noses are turned up like old shoes, women wear skillets for hats, and men screw their breeches on, and where people are so proper they eat with little fingers pointing, and one pea at a time. Father rarely missed a chance to preach us a sermon.

"We've got to haste," Elvy pled.

"Do you know the road to Biggety Creek?"

Elvy nodded.

Father keened his eyes to see what manner of child was his own, his face lengthening and his patience wearing thin. He grabbed his hat off and clapped it angrily against his leg; he strode into the barn, fed the mules, and came to the house with Elvy tagging after and weeping.

"Fix an early supper," he told Mother.

Father's jaws were set as he drew his chair to the table. The day was still so bright the wall bore a shadow of the unkindled lamp. Elvy had hidden behind the stove, lying on the cat's pallet, crying. "Come and eat your victuals," Mother begged, for her idea was to humor children and let them grow out of their notions. But Elvy would not.

We knew Father's hand itched for a hickory switch. Disobedience angered him quicker than anything. Yet he only looked worried. The summer long he had teased Elvy, trying to shake her belief. Once while shaving he had asked, "What ever made you marry a lump of a husband who won't come home, never furnishes a cent?" Morg and I stood by to spread leftover lather on our faces and scrape it off with a kitchen knife. "I say it's past strange I've not met my own son-in-law. I hunger to shake his hand and welcome him to the family, ask him to sit down to our board and stick his feet under."

Father had glanced slyly at Elvy. "What's his name? Upon my honor, I haven't been told."

Elvy looked up. Her eyes glazed in thought. "He's called Razor."

"Given name or family?"

"Just Razor."

"Ask him to visit us," Father urged in mock seriousness. "Invite him up for Sunday dinner."

Elvy had promised that her husband would come. She had Mother fry a chicken, the dish he liked best, claiming the gizzard was his chosen morsel. Nothing less than the flax tablecloth was good enough, and she gathered day-eye blossoms for the centerpiece. An extra chair was placed, and we waited; we waited noon through, until one o'clock. Then she told us confidentially, "Go ahead and eat. Razor allus was slow as Jim Christmas."

She carried a bowl of soup behind the Cincinnati stove to feed her children. In the evening she explained, "I've learnt why my man stayed away. He hain't got a red cent to his pocket and he's scared of being lawed for not supporting his young 'uns."

Father had replied, "I need help—need a workhand to grub corn ground. A dollar a day I'll pay, greenback on the barrel top. I want a feller with lard in his elbows and willing to work. Fighting sourwood sprouts is like going to war. If Razor has got the measure of the job, I'll hire him and promise not to law."

"I ought never to a-took him for a husband," Elvy confessed. "When first I married he was smart as ants. Now's he turned so lazy he won't even fasten his gallus buckles. He's slouchy and no 'count."

"Humn," Father had grunted, eyeing Morg and me, the way our clothes hung on us. "Sloth works on a feller," he preached. "It grows roots. He'll start letting his sleeves flare and shirttail go hang. One day he gets too sorry to bend and lace his shoes, and it's a *swarp, swarp* every step. A time comes he'll not latch the top button of his breeches—ah, when a man turns his potty out, he's beyond cure."

"That's Razor all over," Elvy had said.

Father's teasing had done no good. As we sat at supper that late afternoon, listening to Elvy sob behind the stove, Morg began to stare into his plate and would eat no more. He believed Elvy. Tears hung on his chin.

Father's face tightened, half in anger, half in dismay. He lifted his hands in defeat. "Hell's bangers!" he blurted. Morg's tears fell thicker. I spoke small into his ear, "Act it's not so," but Morg could never make-like.

Father suddenly thrust back his chair. "Hurry and get ready," he ordered, "the whole push of you. We're going to Biggety Creek." His voice was dry as a stick.

Elvy's sobbing hushed. Morg blinked. The room became so quiet I could hear flames eating wood in the firebox. Father arose and made long-legged strides toward the barn to harness the mules.

We mounted the wagon, Father and Mother to the spring seat, Elvy settling between; I stood with Morg behind the seat. Dusk was creeping out of the hollows. Chickens walked toward the gilly trees, flew to their roosts, sleepy and quarrelsome. Father gathered the reins and angled the whip to start the mules. "Now, which way?" he asked Elvy. She pointed ahead and we rode off.

The light faded. Night came. The shapes of trees and fences were lost and there were only the wise eyes of the mules to pick the road when the ground had melted and the sky was gone. Elvy nodded fitfully, trying to keep awake. We traveled six miles before Father turned back.

The Sharp Tack

Standing Rock, Kentucky
March 2, 1946

Mr. Talt Evarts
Wiley, Ky.

Dear Mr. Evarts:

I wouldn't know you from Adam's off-ox, and I'm not the pattern of a man to butt into the affairs of others. Say I, Let every man-jack attend to his own affairs and stay out of the shade of the next fellow. What's not a body's business, play deaf and dumb to it. But lately strange tales have been drifting from Wiley Town, lies strong enough to melt the wax in a body's ears. They concern the Man Above, and what concerns Him concerns me. As his disciple, whoever steps on His toes mashes mine.

For half of a lifetime I've preached amongst the hills and hollows of Baldridge County. I've served more folks than you have reckoning of. Married them, buried them, and tried to save their souls betwixt and between. There isn't a church-house or oak bower in Baldridge County in which I haven't trod the pulpit and preached the Book. It's my burden on earth to be watchdog to the sheep, unfrocker of the world wearing the lamb's clothing, scourger of the wicked. Well, sir, I'm writing to you on your behalf. I take my pen in hand to say that you are within singeing distance of hellfire and eternal damnation.

Our soldier boys have come home telling a mixture of things. Most handle only the truth and if wonders they viewed grow a mite big in their mouths I lay it to high spirits. Didn't they fit the good fight across the waters, risk their necks to slay the heathen? Didn't they send money home? To their reports I'm all ears. I grunt and I say "Oh!" and "Ah!" A grandson of mine climbed a tower in Italy called Pisa, and to hear him tell it, it was out of whanker, leaning on air, against nature and the plan of the Almighty. Plumb si-goggling! An anticky falsehood, I figure. Trying to see how big he could blow the pig's bladder before it busts. But your tale—yours is humbug of a different character. I've had it direct you've returned bearing a mortal untruth. And some are believing it. To learn of it jarred my heart.

People inform me you are claiming to have been to the Holy Land. They say you've brought a cedar sprout from Lebanon where King Solomon cut his temple timber and aim to plant it in Baldridge County soil. Upon my word and deed and honor! This cross-grains my fifty-one years of ministry in His Name. It sets to naught my long and weary labors.

Now, listen, mister boy. I'm a Bible worm. I've read it lid to lid. I testify only the dead and the saved ever journey to that Country—those risen from the grave, and that's not to be until Resurrection Day. The Holy Land is yonder in the sky and there's no road to it save by death and salvation. The fashion you spout lies, any minute I expect to hear of you passing through Jericho on an ass visiting Zion. As for the cedar bush, where you hooked it is not where you claim. Our hills and hollows have as much need for it as a boar has for tits. Jump on it. Tramp it into the ground.

I have a sermon which fits you like bark fits a tree. But it would use up a horn of ink to pen it. Besides, writing it I'd have to leave off the singing. My text would be on sharp tacks who twist Scripture to confound people and abet the Serpent. For one particular, they declare the world is round as a mushmelon, while the Book says plainly it has four corners. They start new congregations to peddle their corkscrew religion. They can quote you chapter and verse, aye-o, but they bear no fruit. They preach, and Old Horny reaps the benefit. I say, There's just one sect—the True Church. The rest are insects.

My advice to you is to hush your wild talk and line up behind common sense. You're riding a horse with the blind staggers. Saddle a fresh mount, say I. If you're bound to foam at the mouth, tell of seeing twenty-foot snakes as a soldier boy hereabouts vows he saw in Africa. Or of a people with lips the size of saucers. Or of a tombstone in the land of Egypt covering thirteen acres. Tall stories of that sort are evil, yet not fatal to the soul. Hark my counsel, or you're going as straight to hell as a martin to its gourd. And hell is not a haystack.

Jerb Powell

Standing Rock
March Eleventh

Talt Evarts
Wiley, Ky.

Let you open your mouth and out jumps a toad-frog. What further demon-gotten claims are to leap forth? The news comes you are now showing a chunk of marble you say was dug from King Solomon's quarry under the city of Jerusalem. Dug where Old Sol got his building rock for the Temple's foundations. Great balls of thunder! Can't you learn to separate heaven from earth?

Why didn't you follow the pattern of other soldier boys and bring home fighting knives and German guns and Jape swords? There are enough brought-on weapons in and about Standing Rock to wage a battle. Aye gonnies, the Silver War might of come out different did our side have them then. You should have latched on to honest relics. Cephus Harbin's Rufus had a chip off the rock of Gibraltar. A couple more wars and Gibraltar won't be of a size to strike a match on. My grandnephew sports a watch charm made from a toe he knocked off of a statue in France. Yet you couldn't be satisfied unless you fetched something fiendish. Hasn't a bloody war contented your mind? What else will it take to satisfy your lust for chicanery?

Your falsehoods are spreading like the Spanish grippe and some dumb-heads are believing them. It appears you could paint goose manure and sell it for gold. You've already caused me two run-ins. Our plug of a postmaster said I ought to crawl out of my terrapin shell and join the universe. Said I hadn't done my "home work"—whatever that means. I fixed the jasper. Told him did he swap brains with a jaybird it would fly backward. And I've tilted with our ignorant schoolteacher. He's a round-earth believer. Oh they're scratching under rocks to find schoolmasters nowadays.

The teacher started it. Said, "Reckon you've heard about the soldier boy from Wiley visiting the Holy Land." Says I, "I've heard the world is the shape of a crab apple, but that's not speaking I'm believing it. It's contrary to the Teachings. If I swallow that I'll have to agree water runs uphill and Chinamen walk with their heads hanging." He insisted, "The boy was on the very spot. No two ways talking." Spake I, "A host of the righteous will rise from the grave on Judgment Day and fly there. None now treading the earth has passed through the gates of pearl and retuned to tattle about it." You ought to of seen his countenance when I wised him up. His jaws sagged like a gate.

In olden time Noah sent a bird flying the waters. He sent a dove on particular business. But hey! Who sent you? Old Scratch? Lucifer incarnate? Old Gouge? The Book speaks of the behemoth. Why didn't you snatch a behemoth whisker? And I ask, Has any other traveler matched your claim of visiting Up Yonder? Now, no. A thousand counts no.

I'm not scorning the miracles of the age. Some truths are evident, known without witnessing. Joab Gipson's eldest son flew over Germany and dropped bombs down the throats of the enemy. Roan Thomas's son bore no gun in the fray. He fit with balls of fire spouted from a nozzle. Dial Roberts was an underwater sailor, traveled the bowels of the seas in a vessel. I fling my hat to the boys who punished the followers of the crooked cross.

Harken. Cease your blasphemy. Quit *baaing* on the order of a broken-mouth ram. Destroy the cedar sprout as you would a copperhead snake. And hey! A chunk of marble makes the best sort of hone to sharpen razors.

Jerb Powell

March Twenty-First

Talt Evarts:
A dunce I was to even mention a behemoth. I hear you are declaring them hippopotamuses, critters that live somewhere on this earth. Hell's bangers! Are you in cahoots with Beelzebub? Aye, your tongue is a viper which

continues to wiggle even after its head is cut off. I'm here to announce you are shoving yourself into a picklement. When you die, my opinion, there won't be a preacher worthy of the name willing to hold a service over your carcass.

A thought keeps itching my mind. While you were soldiering how did you manage to traipse all over the map. Why weren't you busy pumping bullets into the gizzards of the adversary? Throughout the war I had my ear glued to the news. As I recollect, no armies shot lead mines at each other in a country called Holy Land. Wheresoever it was you journeyed, did you sneak away to it from the battle? Upon my honor, I believe you white-eyed.

I'm a preacher, bear in head. The promise of Hereafter is a rapture to my heart, reckless tidings such as you bear a pain and a sorrow. Had I half a suspicion you had been to the real On High, a yoke of oxen couldn't of held me here at Standing Rock. To Wiley Town I would have hied. On hands and knees if necessary. Crawled if no other way. A peck of questions I would of asked: How wide the streets of gold? How sounded the trumpets of Tomorrow? How fared the blessed where ten thousand years is but a day? Being in my right mind, I stayed at home. Naturally. I wasn't born yesterday.

Talt Evarts, I've strove earnestly with you. I've written you letters you never answered, licked stamps and wasted paper trying to purge your stony heart. To no profit. You're buckled to the Devil. I've cut out toe-holds for you on the down-road, still you insist on sliding toward perdition. The time is short. My patience has worn thin as a dime. I won't struggle with you eternally.

Jerb Powell

April Second

Mr. Talt Evarts:
I would have bet my thumbs I'd not again black paper in your behalf. I had capped the ink bottle. But I've met with something which puts a different cast on matters. It came out of another argument with the Standing Rock teacher. I learnt a speck. I'll admit it. Aye, I aim to keep learning till my toes turn up. The teacher stayed mired in his own folly while I began to spy a ray

of daylight. The teacher—you might know him. I won't handle his name. I wouldn't want to dirty my tongue.

Well, sir, this jasper pulls a geography on me. He opened her up to a map where a dot stood for Jerusalem, a dot for Tiberius, a patch for the Dead Sea, a streak for the river Jordan. Printed up plain as my nose. For the split of a second I was stumped. What were these precious names doing in a book taught scholars at the tender age? Had the sharp tacks been at work? Then wisdom struck. It knocked me like the bolt which hit Paul on the Damascus Road. The whole thing came as clear as a baby's eye. I said, "Anybody two inches wide between the ears ought to be able to figure how these names got into a geography. I still say the soldier is bad wrong. To this I stick." More I wouldn't argue. I left the teacher with his eyebrows crawling.

So I'm back to declare there may be hope for you yet. You can plead ignorance. Ignorance pure and simple. The Creator is not stingy with His mercy. Witties are granted compassion, lackers of knowledge given a season to catch up. Is it your fault you missed the wagon? I count it my obligation to set you aright.

Jerb Powell

April Thirteenth

Dear Talt Evarts:

I'm in the worse calamity ever was. The Standing Rock schoolteacher and his bunch are low-rating me amongst the people. They've started a mud ball rolling. They say I vilified you when I pronounced your trip to the Holy Land a snare and a delusion. They howl I'm blaming you for keeping your eyes wide while serving your country. Our transgressor of a postmaster badmouthed me with, "All he knows is a chew tobacco."

A sorry come-off for a man to have dirt slung on his name after a life of snatching souls from the Devil's paws. I've strayed seldom from the straight and narrow. I married one woman and clung to her. I never sold my vote. No man has ever been skinned by me, except in a horse trade, and that doesn't count. Aye, the jaspers deserve to swallow their tongues and gag to death.

Pick your ears. Mark me well. I'm not claiming now you didn't go to a country bearing the name "Holy Land." I'm a fellow with brains enough to turn around when I've learnt I'm heading a wrong direction. What lodges in my craw is the mixing of Up Yonder with a place in this world. I'm willing to allow you visited a town called Jerusalem. I hold it was labeled after the city On High—like Bethlehem, Nebo and Gethsemane here in Kentucky. The Holy Land on earth is the namesake of the Country Above. That you didn't actually go to Glory Land was what I was trying to drive into skulls.

To show I'm of a notion to forgive you, I'll say I hope the cedar lives. Shovel barnyard dirt to it. That will make it walk. It promises to become the hurrah of the mountains, a living sermon, a foretaste of eternal life. I wish I had a sprig of it as a token.

I've been spying into your army record. You were a brave soldier by all my hears. You held your ground square in the whiskers of the foe.

Respectfully,
Jerb Powell

April Seventeenth

Dear Brother Evarts:

The cedar sprig you mailed reached me as green as the olive branch Noah's dove fetched to the ark. I dangled it before the schoolteacher and he threw up his hands and said, "I've hushed." And our postmaster allowed, "If the soldier can overlook your views, I reckon I can." Yes, sir, it takes a while to hammer straight warped minds. I'll hang the sprig over the door where it will feast my eye.

The next occasion I'm over to Wiley Town I'll stop by and shake your hand. I've heard you brought a gill of water from the river called Jordan. Not the real Jordan, of course. A river named after it. I aim to beg a drop or two. And I have a host of questions to ask. A country named for the heavenly one ought to be a pattern for folks living everywhere.

Eternally,
Jerb Powell

Maybird Upshaw

To the day I perish I will recollect Maybird Upshaw being hauled into my yard on Shepherds Creek in a wagon. She was my wife's kin, widowed by her second husband's death at the mines; she was the largest woman ever I set eyes upon.

The threshold creaked as Maybird pushed into the house. She sat on a trunk as we had no chair of a size to hold her. She dwarfed my wife and made a mouse of the baby. I recollect she sighed, "I've come to visit awhile," and breathed deep with satisfaction. "I aim to rest me a spell."

"You're welcome if you can live hardscrabble," said Trulla, fastening cold eyes on me, eyes blue as gun-metal. I knew she was thinking Maybird might be on our hands for life.

"We have only old-fashioned comforts," I spoke, brushing a hand behind my ears, for I stood in mortal need of a haircut. My eyes roved the log walls, coming to rest on Maybird, her large fair head with tresses rich as fire, the drapes of flesh hanging from her arms, knees dimpled as the baby's cheeks. I tried to figure her weight. She was as big as a salt barrel. She had the world beat.

A smile caught Maybird's face. "I'm not picky," she declared, "and anywhere's better than a coal camp." She made a book of her hands. "I'll stop off here awhile, then be moving on. I don't intend to burden."

"You'll miss the camps," I reminded, feeling Trulla's stare boring my skull. "Credit at the commissary when you're of a notion to buy, green money on payday, picture shows and circuses. They say when you've breathed gob smoke you're ruined for country air. And Shepherds Creek is as lorn a place as a body can discover."

"I'm not of a mind to stay long in any single spot," Maybird said. "I can't live content in a valley for wondering what's yonder side of the mountain. Ah, I've lived in a lot of camps—Blue Cannel, Hardblock, Alicecoal, Oxeye. And if

I had my rathers, I'd not stick my feet more than once under any table. During the days of my life I aim to see the whole of creation."

"A widow-woman would starve," Trulla argued, "traveling here and yon."

Maybird's face lit. Gold freckles shone on her nose. "My mother taught me to make wax blossoms when a child, window bouquets, mantel dressing and funeral wreaths. Why, I'll earn my way selling false flowers. The Turks-cap lilies and roses I pattern would fool butterflies. One sight of a blossom and I can shape a match to it."

"I've never yearned to travel," Trulla said, snatching up the baby and jouncing it nervously. "My longing is for a house with high ceilings and tall windows. But here stands the log pen of a homeseat I married. I'm tied to a man who is satisfied to live the same as his grandsire."

I let pass Trulla's complaint, being proud of the old-timey log dwelling which had been in the family more than a hundred years; I kept feasting my eyes on Maybird, and rousing courage to ask her weight.

"It's not my notion to settle down," Maybird went on. "I weary of viewing the same things over and over. Soon I'll be wandering along."

"While you're relaxing," Trulla suggested, "you might begin to make false flowers. We'll rob our bee gums and have wax in plenty."

Maybird chuckled. "Then I can start laying-by for my rambling." She began to laugh. Joy rose in her as cream to the lip of a milk jar. "Only would somebody peddle my bouquets at the camps. Thirty-five cents they ought to bring, fifty if the mines are working double shifts."

Trulla's face sharpened. "My man can go sell the flowers. He needs mightily to discover a barber anyhow. He has played Sampson long enough."

I squirmed. "A man drumming flowers? To sell firewood, or corn, or garden sass, I'd not mind. But peddling wax would be bitter hard. It's not man's work."

Maybird stirred and the hinges of the trunk rasped. She lifted a huge hand. "Just say they're Maybird Upshaw's pattern. Summer blooms for dresser tops. Blossoms to brighten a table, never to fade. They'll remember. Oh I'd go myself if I could get about handy." She cast a spiteful glance at the narrow door.

I hummed and hawed, and finally to change the talk I plucked courage and asked, "Maybird, how much do you weigh?" I didn't want to hear more about flower peddling. And if Trulla's quick look had been a blade my throat would have been cut.

But Maybird was proud of her size. She tossed her great head. "The day I was born," she said, "I tipped the scales at three pounds and a quarter—so tiny I was bedded on a pillow. At eighteen I weighed two hundred and eighty-five on the steelyards, yet for the past six years I've had no way to learn. The check-weigh-man's scales at the mines won't register under a thousand. My opinion, I'm safe to weigh four hundred."

"Your weight might hinder travel," Trulla remarked sharply.

"Now, no," Maybird declared, "I'll go the world around. In Kentucky I aim to see where the Frenches and the Eversoles fit their feud, and the Hatfields and the McCoys. I'll look on Natural Bridge and the Breaks of the Big Sandy River. I'll see Abe Linkhorn's birthplace, and where a battle was fit at Perryville. And I've heard afar west the fires of Torment spout from the ground, and the devil's boiling kettle throws up a steam. I'll see what there is to see."

"You ought to of been a gypsy," I said, "living in a cloth house, reading hands for bread, traipsing place to place,"

Maybird laughed softly. She blushed the mad color of her hair.

I walked to Oxeye mine camp the hottest September day in memory; and I felt like a dunce carrying a mess of false flowers. But Trulla's one fixed thought was to make certain of Maybird's departure before she grew too heavy ever to move again. Already it was tuggety-pull to get her through any door.

I knocked at the first house and I was as scared as the day I married. I brushed my hair under the back brim of my hat. Waiting, I spied about. Camp houses marched the hills and gob smoke fed into the sky. Babies were crying. Everywhere hung the smell of soot and dishwater.

A beardy fellow cracked the door, his woman crowding behind him. I lifted a bouquet. "Maybird Upshaw—" I began, and my throat frogged.

"Big May?" he asked.

His wife snatched the blossoms. "One thing about the large," she said, "they have good hearts. Generous, gee-o! Maybird always gave us flowers. We were neighbors. Thank Maybird. Thanks."

The door slammed and I was not a chip the richer.

A miner came along, his cap lamp burning in broad daylight. I inquired, "Are there double shifts working these days?"

"Yis." He stared as if he'd met a witty. "Are you drumming them flowers?" I was holding a bunch as you might a dead cat by the tail.

I dipped my head.

"A carnival has pitched at the ballground and folks won't spend a dime else-wheres. Oxeye Camp has gone show-crazy."

I knocked on many a door, not selling a blossom. "For sale?" they would say. "That doesn't sound like Maybird. She used to give us a vase full. To my knowledge she never sold a petal. She was that freehearted." Or, "I've only the price of the carnival, else I'd buy." An old-faced child said, "Maybird is the big-gest show ever I seed. The awfulest foot! I bet she weighs a jillion." And she stared at the hair escaping my hat.

In mid-afternoon a woman called after me. She bought a bouquet and paid two dimes and a nickel. "I'll pitch in to help a widow-woman good days or bad," she said. "Anyhow, nobody but Maybird can pattern flowers so real-like." And then I heard music afar and saw tents on the ballground, and a mighty wheel turning and with lights ringing it. People hurried by, and I followed.

The carnival folk yawned in the sun, blinking like owls. A music engine played. A weight-guesser held his hat in the crook of an elbow and shouted among a thicket of walking sticks: "I come within three pounds! Your weight within three! A gentleman's cane if I fail!" Miners and their women and chil-dren shucked out money to see MAN OR BEAST and MARVELS OF AMERICA.

I held the flowers behind me, and I asked the guesser a question. "Can you figure a woman's weight, sight unseen?"

He spoke swiftly, "If I'm given an idea of her measurements."

"I'll pay a quarter."

"Hand over. Right-tow. How tall? Broad of beam? Size of shoe?"

I told the best I could. I spread my arms, holding forth the flowers, though I couldn't circle so great a space as Maybird covered. I took a walking stick and drew on the ground. "She's so stout she looks notable," said I.

The weight-guesser blew between his teeth. "She's a whale," he cried. "Gaffney ought to hear about her."

"It's my belief she's a finer view than any you have here," I bragged.

He jerked an elbow toward MARVELS OF AMERICA.

"We have a dame weighing four hundred and twenty, but no match to the madam you've reported." He clapped the quarter back into my hand, and a ticket beside, and told me to see the show tee-total. "And take a gander at Mary Mammoth," he said. He didn't try to guess Maybird's weight.

"I ought to be going," I said, but I stayed to watch the acting dogs. I saw a fool swallow a sword; a lack-brain ate fireballs; a human creature reposed on a bed of spikes. I saw Mary Mammoth sitting on a platform, eating a meal. She nibbled a dish of lettuce leaves and drank from a nail hole in a can. Compared to Maybird she looked puny.

The weight-guesser called me over when I quit the tent. "Shake hands with Gaffney, the boss," he said. And Gaffney asked, "What's your opinion of Mary?"

"She'll do in a pinch," I said, and I felt a wax petal strike my shoe. The flowers were melting in the heat. "But my wife's sister-in-law dwarfs all womankind—firm-fleshed, plump cheeks, the picture of life. More pounds to her statue than ever I saw a human pack. Why, it took a two-horse wagon to haul her to Shepherds Creek."

Gaffney lifted an arm. "The lady belongs in a side show. She'd draw customers like honey draws flies."

"My belief," I agreed.

Maybird kept gaining weight. And was she an eater! She could stash away a peck at a sitting. She stripped the garden, emptied the meatbox. People came to look at her, and they ate also. I ran up a store debt. And I got joshed. A wag at the post office said, "I hear there's going to be a trial in the magistrate's court next Saturday." I bit, "What over?" Laughed he, "To try and see if Big May can sit in a number two washtub." The joke was on him. Even a number four tub would have been tight squeezing.

You could nearly see Maybird gaining. Before Gaffney came it got to where she couldn't pass through the door. We tugged and pulled, shoved and pushed, to no success. Trulla wanted me to widen the opening but I vowed it would destroy the house pattern. You mustn't fiddle with a butt-notched log dwelling. The building would have to be torn down ridgepole to sleepers to deliver Maybird. She was as trapped as a fox in a hen coop.

Trulla worried and grew cross. She would moan to me, "Of what use for the head of the carnival to come now that Maybird's prisoned inside." And Trulla turned hard to live with. The least thing and she took the rag off the bush. I couldn't glance at Maybird, much less carry on a conversation with her, without Trulla flying off the hinges. Never could I figure a woman's mind. Once she got the fidgets and took a notion to cut my hair. I stood in uncommon need of a trimming. But I saw the metal in her eyes, her chin trembling. I inched away, scared to have her near me with anything sharp in hand.

The carnival people came on a Thursday. I was in the barn, spying into a piece of looking glass, trying to crop my temples with mule shears. I heard hoofs rattle rocks, a singing of wheels, and a voice cry, "Whoa-ho!"

I hustled across the lot and sprang over the fence. A wagon and team stood in the yard. I heard Gaffney and the weight-guesser talking to Maybird inside the house. Maybird was sighing, "I'm held here everlastingly. I can't get out." Gaffney answered, "I didn't wrestle ferris wheels and cyclodromes thirty years for nothing. A way will be devised." The weight-guesser nodded.

I went in to bid the visitors welcome and offer chairs. Trulla stood back, shut-mouthed, too timid before strangers to practice manners. The first chance I whispered to the weight-guesser, "How much do you figure Maybird will pull on the scales?"

The weight-guesser calculated, one eye squinted to sharpen his view; he dug fingers into his scalp. "Five hundred and seven," he blurted, "and I've not missed three pounds."

Gaffney snapped his fingers with satisfaction. "We'll bill her as THE WORLD-LY WONDER," he said. And directly he set about inspecting the butt-locked logs of the front wall. He surveyed inside and out.

I was uneasy. I said, "Could we get a block and tackle, we might lift her up through the roof. No harm done to tear off a few shakes."

"Ah, no," he said. "Twisting the wrist is my calling. And all I'll need is a crowbar and a hammer." With a hammer's claws he pried loose the door facing and set it aside. The logs to the height of the door were left supported only at the corner.

I swallowed air. My Adam's apple jerked. I was in misery.

"We'll not damage," he said, and he and the weight-guesser worked the bar between the bottom log and the sleepers and prized up and forward.

I expected the worse. My breath caught.

The walls budged. Five logs raised in their notches and swung gate-fashion. The house opened like a turkey crate. A passage was made and Maybird walked through. Then the logs were jimmied back into place and the facing restored.

We hoisted Maybird into the wagon. She sat on the wagonbed and laughed, her face bright as a wax blossom, her hair wealthy as the sun.

Gaffney and the weight-guesser climbed onto the spring seat, and they rode away. And Trulla began to cry. She clapped a hand on my shoulder and her eyes had the glint of new nails. She got me into the house, found scissors, and worked me over. She whacked and gapped. She nearly ran out of hair. She skinned me alive.

Pattern of a Man

Salt Springs, Kentucky, May 17th

Mr. Perry Wickliff,
Roaring Fork, Ky.

Sir:

I take my pen in hand to ask your support of my candidacy for jailor of
Baldridge County on August 5th. I've heard you lost out in a school shuffle
last year. They say you were ousted as teacher at Spring Branch in the middle
of the term and have rented land off of Zeb Thornton and are trying to farm.
It chokes my heart to think of one with your learning digging holes and
plowing balks. A schoolteacher with paper hands battling dirt!

If any county needs top scholars, it's Baldridge. I'm bound there's a
politician behind the deal, and it stands to reason you're bitter as an oak gall.
When elected I'll use my power in your behalf. Whoever the gentleman who
frisked you out of a job, I'll have him out on a limb like a screech owl shoving
a chicken.

In a jailor race any hound dog can run and candidates are thicker than
yellow jackets at a stir-off. You don't have to know book letter from cow
horns, or to have ever darkened a schoolhouse door. On that account a big
bunch will file for office. I've underwent six years of education and I'm no
dumb-head. I'll be the only candidate who can make out print bottom up—a
trick I learnt reading newspaper wallpaper in boyhood. Many a deputy sheriff
has scratched his head at my recital of a warrant in this fashion. I've been
unlucky in the way of getting indicted for this and that and have spent more
time in jail than any other innocent man in the mountains. Point a finger at
me and I look guilty. Yet I've kept my name clear. Nothing ever stuck on me.

Before the election ends you'll hear lies, candidates smutting each other's reputations. They'll wear the hollows out slick rooting for votes. Oh you can't run a race without getting banged. The strongest they'll hit the hardest. Already they're spreading a tale about me and a gum of bees. I ask Justice, Can I rule what bees will do? I sold gum to a neighbor and nine days later the critters came swarming home.

On account of the contrariness of bee nature I suffered a month's confinement in the Crossbar Hotel. That's what the jaspers on the inside call it. I ate victuals Lazarus would of culled, slept on a mattress jake-walking with chinch bugs. And fleas! The cracks were hopping with them! As we'd say, if the flats don't bite you the sharps will. And hear me. Floors and walls begged for lye soap and shuck mops. The grub was so rough we used to swear you had to wear gloves to eat it. And that's where I struck my notion.

I struck on a notion to become the jailor. I swore to myself I would run for it next go-round, and when I'd nailed the job down, to bring my woman and live in the jailhouse. My woman would keep the place as clean as snow. Where my dough-beater has a hand you'll not find a speck of dust big enough to put in your eye. And we would feed meals a man could enjoy picking his teeth after. Chicken and dumplings every Sunday. A county lock-up needs a woman's fussing, and a woman's hate of gom.

I crave your vote and influence, for I hear you're well thought of over there. Canvas the Roaring Fork people in my behalf and I'll pull ropes to win you back a school job. Once I knew Roaring as I know my *a-b-ab's*, and many the woman will recollect me and my rounding ways. It happens I've not set foot in the section for a couple of years. But I found my wife on Fern Branch, a prong of Roaring, and I'm married-kin to plenty of folks in your territory.

Now, listen to me. While canvassing you might see a girl fair to the eye who can be talked into matrimony. I hear you live by your lorn self. Twenty-six years old and not wed! What in thunder! Can you stand to eat your own cooking?

Till I get there myself to clap the hands of the voters, begin swinging them in my favor. I stand well in the opinion of all, except Zeb Thornton—a tough one to deal with, as you may have discovered. A hard number, that Zeb.

It's my aim to travel the length of Roaring Fork, up every draw and trace and hollow. First my pieded pony must be shod before she walks the rocks, and I'm waiting to see who and how many join the race. The county court clerk says sixteen have filed and a big lot are on the borders of it. The more candidates, say I, the better.

I lay down my pen.

Crafton Rowan

Salt Springs, Ky, May 28th

Dear Perry Wickliff:

I've been plaguing the mail rider ten days. After the trouble I took writing to you I feel a reply is my right. Has a body spoken against me, or are you busy trying to raise a crop? A farming life is contrary to education. Why, I bet you don't know what makes a pig's tail curl. And you may be one of these sharp tacks who scorn to plant by the almanac. Being Zeb Thornton owns the land, I'm bound he has put his worst off on you. Land so clayey you can hear corn sprouting at thirty yards. Did my pony have shoes, I'd trot over and see how you fare.

Now, before Zeb Thornton poisons your mind against me I'll tell you the law trouble we had three years ago. Zeb, to my shape of thinking, is a form of cattle buyer it pays to have few dealings with. Mealy-mouthed, two-faced, slick as a dogwood hoe handle. That's Zeb all over.

I had a heifer growing into a cow, nubbins of horns blossoming, petted nigh to death. My woman had set stake on keeping her for milk and butter. Comes Zeb knocking at the door of a winter evening, trailed by a drove of cattle. I welcomed him under my roof as I would any of God's creations, and I fed and quartered his stock. Next morning he spied my heifer and took advantage of being company. He wore my mind down bargaining and paid me eight dollars. Cold robbery, ever I named it, and my woman came within a pea of leaving me.

Zeb mixed my calf amongst his brutes and went herding downcreek, acting like the king of the pen-hookers. But my heifer had a will of her own. She stole away and hid in my barn. The next shot out of the barrel Zeb arrived with a deputy sheriff, bearing a warrant. Nine days I suffered the lock-up before making bail, although I later proved my innocence in court. Was Zeb Thornton the last man earthly, I wouldn't do another lick of trading with him.

Twenty-one candidates have filed in the jailor race and a rumor goes a wad more are ready to jump in. There's even a woman on the ticket, with about as much chance as a snowball in Torment. She's as pretty a fixing as I ever saw, but that won't help her at the polls. In my time Baldridge County won't vote itself under a petticoat government. I say, let as many as wants pitch in their hats, be they hens or roosters, boars or sows. They'll split the vote more directions than a turkey's foot. They'll whittle their following to a nub.

All the main creeks have one candidate at least, except Roaring. Roaring Fork is virgin territory. Broad Creek has five, Grassy Branch three. Big Ballard has nine. Others here and there. I'm counting to go solid around Salt Spring as I'm kin to everybody and his pappy, kin through my wife. And in spite of Garlan Hurley who has filed against me. My opinion, he'll get two votes, his own and his woman's. Beyond that he won't stain paper. And I ought to run well on Roaring due to my wife. Aye, could I stack Roaring's votes on top of Salt Springs I'd be as good as elected. For once I'd go into jail by law and right, the key in my hand.

Work for my election and I'll have you principal of a school even if it croaks every politician in the county. I'll have you teaching young 'uns quicker than hell can singe a feather. It smothers my heart to know hard learning is being dragged along a furrow, wasting to moles and crows. My old teacher used to say that once a body breathed chalk dust and pounded the Big Thick Dictionary he was spoiled for common labor. Name the schoolhouse you would be master of. I'll ring you.

Hear me. I'll be coming to Roaring Fork the minute I find shoes to fit my nag. She's finicky as a woman and won't travel barefooted.

Keep your eyes skinned for a wife.

Faithfully,
Crafton

The Hills Remember

Perry Wickliff:

I've got wits that beat seven indictments, I've had lawyers walking on pencils, but danged my eyes if I can make sense of why you answered my letter by word of mouth. I've been of the belief mail carriers were paid to haul messages in envelopes, not in their skulls. How much postage did you stick on his upper lip?

How big the yarn swelled in the carrier's head is ontelling. When a tale passes teeth twice you won't recognize it. Anyhow, what he told I wouldn't have made public for a war pension. I figure it has cost me in the neighborhood of a dozen votes. The gist of it was I had attempted to bribe you into working for my election—a falsehood and you know it. I asked you free will, no strings tied.

My burden in life to be misjudged. I aimed to help you stop farming, a trade you couldn't master to the day you die. I get my jowls slapped. Worry you not, I'll win the race beholden to none, fair field and no favor. Of the thirty-two candidates at the writing I'm the only one with the policy of moving into the jailhouse stick, stove, bed and wife. I'm the pattern of a man who understands what a lock-up needs. From cold experience I know the head-down feet-up way it's now being operated. They don't know dirt from horse manure.

At last Roaring Fork has a candidate, some jasper who calls himself Muldraugh. My opinion, a stalking horse put in by Zeb Thornton to snag my votes. Like the female candidate, he hasn't an icicle's chance in a hot skillet. Muldraugh, aye. What kind of a name is that? He was born yonside Pound Gap, in Virginia, a full sixty-five miles from here, and didn't move into our country until he was a right smart sized boy. The day hasn't come when this county will support a foreigner for public office.

Perry Wickliff, if you still want to climb on my bandwagon, I've left the tailgate down. Yet mount of your own accord. I'll plague you no longer for scattering your brains to the sparrows and living in a bachelor's hell. A final offer I make. Would you take the school at Dirk, a hop and jump from your scarecrow farm? Whoever is the teacher, I'll have him flagged out.

Forty-three candidates had filed by the day they closed the books. So many running the winner won't need more than a double handful of votes. I figure I'll win by a basket full.

Faithfully,
Crafton Rowan

Salt Springs, June 8th

You, there, Perry Wickliff:

I got the postcard and have sized you up as a fellow with no more political sense than a dry-land goose. Are you too stingy to paste a stamp on a letter? Why, mail carriers spend half the day reading postcards and spreading the news. So you advise me to hurry shoes on my spoiled nag and come speak for myself. And you hint Roaring Fork hasn't seen my face in forever. This coming from a man who beyond a doubt was rode out of a schoolhouse on a rail.

My opinion, you've fallen into Zeb Thornton's trap head and ears. The reason I haven't been over for a spell is a personal matter not a whit ruled by the oath Zeb swore at the time of our calf trouble, his threatening my life did I so much as set a toe in the Roaring valley. A free country. I'll travel anywhere I get a ripe notion, and if I choose to shun a mother-in-law's district to keep the family peace, that's my right too. I vow I've had my last trade and traffic with Zeb Thornton.

On behalf of my pieded pony, I'll say she's less spoiled than the common run of folks. Has more sense than a tub of educated fools playing farmer. She can do everything but talk, and so gentle you can sit in a chair and curry her. She's bare-hoofed as a tenderfooted critter ought to be until her true size is located. If it comes to a force put, I'll forge a pair of shoes for her my own self.

Wickliff, I'm seeking the full facts of why you were cut loose from that teaching job. I smell a rat hide. Upon my word and honor, it appears the political foxes of Baldridge County done a good deed for once. They got rid of a sorry schoolmaster.

I'd stake my hat the crows are starving in your fields.

Crafton Rowan

Salt Springs, July 10th

Dear Perry:

During the past month you have caused me trouble and sorrow beyond my human due. After the varmity manner you treated my jail race I sunk so low in spirit I let Garlan Hurley talk me out of running for the office. He figured to heir my Salt Spring votes. He wore me down into accepting forty-five dollars. But ho! Before I could get to the clerk's office to withdraw, my name had been sent to the printers. My name was on paper.

Could I lie down on a legal ballot? It was run whether or no. No two ways talking. I had to repay Garlan or stand up to bullets. But I'd already been fleeced of the money. The son of a gun who owns the land adjoining mine claimed I'd swung over on his side and cut timber. I ask, Who knows where lines run nowadays with the landmarks gone, the streams changed course? Any jury would have handed in a verdict in my favor. Yet you can't fight law battles while running races. My neighbor got my forty-five dollars, Garlan Hurley my pieded pony.

Are you a fellow who will acknowledge an honest debt? Recollect the message you sent by the mail carrier early in June, and the postcard shortly thereafter? By my soul, they cost me at least thirty-six votes. I'm of a mind there are three dozen uncommitted you could swing to me. A word said in my behalf would drop them into my pocket—enough with Salt Springs's backing to ring me in. I'm counting on you to settle your obligation.

With crops layed-by it would do you pleasant to travel the waters of Roaring head to mouth. You stir out little, goes the talk. Folks rarely see a hair of you. That's not right, living like you do. Marry, say I. Any good woman will do. Marry and start filling up the house with babies. Then you'll have something to live and work for.

Listen to me, Perry. Old Stedam Byrd, a mile downcreek, has two single daughters, twenty years old or so. Big, hefty girls, not yet claimed. Spruce up your horse, angle your hat, and go visit them Sunday. Begin lining things up for yourself and my candidacy. They'll pour the fried chicken to you, with a horn of something to drink beforehand to make it slick down easy. Stedam controls four votes.

I've come on the true reason you left that teaching job in the middle of the school term. A trustee reports you waked him at midnight to say that after six years of teaching you were bone-tired of minding other people's young 'uns. I declare you justified, remembering when a chunk of a boy I ran teachers distracted. Why, I struck a match once that burnt a schoolhouse down.

The reports lately claim your cornfields are the blackest and the growingest in the mountains, due to the extra seasoning of rain Roaring Fork alone enjoyed this year.

Faithfully,
Crafton

Salt Springs, July 21

Dear Perry:

I would travel to Roaring and start canvassing if I had a beast to ride, and if I didn't have to keep a lookout here. With candidates thicker than horseflies at a stock sale, I daren't take eyes off my voters. Garlan Hurley and others of his sorry pattern are trying to wean the loyalty of my blood kin. Who Garlan's kin is, don't ask. He couldn't name his own pappy.

What hurts, these jaspers are imping my policy, declaring for a clean jail and home cooking. Trying to cut my throat with my own butcher knife.

I believe to my heart Garlan's another stalking horse put in by somebody. Everything's in a rigamaroar. A misery to win a vote and then have to turn sheepdog and guard it against thieves. Bat an eye and you've lost lambs.

My faith in humankind tells me you are working in my behalf. Let it out about the candidate on your creek being a foreigner, not of this country. And don't forget Ben Manley's influence—the Ben at the mouth of Buckeye Branch. I've learnt he has two daughters pretty enough to draw skims across a male's sight. I recollect their mother, a picture-piece at sixteen with catbird's eggs for eyes. And she'll remember me, though won't admit it. I recollect she plaited her hair into two big plaits. I'd take and tie 'em together, and latch them under my chin. Aye, the good old days! Ben Manley votes three.

Oh I miss my pieded pony as I would my feet. I've walked until my hamstrings are rebelling.

Faithfully,
Crafton

Salt Springs, July 30th

Perry:

Seven days until the election. Time's burning. Hurry along to Moab Colley's place on Oak Trace. One daughter left untaken in his household. She's not a pullet, has shed her pinfeathers, but bear in head you're on the high side of the twenties. The thing is, Moab gives his daughters fifty dollars, a cow, a walnut bedstead and nine quilts to start them in life. He votes five.

The way the signs are reading the old jailor can prepare himself to clap the big key into my hand come the first of the year. With forty-three candidates tearing up the patch a small wad of votes will fan a body in. Aye, my election is safe as gold. My solid Salt Springs following, stacked onto the votes tricked from under the whiskers of candidates elsewheres and laid alongside the Roaring Fork support, ought to raise a pile nobody can top. When they open the ballot boxes—heepee! Watch the geese fly out.

The master crop of corn you've raised is the wonder of the county. A rumor says it might run to sixty-five bushels to the hillside acre. In this world the Man Above throws a mighty weight to the side of those who know not what they are doing.

Faithfully,
Crafton

Salt Springs, August 4th

Perry:

I hasten this postcard, the only rag of paper in the house. A last favor I ask. Go to the polls tomorrow, stand as close to the ballot box as the law allows, and a span closer, and urge the folks to pile on a winner. Say I'm the pattern of a man to elect.

I figure I've got the jail job in the frog of my hand. Hurrah for me!

Craft

Baldridge County Jail
August 11th

Dear Perry:

I've borrowed this sheet of paper off the jailor to let you hear my side of the case against me. I ask Justice, Can I rule what a spoiled pony will do? Can a body legally be jailed for giving a critter food and shelter when it turns up hungry and barefooted at his barn gate? Garlan Hurley kept her a solid month and never bothered to nail shoes to her tender feet. Oh he's not got a heart, just a big wart in his chest. But I can read this case bottomside up. I'll come clear in court. Nothing ever got stuck on me.

Perry, I'm trying to raise bail. And the only cattle trader I know of who will buy calves off-season is Zeb Thornton. Let out to him I have a couple of fine heifers, both promising milk- and butter-makers. And he's to deal through me, and not let my wife know. It's a force put.

I can't groan for laughing at the way a female beat out a raft of men in the jailor's race. Thrashed us to a fare-ye-well. Every man jack of us had to go to the bull-hole. She rounded up more votes than the rest of us put together. Yet I don't understand it. All signs seem to fail nowadays.

I'll be here when the woman takes office in January unless I can sell my calves and make bail, and unless the chinch bugs walk off with me plumb. Always I've claimed the county lock-up needs a woman's broom and skillet—a woman with a man standing by. On your behalf I want to report she is fair as a picture, and single.

Faithfully,
Crafton Rowan

School Butter

"If Surrey Creek ever reared a witty," Pap used to tell me, "your Uncle Jolly Middleton is the scamp. Always pranking and teasing. Forever going the roads on a fool horse, hunting mischief. Nearly thirty years old and he has yet to shake hands properly with an ax haft or a plow handle. Why, he'll pull a trick did it cost him his ears, and nobody on earth can stop him laughing."

But Uncle Jolly didn't need to work. He could pick money out of the air. He could fetch down anything he wanted by just reaching. And he would whoop and holler. Folk claimed he could rook the horns off of Old Scratch, and go free. Yet he didn't get by the day he plagued the Surrey Creek School, and for once he couldn't laugh. He bears a scar the length of his nose to mark the occasion. Duncil Burke taught at Surrey the year Uncle Jolly halloed "school butter" at the scholars. A fellow might as lief hang red on a bull's horns as yell that taunt passing a schoolhouse in those days. An old-time prank. If caught they were bound to fare rough.

I attended the whole five-month session, and I was a top scholar. I could spell down all in my grade except Mittie Hyden. And I could read and calculate quicker than anybody save Mittie. But she kept her face turned from me. Mostly I saw the rear of her head, the biscuit of her hair.

The free textbooks I learned by heart, quarreling at the torn and missing pages. My reader left William Tell's son standing with an apple on his head; Rip Van Winkle never woke. I prodded Duncil, "My opinion, if you'll let the superintendent know he'll furnish new texts. Pap says Fight Creek and Slick Branch teachers brought in a load for their schools."

A sixth-grader said, "Ours have done all they come here to do."

"Surrey allus was the tail," Mittie said. She didn't fear to speak her mind. "Had my way, I'd drop these rags into the deepest hole ever was."

Ard Finch, my bench mate, snorted. He could hoot and get by, for he was so runty he had to sit on a chalk box. He could climb the gilly trees beyond the play yard and not be shouted down. He could have mounted to the top of the knob and Duncil not said button. And he was water-boy and could go outside at will. Ard wouldn't have cared if books wore down to a single page.

"New texts will be furnished in due season," Duncil said. He believed in using a thing to the last smidgin. He set us to work. I was put studying a dictionary, and I boasted to Ard Finch, "I'll master every word there be. I'll conquer some jaw breakers." But I got stuck in the *a*'s. I slacked off and read "Blue Beard." Short as it was I had to borrow four readers to splice it together.

The next visit Uncle Jolly made to our house I told of Surrey's textbooks. I said, "Duncil's too big a scrimper to swap them in. A misery to study, hopping and a-jumping." And I spoke of another grievance. "Reader-book yarns are too bob-tailed anyhow to suit my notion. Wish I had a story a thousand miles long."

Uncle Jolly cocked his head in puzzlement. He couldn't understand a boy reading without being driven. He peered at me, trying to figure if I owned my share of brains. He tapped my head, and listened. He said he couldn't hear any.

Uncle Jolly rode past Surrey School on an August afternoon when heat-boogers danced the dry creek bed and willows hung limp with thirst. I sat carving my name on a bench with a knife borrowed from Ard Finch. I knicked and gouged, keeping an eye sharp on Duncil, listening to the primer class blab: "See the fat fox? Can the fox see the dog? Run, fox, run." A third-grader poked his head out of the window, drew in and reported, "Yonder comes Jolly Middleton." There came Uncle Jolly riding bare-bones, his mare wearing a bonnet over her ears and a shawl about her neck.

"Hit's the De'il," a little one breathed, and the primer children huddled together.

A cry of glee rose at sight of a horse dressed like people and scholars would have rushed to the windows had Duncil not swept the air with a pointer. Only Mittie Hyden kept calm. She looked on coldly, her chin thrown.

I crowed to Ard, "I'd bet buckeyes he's going to my house."

Ard's small eyes dulled. He was envious. Being dwarfish he yearned to stand high. He said, "My opinion, he's going to Bryson's mill to have bread ground."

"Now, no," said I. "He's not packing corn."

"Did I have my bow and spike," Ard breathed, "they'd make the finest bull's-eye ever was."

Uncle Jolly circled the schoolhouse. He made the beast rattle her hoofs and prance. He had her trained pretty. Then he halted and got to his feet. He stood on her back and stretched an arm into the air; he reached and pulled down a book. Opening it, he made to read though he didn't know the letter his mare's track made.

Mittie Hyden sniffed, "The first 'un he ever cracked."

Duncil tried to teach despite the pranking in the yard. He whistled the pointer, threatening to tap noggins should we leave our seats. He started the primer class again: "See the fat fox? Can the fox see the dog?" But they couldn't hold their eyes on the page. Scholars chuckled and edged toward the windows. And Ard smiled grudgingly. He would have given the ball of the world to be Uncle Jolly putting on a show. He grabbed the water bucket and ran to the well.

Mittie said, "We're being made a laughingstock."

We quieted a grain, thinking what Fight Creek and Slick Branch children might say.

Uncle Jolly put the book into his shirt and spun the horse on her heels. He pinched her withers and she cranked her neck and flared her lips and nickered. He laughed. He outlaughed his critter. Then he dug heels against her sides and fled upcreek.

"Surrey will be called dog for this," Mittie warned. She wasn't afraid to speak her mind. "It's become the worst school in Baldridge County. Textbooks worn to a frazzle, teacher won't ask for new. Not strange we've drawed a witty."

Duncil's face reddened. He was stumped.

"Uncle Jolly is smart as ants," I defended, "and his mare is clever as people."

Mittie darted a glance at me. She closed her teeth and would say no more.

Hands raised the room over, begging leave to talk. Scholars spoke unbidden:

"I seed a bench-legged dog once, trained to raise and walk on her hind legs. Upon my word and honor, she had a peck o' brains."

"One day my mom passed Jolly Middleton and he was all hey-o and how-are-ye. He tipped his hat, and out flew a bird."

"Biggest fun box ever was, my pap claims."

Rue Thomas began, "Once on a time there was a deputy sheriff aimed to arrest Jolly Middleton—"

Duncil found his tongue. "I grant there's a nag with more gumption than her master. Now, hush."

Ard fetched in a bucket of water. He whispered to me, "Tomorry I'm bringing my bow and spike for shore."

Rue Thomas tried again, "Once the Law undertook to corner Jolly Middleton—"

"Hush!" Duncil ordered. He lifted his chin, rummaging his mind for a way to sober us. He noted the hour—thirty minutes until breaking. He said presently, "We'll have a season of story-telling to finish the day. Accounts of honor and valor." He nodded at Mittie. "Young lady, take the floor and lead with the history of the Trojan horse in days of yore."

Mittie stood and went forward without urging. I harkened although I opened the dictionary and pretended to study. She told of the Greeks building a mighty wooden nag, hollow as a gourd, and with a door in its belly; of the critter getting drawn into Troy-town for a sight to see, and warriors climbing forth at night and sticking spears through everybody. We listened, still as moss eating rocks.

When school let out I ran the whole way home. Pap sat on the porch and the rocker of his chair was scotched by a book. Before I could quit chuffing he announced, "That scamp of an uncle has been here again. And he has confounded creation by doing a worthy deed. He's talked the superintendent into promising new texts for Surrey, and you're to notify Duncil Burke."

I stared at the book, too winded to speak.

Pap bent to free the rocker. Raising the volume he added, "And Jolly says for you to read this till your head rattles."

I seized the book. A giant strode the cover, drawing ships by ropes, and the title read "Gulliver's Voyage to Lilliput." I opened the lid, eyes hasting: "My father had a small estate in Nottinghamshire; I was the third of five sons. . . ."

I wore it like a garment. Under my pillow it rested at night, clutched in my hand it traveled to school of a day. I turned stingy. I wouldn't loan it, declaring, "I'll be the only feller fixed to tell about Lemuel Gulliver and what he done. I'm bound it will cap any old wooden horse yarn."

Ard said, "Rather to see a person cutting up jake on a horse than hear a lie-tale. I'd give a peck o' books would Jolly Middleton come along right now. My bow and spike's waiting under the floor."

I said, "Uncle Jolly could brush off arrow-spikes, the same as Gulliver did."

"Aye gonnies," Ard swore, "I'd make a dint."

But nine days passed before Uncle Jolly returned, and before I had a chance to relate Gulliver's voyage. By then our textbooks were shedding leaves to match frostbitten maples. Come the slightest draft pages flew. Scholars bundled their books and tied them with string, or weighted them with pencil boxes and rulers. Pless Fowley's child stored her primer in a poke.

When I reported Uncle Jolly's message to Duncil he twitted, "Any news that rogue puts out has a sticker in it. Not an earnest bone in his body, to my judgment."

Mittie tossed her head, agreeing. Yet she mumbled, "I wish a whirly-wind would blow our books to nowhere. Then somebody would be bound to do something."

"The ones on hand will endure a spell longer," Duncil said flatly.

A fourth-grader blurted, "A trustee took notice of my ragtag speller and asked, 'What kind of a pauper place are we supporting at Surrey?'"

"Fight Creek and Slick Branch are making light of us," another said.

"They're calling Surrey a rat's nest."

"Naming us the hind tit."

Duncil's ire raised. He lifted his pointer. "Bridle your tongues," he said, "else you'll taste hickory."

A fifth-grader asked unheeding, "If Jolly comes, what are we aiming to do?" And Rue Thomas opened his mouth to tell of a happening but didn't get two words spoken before Duncil's pointer whistled and struck a bench and broke.

Still when Uncle Jolly passed on a Tuesday morning with corn for Bryson's mill, Duncil gave over teaching. Uncle Jolly rode feet high and legs crossed, and he came singing "Meet Little Susie on the Mountain Green." A sack petticoat draped the mare's hindquarters, a bow of ribbon graced her headstall, and her face was powdered white.

Pless Fowley's child moaned, "Hit's the De'il, hit is." She gathered her primer into a poke. Scholars watched, mouths sagged in wonder. Ard breathed to me, "I'm seeing my pure pick of a bull's-eye."

Uncle Jolly rode into the schoolyard and bowed, and the mare bent a knee and dipped her head. He set her sidestepping, hoof over hoof, shaking her hips, flapping the skirt. She ended in a spin, whirling like a flying-jenny. Then, pinching her withers, he cried, "Fool stutter!" The mare nickered, and Uncle Jolly laughed. He laughed fit to fall. And away they scampered, and while still in view the critter lost her petticoat.

A scholar sang out, "He yelled school butter!"

"School butter wasn't named," I said.

"The next thing to it."

The upper grades boys leaped to their feet, angry and clamorous, thinking their ears might have deceived them. They would have taken after Uncle Jolly had not Duncil raised a new pointer—a hickory limb as long as a spear.

Duncil brandished the pointer and the scholars quieted. They settled, knowing Uncle Jolly would return directly when Bryson had ground his corn. Duncil closed the grammar he held. Until Uncle Jolly went his way it was useless to try to teach. Forthwith he inquired, "Which of you is prepared to entertain us with a narrative of ancient days? A tale to discipline our minds."

Rue Thomas said, "I can speak of a deputy aiming to capture a mischiefmaker and what happened. Aye, hit's a good 'un."

"It's not what I requested," Duncil said sharply.

Ard's hand popped up. "Here's a feller ready with a tale about Old Gulliver. A back-yonder story." He wagged his thumb toward me.

"Come forward," Duncil invited.

I played shy. I let him beg twice, not to seem too eager. Then I strode to the front. I told of Gulliver riding the waters, of the shipwrecking, and of his swimming ashore. "He took a nap on dry land and tiny folks no bigger than a finger came and drove pegs and tied him flat with threads. They fastened him to the ground limb and hair. And a dwarf mounted Gulliver's leg bearing a sword, and he was a soldier, and brave . . ."

I related the voyage to Lilliput beginning to end, though scholars barely attended my words and kept staring along the road. Whether Mittie listened I couldn't discover, for she loosened the biscuit on her head and let her hair fall over her face.

"Be-dog," a voice grumbled as I finished, "I'd ruther hear the truth."

"Ought to hear of Jolly Middleton nearly getting jailhoused," Rue Thomas said. "A gospel fact."

Duncil groaned. And he checked the clock. There was still time to reckon with. He gave in. "Maybe we can have done with the subject by talking it to death, wearing it out plumb. Say on."

Rue Thomas babbled, "Once Jolly Middleton took a trip to town. Rode by the courthouse and blocking his path was a deputy sheriff ready to arrest him for some antic. There stood the Law, a warrant in his fist. You think Jolly would turn and flee? Now, no. Not that jasper. Up he trotted into the Law's teeth, and he jabbed his beast in the hip, and low she bent to the balls of her knees. He reached and shook the deputy's hand, and was away and gone ere the Law could bat an eye."

A primer child whimpered, "What air we aiming to do when the De'il comes?"

We heard a clop-clop of hoofs and saw Uncle Jolly approaching. He lay stretched the length of his critter's back, a poke of meal for a pillow, lolling in ease. His feet were bare and his shoes dangled at the end of the mare's tail.

Bull yearlings couldn't have held us. We rushed to the windows. Even Mittie craned her neck to see, her mouth primped with scorn. And Ard snatched the water bucket and ran outside. I thought to myself, "Ard Finch couldn't hit a barn door with an arrow-spike."

The mare drew up in the schoolyard and Uncle Jolly lay prone a moment. Then he stretched his arms and legs and made to rise. He yawned near wide enough to split. And, in the middle of a yawn, he gulped unaccountably, his eyes bulged, his tongue hung out. He seemed stricken. He began to twist and toss. He yelled, "Oh," and, "Ouch!" and, "Mercy me!" As in torment he slapped his breeches, his chest, his skull.

The scholars watched, not knowing whether to pity or jeer.

Uncle Jolly reached inside his shirt and drew out four crawdabbers. He pulled a frog from one pocket, a grannyhatchet from the opposite. His breeches legs yielded a terrapin each, his hat a ball of June bugs. He rid himself of them and breathed a sigh of relief. Then he straddled his mare, spoke "Giddy-yap," and started away.

"Humph," came a grumble, "I thought he was going to do a real something."

Uncle Jolly gained the road and halted. He looked over his shoulder and a wry grin caught his mouth and he shouted,

School butter, chicken flutter,
Rotten eggs for Duncil's supper.

Boys hopped through the windows before Duncil could reach for the pointer. Girls and primer children struck for the doors. And Ard came around a corner with a spike fitted to his bow and let fly. The spike grazed the mare's hip and she sank to her knees, and caught unawares Uncle Jolly tumbled to the ground headforemost. The poke burst, the meal spilled. Up they sprang as scholars sped toward them. The mare took flight across the bottom behind the schoolhouse, Uncle Jolly at her heels. They ran to equal Sooners. Duncil Burke was left waving a pointer in the yard.

I kept pace with the swiftest. I went along for the running, satisfied we could never overhaul Uncle Jolly, and I traveled empty-handed, having forgotten my book. Uncle Jolly and his beast outdid us, the way we shook the short-legged scholars. They took three strides to our one. And on nearing the creek they parted company, the mare veering along the bank, Uncle Jolly plunging into the willows. When last we saw him he was headed toward the knob.

At the creek we searched the dry bed for tracks. We combed the willows and the canes beyond. We threshed the thicket between the creek and the foot of the knob. And up the knob we went, fanning out, Rue Thomas warning, "Keep your eyes skinned, you fellers. What that mischief will do is untelling."

We climbed to the first bench of the knob and paused to catch our breaths. We looked abroad. We stared upon the schoolhouse roof; we could almost spy down the chimney. From somewhere Duncil's voice lifted, calling, calling. Of a sudden we saw scholars hurrying back across the bottom, crying shrilly. We saw Uncle Jolly run out of the schoolhouse and papers fluttered from his arms like butterflies.

We plunged downhill. We fell off of the knob, mighty near, and tore through the canes. We scurried to join the scholars gathering beyond the play yard. And there under a gilly tree Uncle Jolly lay snoring, a hat covering his face, bare feet shining. The mare was nowhere in sight. Ard Finch stood close, but only Mittie Hyden wasn't the least afraid. She walked a ring around him, scoffing, "He's not asleep. Hit's pure put-on."

The bunch crept closer.

A little one asked, "What air we aiming to do?"

"We'd duck him in the creek if it wasn't dry," Rue Thomas said.

"It would take a block and tackle to lift him," a scholar said.

"He's too heavy to rail-ride," another made excuse.

Mittie accused, "I'm of a mind you fellers are scared."

"I hain't afraid," Ard said, and he moved alongside Uncle Jolly to prove it.

"Better not tip Old Scratch," Pless Fowley's child wailed, and she ran away to the schoolhouse.

Ard said, "I know a thing we can do. Fix him the same as the Lilliputians done Old Gulliver. Snare him plug-line."

"Who'll tie the first string?" Rue Thomas posed.

"I will," said Ard. "Fetch me some sticks for pegs and I'll show you who's game." And after they were brought he pounded them into the ground beside Uncle Jolly's feet. He cut his bowstring into lengths and staked the toes.

Uncle Jolly snored on.

The scholars grew brave. They dug twine and thread out of pockets. They unwound three stocking balls. They fenced Uncle Jolly with pegs and made fast his legs, arms, neck and fingers. Fishing lines crisscrossed his body, pack threads tethered locks of his hair. Even the buttons of his shirt suffered tying. They yoked him like a fly in a web, and still he kept snoring.

And when they had him bound Ard played soldier. He stepped onto Uncle Jolly's thigh and mounted proudly to his chest; he balanced his feet and drew forth his knife and brandished it for a sword.

The hat slid from Uncle Jolly's face. His eyelids cracked. His eyes flew wide at sight of the blade. And of a sudden he bucked. Strings parted and strings went flying, and Ard teetered. He bucked again and Ard upset and fell, and the blade raked Uncle Jolly's nose from saddle to tip.

We stared, not moving though we heard the mare's hoofs rattling, though we saw Duncil coming pointer in hand. Pless Fowley's child ran among us, holding an empty poke, crying, "All the books have been dropped into the well. Nary a scrap is left." And Mittie Hyden looked squarely at me. She said, "Jolly Middleton is the best devil ever was."

Uncle Jolly sat up. He pinched his nose together, and his face wrinkled with joy. "I can't laugh," he said. "Upon my honor, I can't."

The Nest

Nezzie Hargis rested on a clump of broomsage and rubbed her numb hands. Her cheeks smarted and her feet had become a burden. Wind flowed with the sound of water through trees high on the ridge and the sun appeared caught in the leafless branches. Cow paths wound the slope, a puzzle of trails going nowhere. She thought, "If ever I could see a smoke or hear an ax ring, I'd know the way."

Her father had said, "Nezzie, go stay a night with your Aunt Clissa"; and Mam, the woman her father had brought to live with them after her mother went away, explained, "We'd take you along except it's your ailing grandpaw we're to visit. Young 'uns get underfoot around the sick." But it had not been the wish to see her grandfather that choked her throat and dampened her eyes—it was leaving the baby. Her father had reminded, "You're over six years old, half past six by the calendar clock. Now, be a little woman." Buttoned into a linsey coat, a bonnet tied on her head, she had looked at the baby wrapped in its cocoon of quilts. She would have touched its foot had they not been lost in the bundle.

Resting on the broomsage she tried to smile, but her cheeks were too tight and her teeth chattered. She recollected once kissing the baby, her lips against its mouth, its bright face pucked. Mam had scolded, "Don't paw the child. It's onhealthy." Her father had said, "Womenfolk are always slobbering. Why, smack him on the foot." She had put her chin against the baby's heel and spied between its toes. Mam had cried, "Go tend the chickens." Mam was forever crying, "Go tend the chickens." Nezzie hated grown fowls—pecking hens and flogging roosters, clucking and crowing, dirtying everywhere.

Her father had promised, "If you'll go willing to your Aunt Clissa's, I'll bring you a pretty. Just name a thing you want, something your heart is set on." Her head had felt empty. She had not been able to think what she wanted most.

She had set off, her father calling after, "Follow the path to the cattle gap, the way we've been going. And when we're home tomorrow, I'll blow the fox horn and come fetch you." But there were many trails upon the slope. The path had divided and split again, and the route had not been found after hours of searching. Beyond the ridge the path would wind to Aunt Clissa's, the chimney rising to view, the hounds barking and hurrying to meet her, and Uncle Barlow shouting, "Hold there, Digger!" and, "Stay, Merry!" and they would not, rushing to lick her hands and face.

She thought to turn back, knowing the hearth would be cold, the doors locked. She thought of the brooder house where diddles were sheltered, and where they might creep. Still across the ridge Uncle Barlow's fireplace would be roaring, a smoke lifting. She would go to the top of the ridge and the smoke would lead her down.

She began to climb and as she mounted her fingers and toes ached the more. Briers picked at the linsey coat and tugged at the bonnet. How near the crest seemed, still ever fleeing farther. Now more than half of the distance had been covered when the sun dropped behind the ridge and was gone. The cold quickened, an occasional flake of snow fell. High on the ridge the wind cried, "O-oo-o."

Getting out of breath she had to rest again. Beneath a haw where leaves were drifted she drew her coat tight about her shoulders and closed her eyes. Her father's words rang in her ears:

"Just name a thing you want. . . . . I'll bring you a pretty."

Her memory spun in a haste like pages off a thumb. She saw herself yesterday hiding in the brooder house to play with newly hatched diddles, the brooder warm and tight, barely fitting her, and the diddles moist from the egg, scrambling to her lap, walking her spread palms, beaks chirping, "Peep, peep." Mam's voice had intruded even there: "Nezzie! Nezzie! Crack up a piece of broken dish for the hens. They need shell makings." She had kept quiet, feeling snug and contented, and almost as happy as before her mother went away.

Nezzie opened her eyes. Down the slope she saw the cow paths fading. Too late to return home, to go meeting the dark. She spoke aloud for comfort,

"I ought to be a-hurrying." The words came hoarsely out of her throat. She climbed on, and a shoe became untied. She couldn't lace it anew with fingers turned clumsy and had to let the strings flare.

And she paused, yearning to turn back. She said to herself, "Let me hear a heifer bawl or a cowbell, and I will. I'll go fast." The wind moaned bitterly, drafting from the ridge into the pasture. A spring freezing among the rocks mumbled, "Gutty, gutty, gutty." She was thirsty but couldn't find it. She discovered a rabbit's bed in a tuft of grass, a handful of pills steaming beside it. The iron ground bore no tracks.

Up and up she clambered, hands on knees, now paying the trails no mind. She came to the pasture fence and attempted to mount. Her hands could not grasp, her feet would not obey. She slipped, and where she fell she rested. She drew her skirts over her leaden feet. She shut her eyes and the warmth of the lids burned. She heard the baby say, "Gub."

The baby said, "Gub," and she smiled. She heard her father ask again, "You know what 'gub' means? Means, get a move on, you slowpokes, and feed me."

She must not tarry. Searching along the panels she found a rail out of catch and she squeezed into the hole. Her dress tore, a foot became bare. She recovered the shoe. The string was frozen stiff.

A stretch of sassafras and locust and sumac began the other side of the fence. She shielded her face with her arms and compelled her legs. Sometimes she had to crawl. Bind-vines hindered, sawbriers punished her garments. She dodged and twisted and wriggled a passage. The thicket gave onto a fairly level bench, clean as a barn lot, where the wind blew in fits and rushes. Beyond it the ground ascended steeply to the top.

Dusk lay among the trees when she reached the crest of the ridge. Bending against the wind she ran across the bit of plateau to where the ridge fell away north. No light broke the darkness below, no dog barked. And there was no path going down. She called amid the thresh of boughs: "Aunt Clissa! Uncle Barlow! It's Nezzie."

Her voice sounded unfamiliar. She cupped her hands about her mouth: "Nezzie a-calling!" Her tongue was dry and felt a great weariness. Her head dizzied. She leaned against a tree and stamped her icy feet. Tears threatened, but she did not weep. "Be a little woman," her father had said.

A thought stirred in her mind. She must keep moving. She must find the way while there was light enough, and quickly, for the wind could not be long endured. As she hurried the narrow flat the cold found the rents in the linsey coat and pierced her bonnet. Her ears twinged, her teeth rattled together. She stopped time and again and called. The wind answered, skittering the fallen leaves and making moan the trees. Dusk thickened. Not a star showed. And presently the flat ended against a wall of rock.

How thirsty she was, how hungry. In her head she saw Aunt Clissa's table— biscuits smoking, ham fussing in grease, apple cake rising. She heard Uncle Barlow's invitation: "Battle out your faces and stick your heels under the table; keep your sleeves out of the gravy and eat till you split." Then she saw the saucer of water she had left the diddles in the brooder. Her thirst was larger than her hunger.

She cowered by the wall of rock and her knees buckled. She sank to the ground and huddled there, working at the bow of her bonnet strings. Loosening the strings she chafed her ears. And she heard her father say: "A master boy, this little 'un is. Aye, he's going somewhere in the world, I'd bet my thumb."

Mam's sharp voice replied, "Young 'uns don't climb much above their raising. He'll follow his pappy in the log woods, my opinion."

"If that be the case, when he comes sixteen I'll say, 'Here,' and reach him the broadax. He'll make chips fly bigger'n bucket lids."

"Nowadays young 'uns won't tip hard work. Have to be prized out of bed mornings. He'll not differ."

"I figure he'll do better in life than hoist an ax. A master boy, smart as a wasper. Make his living and not raise a sweat. He'll amount to something, I tell you."

Nezzie glimpsed the baby, its grave eyes staring. They fetched her up. She would go and spend the night in the brooder and be home the moment of its return. And she would drink the water in the diddles' saucer. She retraced her steps, walking stiffly as upon johnny-walkers, holding her hands before her.

The ground had vanished, the trees more recollected than seen. Overhead the boughs groaned in windy torment.

Yet she did not start down directly, for the pitch of the slope was too fearful. She tramped the flat, going back the way she had come, and farther still. She went calling and listening. No spark broke the gloom. The dogs were mute. She was chilled to the bone when she squatted at the edge of the flat and ventured to descend. She fell in a moment, fell and rolled as a ball rolls. A clump of bushes checked her.

From there to the bench she progressed backward like a crawdabber, lowering herself by elbows and knees, sparing her hands and feet. She traveled with many a pause to thresh her arms and legs and rub her ears. It seemed forever. When she reached the bench snow was spitting.

She plodded across the bench and it had the width of the world. She walked with eyes tight to shun the sting of snowflakes. She went on, sustained by her father's voice:

"Let this chub grow up and he'll be somebody. Old woman, you can paint yore toenails and hang 'em over the banisters, for there'll be hired girls to do the work. Aye, he'll see we're tuk care of."

"He'll grow to manhood, and be gone. That's about the size of it. Nowadays . . ."

Sitting on a tuft she blew her nose upon her dress tail. Then she eased herself upon the ground with her head downhill. She began squirming left and right, gaining a few inches at each effort. She wallowed a way through briery canes, stands of sumac, thorny locusts. She bumped against rocks. Her coat snagged, her breath came in gasps. When snow started falling in earnest she was barely aware of it. And after a long struggle she pressed upon the rail fence. She groped the length of two panels in search of a hole before her strength failed.

Crouched against the fence she drew herself small into her coat. She pulled the ruffle of her bonnet close about her neck and strove against sleep. The night must be waited out. "Tomorrow," she told herself, "Pap will blow the fox horn and come for me. He will ride me on his head as he did upon an occasion." In her mind she saw the horn above the mantelpiece, polished and brass-tipped; she saw herself perched on her father's head like a topknot.

"What, now, is Pap doing?" She fancied him sitting by the hearth in her grandfather's house. "What is Grandpaw up to?" He was stretched gaunt and pale on a featherbed, his eyes keen with tricks. Once he had made a trap of his shaky hands, and had urged, "Nez', stick a finger in and feed the squirrel." In had gone her finger and got pinched. "'T'was the squirrel bit you," he had laughed. And seeing her grandfather she thought of his years, and she thought suddenly of the baby growing old, time perishing its cheeks, hands withering and palsying. The hateful wisdom caught at her heart and choked her throat. She clenched her jaws, trying to forget. She thought of the water in the diddles' saucer. She dozed.

"Nezzie Hargis!"

She started, eyes wide to the dark.

"I'll bring you a pretty. . . . Just name a thing you want."

She trembled and her teeth chattered. She saw herself sitting the baby on her lap. It lay with its fair head against her breast.

"Name a thing . . . something your heart is set on."

Her memory danced. She heard her father singing to quiet the baby's fret. "Up, little horse, let's hie to mill." She roved in vision, beyond her father, beyond the baby, to one whose countenance was seen as through a mist. It was her mother's face, cherished as a good dream is cherished—she who had held her in the warm, safe nest of her arms. Nezzie slept at last, laboring in sleep toward waking.

She waked to morning and her sight reached dimly across the snow. An ax hewed somewhere, the sound coming to her ears without meaning. She lifted an arm and glimpsed the gray of her hand and the bloodless fingers; she drew herself up by the fence and nodded to free her bonnet of snow. She felt no pain, only languor and thirst. The gap was three panels distant and she hobbled toward it. She fell. Lying on the ground she crammed snow into her mouth. Then she arose and passed under the bars, hardly needing to tilt her head.

Nezzie came down the slope. She lost a shoe and walked hippity-hop, one shoe on, one shoe off. The pasture was as feathery as a pillow. A bush plucked her bonnet, snatching it away; the bush wore the bonnet on a limb. Nezzie laughed. She was laughing when the cows climbed by, heads wreathed in a fog of breath, and when a fox horn blew afar. Her drowsiness increased. It grew until it could no longer be borne. She parted a clump of broomsage and crept inside. She clasped her knees, rounding the grass with her body. It was like a rabbit's bed. It was a nest.

A Master Time

Wick Jarrett brought the invitation of his eldest son, Ulysses. "He's wanting you to come enjoy a hog-kill at his place next Thursday," Wick said. "Hit's to be a quiet affair, a picked crowd, mostly young married folks. No old heads like me—none except Aunt Besh Lipscomb, but she won't hinder. 'Lysses and Eldora will treat you clever. You'll have a master time."

Thursday fell on the eve of Old Christmas, in January, a day of bitter wind. I set off in early afternoon for Ulysses's homeseat on Upper Logan Creek, walking the ridge to shun the mud of the valley road. By the time I reached the knob overtowering the Jarrett farm my hands and ears were numb, my feet dead weights. A sheep dog barked as I picked my way down and Ulysses opened the door and called, "Hurry in to the fire." I knocked my shoes at the doorsteps. "Come on in," Ulysses welcomed. "Dirt won't hurt our floors."

A chair awaited me. Before the living-room hearth sat Ulysses's cousins, Pless and Leander Jarrett, his brothers-in-law, Dow Owen and John Kingry, a neighbor, Will Harrod, and the aged midwife, Aunt Besh Lipscomb, who had lived with Ulysses and Eldora since the birth of their child. From the kitchen came sounds of women's voices.

"Crowd to the fire and thaw," Ulysses said, "and pull off your jacket."

"Be you a stranger?" Aunt Besh asked.

"Now, no," Ulysses answered in my stead. "He lives over and across the mountain."

"He's got a tongue," Aunt Besh reproved. And she questioned, "Was I the granny-doctor who fotched you?"

Ulysses teased, "Why, don't you remember?"

Aunt Besh said, "I can't recollect the whole push."

The fellows chuckled under their breaths, laughing quietly so as not to disturb the baby sleeping on a bed in the corner.

The heat watered my eyes. My hands and feet began to ache.

"You're frozen totally," Aunt Besh declared. "Pull off your shoes and socks and warm your feet. Don't be ashamed in front of an old granny."

"Granny-doctors have seen the world and everything in it," Ulysses said.

"Hush," Aunt Besh cried, and as I unlaced my shoes she said, "'Lysses, he needs a dram to warm his blood."

Ulysses shrugged. "Where'd I get it?"

"A medicine dram. Want him to catch a death cold?"

"I ought to of got a jug for the occasion," Ulysses said. "We're all subject to take colds. I forgot it plumb."

"I'd vow there's a drap somewhere."

"This is apt to be the driest hog-kill ever was," Ulysses said.

"Humph," Aunt Besh scoffed.

I had my shoes on again when the wives gathered at the fire. Eldora took up the baby, scolding Ulysses. "You'd let it freeze. Its little nose is ice." And Ulysses said, "We men, we might as well allow the petticoats to hug the coals a spell. Let's get some air." We followed him through the front door, and on around to the back yard. The wind tugged at us. We pulled our hats down until the brims bent our ears.

Ulysses led us into the smokehouse. "Look sharp," he said, "and see what there is to see." We noted the baskets of Irish and sweet potatoes, cushaws and winter squash, the shelves loaded with conserved vegetables and fruits. "Anybody give out of table stuff," he went on, "come here and get a turn." Will Harrod glanced about impatiently, and Dow Owen uncovered a barrel. Ulysses said, "Dow, if you want to crack walnuts, the barrel is full." Pless and Leander Jarrett took seat on a meatbox and grinned.

"Ah, 'Lysses," Will Harrod groaned, "quit your stalling."

"Well, s'r," Ulysses said, "I've got some sugar-top here, but it's bad, my opinion. I hate to poison folks." The bunch livened. Pless and Leander, knowing where to search, jumped off the saltbox and raised the lid; they lifted a churn by the ears. Will said, "Say we drink and die." Ulysses cocked his head uncertainly at me. I said, "Go ahead, you fellows."

A gourd dipper was passed hand to hand, and Will, on taking a swallow, yelled joyously. Ulysses cautioned, "Don't rouse Aunt Besh. We'd never hear the last." The gourd was eased from Dow Owen's grasp, Ulysses reminding, "A job of work's to do. We'll taste lightly right now." A jar of pickled pears was opened to straighten breaths.

We returned to the fire and the wives laughed accusingly, "Uh-huh" and "Ah-ha." Leander's wife clapped a hand on his shoulder, drew him near, and sniffed. She charged, "The sorry stuff and don't deny it."

"Pear juice," Leander swore. "Upon my honor."

"You've butchered the swine quick," Aunt Besh said scornfully. No attention was paid to her and she jerked Ulysses's coattail. "Are ye killing the hogs or not?"

"Can't move a peg until the women are ready," Ulysses answered.

"It's you men who are piddling," one of the women reported. "We've had the pots boiling an hour."

Eldora spoke, "Who'll mind the baby? I won't leave it untended."

Aunt Besh said, "Don't leave me to watchdog it."

Pless's wife volunteered to stay. She was the youngest of the wives, sixteen at most.

"Aunt Besh," Ulysses petted, "you just set and poke the fire."

"Go kill the hogs," Aunt Besh shrilled.

"She's the queen," Ulysses told us.

"Go, go."

Ulysses got his rifle. "John," he said, "you come help." And they made off.

There being two hogs for slaughter we waited until the second shot before rushing toward the barn, men through the front entrance, women the rear. The hogs lay on straw, weighing between 350 to 400 pounds. The wind raced, flagging the blazes beneath three iron pots. An occasional flake of snow fell. We men scalded the carcasses in a barrel; we scraped the bristles free with knives while the women dabbled hot water to keep the hair from setting. The scraping done, gambrels were caught underneath tendons of the hind legs and the animals hefted to pole tripods; they were singed, shaved, and washed, and the toes and dewclaws removed. Ulysses and John served as butchers, and as they labored John questioned:

"Want the lights saved?"

"Yes, s'r," Ulysses replied.

"Heart-lump?"

"Yip."

"The particulars?"

"Nay-o."

"Sweetbreads?"

"Fling them away and Aunt Besh will rack us. The single part she will eat."

Will Harrod laid a claim: "The bladders are mine. I'll make balloons."

The sheepdog and a gang of cats dined well on refuse.

The wind checked and snow fell thicker. The women hurried indoors, carrying fresh meat to add to the supper they had been preparing nearly the day long. Ulysses and John hustled their jobs, the rest of us transporting hams, loins, shoulders, and bacon strips to the smokehouse. No hog-kill tricks were pulled. Nobody had a bloody hand wiped across his face; none dropped a wad of hog's hair inside another's breeches.

John complained to Ulysses, "The fellers are heading toward the smokehouse faster'n they're coming back."

"We'll join 'em in a minute," Ulysses said.

When I entered the living room Aunt Besh asked, "Got the slaughtering done finally?" And seeing I was alone she inquired, "Where are the others?"

"They'll come pretty soon," I said, removing my hat and jacket and brushing the snow onto the hearth. "We put by the sweetbreads," I added.

Aunt Besh gazed at me. Pless's wife clasped the baby and lowered her face. Aunt Besh said, "Son, speak while 'Lysses hain't here to drown you out. Was I the granny-doctor who fotched you into the world?"

"Aunty," Pless's wife entreated, "don't embarrass the company."

"Daren't I ope my mouth?" Aunt Besh blurted.

I said, "Who the granny was, I never learned."

"Unless you were born amongst the furrin I'm liable to 'a' fotched you. I acted granny to everybody in this house, nigh everybody on Logan Creek."

Pless's wife blushed. She stirred in her chair, ready to flee.

"There's a way o' telling," Aunt Besh went on. "I can tell whether I tied the knot."

Up sprang Pless's wife, clutching the infant. She ran into the kitchen.

"I wasn't born on Logan," I explained.

"Upon my word and honor!" Aunt Besh cried. "Are ye a heathen?"

Eldora brought the child back to the fire, and she came laughing. The husbands tramped in, Dow walking unsteadily, for he had made bold with the churn dipper. Will dandled two balloons. Hearing mirth in the kitchen John asked, "What has put the women in such good humor?"

Aunt Besh watched as a chair was shoved under Dow, and she began to wheeze and gasp. Presently Ulysses queried, "What's the trouble, Aunt Besh?"

"My asthma's bothering," she said. "The cold is the fault."

"Why, it's tempering," Ulysses remarked. "It's boiling snow, but the wind's stilling."

"My blood is icy, no matter."

"I'll wrap you in a quilt."

"No."

"I'll punch the fire."

"Devil," Aunt Besh blurted, "can't you understand the simplest fact?"

Eldora scolded, "'Lysses stop plaguing and go make a cup of ginger stew to ease her."

Ulysses obeyed, and Aunt Besh raised her sleeves and poked forth her arms. "See my old bones," she whimpered. "There's hardly flesh to kiver 'em. I need good treatment, else I'm to bury." Tears wet her eyes.

"Aunty," Will comforted, "want to hold a balloon?"

"Keep the nasty things out of my sight," Aunt Besh said.

Ulysses fetched the stew—whiskey in hot water, dusted with ginger and black pepper. Aunt Besh nursed the cup between quivering hands and tasted. "'Lysses," she snuffed, "your hand was powerful on the water."

Supper was announced and Ulysses told us, "Rise up, you fellers," and Eldora said. "You'll find common victuals, but try to make out." We tarried, showing manners. Ulysses insisted, "Don't force us to beg. Go. Go while the bread is smoking."

After further prompting we trooped into a narrow gallery lighted by bracket lamps, which was the dining room. John hooked a wrist under Dow's arm, leading him. Aunt Besh used the fire-poker for a walking stick.

"Why don't you eat with us women at the second table?" Eldora asked Aunt Besh.

"I don't aim to wait," Aunt Besh said. "I'm starving."

We sat to a feast of potatoes, hominy, cushaw, beans, fried and boiled pork, baked chicken, buttered dumplings, gravy, stacks of hand-pies, and jam cake. Ulysses invited, "Rake your plates full, and if you can't reach, holler."

As we ate, laughter rippled in the kitchen. Leander's wife came with hot biscuits, and her face was so merry, Leander inquired, "What's tickling you feymales?" She made no reply.

John said, "They've been gigglng steady."

"We ought to force them to tell," Leander said. "Choke it out."

"If you'll choke your woman," John proposed, "I'll choke mine."

"Say we do," Leander agreed. "And everybody help, everybody strangle his woman, if he's got one. But let's eat first."

A voice raised in the kitchen. "You'll never learn, you misters." The laughter quieted.

"We'll make them pray for air," Leander bragged loudly. He batted an eye at us. "We'll not be outsharped."

"Cross the women," Ulysses said, "and you'll have war on your hands."

"Suits me," Leander said, and Pless and John vowed they didn't care. Will, his mouth full, gulped, and nudged Dow. Dow, half asleep, said nothing.

Of a sudden the women filed through the gallery, their necks thrown, marching toward the fire. Only Eldora smiled.

Ulysses said, "You big talkers have got your women mad. But I didn't anger mine, you may of noticed."

"Ah," Pless said, "they know we're putting-on."

"Eat," Aunt Besh commanded, "eat and hush."

Dow nodded in his chair and Ulysses arose and guided him to a bed.

While we were at table the wives hid the churn, and when they joined us in the living room later in the evening the four estranged couples sat apart, gibing each other. Ulysses tried making peace between them. The wives wouldn't budge, though the husbands appeared willing.

John sighed, "Gee-o, I'm thirsty," and his wife asked sourly, "What's against pure water?" "Hit's weaky," was the reply.

Finally Ulysses threw open the door. The wind had calmed, the snowing ceased. Moonlight behind the clouds lighted the fields of snow. Every fence post wore a white cap. Ulysses said, "Maybe the way to end the ruckus is to battle. Who's in the notion to snowball-fight?"

"Anything to win the churn back," Leander said.

"The churn is what counts," Pless baited, "the women don't matter."

"A fight would break the deadlock," Ulysses declared.

The four wives arose.

Will groaned, "I'm too full to move," and John testified, "I can't wiggle." Pless and Leander were as lief as not, yet Pless reminded, "Me and Leander are old-time rabbit rockers."

Ulysses urged, "Tussle and reach a settlement."

The wives pushed John and Will onto the porch and shoved them into the yard. "Get twenty-five steps apart," Ulysses directed, "and don't start till I say commence." He allowed the sides to prepare mounds of snowballs.

I had followed to witness the skirmish, as had Eldora and Dow's wife. Behind us Aunt Besh spoke, "Clear the door. Allow a body to see."

Ulysses yelled, "Let 'em fly," and the wives hurled a volley. A ball struck Will's throat and he appealed to Ulysses, "Rocks, unfair." Aunt Besh hobbled to the porch, the better to watch; she shouted and we discovered the side she pulled for. Will and John fought halfheartedly, mostly chucking crazy; Leander and Pless, deadeye throwers, practiced near-hits, tipping their wives' heads, grazing shoulders, shattering balls poised in hands. The women dodged and twisted and let fly.

Will sat in the snow when the hoard of balls was exhausted, and John quit— quit and yanked up his collar. Leander and Pless stopped tossing and batted the oncoming missiles with their hands.

The women crept nearer, chucking point-blank. They rushed upon Will and before he could rise to escape had him pinned. They stuffed snow in his mouth and plastered his face. Then they seized John, a docile prisoner, rolling him log-fashion across the yard. And they got hands on Pless. Pless wouldn't have been easily caught had not Leander grabbed his shoulders and shielded himself. Leander stood grinning as snow was thrust down Pless's neck.

Leander's feet wouldn't hold at his turn. It was run, fox, run around the house, the women in pursuit. He zigzagged the yard, circled the barn, took a sweep through the bottom. They couldn't overhaul him. His wife threatened, "Come take your punishment, or you'll get double-dosed." He came meekly and they buried him in snow. They heaped snow upon him and packed and shaped it like a grave. He let them satisfy themselves until he had to rise for air.

The feud ended and all tramped indoors good-humoredly, the wives to comb rimy hair, the husbands to dry wet clothes and accuse Aunt Besh of partiality. Hadn't Aunt Besh bawled "Kill 'em" to the women. An argument ensued, Aunt Besh admitting, "Shore, I backed the girls."

The husbands fire-dried, chattering their teeth exaggeratedly, and their wives had the mercy to bring the churn from hiding and place it in the gallery. The dipper tapped bottom as its visitors heartened themselves. Aunt Besh eyed the gallery-goers. "I got a chill watching you fellers," she wheezed.

Ulysses said, "I don't hear your gums popping."

"Are ye wanting me to perish?" she rasped.

Eldora chided Ulysses into brewing another ginger stew, and Aunt Besh instructed, "This time don't water it to death."

It was Leander who remembered to inquire, "Now, what was it tickled you feymales back yonder?"

The women turned their heads and smiled.

The night latened, and Aunt Besh dozed. Husbands and wives, reconciled, sat side by side. The balloons were kept spinning aloft. Apples were roasted on the hearth, potatoes baked in ashes, popcorn capped, and pull-candy made.

Past one o'clock Eldora made known the retiring arrangements. Aunt Besh would sleep in her chair, on account of asthma. Two beds in the upper room would hold the women, two in the lower provide for the men. Ulysses and Eldora, occupying the living-room bed, could keep the child near the fire and attend Aunt Besh's wants in the night.

My roommates sauntered off. When I followed they were snoring. John, Will, and Dow lay as steers strawed to weather a blizzard; my assigned bed-fellows were sprawled, leaving little of the mattress unoccupied. I decided to go sleep in front of the hearth, though I waited until the house quieted, until smothered laughter in the upper room hushed.

I found the coals banked, the lamp wick turned low. Aunt Besh sat wrapped in a tower of quilts and I thought her asleep. But she uncovered her face and spoke, "See if there's a drap left in the churn." I investigated, and reported the churn empty. She eyed me coldly as she might any creature who had not the grace to be born on Logan Creek. "I'll endure," she said.

A Ride on the Short Dog

We flagged the bus on a curve at the mouth of Lairds Creek by jumping and waving in the road and Dee Buck Engle had to tread the brake the instant he saw us. He wouldn't have halted unless compelled. Mal Dowe and I leaped aside finally, but Godey Spurlock held his ground. The bus stopped a yard from Godey and vexed faces pressed the windows and we heard Old Liz Hyden cry, "I'd not haul them jaspers."

Dee Buck opened the door and blared, "You boys trying to get killed?"

We climbed on grinning and shoved fares to Roscoe into his hand and for once we didn't sing out, To Knuckle Junction, and Pistol City, and Two Hoots. We even strode the aisle without raising elbows to knock off hats, having agreed among ourselves to sort of behave and make certain of a ride home. Yet Dee Buck was wary. He warned, "Bother my passengers, you fellers, and I'll fix you. I've put up with your mischief till I won't."

That set Godey and Mal laughing, for Dee Buck was a bluffer. We took the seat across from Liz Hyden and on wedging into it my bruised arm started aching. Swapping licks was Godey's delight.

The bus wheezed and jolted in moving away, yet we spared Dee Buck our usual advice: Feed her a biscuit and see will she mend, and, Twist her tail and teach her some manners. The vehicle was scarcely half the length of a regular bus. "The Short Dog" everybody called it. It traveled from Thacker to Roscoe and back twice a day. Enos Webb occupied the seat in front and Godey greeted, "Hey-o, chum. How's your fat?" Enos tucked his head, fearing a rabbit lick, and he changed his seat. He knew how Godey served exposed necks. Godey could cause you to see forked lightning and hear thunder balls. Though others shunned us, Liz Hyden gazed in our direction. Her eyes were scornful, her lips puckered sour. She was as old as a hill.

Godey and Mal couldn't sit idle. They rubbed the dusty panes with their

318

sleeves and looked abroad and everything they saw they remarked on: hay doodles in Alonzo Tate's pasture, a crazy chimney leaning away from a house, long-johns on clotheslines. They kept a count of the bridges. They pointed toward the mountain ahead, trying to fool, calling, "Gee-o, looky yonder!" But they couldn't trick a soul. My arm throbbed and I had no notion to prank, and after a while Godey muttered, "I want to know what's eating you."

"We'd better decide what we can do in town," I grouched. Roscoe folk looked alive at sight of us. And except for our return fares we hadn't a dime. The poolroom had us ousted. We'd have to steer clear of the courthouse, where sheriffs were thick. And we dare not rouse the county prisoners again. On our last trip we had bellowed in front of the jail, "Hey-o, you wife beaters, how are you standing the times?" We'd jeered and mocked until they had begged the turnkey to fetch us inside, they would notch our ears, they would trim us. The turnkey had told them to be patient, we'd get in on our own hook.

Godey said, "We'll break loose in town, no two ways talking."

I gloomed, "The Law will pen us for the least thing. We'll be thrown in amongst the meanest fellers who ever breathed."

Godey screwed his eyes narrow. "My opinion, the jailbirds have you scared plumb. You're ruint for trick-pulling." He knotted a fist and hit me squarely on my bruise.

My armed ached the fiercer. My eyes burned and had I not glanced sideways they'd come to worse. "Now, no," I said; but Godey's charge was true.

"Well, act like it," he said. "And pay me."

I returned the blow.

Old Liz was watching and she blurted, "I swear to my Gracious. A human being can't see a minute's peace."

Godey chuckled, "What's fretting you, old woman?"

"Knock and beat and battle is all you think on," she snorted.

"We're not so bad we try to hinder people from riding the bus," he countered. "Aye, we heard you squall back yonder."

Old Liz's lips quivered, her veiny hands trembled.

"Did I have the strength to reach," she croaked, "I'd pop your jaws. I'd addle you totally."

Godey thrust his head across the aisle and turned a cheek. He didn't mind a slap. "See your satisfaction," he invited.

"Out o' my face," she ordered, lifting her voice to alert Dee Buck. She laced her fingers to stay their shaking.

Dee Buck adjusted the rearview mirror and inquired, "What's the matter, Aunt Liz?"

"It's these boys tormenting me," she complained. "They'd drive a body to raving."

Dee Buck slowed. "I told you fellers—"

"What've we done now?" Godey asked injuredly.

"Didn't I say not to bother my passengers?"

"I never tipped the old hen."

"One more antic and off you three go."

Godey smirked. "Know what?" he blatted. "We've been treating you pretty and you don't appreciate it. Suit a grunt-box, you can't."

"You heard me," Dee Buck warned.

When the bus stopped for a passenger at the mouth of Willow Branch, Dee Buck called back to Aunt Liz. "How are ye, Aunty?"

"Doing no good," said Aunt Liz.

The twins got on at Lucus. They were about nine years old, as alike as two peas, and had not a hair on their heads. Their polls were shaven clean. Godey chirruped, "Gee-o, look who's coming," and he beckoned them to the place quitted by Enos Webb. Dee Buck seated the two up front and Godey vowed, "I'll trap the chubs, just you wait," and he made donkey ears with his hands and brayed. The twins stared, their mouths open.

Mal suggested, "Why don't we have our noggins peeled?"

"Say we do," laughed Godey, cocking a teasing eye on me. "They can't jail us for that shorely."

I replied, "We're broke as grasshoppers, keep in mind."

It didn't take Godey long to entice the twins. He picked nothings out of the air and chewed them, chewed to match sheep eating ivy; he feigned to pull teeth, pitch them back into his mouth, to swallow. The twins stole a seat closer, the better to see, and then two more. Directly Godey had them where he wanted. He greeted: "Hey-o, dirty ears."

The twins nodded, too shy to answer.

"What is you little men's names?" he asked.

They swallowed timidly, their eyes meeting.

"Ah, tell."

"Woodrow," ventured one. "Jethro," said the other. They were as solemn as fire-pokers.

"Hustling to a store to spend a couple of nickels, I bet."

"Going to Cowen," said one. "To Grandpaw's," said his image.

"Well, who skinned you alive, I want to know?"

"Pap," they said.

Godey gazed at their skulls, mischief tingling him. He declared, "Us fellers aim to get cut bald in Roscoe. Too hot to wear hair nowadays."

I slipped a hand over my bruise and crabbed, "I reckon you know haircuts cost money in town." Plaguing Godey humored me.

"Witless," Godey said, annoyed, "we'll climb into the chairs, and when the barbers finish we'll say, 'Charge it to the sand bank.'"

"They'd summons the Law in an eye-bat."

"Idjit," he snapped, "people can't be jailed for a debt." Yet he wouldn't pause to argue. He addressed the twins: "You little gents have me uneasy. There are swellings on your noggins and I'm worried on your behalf."

The twins rubbed their crowns. They were as smooth as goose eggs.

"Godey's sharp on this head business," said Mal.

"Want me to examine you and figure out your ailment?" asked Godey.

The twins glanced one to the other. "We don't care," said one.

Godey tipped a finger to their heads. He squinted and frowned. And then he drew back and gasped, "Oh-oh!" He punched Mal and blabbed, "Do you see what I do? Horns, if ever I saw them."

"The tom truth," Mal swore.

"Sprouting horns like bully-cows," Godey said. "Budding under the skin and ready to pip."

"You're in a bad way," Mal moaned.

"In the fix of a boy on Lotts Creek," Godey said. "He growed horns, and he turned into a brute and went hooking folks. Mean? Upon my word and honor, the bad man wouldn't claim him."

"A feller at Scuddy had the disease," Mal related. "Kept shut up in a barn, he was, and they fed him hay and cornstalks, and he never tasted table food. I saw him myself, I swear to my thumb. I saw him chewing a cud and heard him bawl a big bawl."

Godey sighed. "The only cure is to deaden the nubs before they break the skin."

"And, gee-o, you're lucky," Mal poured on. "Godey Spurlock is a horn-doctor. Cured a hundred, I reckon."

"Oh I've treated a few," admitted Godey.

"Spare the little masters," pled Mal.

Dee Buck was trying to watch both road and mirror, his head bobbing like a chicken drinking water. Old Liz's eyes glinted darkly. I poked Godey, grumbling, "Didn't we promise to mind ourselves?" But he went on: "They may enjoy old long hookers, may want to bellow and snort and hoof up dirt."

"We don't neither," a twin denied.

Godey brightened. "Want me to dehorn you?"

The boys nodded.

Though I prodded Godey's ribs, he ignored me. He told the twins, "The quicker the medicine the better the cure," and he made short work of it. Without more ado he clapped a hand on each of their heads, drew them wide apart, and bumped them together. The brakes began to screech and Old Liz to fill the bus with her groans. The twins sat blinking. Dee Buck halted in the middle of the road and commanded: "All right, you scamps, pile off."

We didn't stir.

"You're not deaf. Trot."

"Deaf in one ear, and can't hear out of the other 'un," Godey jested.

Dee Buck slapped his knee with his cap. "I said go."

Old Liz was in a fidget. "Get shut of them," she rasped her arms a-jiggle, her fingers dancing. "See that they walk. Make 'em foot it."

"Old Liz," Godey chided, "if you don't check yourself you're liable to fly to pieces."

"Rid the rascals," she shrilled to Dee Buck. "Are ye afraid? Are ye man enough?"

Godey scoffed, "He'll huff and he'll puff—all he ever does. He might as well feed the hound a sup of gas and get traveling."

Dee Buck blustered, "I've had a bait of you fellers. I'm offering you a chance to leave of your own free will."

"Collar and drag 'em off," Old Liz taunted. "A coward, are ye?"

"Anybody spoiling to tussle," Godley challenged, "well, let 'em come humping."

Dee Buck flared, "Listen, you devils, I can put a quietus on you and not have to soil my hands. My opinion, you'll not want to be aboard when I pull into town. I can draw up at the courthouse and fetch the Law in two minutes."

"Sic a sheriff on us," Godey said, "and you'll wish to your heart you hadn't. We paid to ride this dog."

"Walk off and I'll return your fares."

"Now, no."

"I won't wait all day."

"Dynamite couldn't budge us."

Dee Buck swept his cap onto his head. He changed gear, readying to leave. "I'm willing to spare you and you won't have it."

"Drive on, big buddy."

The bus started and Old Liz flounced angrily in her seat. She turned her back and didn't look 'round until we got to Roscoe.

We crossed two bridges. We passed Hilton and Chunk Jones's sawmill and Gayheart and Thorne. Beyond Thorne the highway began to rise. We climbed past the bloom of coal veins and tipples of mines hanging the slope; we mounted until we had gained the saddle of the gap and could see Roscoe four miles distant. Godey and Mal cut up the whole way, no longer trying to behave. They hailed newcomers with, "Take a seat and sit like you were at home, where you ought to be," and sped the departers, "I'll see you later, when I can talk to you straighter." The twins left at Cowen and Godey shouted, "Good-bye, dirty ears.

Recollect I done you a favor." We rolled through the high gap and on down the mountain.

I nursed my hurt and sulked, and eventually Godey growled, "I want to know, did you come along just to pout?"

"You've fixed us," I accused bitterly, and I openly covered my crippled arm.

Godey scoffed, "Dee Buck can't panic me. You watch him turn good-feller by the time we reach town, watch him unload in the square the same as usual. Aye, he knows what suits his hide." He grabbed loose my arm and his fist shot out.

It was too much. My face tore up, my lips quivered and tears smeared my cheeks. Godey stared in wonder. His mouth fell open. Mal took my part, rebuking him, "No use to injure a person."

"I don't give knocks I can't take myself," Godey said; and he invited, "Pay me double. Hit me a rabbit lick, I don't care. Make me see lightning." He leaned forward and bared his neck.

I wiped the shameful tears, thinking to join no more in Godey's game.

"Whap him and even up," Mal said. "We're nearly to the bottom of the mountain."

"Level up with me," said Godey, "or you're no crony of mine. You'll not run with my bunch."

I shook my head.

"Hurry," said Mal. "I see town smoking."

I wouldn't.

Mal advised Godey, "Nettle him. Speak a thing he can't let pass. Make him mad."

Godey said, "Know what I'm in the opinion of? Hadn't it been for Mal and me you'd let Dee Buck bounce you off the bus and never lifted a finger. You'd have turned chicken."

"I'd not," I gulped.

"Jolt him," Mal urged. "What I'd do."

"You're a chicken leg," Godey said, "and everybody akin to you is a chicken leg, and if you're yellow enough to take that I'll call you 'Chicken Leg' hereinafter."

I couldn't get around Godey. Smite him I must, and I gripped a fist and struck as hard as I could in close quarters, mauling his shoulder.

"Is that your best?" he belittled. "Anyhow, didn't I call for a rabbit lick? Throw one and let me feel it; throw one, else you know your name." Again he leaned and exposed his neck.

"He's begging," Mal incited.

I would satisfy him, I resolved, and I half rose to get elbowroom. I swung mightily, the edge of my hand striking the base of his skull. I made his head pitch upward and thump the seat board in front; I made his teeth grate. "That ought to do," I blurted.

Godey walled his eyes and clenched his jaws. He began to gasp and strain and flounder. His arms lifted, clawing the air. Tight as we were wedged the seat would barely hold him. Mal was ready to back up a sham and he chortled, "Look, you good people, if you want to see a feller croak." None bothered to glance.

Then Mal and me noticed the odd twist of Godey's neck. We saw his lips whiten, his ears turn tallow. His tongue waggled to speak and could not. And of a sudden we knew and sat frozen. We sat like posts while he heaved and pitched and his soles rattled the floor and his knees banged the forward seat. He bucked liked a spoiled nag. . . . He quieted presently. His arms fell, his hands crumpled. He slumped and his gullet rattled.

We rode on. The mountain fell aside and the curves straightened. The highway ran a beeline. We crossed the last bridge and drew into Roscoe, halting in the square. Dee Buck stood at the door while the passengers alighted, and all hastened except Old Liz and us. Old Liz ordered over her shoulder, "Go on ahead. I'll not trust a set of jaspers coming behind me." We didn't move. She whirled and her eyes lit on Godey. She sputtered "What's the matter with him?"

Mal opened his mouth numbly. "He's doing no good," he said.

The Fun Fox

The day I opened the Keg Branch School I rolled my sleeves to display my muscles, and I kept a pointing-stick handy.

Keg Branch was in the upper part of the county—"the jumping-off-place," some folk call it. The highway played out miles this side, and the creek bed served as the road. The behavior at the school was notorious; but I was eighteen, anxious to undertake my first teaching job, and the Keg Branch position was the only one open.

The superintendent of county schools had given me ample warning. "All sorts of chicanery will be attempted," he had said, "even to riding you on a rail. Yet my rule is: a rail ride is a discharge, for a teacher must stay master. And an old citizen may plague this term—one I angered by my refusal to authorize a new schoolhouse. The building is in bad condition, I'm bound to admit. Still, I'll not sanction another until the children mend their ways. He swore he'd bring a fool's look to somebody's face."

"The children won't wrap me around their thumbs," I had boasted, "and I'll get at the root of the trouble. I'll stand shy of the old fellow."

"They've run off even experienced teachers," the superintendent had explained, "but I feel I should give you a trial, in spite of my doubt you can last. Prove me wrong if you can, and hang on at least until I find a substitute."

The surprise that greeted me when I arrived on Keg Branch took me aback. The schoolhouse was brand-new! It sat on the foundation of the old one, upon a wedge of land between a cliff and a swamp and the creek, with scarcely space, as the saying goes, to swing a hungry cat. My surprise was so great that the lack of a playground didn't strike me at once. At Argus Bagley's, where the teacher customarily lodged, I expressed my astonishment over the building.

Argus explained, "Up until a few sessions ago, the discipline of the scholars was fair, but for some reason it worsened. They've turned the school into a hurrah's nest. We rebuilt in the expectation it might improve matters."

I inquired, "Why was it done without the county's support and knowledge?"

Argus chuckled. "Ever hear of Mace Crownover?"

I shook my head, wondering.

"Well, you're in his territory," Argus said. "The new building was his notion, and when the superintendent refused to help, the community humored Mace by providing lumber and labor. What Mace wants he usually gets."

Then I knew. "I've heard mention of Crownover," I said. "He's got the superintendent fooled, certainly."

"Confounding folks is Old Mace's trade," Argus said. "What that fun fox will do is beyond guessing. Still, he's not so feisty as he used to be, not so ready with pranking and telling tales. Declares his wife is beginning to draw a tight rein and that he's on the borders of swearing off tricks and tales for life. No matter. If ever you cross his path, keep your eyes skinned."

"I understand he's apt to make my job the harder," I said.

"Oh I reckon not," Argus said. "Yet I doubt he'd let pass a chance to hocus any person. Always up to mischief, that's his history. Why, right now he has a forty-dollar collect package in the post office and he vows he'll clear it. He'll clear it, says he, and I'd swear he hasn't a cent to his pocket. A trick, I'd bet my ears."

"What does the package contain?" I inquired, mildly curious.

Argus grinned. "He says it's for him to know and for us to find out."

Forty-eight children, raging in age from six to sixteen, from tads in the primer to overgrown eighth-graders, attended school the first day, and they came with eyes gleaming. They acted as I'd been told to expect. Spitballs rained, erasers zoomed, tricks were rife. Antics were pulled under my very nose, though catch a body I could not. Unwittingly I wore a sign on my back: "Hello the rabbit!" They laughed when I flexed my arms, when I whistled the pointing-stick, when I threatened or scolded. A good thing Mace Crownover didn't show up, for I already had my hands full.

The next day, I learned I was truly in for a bug race. A chair collapsed under me, soot blackened my fingers when I reached into a crayon box, the pointing-stick broke when I lifted it. Wasps in my lunch basket stung me, and the water in the well turned inky.

Again I caught nobody at mischief—none save a primer child sewing together the pockets of a coat I'd hung on a peg. Bad deportment to the contrary, the children were eager and bright at their studies, and they were respectful toward the new building, neither marking nor scarring it. At recess and at noon they jostled in the small area before the door. There was no room for even marble games or hopscotch, and I gazed covetously at Argus Bagley's posted land across the creek. Argus was the principal landowner in the section.

They kept me walking on pencils the week long, and such was my torment I almost forgot about Mace Crownover. Thorns were in my chair, cockleburs in my pockets, a fresh bouquet of sneezeweeds atop my desk daily. My hat was regularly glued to the wall, and a greased plank sprawled me twice. Yet the scamps were cunning enough to escape detection.

However, on Thursday afternoon I found a clue to their misbehavior. A student read a theme, which began: "A man bought a horse off Mace Crownover. The critter was blue or green or purple. You couldn't tell which. You couldn't learn till rain washed away the pokeberry and madder dye. The beast was gray. Gray as teeth."

The children listened, eyes round and mouths ajar. At the completion one said, "Old Mace's tricks are the best a-going."

And another chirruped, "Ought to hear him tale-tell. He can spin them from now till Sunday, and every word the truth."

I thought, Ah-ha, so it's Crownover's example they're following. I hushed them abruptly and would permit no further mention of him. The children took it ill. They batted their eyes at each other and closed their textbooks with a snap. They acted as though the final day of the term had come.

And Friday morning, on opening the door, I discovered a fence rail leaning in a corner.

I knew by now I couldn't fend off four-dozen children. The eighth-graders alone could handle me. But come what may, I'd not surrender without a tussle. I'd stick till the last pea hopped out of the pod. I ignored the rail, feigning not to see it, and I schemed to delay the reckoning. I conducted a three-hour spelling bee—spelling was their delight. I skipped recess and held the lunch period indoors, in the meantime reading to them from *Tom Sawyer*. I read all afternoon, and they could not tear their ears away. Thus I squeezed through till closing.

In the evening, while I was cudgeling my mind to decide what to do Monday, Argus brought a message. He reported: "Old Mace announces he'll clear the package at the post office tomorrow, and he's inviting the doubters to come witness it. Says he wants the schoolteacher there in particular."

I replied bitterly, "He's setting the stage for a hoax."

Argus chuckled, "That fox would saw off a toe for a laugh. He's the cat's beard."

"In my opinion," I blurted, "he's the downfall of the Keg Branch School."

Argus jerked his chin, surprised at my accusation, and he defended Crownover. "Had it not been for him, you'd be teaching in a shack," he said. "Squirrels used to steal the lunches through the cracks. Come a high wind, shingles scattered like leaves. Walk the floor, you made a noise like a nest of crickets."

To argue would serve no purpose, I decided. I smothered my rancor and said, "The package doesn't concern me."

"A trick, naturally," Argus said, "and he may pull it on you. Nevertheless, be on hand and show you're not bluffed out. Remember that courage goes a long way in this community."

Though tempted, I said, "I've borne enough misdoings for one week."

"Humor the old gent," Argus advised. "I'll go along and start him talking so he won't rack you too heavy. Go, and count it a part of your education."

The post office occupied a corner of the general store just above the schoolhouse. Saturday morning early, when Argus and I arrived, the counters and feedbags and barrels were covered with men, and the crowd overflowed onto the porch. Argus found a seat on a sack of salt, and Zack Tate, postmaster and merchant, furnished a crate for me to sit on. A stool stood bare, awaiting Mace.

Argus proposed to Zack, "Let's try loosening Mace's tongue. Before he locks his lips absolutely, we ought to hear him relate one more tale."

Zack agreed. "Say we do. We'll try, though it seems nowadays his wife has him twisted down tighter'n a nut on a bolt."

The crowd smiled expectantly.

"You believe he'll have money enough to free the package?" someone asked.

Zack said, "He's just wagging you fellers. Haven't you learned that?"

"I know him well enough not to read him off too quick," came the reply.

A man inquired, "Anybody made a reasonable guess what's in the bundle?"

"Maybe the devil's eyeteeth," a joker said.

Time passed. Eight o'clock came without a glimpse of Mace. At eight-thirty, the mail rider reported he'd seen nobody along the creek road. By nine, the men had become restless.

To hold them, Argus said, "Mace is giving the crowd a while to swarm and will appear right shortly."

Right as a rabbit's foot! It wasn't long before a cry arose outside. "Yonder comes Old Scratch!" And presently Mace was standing in the doorway. The walk had winded him, and he was panting. He was about sixty-five years of age, wide-faced and bushy-browed. His eyes were as blue as a marsh wren's eggs in a ball of grass.

Argus shoved the post office stool forward, greeting, "You're late, old buddy. Sit and rest and give an account of yourself."

"I promised my wife I'd do my duty and hurry home," Mace answered. He scanned the crowd, his gaze settling on me.

"What antic delayed you?" Argus baited. "Confess up."

"Why, I'm a changed character," Mace snorted. He accepted the offered seat, still looking in my direction. When he'd regained his breath he addressed me, "I figure you're the new teacher."

I nodded coldly.

"I'm hoping to thresh out and settle a matter today," he spoke gravely.

Zack Tate broke in, "The package is ready any time you are, Mace."

"It'll preserve an extra minute," Mace replied.

Argus caught his chance. "Tell us a big one while you rest. Tell of the occasion you turned the tables on the town barber after he'd short-shaved you."

Mace jerked his head as if slapped. "Never in life has a razor touched my jaws."

"You singe them off, aye?"

"Now, no," Mace said. "I climb a tree, tie my whiskers to a limb, and jump out." While the crowd guffawed, he pinned me with a stern glare and said, "The word comes the scholars are running you bowlegged. Still, their behavior has improved mightily over last session. Not a window broken, not a desk whittled, not a peephole drilled through the walls."

Argus spoke quickly to draw Mace's attention. "Come on and relate some rusty you've pulled and we'll not bother you more. You be the chooser. Anything."

Mace's eyes sparkled despite himself. "Let me name the word 'rusty' and my woman will wring my neck. And remember, I'm trying to conquer my trifling."

The men batted eyes at each other. Mace was a slick hand at double talk.

"Ah, quit stalling," Argus begged. "Tell of the foot logs you doctored to snap in two under people, the gallus straps cut during election rallies, the 'dumb-bulls' you fashioned to stampede cattle. Or tell of you dying—playing stone dead purely to hear your kin hallo and bawl."

But Mace would not. He went on talking to me. "I decided last spring, if matters rode unhindered, the Keg Branch children would grow into bad citizens."

"Hark! Hark!" Zack Tate cried.

"Somebody had to take hold of the problem," Mace said, "and I did. I took to spying on other schools to learn why ours didn't prosper. It boiled down to a couple of needs: a new schoolhouse, and a collection of stuff. The schoolhouse is built. Lastly, the stuff's here."

The crowd smirked.

Mace rose, hat in hand. "You know me, my friends, and surely you don't want your young 'uns marching in my tracks. You have a chance to straighten them out, so unknot your money sacks and give till it pinches." He held his hat brim up, dug a half-dollar from his pocket, and dropped it in. At sight of the coin, both Zack and Argus gasped.

"What's in the bundle?" a complaint sounded. "We're buying a pig in a poke."

"Don't you trust me?" asked Mace.

"Gee-o, no!" was the reply.

"Well, my wife doesn't either," Mace sighed. "The reason I've got to hurry." He passed the hat, cajoling and pleading. "Cough up, you tightwads, you eagle chokers. Forty dollars will buy peace. And recollect it's in your children's behalf."

None took Mace seriously, though most were willing to help the prank along. They flung money into the hat and laughed.

But to Argus, who shucked loose a dollar bill, Mace said, "We'll not accept a penny from you."

Argus was puzzled. "My money will spend the same as the next person's," he said.

"Hold your 'tater," Mace said, "and directly I'll tell what you're assessed. You're to give the most."

"Huh!" grunted Argus in bafflement.

When it appeared the last dime had been bled out of the crowd, the money was counted. It lacked ninety cents of reaching the full amount.

Argus offered, "I'll finish the pot."

Mace shook his head.

Zack volunteered, "Mace, I'll throw in the remainder if you'll agree to one simple thing."

"Say on," bade Mace.

"Confess how you came by your half-dollar."

"You wouldn't believe the truth, did you hear it."

"Speak it, and I'll try."

Mace squirmed on the stool. He moaned, "I oughten to throw away a precious secret. After you know, you'll all follow the practice, and money will get too common. It won't buy dirt."

"Tell and be done."

"I hate to."

"We're listening."

Mace yielded grudgingly. "Fetching that fifty-cent piece was the cause of my tardiness," he said. "I had to travel clear to the breaks of the mountains to upturn a rock I'd spit under six months ago. A pity I couldn't have waited a year. By then it would have grown to a dollar."

The package was brought. The crowd moved warily aside as Mace unclasped his knife, thrust the handle toward Zack, and said, "Cut the twine and open it."

"Aye, no," Zack refused. "Someone else can play the goat."

"Upon my word and deed and honor!" Mace blared. "Do you think it's full of snakes?"

"It's untelling," Zack said.

Mace appealed to Argus. "Open it quick. I'm bound to hustle."

"Scared to," Argus replied honestly.

Mace lifted his hands in sorrow. He groaned, "I've come on a bitter day. I've totally lost the confidence of my fellowman." As he spoke, he moved toward me, proffering the knife. "Here," he said, "prove I'm not a false speaker."

I shrugged. I'd as lief as not. Hadn't Argus said courage was honored on Keg Branch? I accepted the knife, and mouths in the crowd stretched to laugh. I cut the twine and broke the wrappings, and out rolled a volleyball, a basketball, baseballs, nets, and bats.

As we blinked Mace told Argus, "You're to donate the playground—a piece of the land you own across from the schoolhouse. The scholars need elbow room to burn up their surplus energy."

All stared in wonder, but mine was the only face that bore a fool's look.

Mace clapped on his hat and strode toward the door. At the threshold he glanced 'round, his eyes shining. "I'm going home and tell my wife to skin me alive for mixing in sorry company."

It turned out that I taught through the entire session on Keg Branch—and two more besides.

The Burning of the Waters

We moved from Tullock's lumber camp to Tight Hollow on a day in March when the sky was as gray as a war penny and wind whistled the creek roads. Father had got himself appointed caretaker of a tract of timber at the far side of the county, his wages free rent. We were to live in the one-room bunkhouse of an abandoned stave mill.

Father rode in the cab with Cass Tullock, and every jolt made him chuckle. He laughed at Cass's complaint of the chugholes. He teased him for holding us up a day in the belief we might change our minds. Beside them huddled Mother, the baby on her lap, her face dolesome. Holly and Dan and I sat on top of the load and when a gust blew my hat away I only grinned, for Father had promised us squirrel caps. Holly was as set against moving as Mother. She hugged her cob dolls and pouted.

The tract lay beyond Marlett and Rough Break, and beyond Kilgore where the settlements ended—eleven thousand acres as virgin as upon the first day of the world. Father had learned of it while prospecting timber for Cass and resolved to move there. To live without work was his dream. Game would provide meat, sugar trees our sweetening; garden sass and corn thrive in dirt black as a shovel. Herbs and pelts would furnish ready cash.

Father had thrown over his job, bought steel traps and gun shells and provisions, including a hundred-pound sack of pinto beans. He had used the last dime without getting the new shoes he needed. He told us, "Tight Hollow is a mite narrow but that's to our benefit. Cold blasts can't punish in winter, summers the sun won't tarry long enough overhead to sting. We can sit on our hands and rear back on our thumbs."

Once Father made up his mind, arguing was futile. Still Mother had spent her opinion. "Footgear doesn't grow on bushes to my knowledge," she said.

"You tickle me," Father had chuckled. "Why, ginseng roots alone fetch thirteen dollars a pound and seneca and goldenseal pay well. Mink hides bring twenty dollars, muskrat up to five. Aye, we can buy shoes by the rack. We'll get along and hardly pop a sweat."

"Whoever heard of a feller opening his hand and a living falling in it?" Mother asked bitterly. "My reckoning, you'll have to strike more licks than you're expecting."

Mother's lack of faith amused Father. "I'll do a few dabs of work," he granted. "But mostly I'll stay home and grow up with my children. Kilgore post office will be the farthest I'll travel, and I'll go there only to ship herbs and hides and rake in the money." He poked his arms at the baby, saying, "Me and this chub will end up the biggest buddies ever was."

The baby strained toward Father, but Dan edged between them. Dan was four.

Mother inquired, "What of a school? Is one within walking distance?"

Holly puffed her cheeks and grumbled, "I'd bet it's a jillion miles to a neighbor's house."

"Schools are everywhere nowadays," Father said, his face clouding. "Everywhere." He was never much for jawing.

"Bet you could look your eyeballs out," Holly said, "and see nary a body."

Annoyed, Father explained, "A family lives on Grassy Creek, several miles this side. Close enough, to my fancy. Too many tramplers kill a wild place."

"Tullock's Camp is no paradise," Mother said, "but we have friendly neighbors and a school. Here we know the whereabouts of our next meal."

Father wagged his head in irritation. He declared, "I'll locate a school by the July term, fear you not." And passing on he said, "Any morning I can spring out of bed and slay a mess of squirrels. We'll eat squirrel gravy that won't quit. Of the furs we'll pattern caps for these young 'uns, leaving the tails for handles."

"Humph," said Holly. "I'll not be caught wearing a varmint's skin."

Mother would not be denied. "Surely you asked the Grassy folks the nearest school?"

Father's neck reddened. "I told them we'd move the first Thursday in March," he spoke sharply. "They acted dumfounded and the man said, 'Ah!' and his woman mumbled, 'Well! Well!' The whole of the conversation."

"They don't sound neighborly," Mother said.

"Now, no," agreed Holly.

"Upon my word and honor!" Father chuffed. "They're good people. Just not talky." And on his own behalf, "Let a man mention the opportunity of a lifetime and the women start picking it to pieces. They'd fault heaven."

Mother had sighed, knowing she would have to allow Father to whip himself. She asked, "When you've learned we can't live like foxes will you bow to the truth? Or will you hang on till we starve out?"

Of a sudden Father slapped his leg so hard he startled the baby and made Dan jump. "Women aim to have their way," he blurted. "One fashion or another they'll get it. They'll burn the waters of the creek, if that's what it takes. They'll up-end creation."

"Men can be pretty hardheaded," Mother had said.

Daylight was perishing when we turned into Tight Hollow. The road was barely a trace. The tie rods dragged and Cass groaned; Cass groaned and Father chuckled. The ridges broke the wind, though we could hear it hooting in the lofty woods. Three quarters of a mile along the branch the stave mill and bunkhouse came to view, and, unaccountably, a smoke rose from the bunkhouse chimney. The door hung ajar, and as we drew up we saw fire smoldering on the hearth.

Nobody stirred for a moment. We could not think how this might be. Father called a hey-o and got no reply. Then he and Cass strode to the door. They found the building empty—empty save for a row of kegs and an alder broom. They stood wondering.

Cass said, "By the size of the log butts I judge the fire was built yesterday."

"Appears a passing hunter slept here last night," Father guessed, "and sort of fanned out the gom."

We unloaded the truck in haste, Cass being anxious to start home. Dan and I kept at Father's heels and Holly tended the baby and her dolls, the while peering uneasily over her shoulder. Our belongings seemed few in the lengthy room, and despite lamp and firelight the corners were gloomy.

At leaving, Cass counseled Father, "When you stump playing wild man you might hanker to return to civilization. Good sawsmiths are scarce." And he twitted, "Don't stay till Old Jack Somebody carries you off plumb. He's the gent, my opinion, who lit your fire."

"I pity you working fellers," Father countered. "You'll slave, you'll drudge, you'll wear your finger to nubs for what Providence offers as a bounty."

"You heard me," Cass said, and drove away.

The bunkhouse had no flue to accommodate the stovepipe, and Mother cooked supper on coals raked onto the hearth. The bread baked in a skillet was round as a grindstone. Though we ate little, Father advised, "Save space for a stout breakfast. Come daybreak I'll be gathering in the squirrels."

Dan and Holly and I pushed aside our plates. We gazed at the moss of soot riding the chimney-back, the fire built by we knew not whom. We missed the sighing of the sawmill boilers; we longed for the camp. Mother said nothing and Father fell silent. Presently Father yawned and said, "Let's fly up if I'm to rise early."

Lying big-eyed in the dark I heard Father say to Mother, "That fire puzzles me tee-totally. Had we come yesterday as I planned, I'd know the mister to thank."

"You're taking it as seriously as the young 'uns," Mother answered. "I believe to my heart you're scary."

"Not as much as a man I've been told of," Father jested. "He makes his woman sleep on the outer side of the bed, he's so fearful."

When I waked the next morning Mother was nursing the baby by the hearth and Holly was warming her dolls. Dan waddled in a great pair of boots he had found in a keg. The wind had quieted, the weather grown bitter. The cracks invited freezing air. Father was expected at any moment and a skillet of grease simmered in readiness for the squirrels.

We waited the morning through. Toward ten o'clock we opened the door and looked upcreek and down, seeing by broad day how prisoned was Tight Hollow. The ridges crowded close; a body had to tilt head to see the sky. At eleven, after the sun had finally topped the hills, Mother made hobby bread and fried salt meat. Bending over the hearth, she cast baleful glances at her idle stove. Father arrived past one and he came empty-handed and grinning sheepishly.

"You're in good season for dinner," Mother said.

Father's jaws flushed. "Game won't stir in such weather," he declared. "It'd freeze the clapper in a cowbell." Thawing his icy hands and feet he said, "Just you wait till spring opens. I'll get up with the squirrels. I'll pack 'em in."

The cold held. The ground was iron and spears of ice the size of a leg hung from the cliffs. Drafty as a basket the bunkhouse was, and we turned like flutter-mills before the fire. We slept under a burden of quilts. And how homesick we children were for the song of the saws, the whistle blowing noon! We yearned for our playfellows. Holly sulked. She sat by the hearth and attended her dolls. She didn't eat enough to do a flaxbird.

Father set up his trap line along the branch and then started a search for sugar trees and game. Straightway he had to yield in one particular. There was scarcely a hard maple on the tract. "Sweetening rots teeth anyhow," he told us. "What sugar we need we can buy later." Hunting and trapping kept him gone daylight to dark and he explained, "It takes hustling at the outset. But after things get rolling, Granny Nature will pull the main haul. I'll have my barrel full of resting."

When Father caught nothing in his traps two weeks running he made excuse, "You can't fool a mink or muskrat the first crack. The newness will have to wear off the iron." And for all of his hunting, my head went begging a cap. Rabbits alone stirred. Tight Hollow turned out pesky with rabbits. "It's the weather that has the squirrels holed," he said. "It would bluff doorknobs."

"Maybe there's a lack of mast trees too," Mother said. "Critters have sense enough to dwell where there's a living to be got. More than can be said for some people I know."

Holly said, "I bet it's warm at the camp."

"It's blizzardy the hills over," Father chuffed edgily. "I don't recollect the beat."

Mother said, "Not a marvel the hollow is cold as a froe, having sunlight just three hours a day. For all the world like living in a barrel."

"At Tullock's Camp," Holly said, "you could see the sun-ball any old time."

"And the houses were weather-boarded," Mother joined in. "And my cook-stove didn't sit like a picture."

338

"Now, yes," chimed Holly.

Father squirmed. "Have a grain of patience," he ordered. And to stop the talk he said, "Fetch the baby to me. I want to start buddying with the little master."

During March Dan and I nearly drove Mother distracted. We made the bunkhouse thunder; we went clumping in the castaway boots. The stave mill beckoned but the air was too keen, and we dared not venture much beyond the threshold. Often we peered through cracks to see if Old Jack Somebody were about, and at night I tied my big toe to Dan's so should either of us be snatched in sleep the other would awake.

In a month we used more than half of the corn meal and most of the lard. The salt meat shrank. The potatoes left were spared for seed. When the coffee gave out Father posed, "Now, what would Old Dan'l Boone have done in such a pickle?" He bade Mother roast pintos and brew them. But he couldn't help twisting his mouth every swallow. Rabbits and beans we had in plenty and Father assured, "They'll feed us till the garden sass crosses the table." Holly grew thin as a sawhorse. She claimed beans stuck in her throat, professed to despise rabbit. She lived on broth.

The traps stayed empty and Father said, "Fooling a mink is ticklish business. The idea is to rid the suspicion and set a strong temptation." He baited with meat skins, rancid grease, and rabbit ears; he boiled the traps, smoked them, even buried them awhile. "I'll pinch toes yet," he vowed, "doubt you not."

"The shape your feet are in," Mother remarked, "the quicker the better."

"We're not entirely beholden to pelts," Father hedged. "Even if I had the bad luck to catch nothing, the herbs are ahead of us—ginseng at thirteen dollars a pound."

"I doubt your shoes will hold out to tread grass," said Mother.

Coming in with naught to show was awkward for Father and he teased or complained to cover his embarrassment. One day he saw me wearing a stocking cap Mother had made and he laughed fit to choke. He warned, "Shun wood choppers, little man, or your noggin might be mistaken for a knot on a log." Again, spying Holly stitching a tiny garment, he appealed to Mother, "Upon my deed! Eleven years old and pranking with dolls. I recollect when girls her age were fair on to becoming young women."

"Away from other girls," Mother asked, "how can she occupy herself?"

"Stir about," said Father, "not mope."

Holly said, "I'm scared to go outside. Every night I hear a booger."

"So that's it," Father scoffed.

"The plime-blank truth, now."

Mother abetted Holly, "Something waked me an evening or so ago. A rambling noise, a walking sound."

"My opinion," Father said, "you heard a tree frog or a hooty-owl. Leave it to women to build a haystack of a straw."

Mother saw my mouth gape and Dan's eyes round. Without more ado she changed the subject. She prompted Father, "Why don't you go visit the Grassy Creek people? Let them know we're here, and begin to act neighbors."

"They knew we were coming," Father reminded. And he said, "When I have hides for Kilgore post office I might speak howdy in passing."

"The fashion varmints are shying your traps," Mother said. "That'll be domesday."

Father looked scalded. He eyed the door as if on the verge of stalking out. He said, "Stuff your ears nights, you two, and you'll sleep better."

The cold slackened early in April. It rained a week. The spears of ice along the cliffs plunged to earth and the branch flooded. The waters covered the stave mill, lapped under the bunkhouse floor, filled the hollow wall to wall. They swept away Father's traps. When the skies cleared, the solitary trap he found near the mouth of the hollow he left lying.

"Never you fret," Father promised Mother, "herbs will provide. I've heard speak of families of ginseng diggers roaming the hills, free as the birds. They made a life of it."

"I'd put small dependence in such tales," Mother said.

The woods hurried into leaf. The cowcumber trees broke blossoms the size of plates. Dogwood and service whitened the ridges, and wheedle-dees called in the laurel. And one morning Mother showed Father strange tracks by the door. Father stood in the tracks and they were much larger than his shoes. His shoes had lasted by dint of regular mending. He wagged his head. He could only droll, "It would profit any jasper wearing leather to steer clear of me. I'm apt to compel a trade."

"My judgment," Mother said, "we're wanted begone. They're out to be rid of us. They'll hound us off the tract."

"I'm the appointed caretaker of this scope of land," Father replied testily, "and I'll not leave till I get my ready on."

Wild greens spelled the pintos and rabbit. We ate branch lettuce and ragged breeches and bird's-toe and swamp mustard. And again the beans and rabbit when the plants toughened. By late April the salt meat was down to rind, the meal sack more poke than bread, the lard scanty. Father hewed out a garden patch and then left the seeding and tilling to Mother. He took up ginseng hunting altogether. He came in too weary to pick at us and he rarely saw the baby awake. Dan began to look askance at him. As for his shoes, he was patching the patches.

Dan and I gradually forgot Old Jack. We waded in the branch and played at the stave mill. We pretended to work for Cass Tullock, feeding mock logs to saws, buzzing to match steel eating timber. And we chased cowbirds and rabbits in the garden. Rich as the land was, the seeds sprouted tardily, for the sun warmed the valley floor only at the height of the day. Mother fixed a scarecrow and dressed it in Father's clothes. We would hold the baby high and say, "Yonder's Pap! Pap-o!" The baby would stare as at a stranger.

Father happened upon the first ginseng in May and bore it home proudly. We crowded to see it—even Holly. Three of the roots were forked and wrinkled, with arms and legs and a knot of a head. One had the shape of a spindle. Tired though he was, Father boasted, "The easiest licks a man ever struck. Four digs, four roots."

"Dried they'll weigh like cork," Mother pronounced; and she asked, "Why didn't you hit more taps, making the tramping worth the leather?"

His ears reddening, Father stammered, "The stalks are barely breaking dirt. Hold your horses. You can't push nature."

Mother said, "I believe to my soul your skull is as hard as a ball-peen hammer."

Father glanced about for the baby, thinking to skip an argument. The baby was asleep. He complained, "Is the chub going to slumber its life away?" He eyed Dan leaning against Mother and said, "That kid used to be a daddy's boy, used to keep my knees rubbed sore." And he took a square look at Holly and inquired, "What ails her? I want to know. She's bony as a garfish."

"You're the shikepoke," Mother replied. "You've walked yourself to a blade." And she said, "Did you come home early as at Tullock's Camp you'd find the baby wide-eyed."

Holly snatched the ginseng and fondled it. "Gee-o," she breathed in delight.

Father caught the baby awake the day he got up with the squirrels. He arrived in midafternoon swinging two critters by their tails, and he came grinning in spite of having found no ginseng. He crowed, "We'll allow the beans and bunnies a vacation. We'll feast on squirrel gravy." He jiggled them to make the baby flick its eyes. After skinning the squirrels, he stretched the hides across boards and hung them to cure.

The gravy turned out weak and tasteless. Lacking flour and milk there was no help for it. Yet Father smacked his lips. He offered the baby a spoonful and it shrank away. He ladled Dan a serving and Dan refused it. Tempting Holly he urged, "Try a sop and mind you don't swallow your tongue." Holly wrinkled her nose. "Take nourishment, my lady," he cajoled, "or you'll fair dry up and blow away."

"Humph," Holly scoffed, leaving the table.

Father's patience shortened. "Can't you make the young 'un eat?" he demanded of Mother. "She's wasting to a skeleton."

"We'll all lose flesh directly," Mother said.

Holly said, "Was I at Tullock's Camp, I'd eat a bushel."

Father opened his mouth to speak but caught himself. He couldn't outtalk the both. He gritted his teeth and hushed.

When ginseng proved scarce and goldenseal and seneca thinly scattered, Father dug five-cent dock and twenty-cent wild ginger. He dug cohosh and crane's bill and bluing weed and snakeroot. He worked like a whitehead. Mornings he left so early he carried a lantern to light his path and he returned after we children had dozed off. Still the bulk of the herbs drying on the hearth hardly seemed to increase from day to day. Again Mother reported strange tracks but Father shrugged. "It's not the footprints that plague me," he said, "it's the puzzle."

The garden failed. The corn dwarfed in the shade, the tomatoes blighted. The potato vines were pale as though grown under thatch. We ate the last of the bread and then we knew beans and rabbit plain. Father hammered together box traps and baited for groundhogs. A covey of whitebacks sprung the stick triggers and we had a supper of them. Dry eating they made, aye-o! The groundhogs were too wise.

Awaking one evening as Father trudged in, I heard Mother say direfully, "We'll have to flee this hollow, no two ways talking. They'll halt at nothing to be rid of us."

"What now?" Father asked wearily.

"Next they'll burn us out," Mother said, displaying a bunch of charred sticks. "Under the house I found these. By a mercy the fire perished before the planks took spark."

"May have been there twenty years," Father discounted. "Who knows how long?"

"Fresh as yesterday," Mother insisted. "Smell them."

"To my thinking," Father ridiculed, "scorched sticks and big tracks are awful weak antics. The prank of some witty, some dumb-head."

"We can't risk guessing," Mother begged. "For the sake of the children—"

"Women can read a message in a chicken feather," Father declared. "They can spin riddles of rocks. For my part, I have to see something I can understand. A knife brandished, say. Or a gun pointing in my direction."

Mother threw up her hands. "You're as stubborn as Old Billy Devil!" she cried.

Father yawned. He was too exhausted to wrangle.

The day came when Father's shoes wore out completely. He hobbled home at dusk and told Mother, "Roust the old boots. My shoes have done all they came here to do."

"They'll swallow your feet," Mother objected. "They'll punish." She was close to tears.

"It's a force put," Father said. "I'll have to use the pair do they cost me a yard of skin."

Reluctantly Mother brought the boots and Father stuffed the toes with rags and drew them on. They were sizes too large and rattled as he walked. Noticing how gravely we children watched, he pranced to get a rise out of us. Our faces remained solemn.

"I'll suffer these till I can arrange otherwise," he said, "and that I aim to do shortly. I'll fetch the herbs to the Kilgore post office tomorrow."

"They may bring in enough to shod you," Mother said, "if you'll trade with a cheap-John." She dabbed her eyes. "A season's work not worth a good pair of shoes!"

His face reddening, Father began sorting the herbs. But he couldn't find the ginseng. He searched the fireplace, the floor. He looked here and yon. He scattered the heaps. Then he spied Holly's dolls. The forked ginseng roots were clothed in tiny breeches, the spindle-shaped ones tricked in wee skirts. They were dressed like people. "Upon my deed!" he sputtered.

Father paced the bunkhouse, the boots creaking. He glared at Holly and she threw her neck haughtily. He neared Dan and Dan sheltered behind Mother. He reached to gather up the baby and it primped its face to cry. "Upon my word and deed and honor!" he blurted ill-humoredly and grabbed his hat and lantern. "Even the Grassy folks wouldn't plumb cold-shoulder me. I'm of a notion to spend a night with them." He was across the threshold before Mother could speak to halt him.

Father was gone two days and Mother was distraught. She scrubbed the bunkhouse end to end; she mended garments and sewed on buttons; she slew every weed in the puny garden. And there being nothing more to do she gathered up the squirrel skins and patterned caps.

The afternoon of the second day she told us, "I'm going downcreek a spell. Keep the baby company and don't set foot outside." Taking Father's gun she latched the door behind her. We watched through cracks and saw her enter the garden and strip the scarecrow; we saw her march toward the mouth of the creek, gun in hand, garments balled under an arm. She returned presently, silent and empty-handed, and she sat idle until she saw Father coming.

Father arrived wearing new shoes and chuckling. I ran to meet him, the tail of my fur cap flying, and he had to chortle a while ere he could go another step. He chirruped, "Stay out of trees, mister boy, or you may be shot for a squirrel." But it wasn't my cap that had set him laughing. Upon seeing Mother he drew his jaws straight. He wore a dry countenance though his eyes were bright.

Mother gazed at Father's shoes. "What word of the Grassy people?" she asked coolly.

"They're in health," Father replied, hard put to master his lips. He had to keep talking to manage it. "And from them I got answers to a couple of long-hanging questions. I learned the nearest schoolhouse; I know who kindled our fireplace."

Dan, hiding behind Mother, thrust his head into sight. Holly let her dolls rest, listening.

"Kilgore has the closest school," Father said. "A mite farther than I'd count-ed on. As for the fire, why, the Grassy fellow made it to welcome us the day he expected us to move here. But he's not the Mischief who planted tracks and pitched burned sticks under the house. Nor the one who waylaid me at the mouth of the hollow a while ago."

Mother cast down her eyes.

Father went on, struggling against merriment. "A good thing I made a deal with Cass Tullock to haul our plunder back to the camp. Aye, a piece of luck he advanced money for shoes and I had proper footgear to run in when I blun-dered into the ambush." He began to chuckle.

Mother lowered her head.

Swallowing, trying to contain his joy, Father said, "Coming into the hollow I spied a gun barrel pointing across a log at me—a gun plime-blank like my own. Behind was a bush of a somebody rigged in my old coat and plug hat. Gee-o, I traveled!" His tongue balled, cutting short his revelations. His face tore up.

Mother raised her chin. Her eyes were damp, yet she was smiling. "If you'd stop carrying on," she said, "you could tell us how soon to expect Cass."

A gale of laughter broke in Father's throat. He threshed the air. He fought for breath. "I can't," he gasped. "You've tickled me."

Chicken Roost

A horseman broke out of a cove into the road as Godey and Mal approached, declaring to the world, "I've been here and I'm done gone." That this was the new jockey ground was evident from the squeals and neighs issuing from it.

"What's the trouble, old son?" Godey inquired. "Too early to be skipping off."

"Two hours from now there won't be a soul hereabouts."

"Don't go away mad," said Godey.

"Mad?" cried the horseman, giving his mount a cut with a switch. "I'm madder'n forty hornets."

At the behest of Judge Solon Jones, the county agriculture agent had chosen Chicken Roost Hollow as a makeshift swapping area, the judge paying four dollars out of his pocket for a day's rent, as well as putting up five as a prize for the log-pulling contest. The hollow was some eighteen poles in length, three at the widest, hemmed by wooded slopes. The lower reaches were mostly cleared, with a tree standing here and there. Save for the dry bed of the branch there was not a level spot in it, and a spring for watering man and beast was lacking. Drovers used it for an overnight cattle pen. Giant beeches higher up filtered the light, permitting the sun to look in only at midday.

A pair of horsemen were in parley at the entrance, wheeling and turning, barring the way, one astride a stud with fuzzy ears, whiskery muzzle, and bulging hindquarters, the mount of the other a slight blue-hued mare with little except color in the course of distinction.

"Hod dammit, I aim to swap," blared the master of the blue.

"Offer me something," returned the owner of the stud.

The boys drew up to listen.

"Even."

"Give me ten."

"I said, even."

"Ten."

"Even."

"Ten. Not a chip less."

"Five."

"You heard me. Ten."

"Five."

"Ten."

"Five, dammit, five."

The rider of the stud broke off suddenly, mouthing, "I haven't lost a thing in this hollow," and deserted it at a smart pace, with the owner of the mare blatting after, "If you go, I'll cry."

Seizing the opportunity, Godey made a pitch. "Want to buy a gentleman mule?"

The man on the mare gave the animal a swift appraisal, pointed into the hollow and notified, "The grease buyer is up in there waiting for you sports," and jerking rein was away in pursuit of the stud.

Hardly had the boys started than a rider bore down upon them and spun 'round with the warning, "Watch yourself, you tads, these heels can't see," and slapped his mount and loped up the bed of the stream shouting, "Hoo-oo-ee, look what I've got." He rode a chestnut mare in tolerable flesh and coat, tail plaited, a pompom on her bridle, and on gaining at least momentary attention from an otherwise distracted crowd, made his cry:

"Round and sound and slick as a mole,
Two good eyes and heavy in foal."

A horseman offered chase, yelling "Can she work?" and received the answer, "You dadjim right she can work, and she will work." The run ended abruptly; a haggle ensued.

Godey and Mal stopped to get their bearings. The traders seemed numerous due to the lot of them being in view at once, not scattered, as formerly, throughout town. To Mal's satisfaction, the only person from home they sighted was Fester Shattuck—Fester astride a peeled log, a saddle beside him, swapped out. The medicine hawker and his sidekick were not to be discovered, or the watch seller with chains dangling from his pockets, although the grease buyer representing a rendering factory downstate was present and had a couple of shikepokes tethered to a tree. Something was amiss, for trading did not appear the first order of business. Riders were drawn up in circles, twisting in saddles, jawing and spitting, and what they had to say was uttered for the entire gathering.

"If you're hunting yellow dogs, the courthouse is packed with them, the fellers we elected."

"Amen, brother. You've spoken a parable."

"To the bull-hole with 'em, the whole shebang."

"Except for Judge Jones. Spare him. He stayed to the bottom with us."

"Him, too, by grabbies. Out with the danged push. If Solon Jones hasn't the power to control the others, he's clogging the works."

"That's the right talk. The old doddler has warmed the bench too long, nigh about burnt a hole in it."

"You have the judge wrong. He went the distance for us."

"What took place, I'll tell you; the politicians let the storekeepers put it over on us. They've shoved us beyond sight and sound."

Yet Chicken Roost was serving well in two particulars: There was no necessity to duck or hide to take up a drink of spirits, and shaded by towering beeches, the hollow was as cool as a cellar. From a variety of containers—bottles, jugs, fruit jars—whiskey was openly imbibed and shared.

"I'm wroth enough to set off dynamite," a trader swore.

A raucous laugh followed, and an admonishment, "Go ahead and poot. The biggest noise you'll ever make."

"Damn your eyes," was the reply.

The rings broke up, several horsemen departing the hollow, the rest to see what they could manage under the circumstances. A scattering of complainers remained to grumble, ire unspent.

"Next year I'll stick my dinner in my pocket and I won't leave a copper cent in town."

"There won't be another year, sky bo. Jockey Day is deader'n a nit."

"You've said it. As finished as four o'clock." "What struck me on the hairy side was the hiring of the skunk of the universe to do their dirty work." "I'll go along with you on that, even if you are a tight-fisted Republican."

"And I'll agree with a spending Democrat this final once. Next election I'll wade manure to my knees if I have to go vote against 'em, be they Democrat, Republican, or straddle-pole."

"Amen, rat's nest. Keep a-talking the truth and you'll go to Heaven directly, like Elijah done." "I am too, pumpkin head."

Mal, still wary lest someone who might recognize them had been overlooked, breathed to Godey, "Are you seeing anybody we know?"

"Nobody," said Godey, "so stop sweating." He had spotted the county agent watching the proceedings from a stump on the rise above Fester, collar buttoned, a tie at his throat, shirt pockets stuffed with pamphlets and pencils. Fester didn't count.

Fester Shattuck sat astride a beech trunk that had been felled and barked for the log-pulling contest. The skinned tree was an act of foresight on the part of the county agent, who had the grabs, the harness, and the swingletree in readiness as well. Fester had swapped out within forty-five minutes of his arrival, the nag he came on, a spavined horse, and a jenny passing through his hands in quick succession. Yet he was not completely flat. In ridding himself of the jenny, which he subsequently learned favored a leg in walking, a handicap difficult to observe on uneven footing, he had come by a hand-tooled copper-trimmed saddle that should sparkle the hardest eye. Confidence supported by nips of the sugar-top stored in his saddlebags, he probed about for chances to get back into the swapping game; he had not traveled out of his way, by Shade Muldraugh's on Dead Oak, for nothing. He had spied Godey and Mal before they did him. And Riar's mule was no stranger.

"Hoo-oo-ee, look at this."

The owner of the chestnut mare was making a second run up the hollow, terms offered after the first sally having proved unacceptable. He varied his cry:

"Round and sound, tough as whang,
Two good eyes, and four in the spring."

Carping finally put aside, the remainder of the complainers joined the trafficking. The hollow was too crowded for much free movement, particularly along the bed of the branch.

A person on foot had to look alive to avoid being bowled over, trampled, a tail switched in his face, or salted. Where the mounts stalled the earth was slick. Departures were frequent. A horseman would give up and declare, "Today I ought to of stayed home. My bones told me and I didn't heed." But there was no lack of calls of "Hoo-oo-ee," and "Y-u-u-p, follow me," and "Check her, noot. Shoot her up in through there and let me see her action." Runs were often aborted. As a consequence of the new officer, Lafoon Magoffin, putting a quietus on the town, a rabble of young men and boys had climbed the slope behind the courthouse, skirted the bench of the ridge to the upper end of Chicken Roost, and descended to spectators' positions above the throng.

Godey and Mal had dismounted, Godey leading the mule, Mal keeping to the rear for what cover the animal afforded, when they were spotted by the grease buyer. The buyer hailed, "I'm here, you short fellers. The high dollar is over here."

Without turning his head, Godey answered, "Hold your 'tater, brother fox. Be it I need you, I'll pull your chain."

Breaking from the press, a trader split for the entrance muttering, "If ever I visit this place again it will be when two Sundays come together. Plague take such a combobulation." Two horsemen of like mind accompanied him.

A man on a jack drew rein in the boys' path and gave Riar's mule calculated inspection. He wore woolen army pants, a flannel shirt. His steed was fitted out in a platted cornshuck collar with buckeye hames. Folded coffee sacks served as both pad and saddle and surmounted ribs as prominent as barrel staves. He gazed and did not speak.

"How does he look to you, friend," Godey inquired, though outwardly the man appeared not to possess a copper.

The man reached into his shirt and scratched the small of his back. "He's a brother to Methusalem" was his slow reply. "He's been here."

Godey's chin cranked. "Are you some sort of sharp tack?"

The man blinked. "Could be," he acknowledged, and then, "Wicked, hain't he—your plug. A wild ass. Mean as Lafoon Magoffin."

"He's no plug," Godey said levelly. His questioner might be another Tight Wad Thomas with pants full of money. "Of purebred stock, and so gentle you can sit in a chair and shoe him."

"Oh yeah?" came the scoff. "I'd bet different. A mule will play the gentleman for years just to get into a prime position to kick your brains out. I'm knowance to the fact."

"Tell me," snapped Godey, "are you wanting to trade, or are you talking to hear your head rattle?"

"Raised in the Devil's barn," the man continued. "I can read it in his eye."

"A mule is a mule," blurted Godey, and he urged, "Let's talk turkey. I'll sell him hide and ears for twenty dollars. And throw in the eyeballs."

"Twenty is too rich for my blood."

"All right. What about a swap? I'm asking ten to boot."

The man furrowed his brows until they met. He clawed where the tail of his woolen shirt was eating him. "I can't stand the pressure," said he.

His patience ending, Godey crackled, "Then keep him, keep him. Cheapjacks belong together."

"You've branded yourself with your tongue," the man reprimanded, clucking his mount toward the entrance, and he grumbled, "Everybody is wearing boots today."

Cupping his hands about his mouth, the grease buyer blatted, "You youngsters, you with the gray, guide him over here."

"You heard me, snakebrains," Godey reminded. "I said, 'Hold your 'tater.'"

The owner of the chestnut executed a deal, swapping for a filly and receiving thirty dollars in the exchange, a halving of the earlier asking price for the claimed reason "It's worth it to fly out of this hurrah's nest." Dismounting, switching rigs, he slapped the chestnut's rump and said, "Good-bye, old girl," and the jockey ground was short two more traders. Others followed, and the gathering had the aspect of breaking up.

A walker had a foot stepped on and let out a yowl that brought the county agent humping. Only a broken toe had been suffered and the score evened by a drink from the bottle of the offending animal's master. The agent delayed the return to his seat as a general exodus seemed imminent, and taking stance midway the hollow, attempted to dissuade those leaving, plumping for the log-pulling contest, his inducement the five-dollar award to the winner. None turned back, the main excuse being thirsty mounts, and not a few seized the chance to pour scorn on the head of the unknown witty who had picked Chicken Roost for a stamping ground. Avowed one, "If he had the brains The Man gave a chicken, he'd lay doorknobs." Several such scaldings launched the agent toward his stump, and he did not leave it again until a horseman forgot to duck in galloping under a tree.

By the time Godey and Mal approached Fester Shattuck, he had slipped from the beech and lay dozing in the leaves, the fancy saddle propping his shoulders. Having downed the best part of a pint of sugar-top, maintaining a balance on a skinned log was tedious business.

"Hey-o, neighbor," Godey hailed. "What are you doing sleeping in the middle of creation?"

Fester's lips parted. He blinked himself awake.

"Swapped out already?" Mal breathed in awe. "Gosh a'mighty." Fester was a Ballard Creeker he could trust, having much to account for himself.

Fester's eyes rounded. They were like holes in the sky. "Ho," he managed drowsily.

"It's his history," Godey joshed, "and the worst of it is he runs out of ear tobacco, the Old Maud brand"; and taking the hapless Fester to task he scolded, "Fes, old neighbor, I swear to my heart if I had a smoke-grinder for sale you'd be my first customer."

Sitting up, Fester rubbed his face.

Mal said, "He's proving his wife's complaint. She swears he'll begin with a fat horse and finish owning a pair of dogwood hames. And he can't seem to mend."

Chuckling, Godey said, "His woman—why, he'd swap her for a whimmy-diddle did somebody make him an offer."

Fester swallowed, his Adam's apple jerked. Doddling his head he disagreed, "Uh-uh, I wouldn't do that. Couldn't. Couldn't. She's all I've got—her and our babies." His eyes watered; he hiccupped. Then he reflected, "I have this pretty rig to trade on, and the day hain't started hardly. The sun sets late in July." Not one to borrow trouble, he ignored the presence of Riar's mule.

"Ah," jabbered Godey, "a Sunday saddle," and he bent to examine the tooling and brasswork. Sobering suddenly and winking at Mal, he cried in feigned wonder, "Fes, my buddy, you've done it finally. You've tricked some unlucky soul out of his drawers, robbed him totally. A bluegrass quarterhorse wouldn't be a fair swap to it."

On cue, Mal slavered, "A plumb doll."

Fester livened and gulped. "You reckon?" But he knew the boys too well for much assurance. He made an honest plaint, "People won't usually swap a horse for a rig and have nothing to haul it." He thrust an arm into his saddlebag and found his bottle, and thinking better of it, withdrew his hand empty.

"Unload it," cheered Godey. "Sell for cash and buy what suits your fancy," and for backing appealed to Mal, "Am I speaking the truth, knucklehead?"

"You're right as a rabbit's foot," said Mal.

"You can't miss with a gold mine," continued Godey, patting the leather, tracing the tooling with a finger, stroking the pad. He fiddled with the saddle until he had deposited his ball of cockleburs between the pad and the seat. "I'd call it the fastest saddle in seven counties. Throw it onto a brute and they'll take off like Lindbergh."

"As certain as the mumps," said Mal, and in the next breath, "Have you seen anybody else besides us from over on our creek?"

Fester shook his head, and he had a question of his own. "You boys," he inquired, "did you come through town, past the new Law?" He poked a hand into the saddlebag against the moment the boys would go.

"Naturally," answered Godey. "Right down the street, could have knocked his hat off with my elbow. No other way to get here except fly."

Fester's voice sank. "Aye, not me. I cut in behind the stores when I had wind of him. My life long I've heard bad on Magoffin. No heart in his breast, a de'il on earth. Folks shun him the fashion they would a copperhead."

"That shikepoke of a policeman?" ridiculed Godey. "Why, I done every-thing but spit in his face and here I stand, untipped, living proof. All a body needs is nerve."

"Shorely, shorely, you didn't," insisted Fester. "You're rigging me. Forever people have told me—"

"I said, 'Hey-o, Jack nasty,' and he grinned fit to pop."

Said Mal, "Godey is spilling the gospel, Fes, every word the truth."

"Eternally I've heard—"

"You heard like Litt," said Godey. "I believe to my soul if I'd o' called him by his nickname he'd have busted out laughing."

Fester yielded again to the support of the saddle, clutched the bot-tle, and puzzled, "Magoffin must o' joined the church, must o' repented his sins. No other accounting for it. Not his regular nature." He closed his eyes against the light. "But I'll not risk him. Now, no. He might backslide. I'm go-ing home the course I got here, by the offside of Roscoe." Godey's stomach growled. Tugging on the mule's halter, he said, "Play chicken then, if that's your nature. You can't cure a coward." And moving on, he babbled, "We'll see you later when we can talk to you straighter."

The trading continued, diminished though it was, and from his vantage point, the county agent concluded it would hold out only as long as the drink. But if the ranks of the traders thinned, there was a gain in onlookers from the town roosting above the commotion, apparently awaiting the log-pull, as nothing else promised.

"Hey, hey. You're beholding something. Ya-hoo-oo."

The shouter was halted within twenty feet of the beginning of his run.

"What's your price?" a walker demanded.

"A ginger-wine beauty, worth the candy, and I wouldn't part with her ex-cept I can't feed both a horse and an automobile."

"Don't tell me your troubles, I have my own. Name your lowest figure."

"Seventy-five cash—cash on the barrelhead. And she'll bring it, my fellow citizen, every formal dollar." "Don't citizen me. Now, that's your first offer. Skip the bragging and let me hear your last 'un, and don't stutter."

"You hain't deaf, you son-of-a-gun. I'm wanting seventy-five and I'm get-ting it, or I'm taking her to the barn."

"Then keep her, for you're the feller who can't afford to. Stall her and feed her on ten-dollar bills this winter."

"I might do 'er, fat mouth. I might."

Godey and Mal had stopped, Mal still searching for recognizable faces, Godey attending the hagglings in the vicinity. Tongues were thickening, and an occasional finished bottle sailed into the timber with the bawl, "There goes a dead soldier."

"Your stud is too active. Been high-lifed, my opinion. Watch him walk, wagging his hips, picking up them knees. Tomorrow you'll have to snake him out of the stable."

"That cob—hoofs split like stovewood. Huh, you're not talking to me. No foot, no horse."

A medley of voices rose.

"Hey, you folks, crowd up to my filly. Pass a hand across her flanks. They're as soft as a woman's glove. She's a picture, I'm telling you. Was she people, I'd marry her."

"Yeah, she's got freckles on her butt. She's pretty."

"Did you say boot? Is boot all the word you know?"

"Turn the critter into soap and I'll bath myself next Christmas."

"The only bath you ever had was one time you fell in the creek."

The parleys broke up suddenly, nothing bought, nothing sold or traded, and with three bottles flung into the trees and a shout, "Old Aunt Dosha, if you don't keer I'll leave my demijohn setting right here." In a troop the contenders rode out of the hollow, and a bystander observed, "Appears everybody has come here today a-leaving."

The county agent fidgeted on his stump. It was nine forty-five, and by rough count only twenty-seven traders remained. He noted that the man formerly occupying the skinned log had abandoned it for a seat on the ground, the saddle his support, and that farther down the hollow another was sprawled in the leaves, overcome by drink. The latter lay upslope, out of harm's way.

"Who owns this plug?"

The grease buyer had tapped Godey's elbow and stood calculating the weight of the mule. He had a choked countenance, and his lips were as long and as mobile as a sheep's. Following this strike he intended to depart, for the pickings had grown too slim to bother remaining.

"Who's holding the lines?" Godey snapped.

"I mean is he yours—your property?"

"Anybody claim he hain't?"

The buyer's lips unfolded. "Nobody, sprout. I'm trying to establish ownership before I bargain."

"Bargain, aye. What's on your mind?"

"Ah," cozened the grease buyer, "let's cut the gab and get to cases. I want to buy, and you want to sell. Correct?"

"You're the one popping fool questions."

Not completely satisfied, the buyer turned toward Mal. "Does your partner own the animal, or have the authority to dispose of it?"

Casting a glance toward Godey, Mal answered, "Figure he'd come with him if he didn't?"

Godey diverted his attention, feigned to go. He advised, "Trot along and see to your bone-bags, snakebrains. We're wasting breath."

The long lips of the buyer worked for a moment. Whipping out a checkbook, he spieled, "I'll pay three dollars."

"Three dollars," blatted Godey. "You're laughing me to death. Are you counting me a dumb-head?"

"Four."

"Fifteen," countered Godey.

"Seven."

"Sixteen."

"Whoa," cried the buyer. "Whoa. You're going up, getting higher. You're supposed to come meet me."

"Eighteen" was Godey's level reply, "and my next price will be twenty."

"Eighteen. Gosh a'mighty. Too much."

"You paid twenty last year. I have the facts on you. But I'll take eighteen if you'll hush."

The buyer's lips were busy. "You're a sharp duck," he uttered, and flaring the checkbook against a tree inquired, "How do you sign?"

"What's it to you?" asked Godey.

"I . . . I want to write your name on the draft so you can get your money at the bank." He hesitated, brows furrowed, checkbook poised in air. "Do they know you at the Bank of Roscoe?"

Godey grunted. "The big question is do they know you."

The buyer's hand fell. "Any check I sign is gold, for I'm acquainted hereabouts and have trafficked in these parts many a season."

"The only paper I'll accept is colored green," asserted Godey. "You pay others cash. Why cull me?"

"I'll require your name for my record anyhow."

Agreeing promptly, Godey said, "You can have it. You're paying eighteen cash dollars to Hebron Watley. I'm him. Now, are you suited?"

The grease buyer mulled the matter over, lips champing. After an interval he explained, "I'm not wholly persuaded you have title to the animal, and paying by draft is proof I acted legally. My checks are as negotiable as greenbacks. The bank and Roscoe merchants will honor them. So it's a check, I'm afraid, or no deal."

Godey laughed sourly. "A check of yours wouldn't be as good as a page of the Sears and Rearback catalog. Wouldn't cover as much ground. Even a cob is worth more."

Without further ado the buyer pocketed the checkbook and turned away. "I'll be seeing you around," said he, and, "Don't stuff any beans up your noses."

"We're not about to, snakebrains," returned Godey, "and don't you be eating any horse apples."

Almost directly the boys encountered a trader who had a bridle draping his shoulders, a token of his having sold out and in the market. The corners of his mouth headed a riverlet of ambeer, a gray tousle stuck through a rent in his hat. The man paused to scrutinize Riar's mule, to remark, "Where'd you dig up the brother to Methuselum?" and to twist open the animal's lips and observe, "Could stand a new set of grinders the same as myself."

"He's got four legs, and he walks on all of them," Godey replied. "He's been over the road but there's a lot of plowing in him yet."

"Very little, to my notion" came the judgment, and the man continued, "I won't work myself, and something or somebody has to."

"He'll surprise you, old son. He's the berries."

Mal chimed, "He's a clod buster."

"He won't do," declared the man, passing on. "I can't afford a brute as worthless as I am."

Fester improved his resting place after the boys left him by wadding the saddle cloth into a cushion for his head. The sleeper downhollow lacked such comfort, the earth his pillow. Fester took repeated sups from the dwindling half-pint of sugar-top, squinting to gauge the hour. Although he could not discover the sun, the glistering leaves at a point along the ridge proclaimed it not quite ten o'clock. Ample time remained to mend his fortune. He drowsed, chin in his collar, and when he did stir briefly and crack his lids, he gazed as upon an apparition. A Tennessee walking horse, with pen-hooker Rafe Shanks astride, was entering the hollow. The horse was on parade, a showing-forth of equine perfection, a display of grace and poise by both mount and rider.

Fester did not move. Only his eyes shifted, following the pen-hooker, attending the checkreins clasped between fourth and middle finger, the ramrod posture, angle of elbow, bend of knee, shoe in stirrup, the rakish sweep of Rafe Shank's hat. Rafe rode as might the king of horsemasters.

That this was not a vision was attested by the sudden halt in activity. The pair were the cynosure of all eyes as they negotiated the length of the hollow in a single foray, wheeled, and strode out. As they disappeared from Fester's view, his chin drooped and he slept.

The rider who failed to duck in running under a tree had brought the county agent off of his stump in a hurry. Unhorsed, the man lay straddle-legged, to appearances dead, while traders crowded 'round. But he had suffered nothing worse than having the breath knocked out of him and was on his feet within minutes and feeling for his bottle.

"If he hadn't been drunk it would o' killed him" was the repeated comment, and an apologist in the cause of strong spirits averred, "One of the several good things about likker is it limbers a feller and lets him down easy," which encouraged the retort, "From my experience, the limber business is the worst thing to be said for drinking whiskey." The assemblage chortled.

As the grease buyer began his departure and others were following suit, the county agent concluded it was now or never for the log-pulling. Yet Godey Spurlock delayed him by asking, "Do you know a couple of jaspers up Pawpaw on Ballard Creek called Doss and Gobel Colley?"

"I do," responded the agent impatiently. Answering questions was originally his forte, and he shared information with such generosity a criticism of him was that should you ask him a thing he imparted more than you wanted to hear. Preoccupied at the moment, he gave Godey short shrift. "Great boys, the Colleys—hard workers—joined a project of mine—growing strawberries."

"Strawberries," hooted Godey, "my rusty ankles."

The agent amended his statement. "Preparing the land, getting it into shape for a fall planting of a hybrid variety I'm introducing—fruits the size of hens' eggs." He whipped out a pamphlet.

"Aye gonnies, they've hoodwinked you plumb."

Mal, in the dark, assisted. "They've put blinkers on you, them Colleys. They're double-talkers, lie for a living."

Godey went on, "The fact is Doss and Gobel have never thought a thought about strawberries. They were first aiming to raise peaches from seeds Riar Thomas hauled in from South Carolina when a bigger idea struck."

Fidgeting, the agent said, "You're ahead of me on the news."

"I'm trying to wise you and you won't stand."

"I have irons in the fire, my young friends, and must go."

Godey wagged his head mournfully. "They're sinking a hole to China."

The agent spun 'round like a teetotum. His mouth gaped.

Adjusting instantly and spurred by a nudge from Godey, Mal declaimed, "There they were into it, and us eyewitnesses."

"Forty feet down and digging to equal ferrets," said Godey.

The agent peered into the boys' faces. He found them solemn enough. "At forty feet, probably at twenty, they would have struck water," he balked.

"They picked a dry spot on a bench of the ridge."

The strawberry pamphlet fluttered to the ground.

"Is this a put-up?"

"Doss is digging and Gobel hoisting the dirt in a bucket," explained Godey, "and they prophesy they'll reach China come Christmas."

Singling out Godey as the leader, the agent endeavored to arrive at the truth. "You're pulling my leg," he accused.

Godey's forehead wrinkled. "Are you saying I'm telling one?"

"No, no; no offense," hurried the agent, falling over himself, "I mean . . . I mean . . ." But he gave up. With the traders melting away as he watched, he strove to end the conversation. Sputtering, "I'll visit the Colley brothers short-ly—probe into the matter—this week, the latest," he turned to go.

"Hold your 'tater, swifty," bade Godey, "for I haven't finished. There's a second job in your line you can handle while there."

Facing the opposite direction, rattling his soles, the agent inquired, "What now? Speak it. I'm in a bad haste."

"Epizoomicks."

The word turned the agent again. "Epizoomicks?" He batted his eyelids. "Are you referring to an epizootic, an epidemic among animals? Be that the case, it is my province."

"On Bee Tree, at Viney Snow Roseberry's, it's a-happening. Her turkeys are croaking like forty."

The agent started once more, activated by another passing rider. "I'll look into that as well. You have my word—my word."

Of the sixteen traders remaining, three evinced willingness to have their mounts compete in pulling the log, and the agent saw at once a genuine con-test was impossible because the roan stallion entered was a quarter larger than the mare-mule and twice the weight of the pony, the latter two committed by tipsy owners. And the rule must be adjusted to fit the terrain—the winner the animal drawing the log farthest in a minute.

Up pranced the owner of the roan, and while the agent adjusted grabs to the beech, he dismounted and harnessed his animal, hooked swingletree to the chain, and spying up at the gallery of onlookers from town, challenged, "You jaspers got any hats you want to bet?" The number of watchers had swelled until there were about as many of them above as traders below, and an earnest of their age was the total absence of hats. One jeered a reply, "Aye-o, Garfield, big doing, a stud horse battling yearlings," and a companion censured, "Hain't fair, Gar. Shame on you." Having hitched their mounts aside for the occasion, the traders gathered, Godey and Mal in their midst, stepping over the sleeping Fester Shattuck when necessary.

Garfield collected the lines and addressed his beast: "Gee a little bit. Another bit."

"Gee, gee," clamored the gallery, welcoming any excitement.

Pocketwatch in hand, the agent inquired nervously, "Ready, are you?" and without awaiting an answer cried, "Go."

Jerking the lines, Garfield commanded the roan, "Do it, Pete. Hip, hip."

"Hip, hip," echoed the onlookers.

"Come on, daddy boy. Show 'em. Let's me and you show 'em."

The gallery burst out together, "Daddy boy, come on."

The roan dug hoofs into the earth and strained, and twenty-five seconds transpired before the log moved. In the time remaining, with stops and starts, he was able to drag the log a mere four-and-a-half yards, the uphill pitch of the ground a hindrance and the three-foot-through beech a greater burden than calculated. And at this juncture the owner of the mare-mule, addled though he was, withdrew from the competition.

"Coward," rose a caterwaul. "Chicken-legged coward."

The pony's master was no quitter. That an effort to budge the log with so slight an animal was hopeless did not stop him. Yet he dawdled, postponing the showdown. Raising his bottle, he drained and pitched it, and then arranged the traces, which were too ample when buckled their tightest. He ignored the hecklers who had warmed up at the last spectacle, joshing, "She can't stir it, Taylor," and, "You ought to be allowed to push while she pulls."

"Ready?" alerted the agent.

"I hain't," said Taylor Horne. He wouldn't be rushed.

While the pony's owner fiddled with chain and swingletree, a voice lifted among the spectators, ejaculating in mock wonder, "Why, bust my breeches if there ain't Bad Hair from over on Ballard." Godey whirled, intent on catching the culprit with mouth open, while Mal, scalp prickling, not daring to turn and look, stood like a post. With many clamoring at once, Godey could not discover from whose teeth had come the utterance, and no face seemed familiar.

"Ready, sir?"

"Pretty soon." The whiskey blossoms on Taylor Horne's cheeks burned. Casting a glance at his badgerers, he defied, "Any of you birds got money you want to lose? I say she'll do 'er."

"Money, huh?" somebody yawped. "You can't even spell it, much less flash it."

Again the agent spoke, "Ready?" and before a denial could be registered, called, "Go."

"Hup, sweetheart," cried Taylor, urging his pony forward. "Hup. Show 'em."

The gallery mocked, "Sweetheart, hup! Show 'em," and one of them added, "Sweetheart, huh? Now he's gone and told it."

The pony did her best. Her belly barreled, the muscles of her legs grew rigid, rear hoofs dug to the fetlocks in the earth. Her jugular vein swelled to a rope.

"Hup, sweetheart, hup!"

The skinned beech log stayed where it was for all the pony's striving, and still the owner would not relent, pleading, "Jenny Peg, my 'possum baby, do it for me. Hup!" The gallery whooped and slapped thighs and chortled.

The minute up, the agent grasped the pony's bridle, rubbed her nose, and praised, "For your size, you did splendid."

An onlooker called down in derision, "She'll do 'er, won't she Taylor?"

"Go to hell," said Taylor.

The traders moved toward their mounts, and the rabble on the slope arose and stretched and began to leave by the route they had come. So much of jockey day as there was going to be was patently over. Producing his wallet, the agent drew out a five-dollar bill and thrust it at the master of the stallion.

Garfield Wayland peered at the money. "What's that for?" he asked. News of the award had missed his ears, and heretofore victory had been considered honor enough.

"It's the prize," explained the agriculture agent. "You won it, sir, won it fairly."

Since the Red Cross donated him a twenty-four-pound bag of flour in 1933,

Garfield had come by nothing free, and the only money he had ever won was pitching pennies in games of crack-o-loo as a boy. "I heard you," said he, "but you haven't talked yet."

The traders paused; the watchers overhead halted in their tracks.

Hoping to pass the matter off with a jest, the agent cajoled, "If it won't spend, I'll give you another just like it."

"Ah, take it," came from the ridge, "you're holding up creation," and, "Grab it, and buy a gallon."

"What I'm wanting to hear," insisted Garfield, "is whose pocket it's out of. Who put up the five?"

The agent grew earnest. From what he had heard during the morning, the truth would be unpalatable. He bought time before answering by a glance at Fester Shattuck napping in their midst and at the other sleeper sprawled down the hollow, and he saw himself as he surmised these hill farmers viewed him, an upstart who had never grubbed a new-ground or raised corn on land pitched at a forty-five-degree angle, a sharp tack who scoffed at the rural wisdom passed from father to son, who had gathered all he knew out of books, and whose salary was paid out of their sweat. When no solution occurred other than to make a clean breast of it, he said, "Judge Solon Jones, a friend of the people, donated the prize."

Garfield stiffened as if slapped. "You want me to take money off of Judge Jones after how him and the rest of the Roscoe politicians treated us country fellers?" His jaw gripped, his eyes hooded. "Hear me, and hear me straight, I'm not for sale."

"And listen to me," a trader cut in. "We're all for sweeping out the court-house four years coming. To the bull-hole with them, say we everybody."

"Amen, sky bo," came a seconding.

The ridge rang with laughter.

In his confusion the agent found himself saying, "It's yours, the prize, no strings attached, none whatsoever," and, "You have the judge wrong. He argued for holding the trading in town and was overruled."

Garfield Wayland was not listening. "Hand that five back to the old judge and tell him what he can do with it."

From overhead came the prompting, "Give him the particulars, Gar. Plain speaking."

"Tell him," clarified Garfield, "to take it and ram it."

The gathering broke up, and almost in unison the traders swung into saddles and made their departure, flowing around Fester into the natural roadway of the branch bed. The sleeper farther down was lifted, balanced across a saddle, and carried along. Collecting the grabs and swingletree, intent on deserting the scene himself, the agent referred to his timepiece. The affair had ended an hour short of noon.

With heads toward home, the animals hustled and the hollow emptied rapidly. The agriculture agent clanked after them with his gear. And though Mal relaxed, Godey did not. Godey continued to gaze up the slope at the vanishing onlookers who could be observed for some fifteen yards before the woods hid them. Godey was seeing the last of their heels when a cry rang down:

"I smell peaches
I've spied a jasper
With a hole in his breeches."

Although Godey kept his eyes riveted to the ridge until the last of the onlookers had disappeared and the sounds of man and beast had died in Chicken Roost and nobody else was there save Mal and the slumbering Fester, he was unable to single out or guess his taunter. Then, without a word or a glance at Riar's mule, he strode toward the mouth of hollow. Mal trailed him, not venturing to protest the abandonment of the animal, muttering instead, "Nowadays a body can't spit without the world a-knowing."

The boys were a quarter of a mile along the road toward Big Blue and had halted under a locust to await the bus, or perchance to hitch a ride earlier, when Godey broke his silence. He chuffed angrily, "I'll level up with Riar Thomas if it's the final thing I do on the ball of this earth. Dadburn him, and his old hen, and his snotty-nosed young 'uns."

Mal wrestled with himself. The desertion of the mule was a rock in his chest. Dare he suggest they fetch Riar's old gray, take the bypass around Roscoe, and at least turn the animal loose on Ballard? They could claim he had broken fence. "The mule—" he began.

"What about him?" Godey cut Mal off. His eyes were gimlets.

"My opinion," reasoned Mal, "we've already hurt Riar a whole big heap."

"Not half enough," sputtered Godey. "Not by the half." And as a gesture he knotted his fist and said, "If I hadn't sworn not to, I'd warp you one. You . . . you . . ."

Mal's hand raised by habit to shield his arm. His neck reddened, mottling like Tom Peeple's. The color climbed, flushing his cheeks, invading his scalp. Flecks danced before his eyes like the heat devils wrinkling the highway. He gathered his courage to do what he had to do should Godey finish what he had started. The unspoken words hung in the air.

Snickering suddenly, Godey said, "You tickle me. Take your hand down, knucklehead. I swore I wouldn't hit you, didn't I? When Godey Spurlock swears he won't do a thing, he's not liable to."

The tension broke.

His hand still in place, Mal said, "Me and you wouldn't recognize a child of Riar Thomas's did we meet one."

"We wouldn't, huh?" Godey cackled. His face brightened. He beamed. "After all of Tight Wad's cow business? Why, someday we'll see a calf and it'll have a face pine-blank like a Thomas."

"Might," allowed Mal, dropping his arm.

"And speaking of that pinch-nickel," Godey said, "I aim to get up with him right shortly and hear what he has to talk about. We have a right smart-sized crow to pick together."

At midday the sun found the break between the trees shading Chicken Roost, lit the dry branch from mouth to head, and inched across Fester Shattuck's face. He cracked his eyelids and was momentarily blinded by the light. Not a whinny or a knicker reached his ears, and the quiet baffled him. Nothing moved in the heating air. Shifting out of the sun, he let the world take form. Riar's mule came to view, a spool of slobber dangling from its muzzle; horse apples steamed. The hollow was worn slick. When his sight was restored fully, he could discover no other beast or any trader. His tongue was dry, and on groping for his bottle, he found it empty. He stared at the copper-trimmed saddle and could not summon the will to rise.

What brought Fester to his feet finally was the glint of a mason jar on the slope above him. He scrambled to it, the last yards on his knees, and although it was drained, kept it as a collecting vessel, for he now saw glass sparkling on both shoulders of the hollow. Working along the ridge, he caught up any container he found. The majority were dry when discarded, or had landed neck down; few were broken, spared by underbrush and leaves. He collected a drop here, a thimbleful there; a camphor bottle yielded half a gill. When he had enough to constitute a swallow, he upped the jar.

Fester had pressed along to the head of the hollow and was traversing the opposite side before his search was truly rewarded. Where his fellow sleeper had lain were two pint bottles, the first drained, the second three-quarters full with the cork bitten off. It was pure corn whiskey, distilled by the old method, as yellow as the sun. The remainder of the stopper was lodged in the bottle's neck, and when he tried to extract it with his knife, it crumbled as he gouged. In a fever of need, he pushed the cork through and poured the contents into the jar.

The whiskey was too rare to be gulped. He had not encountered its match in years, and the wide-mouthed mason jar was the proper vessel to breath in the aroma as one supped. He imbibed slowly, taking his time.

The hollow began to wake. The beeches rustled. A snake doctor surveyed the dry branch; a towhee made the mast fly; an automobile hooted distantly. Fester himself began to liven. Observed from afar, the burnished brass of the saddle appeared golden. Even Riar's mule acquired a stolid handsomeness. And Fester struck upon a plan. He would return the mule, trafficking along the way, using the saddle as barter, and with any luck be astride a nag of his own by the hour he reached Ballard Creek. Such a saddle should hook any eye. His hopes soared as he drank and presently set himself in motion.

Fester Shattuck knew to exercise caution with a mule. A mule's reckoning was beyond human ken. He approached warily, entreating "Whoa, friend, whoa," and, after cleaning its muzzle with a stick, rubbed its nose and patted its belly, imploring the while, "Old grandpaw, be good to me and I will to you. As certain as Glory is watching, I'll treat you right." A shiver rippled the animal's flanks. Putting the jar aside temporarily, Fester leaned against the critter as against a wall and stroked the roach of mane, but he had enough of his wits not to nibble ears as he might a pony's. The mule flushed its nostrils and stamped. "Stick to me, grandpaw, and you'll see Brushy Branch and your master long before the sun hides. I swear it."

Shaking out the saddle pad, Fester dislodged a ball of cockleburs and pressed it into the earth with a heel. Onto the mule's back went the rig. The girth was adjusted, buckles fastened and tested, the animal circled to make positive everything was secure. Then Fester finished the whiskey. Springing into the saddle with newfound alacrity, he stiffened his spine, grasped reins between fore- and middle fingers, turned elbows outward, set feet lightly into the stirrups, angled his hat, clacked and commanded, "Get up, grandpaw," and rode out of the hollow. He rode kingly.

The blacktop shimmered in the noon heat. Nothing had passed in either direction during the half hour past except the bus returning from Thacker. At the copse of gilly trees below town, Fester gave a long eye to a pony with white stockings tied up in the shade, but nobody was about with whom to bargain. He rode on, the bypath to the rear of the stores slipping his mind until he was in front of Meg Brannon's boardinghouse and saw Lafoon Magoffin looming in the middle of the street. He slowed the mule, yet did not turn back. Had not Godey Spurlock declared, "I believe to my soul if I'd o' called him by his nickname he'd o' busted out laughing"? Fester went forward in the boldness of his drink and curiosity.

Lafoon Magoffin's vigil in the burning sun had gone unrewarded, and his uniform was the darker for being sweated through. His jaws were oily, his chin dripped. The youngsters in the aged Edsel had not pressed their luck by returning, nor had he found occasion to clap hands on any person. Vehicles had been shifted into low gear at sight of him, folk on horseback hightailed to his order, pedestrians allowed him a wide berth. But what had he here? A man on a gray mule approaching, sitting stiff as a poker in the saddle, arms akimbo, heels angled, hat raked to a slant. Holding to the center of the road and veering neither right nor left, the rider jogged squarely up to him, drew rein, and greeted shyly, "Hey-o, baboon."

Magoffin's simian arm shot up even before he smelled the whiskey. His sleeves were skinned to the elbow. Grabbing a wad of shirt, he hauled Fester from the saddle. Down came the billy, up went the knee, and Magoffin's breeches hiked to his shanks as he leaned for a purchase on Fester's belt.

Brad Garner was a witness, as was Elvin Haymond, from Lairds Creek. Elvin had been one of the onlookers in Chicken Roost, having been informed by Brad of Riar Thomas's loss of a load of peaches and urged to check on Godey Spurlock's intentions with Riar's critter. Brad rode the mule through to Brushy and had him in Riar's barn by sundown.

The Run for the Elbertas

As Riar Thomas approached the Snag Fork bridge, the truck lights picked up the two boys sitting on the head wall. Glancing at his watch, he saw it was nearly one o'clock. He halted, pulled the cardboard out of the broken window, and called, "I'll open the door from the inside, it's cranky." The boys sat unmoving. "Let's go," he said, "if you're traveling with me. A body can't fiddle in the peach business."

Godey Spurlock began honing his knife on the concrete, and Mal Dowe got his out too. "Pay us before we start," Godey said. "We hain't going to be slicked."

"What I say," said Mal.

"My grabbies!" Riar chuffed. "You ever know me hiring anybody and failing to settle?"

"They tell you trade out of paying," Godey said. "People didn't name you 'Tightwad' for nothing." Yet it wasn't the money that made Godey stall. He was angling to help drive.

Mal said, "Doss and Wint Colley claim you skinned them the last trip."

Riar snapped the clutch in irritation. "Nowadays," he snorted, "you can hear everything but the truth and the meat a-frying." And he said, "Why do you think I take my own help? To see I get the fruit I buy. Doss and Wint let the loaders short me a dozen bushels. Still I paid off."

"Yeah," said Godey, "in rotten peaches."

"I've tried several fellers," Riar explained, "and the shed crews stole them blind. I need fellers sharp to the thieves. They can trick you and you looking at them."

"Not us they can't," Godey said. "We hain't lived sixteen years for nothing." He slid from the head wall, and Mal followed. "Settle now and we'll guarantee you full measure."

"You know us," said Mal.

"Never in life have I paid for work before it was done," Riar declared, "and I don't aim to begin." He waited. "Are you going or not? Make up your heads."

Edging toward the truck, Godey said, "Promise to let me drive a dab, and we'll risk you."

"Risk me," Riar hooted, slapping the wheel. "If there's another person who'd undertake hauling you jaspers from Kentucky to South Carolina and back I haven't met the witty."

Godey insisted, "Do I get to steer after a while?"

Riar raced the engine impatiently, and the cattle rack clattered behind. "Crawl in," he said, "I can't fool. To deal in ripe peaches and come out you've got to run for them. It's a five-hundred-mile round trip, and I'll have to get there in plenty of time to make arrangements and load by sundown. We've got a splinter of Virginia to cross, a corner of Tennessee, and North Carolina top to bottom."

"I'll give you my knife to drive a speck. It has four blades and all kinds of tricks and things."

Riar shook his head. "I'm gone."

Godey saw Riar meant it and they got in. He warned Riar, "Anybody who beats us will be a-hurting." And he said, "If you want to keep me acting pretty you'd better give me the wheel along the way."

"Now, yes," echoed Mal.

Though it was July the night was chilly. Riar said, "Stuff the board in the window or you'll get aired."

"I'll not ride blind," Godey said.

"When you begin freezing," said Riar, "don't halloo to me."

Mal said, "Let me sit on the board. They's a spring sticking me through the cushion."

Godey laughed. "That makes it mean," he said, and he sat upon the cardboard himself. The truck sputtered in starting, and he teased Riar, "What about a feller who'd hang on to a wreck?"

"She'll run like a sewing machine in a minute," Riar said.

"Too stingy to buy a new, aye? Can't say farewell to a dollar."

Riar said, "You knotheads know the cost of a truck? They'll bankrupt you."

"The fashion you scrimp, you ought to be rich as Jay Goo."

Riar grunted. "Boys don't understand beans," he said, and in his truck's defense, "I've had her repaired for the trip, though I couldn't afford it: brakes relined, spark plugs changed, retreads all round."

"Yeah," Godey ridiculed. "Fenders flopping, windows cracked out. A bunch of screaks and rattles."

"We heard your old gee-haw four miles away," added Mal.

Riar said, "Doubt you not, she'll carry us there and fetch us back—with two hundred bushels of peaches." And he mused, "I used to mule in goods from Jackson. Occasionally my wagon would break down and I couldn't fix it. I'd walk up the road and 'gin to whistle. Fairly soon it would come to me what to do."

"My opinion," said Godey, "the most you calculate on is how to dodge spending money."

"Listen," Riar said gravely, "I've barely my neck above water. Bought the tires on credit, went into debt for repairs. I'll have to make a killing this run to breathe. And if I am a grain thrifty it's on behalf of my family."

"They say," plagued Mal, "you're married to the woman on the silver dollar."

"Let me give you some gospel facts," said Riar.

"We can bear it if you can spare it," sang Godey.

"I try to keep bread on the table and shoes on my young 'uns' feet. And I treat the other feller square. I'm straight as an icicle."

"What about the rotten peaches you put off on Doss and Wint Colley?" reminded Godey. "Preach a sermon on that."

"The fruit at the bottom of the load was mashed shapeless and beginning to spoil," said Riar, "yet the Colleys asked for them instead of pay. Claimed they wanted to plant the seeds and commence an orchard."

"Idjits might swallow that tale," said Godey, "but not us. You believe yourself they actually wanted the seeds?"

"I've come on different knowledge since."

"For what? Tell me."

"You won't hear it from me."

Mal saw light suddenly. "Just one thing they could of done—made peach brandy."

"You reckon?" blurted Godey, his ire rising. "Lied to skip giving us a taste?"

"It's plain as yore nose," said Mal.

"By jacks," Godey huffed, "we'll work on their dog hides."

"What's the profit in revenge?" Riar chided. "Swapping ill with your fellow man?"

"You don't know?" asked Godey in mock surprise.

"No," said Riar.

"Then I'll tell you. It makes you feel a whole heap better."

Mal asked Riar, "Don't you ever get mad and fly off the hinges?"

"I try to control myself," said Riar. And he advised, "You two ought to get some sleep. We'll have no pull-offs for naps along the road."

Mal twisted on the cushion. "Upon my honor," he grumbled, "this seat is eating my breeches up."

Morning found them in the Holston Valley of Tennessee, and the sun got busy early. The moment the ground mist melted, it was hot. The truck was standing at a gasoline pump, the attendant hose in hand and inquiring, "How many?" when Godey woke. Godey's eyes flew open. He said, "Fill her up to the wormholes."

"Five gallons," said Riar.

Godey yawned, bestirring Mal. He said, "I never slept me nary a wink last night."

"Me neither," fibbed Mal.

"You snore just to make the music, aye?" said Riar. "It was hookety-hook between you."

Godey said, "Why don't you fill the tank and not have to stop at every pig track?"

"Ever hear of evaporation?" asked Riar. "A lot goes away before you can burn it."

Godey wagged his head. "Tight as Dick's hatband," he informed the attendant.

Mal said, "Saving as a squirrel."

Directly they were on the road, Godey announced, "I'm hungry, Big Buddy, and what are you going to do about it?"

"We're carrying food the wife prepared," Riar said. "We'll halt at the next black spot."

"You expect to feed us stale victuals?" Godey complained. "Give us a quarter apiece to buy hamburgers."

Riar said, "During my boy days a quarter looked big as a churn lid. Did a body have one he stored it. Now all the young understand is to pitch and throw."

"The truth," mocked Godey. "Saturday I was in town, and I hadn't been there ten minutes when bang went a dime."

"We have food in plenty, I tell you," Riar insisted, "and any we don't use will be wasted."

"So that's the hitch," scoffed Godey. "Before I'd live like you I'd whittle me a bill and peck amongst the chickens."

Riar halted presently in the shade of a beech and hurried out. Mal forced the cranky door on his side and jumped to the ground, and Godey made to pile after—but his breeches caught on the spring. He pulled and still hung. He had to jerk loose. His jaws paled, his mouth twisted to swear, yet he checked himself. He would make it pay later. He hopped down, and none was the wiser.

Mal cautioned Godey under his breath, "You'd better begin greasing Riar up if you're expecting to drive."

"I've already got him right where I want him," said Godey.

Riar put a gunnysack on the grass and spread breakfast: saucer-size biscuits, fried ribs, a wedge of butter. He poured cold coffee from a mason jar into cups shorn of handles.

Godey eyed the meal sourly, keeping turned to hide the rip. "A dog wouldn't eat a mess like that," he caviled. Nevertheless he took a serving. With cheeks full he added, "I wouldn't except I'm so weak I couldn't rattle dry leaves."

"You might do as well at your own table," Riar countered, "but it's not my information."

Hardly were they moving again than Godey broached driving. "I'm ready to steer awhile, big buddy."

Riar grunted noncommittally.

"Last night you let on I could."

"I never made such talk. I promised you two dollars, and have them you will the moment they're earned."

Godey produced his knife. "I'll give you this, and hit's a bargain. Four regular blades, and an awl, and a punch, and a shoe hook, and—"

"All that play-daddle is fit for is to rub a hole in your pocket."

"Then," said Godey determinedly, "I'm going to have my wages now, cash on the barrel."

"Are you making that cry again?" fretted Riar. "They said you were pranky, but I didn't figure on all the mouth I'm having to put up with."

"You heard me."

"My opinion," Mal joined in, "you're not to be confidenced."

Godey declared, "Fork over else we'll allow the shed crews to steal you ragged. Even might help 'em."

"Great sakes!" Riar exclaimed. "Two dollars not yours yet and you growling for them."

"Why, you're behind the times," corrected Godey. "You're paying me an extra three to buy a pair of breeches. Your old cushion has tore a hole in me big as outdoors."

Riar sputtered, "I haven't taken you to raise, mister boy."

"According to law," said Godey, displaying the tear, "I've suffered damage in your vehicle. I know my rights."

"I'll see you to a needle and thread."

Godey had Riar going, and he knew it. He said cockily, "Want to satisfy me and not have to tip your pocketbook?"

"Deliver my life and living into your hands?" Riar chuffed, on to the proposition.

"Turn the truck over to me thirty minutes and I'll forget the breeches. I may even decide to let you off paying me for a while."

Riar groaned. "My young 'uns' bread depends on this machine." But he was tempted. Loading without watchers was a misery, and he couldn't abide further expense.

"It's me drive," Godey said, "or you shell out five dollars."

"Wreck my truck," Riar bumbled, "and I'm ruined. You don't care." But he could see no alternative. "I get along with folks if they'll let me," he said, relenting. And he questioned anxiously, "Will you stay on your side of the road and run steady and not attempt to make an airplane of it?"

"Try me."

Riar slowed and stopped, and he took pliers and bent the point of the broken spring. Godey slid under the wheel, face bright with triumph, and he asked, "Anything coming behind?"

The truck moved away evenly, the gears knuckling without sound. Watch in hand, Riar prompted, "Don't ride the clutch," and "She's not tied up for speed," and "She brakes on the three-quarter pedal." But his coaching was useless, as Godey drove well enough.

Meeting a bus, Godey poked his head out and bawled, "Get over, Joab," and he grumbled, "Some people take their part of the highway in the middle." He reproved Riar. "Why don't you quit worrying? You make a feller nervous."

"I can't," breathed Riar. "Not for my life."

Before Godey's half hour was through he inquired, "Have I done to suit you?"

"You'll get by," grudged Riar.

"How far to the North Carolina line?"

"Another hour should fetch it."

Godey's eyes narrowed. "Want to pet your pocketbook again?"

"What now?" Riar asked skeptically.

"I've decided to swap my pay to drive to there."

"You're agreeing to pass up the money, aye? And after vilifying me about the Colley brothers."

"I aim to," said Godey, "and I won't argue."

Riar shook his head. "I promised cash, and cash you'll have. I'll prove to you June bugs my word is worth one hundred cents to the dollar."

Godey shrugged. "Made up your mind, big buddy?"

"Absolutely."

"Well," said Godey, "let's see can we change it," and without further ado he floored the accelerator. The truck jumped, the cattle rack leapt in the brackets. The shovel hanging from the slats thumped the cab.

"Scratch gravel," crowed Mal. "Pour on the carbide."

"Mercy sakes!" croaked Riar.

Godey spun the wheel back and forth. He zig-zagged the road like a black snake. The rack swayed, threatening to break free.

Riar's mouth opened, but nothing came out. The veins on his neck corded.

Godey cut to the left side of the highway and sped around a blind curve.

Riar could stand no more. "All right," he gasped. "All right."

Godey slackened. Grinning he said, "Why, you break your word fairly easy. Get you up against it and you'll breach."

By early afternoon they had put western North Carolina behind and crossed into South Carolina. The mountains fell back, the earth leveled and reddened, the first peach orchards came to view. The sun beat down, and the cab was baking hot.

Riar charged the boys, "I'm expecting you to keep your eyes skinned when they load my peaches. The fruit goes on several bushels together, and the sharpers can trip you."

Godey and Mal sniggered. Godey said, "Did they know it, it's us they'd better watch."

"What I say," agreed Mal.

"I'm after my honest due," Riar said. "I don't intend to cheat or be cheated." And a thought seized him. Glancing swiftly at the boys he said, "You can count to two hundred, I hope to my soul."

"I can count my finger," jested Godey.

"How much schooling have you had?"

"Aye," said Godey, "I learned who killed Cock Robin."

Mal said, "Godey Spurlock coming up short hain't been heard of."

Beyond Landrum a packing house appeared, the metal roof glaring sunlight. Riar drove past, and Godey clamored, "Hain't you going to stop?"

"They're a contract outfit," Riar said. "They wax and shine their fruits like a pair of Sunday shoes, and some retail at ten cents apiece. They don't deal with the little feller."

"They'd allow us to peep around, I reckon."

To humor them, Riar drew in at the next shed. "Another large operator," he explained, "and we won't buy here either. Just stretch our legs and cool."

A line of ten-wheel trucks was parked at the loading platfom, and Godey breathed, "Gee-o! Look at the big jobs." He teased Riar. "Hain't you ashamed to take your old plug out where people can see it?"

"Not in the least," said Riar.

From the platform Godey and Mal gazed under the shed. They saw the roll conveyors tumbling fruit forward, the workers busy at the picking belts. Hail-pecked and wormy fruits were being shunted aside. The peaches flowed on through sizers and brushes of the defuzzer to the packers, and there seemed no end to them.

Godey's eye lit on a huge peach in a basket, and he snatched it up. A voice behind him spoke, "You're welcome, young fellow, stuff till you bust." Without deigning to turn, Godey held out the great peach and sneered "Pea-jibbit!" and let it fall and stepped on it. But he peeled and ate six others.

When Riar got up with the boys twenty minutes later there was nothing they had not looked at. As they drove away Godey said, "The first ever I knowed peaches have hairs like cats."

"Get them brushings on you," said Riar, "and they'll eat you alive."

"What they told me," said Godey. "Claimed it takes a spell to dig in, but after it does bull nettles hain't a patching to it."

Said Mal, "We'd got some, did we have a poke to put 'em in."

"Of what use is it? I ask you."

Said Godey, "For Doss and Wint Colley a beating is too fine. I want to see them dance."

"Now, yes," said Mal. "They'd throw an ague fit."

Riar frowned. "Hitting back at folks is all you think of."

Two miles beyond Landrum, Riar turned onto a dirt road and the wheels set the dust boiling. The boys' faces were streaked where they wiped the sweat.

Riar stopped at a number of small-growers' sheds, buying at none, saying, "They sell high as Haman," or "Their fruit is too green for my business," or "Most of my customers want Elbertas."

Godey said, "Always I've heard a fruit bought off of you had better be stomached quick, it's so rotty-ripe."

"The mellower the cheaper," said Riar.

Mal said, "You'll travel farther for a dollar than anybody on creation."

"Was I you," said Godey, "I'd take any peaches handy and call 'em Elbertas, and nobody'd know the difference.

Riar shook his head. "When I say a thing is such and such, you can count on it."

"Oh yes?" scoffed Godey. "You point me to a plumb honest feller, and I'll show you a patch of hair growing in the palm of his hand."

"My opinion," gibed Mal, "he's hunting a place where they give away."

"About the size of it," said Godey.

"Even if I had my fruit on order I'd wait until the shade comes over," said Riar. "I don't cook my peaches by hauling in the sun."

The shed where Riar bought was a barn with the sides gone. A single processing unit was operated by the owner's family, and the picking belt was lined with children. Elbertas and Georgia Belles and J. H. Hales lay across the floor in drifts.

With Godey and Mal at his heels Riar inspected the heaps. Encountering a boy, Godey opened his knife and greeted, "Hello, coot, what'll you give to boot?" He lifted a Georgia Belle on the awl, peeled it with the butcher blade, used the shoe hook to pluck the seed. A second youngster hastened to watch, and Godey readied another, bringing the scalper and corkscrew into play.

The owner cast an appraising look at Riar. Noting his eye on a section of Elbertas three days harvested he said, "There's your bargain. A dollar and a quarter a bushel." To explain their being on hand he added, "The whole crop is trying to shape up the same minute."

Riar broke several in half. The flesh was grainy and yellow. He tasted, and they had the sugar. Though much softer than he usually handled, he judged most could bear the trip. They would last the night and the cool of the morning. If he bought them reasonably and peddled them at two fifty, he could clear his debts and have money left. What matter the loss of the bottom layers. He said, "I'll pay seventy cents."

The owner had hardly expected to get rid of the aging fruit. Still he said, "I can't accept less than a dollar."

"Seventy cents," repeated Riar.

"Yesterday they were a dollar fifty."

"Day after tomorrow," parried Riar, "you'll have to scrape them up."

Godey butted in. "People don't call him Tightwad just to beat their gums."

Riar's neck reddened, but he held himself.

Trying to make a stand, the owner said, "I'll drop to eighty, but they'll rot on the floor before I'll accept less."

"Well, then," said Riar, "we can't do business, for I won't pay above seventy for dead-ripe peaches." Shuffling to go he asked, "How far to the next shed?"

The owner changed his tune. He said, "Couldn't we split the difference and meet in the middle?"

Riar gazed at the Elbertas. Only hovering gnats bespoke their advanced maturity. "I'll tell you what I will do," he proposed, "and we can both keep our word. I'll pay eighty for a hundred and seventy-five bushels if you'll throw in the twenty-five that are bound to mash."

"Riar to a whisker," said Godey.

After figuring a moment, the owner grumbled, "But you'd still be getting them at seventy cents."

"What I know," admitted Riar.

Throwing up his arms, the owner groaned, "Take 'em, take 'em."

The sun was still high. Leaving Godey and Mal on their own, Riar rested in the truck, but it was too sultry to sleep. And at sunset he called them with, "My peaches will never be any greener." Godey carried a paper poke, the neck of which was tied with string, and Riar said, "If that's something you've picked up, leave it lay."

"Where I go this poke goes," said Godey.

Guessing the contents, Riar said, "The stuff will not ride in the cab with me." Yet thinking to forbear until he had his peaches aboard, he added, "If you're so set on it, put the poke in the toolbox." He figured to lose it later.

The children loaded the truck, the smaller filling baskets and sending by conveyor to the platform, the larger hoisting them over the rack and emptying. The work quickened upon the arrival of a contract van. Riar counted at the tail gate, and Godey and Mal clung to the slats and sang out the number, and though three measures were often dumped at a time, Riar got his two hundred without a doubt.

The servicing of the van started immediately. And the moment Riar and the owner disappeared into the crib office to settle up, Godey traded his knife to the boys. Five bushels of Georgia Belles headed for the van were switched onto Riar's truck.

At leaving, Riar handed Mal two dollars and advised, "Keep them in your pocket, they won't spoil," and he chided Godey, "You could of had the same if you hadn't got ahead of yourself."

Godey smiled slyly. "I hain't so bad off," he said.

Night caught them on Saluda Mountain in North Carolina. Pockets of fog appeared, and sometimes Riar had to drive with his head through the door. As they crept upward, vehicles passed them, and Godey taunted, "I want to know is this the fastest you can travel?"

"She'd show life," said Mal, "was she fed the gas."

Riar grunted. He was getting used to their gibes.

"Did I have Riar's money," Godey said, "I'd buy me a ten-wheeler. I'd haul a barrel to his peck, put him out of the running."

"They'd no moss grow on the tires either," said Mal.

Riar said, "I'll have to see a profit this trip or I'm already finished. Folks won't have it, but I'm poor as a whippoorwill. I started with nothing, and I'm still in the same fix. You've no reckoning how much a family can run through."

"If I owned a truck," Godey mused, "I'd put in a scat gear, and I'd get gone. I'd whip around curves like a caterpillar. And when I stopped smelling fresh paint I'd trade in on another 'un."

Riar said, "The most I can see you possessing is a bigger foot to step on the gas. Your life long you'll be as penniless as you are now."

Nudging Mal, Godey told Riar, "I won't be broke after you and me do a little trafficking."

"You haven't a thing coming from me," said Riar.

"You'll learn different in a minute," said Godey, "for I aim to buy a stack of hamburgers a span high at the next eating place."

"Can't I beat into you we're carrying food?"

Godey said, "I've missed many a bucket of slop, not being a hog." Then he announced, "I'm about to offer you a chance too good to refuse."

"What are you hatching?" asked Riar.

"I'm telling you five bushels of my own peaches are riding in a corner of the rack. They make yours look like drops."

Riar straightened, suddenly vigilant.

Said Mal, "They're Georgia Belles, the ten-cent apiece kind, size of yore fist."

"They sell two dollars a bushel at the shed," boasted Godey, "and they'll peddle for three. I'll let you have the whole caboodle for five bucks."

"Awfulest bargain ever was," said Mal.

"A pure giveaway," said Godey.

Riar's shoe jiggled on the accelerator, the engine coughed. He blurted, "You've got me hauling stolen goods, aye?"

"Dadburn," Godey swore, "I swapped my knife for them and they're mine."

"You didn't trade with the owner," accused Riar. "I'll not reward chicanery."

Godey's lips curled, but he spoke levelly. "I'm a plain talker, and I'm telling you to your teeth I'll not be slicked out of them."

Mal cautioned Riar, "Was I you, I wouldn't cross Godey Spurlock."

"The truth won't hold still," said Riar.

"By jacks," snarled Godey, "you don't know when you're well off."

"Now, no," said Mal.

"I have my principles," said Riar. "What I get for the Belles I'll return to the owner next season."

Godey said, "Anybody with one eye and half sense would understand they couldn't gyp me and prosper."

"You heard me," said Riar.

"You hain't deef," replied Godey.

They hushed. Nothing was said until the lights of Flat Rock appeared. Mal broke the silence, declaring, "I can smell hamburgers clear to here."

Godey mumbled, "I'm so starved I'm growing together."

"Reach back and get some fruit," Riar said irritably. "All you want."

"Juice is oozing out of my ears already," spurned Godey. And he said, "Big bud, I'm about to make you a final offer. Let me drive to the Tennessee line and you can have my peaches. I'd ruther drive than eat."

"You're not talking to me," said Riar. "I've had a sample of you at the wheel."

"I'll stay on my side of the road, act to suit you."

"Everything has a stopping point," said Riar. "I'll not court a wreck."

"My opinion," said Godey, "when affairs get tough enough you'll break over."

Godey and Mal ate in a café while Riar munched cold bread outside. Before setting off again, Godey held a match to the gasoline meter and said, "You'd better take on a gill. She's sort of low."

"She can read empty," said Riar, "and still be carrying a gallon." Godey would bear watching.

"See do the tires need wind."

"They're standing up," said Riar, pressing the starter.

Riar didn't pause until he reached Fletcher. He had the tank brimmed, for businesses open after midnight were scarce. And he tightened the cap himself. He climbed the rack, the while cocking an eye at Godey. Riar watched Godey so closely Mal had to do the mischief. Mal caught a chance and scooped up a fistful of dirt, crammed it into the tank, and stuck the cap back on.

They passed through Arden and Skyland and Asheville. And nothing happened. The truck ran smoothly. At Weaverville, Riar halted at a closed station to replenish the radiator. A bulb inside threw a faint light. He left the engine idling, but as he poured in water it quit, and feeling for the key a moment later, he found it missing. He spoke sharply: "All right, you boys, hand over."

"Hand what over?" Godey made strange.

"The key. You don't have to ask."

"Why hallo to us. We haven't got it."

Riar struck a match and searched the cab. He blustered, "I don't want to start war with you fellers."

Stretching, Godey inquired, "Are you of a notion we stole the key? You can frisk us." They stepped out and shucked their pockets.

Mal said, "I never tipped it."

"Couldn't have disappeared of itself," said Riar. "One of you is guilty, and I think I know which."

Godey chuckled sleepily. "Why, it might be square under your nose. Scratch around, keep a-looking."

Riar made a second search, and then he said, "Let me tell you boys something. A load of peaches generates enough heat a day to melt a thousand pounds of ice. They have to be kept moving or they'll bake."

"That makes it mean," said Godey.

"Rough as a cob," agreed Mal.

Riar couldn't budge them. He had no choice other than to wire-over the ignition. He got out pliers and a screwdriver, but it was pitch-black under the hood. Offering a penny matchbox to Mal, he said, "Strike them for me as they're needed."

"Do that," warned Godey, "and I'll hang you to a bush."

Breathing deep to master his anger, Riar chuffed, "You jaspers don't care whether my family starves."

"Not our lookout," said Godey, yawning.

Lighting match after match, Riar peered to the farthest the key could have been tossed. He felt along the cab floor again and on the ground beneath. When the matchbox was empty he groped with his fingers.

Godey and Mal were soon asleep, but Riar didn't leave off hunting the rest of the night.

At daybreak Riar loosened the ignition wires and hooked them together. The boys stirred as the truck moved, but did not rouse. Beyond the town limits Riar smartened his speed to an unaccustomed forty-five miles an hour. Then, on the grade north of Faust, the engine started missing, and he had to pump the accelerator to coax it to the top.

Halting in the gap, Riar decided gasoline was not getting through to the carburetor, and inspecting the sediment bulb, he found it choked. His breath caught as he reasoned he had been sold dirty gasoline. In a hurry he cleared the bulb and blew out the fuel pump. Already the truck bed seeped juice and the load was drawing hornets. The day had set in hot.

He rolled downhill, and at the bottom it was the same thing over. The engine coughed and lost power. Again the bulb was plugged, the pump fouled. This time he checked the tank, and the deed was out. The cap barely hung on, and the pipe was rimed with grit. Riar gasped. His face reddened in sudden anger. He threw open the cranky door and glared at Godey and Mal. For a moment he had no voice to speak, but when he could he cried, "You boys think you're pistol balls!"

Godey and Mal cracked their eyelids. Godey asked, "What are you looking so dim about?"

Riar sputtered, "You're too sorry to stomp into the ground."

"Has she tuk the studs on you?"

"Filled my tank with dirt. Intending to make me lose my peaches."

"Are you accusing us? Daggone! To hear you tell it, whatever happens to your old scrap heap we're the cause."

"Don't deny it. You're the very scamp."

"If you mean me," said Godey, "that's where you're wrong. Bring me a Scripture and I'll swear by it."

The veins on Riar's neck showed knots. His cheeks looked raw. "Then you put your partner up to it. Besides, you got my key last night."

Godey chirped, "Where's your proof, tightwad?"

"I have evidence a-plenty," bumbled Riar.

"I'd take oath," vowed Mal, "I never tipped the key."

"When I get mad," confided Godey, "I can see little devils hopping in front of my eyes. How does it serve you?"

Riar was getting nowhere. Slamming the door, he went to work on the pump. He saw the cure was to purge the whole fuel system with fresh gasoline. But getting to a filling station was the question. He tried again and the engine struggled almost a mile before dying.

Godey said, "Give me justice on my peaches and we'll help."

"All you're good for is to gum up," blared Riar. "You're as useless as tits on a boar."

Godey shrugged. He sang, "Suit yourself and sit on the shelf."

"Don't contrary me," Riar begged. "You make me speak things I don't want to."

"Then hurry and fix the old plug, and let's get to some breakfast."

The sun beat upon the peaches as Riar labored. He jockeyed the truck two miles after unclogging it, a half mile next, and each holdup used three quarters of an hour at least. Then several blowings gained less than five miles altogether, and mid-morning found them still in North Carolina and no station in sight. As the day advanced the load settled slowly, the seep of juice became a trickle. Hornets swarmed, and the fainting fruit seemed to beget gnats. Around eleven the truck made a spurt, crossing into Tennessee jerking and backfiring.

They reached a garage at noon. The mechanic came squinting into the sunlight, inquiring, "What's the matter?"

Godey said, "We've run out of distance."

Riar did the job himself, sweat glistening his face and darkening his shirt. He unstrapped the tank and drained it, flushed it with water, and rinsed in gasoline. He removed the fuel line, pump, and carburetor and gave them the same treatment. The mechanic said, "If I had a pump messed up like that I'd junk it and buy a new."

Godey laughed. "Did this gentleman turn loose a dollar, the hide would slip."

While Riar strove, he knew without looking that the lower half of the load was crushing under the weight, the top layers sickening in the sun. The hundred or so bushels in between would hold firm only a few hours longer, and he would never get them to Kentucky. He would have to try selling them in the next town.

Toward three o'clock Riar finished and set off grimly, raising his speed to fifty miles an hour. The machine would go no faster.

Godey crowed, "The old sister will travel if you'll feed her. Pour on the pedal."

Mal asked wryly, "Reckon she'll take another Jiminy fit?"

"Stay on the whiz," cheered Godey, "and maybe she'll shed the rust."

It was fortunate that a rise had slowed them when the tire blew out. As it was, Riar had to fight the wheel to keep to the road. He brought the truck under control and pulled onto a shoulder. He sat as if stricken, his disgust too great for speaking. His stomach began to cramp. Presently he said bitterly, "I hope this satisfies your hickory."

Godey and Mal wagged their heads, though their faces were bright. Godey said, "I reckon it's us you'll blame."

Mal said, "Everything that pops he figures we're guilty."

"Your talk and your actions don't jibe," Riar suffered himself to speak.

On examining the flat, Riar discovered a slash in the tread as straight as a blade could make it. He walked numbly around the truck and took a look at the Elbertas. They had fallen seven slats, the firm peaches sinking into the pulp of the bad, and they were working alive with gnats and hornets. They wouldn't bluff any buyer. He said, "You have destroyed me."

"What do you think I'm getting from the trip?" asked Godey. "Nothing but a hole in my breeches."

Riar said, "I'm ruint, ruint totally."

"Tightwads never fill their barrels," blabbed Godey. "They want more."

Riar swallowed. His stomach seemed balled. "I swear to my Maker," he said, "you have the heart of a lizard." He took his time repairing the tube, using a cold patch and covering it with a boot. He idled, trying to feel better. The shade was over when they started again.

Godey asked, "What are you going to do now?"

Riar was long replying. Finally he said, "If I've burned a blister I'm willing to set on it."

They entered Virginia at dusk, and the evening was hardly less torrid than the day. Ground mist cloaked the road like steam. The boys were snoring by the time they reached Wise.

The enormity of his loss came upon Riar as he neared Kentucky. Cramps nearly doubled him. When he could endure no more he pulled off and cut the lights, and leaving the truck, he walked up the highway in the dark. He pursed his lips and whistled tunelessly. He strolled several hundred yards before turning back.

Riar dumped the peaches at the foot of Pound Mountain. Once he thought he heard his key jingle but was mistaken, for he discovered it later inside the cushion.

It occurred to him that a little food might quiet his stomach, but rummaging the toolbox he found the last crumb gone. He came upon the fuzz and lifted the poke to get rid of it but still didn't let loose. Stepping into the cab he switched on the lights. Godey and Mal slept with heads pitched forward, collars agape. Their faces were yellow as cheese pumpkins in the reflected gleam. Riar untied the poke and shook the fuzz down their necks.

For a distance up the mountain the trees were woolly with fog, but as the truck climbed the mist vanished and the heat fell away. Riar's spirits rose as he mounted, the cramping ceased. The engine pulled the livelier. They had crossed the Kentucky line in the gap and were headed down when the boys began to wriggle.

Encounter on Keg Branch

"You know Adam Claiborne over to Thacker? I mean the welfare Adam who works for the government. Well, sir, I'm wanting to send him some word by you. And I want you to write it down as I say it so you'll get it straight. Tell him that me and that woman has done quit each other and living apart and I want him to see her and learn what she's got to talk about. Tell him not to specify anything. And tell Adam I want to see him on particular business before the next court sets. Tell him to be slick, be slick in his business.

"They swore out a crazy warrant for me, her and her sister. They had me put in jail a spell. Her and her sister, biggest fools of women ever I seed. I aim to damn 'em every chance I get. She's living with another man, been living with him three months. He's got her bigged. Tell Adam to not let nothing out. Tell Adam to specify we hain't married, by God. I aim to down that woman. Aim to have her sent to the asylum. Aye, she's been there before. The man she's living with, he's been there too. I aim to shock him next. A shame-scandal! Her sister tore her dress and swore rape on me—me at my age, seventy-one, and on the old-age draw. Had me put in jail. She told enough lies on me to send her to hell.

"I lived with that woman seven years and she thinks we're married. Why, we drawed up a little old paper and she didn't know any differ. That's how much a dumb-head she is. People like her ought to have their heads pinched off when they're born.

"I'll tell you, they don't know nothing, her and her sister. Nary a one can tell their age. Upon my honor, they don't know what day it is until the school bus runs. Her mother before her couldn't of told how old she was either. The whole drove, they don't know dirt from goose manure. Yet lie! They can lie like a dog a-trotting. They'll get before the county judge over to Thacker and they'll pop their hands and tell the biggest ones ever was.

"I'm building me a house on Short Fork. Tell Adam Claiborne that. The reason I've just come from Bee Tree. Bee Tree is the next hollow to Short Fork, and Short Fork is over yonder ridge. Well, sir, I was over on Bee Tree and I saw another woman. A widow-woman. She's older'n me, five to seven years. She didn't tell me but she has the looks of it. She says, 'I want to get married,' and I says, 'I do too.' So I'm building me a house and I'm going to put her in it."

Plank Town

We were living at Logan's camp when Uncle Jolly appeared on the plank road, heading toward our house. We hadn't seen him since spring. He arrived on an idle Thursday when only the loggers were at work, and folks sat visiting or being visited on porches. The mill operated three days a week. The saws were quiet, the steam boiler sighing instead of puffing. Smoke raised from the burning sawdust mountain as straight as a pencil.

Word had reached Uncle Jolly that Dan had lost two of his fingers and they needed transporting for burial on Sporty Creek. The third and fourth fingers of Dan's left hand had been severed while he played at the mill. For Pap, who was already fed up with eight months of short workweeks, Dan's accident was the last button on Gabe's coat.

Uncle Jolly came riding his anticky horse down the plank road with Jenny Peg prancing sideways. Upon sighting them, Pap announced, "Here comes the witty," and to make Dan brighten sang out:

> The biggest fool you could ever seek
> Dwells in the head of Sporty Creek;
> He puts on his shirt over his coat,
> Buttons his breeches around his throat.

Dan's face lightened. Since losing his fingers, he had become pampered beyond endurance. Any time Pap took seat he climbed onto his knees. He had turned into a worse pet than the baby.

The trick horse bowed. Jenny Peg bowed so low Uncle Jolly slid down her neck to the ground. He caught up Dan, sprang onto the animal's back, and circled the house before saying a *hey-o* or a *howdy-do* to us.

Everybody humored Dan. Although the bandage was long off, the edge of the palm healed, he still drew attention. My playfellows broke off their games to stare at him, to gaze at the stake in the corner of the yard where the fingers were interred in a baking powder can. We had visitors aplenty. Camp folk made our narrow porch their porch.

They came with gifts for Dan: chestnuts, hickory sugar, trifles. Cass Logan, Pap's boss, was a regular caller, dropping in for a moment with popcorn or a trinket, flashing gold teeth, and saying, "There you are, little master." Cass was concerned that Pap might law him.

Uncle Jolly swung Dan to Pap. Pap handled him as carefully as he might a basket of eggs. Teasing, Uncle Jolly inquired, "Does sawdust smell as sweet to you as coal dust?"

"The same difference," said Pap.

Sawmilling was as slack as mining, and on off days Pap had taken to searching the woods for wild herbs. A string of ginseng roots hung from a nail on the porch wall.

To low-rate Uncle Jolly's farming, Pap went on, "Lumbering beats grubbing new-ground in February and pushing a hardtail along a corn furrow in the heat of the gnats."

"I'm hearing you," said Uncle Jolly, "but I'd bet my ears you'll be moving again. Here you are on your honkers in the middle of the week."

"He's talking it," said Mother.

"Yes, sir," admitted Pap. "The hawk appears about to light."

"A born gypsy if one ever walked the earth," breathed Uncle Jolly.

Then Uncle Jolly noticed me, and the baby, and Holly. To me he said, "Hey-o, dirty ears." I regretted not having on my sharp-toed boots. I was barefoot, hardening my soles for the winter. Of the baby he asked, "From what worm tree did you shake this grub?" As many times as he had pranked with it on Sporty, he acted like he'd never glimpsed it before. He keened his eyes at Holly and said, "This young lady is still at home, aye? I'd of sworn some boy rooster would of crowed by now, and she'd of gone a-running."

Holly pitched her chin. "Silly," she scoffed, and turned her back.

Pap reproved her, "I wish you'd change your byword again. I'm getting burnt out on this 'un." And to Uncle Jolly he said, "Speaking of matrimony how's the wife hunt?"

"Courting to marry," chimed Uncle Jolly.

"You've been singing that tune a dozen years."

"The trouble is females don't trip over each other to get to me."

"The switchtail you sparked on Bee Branch four or five seasons—what's become of her?"

"She chose another." Uncle Jolly sighed. "And you know what? I was beginning to like the girl."

"*Like?*" Pap repeated. "Is that the right word?" His chest began to heave. "So you've run out of courting material."

Pap had to laugh a spell before he could go on.

Changing the subject, Uncle Jolly asked Mother, "Are you packing your plunder to move? I'm figuring you're not long for the saw camp."

"With everything in a slump," Mother replied, "it's my hope. It's up to Mr. Hard Skull."

Pap swept an arm toward the string of roots hanging on a nail. "Back to the Old Place some far day," he said, "but not the next go. I'm speculating on something."

Pap turned grave. "Know what ginseng roots fetch nowadays? Thirty-five dollars the pound, and rising. These I found hereabouts, and they're pea-jibbits to what must grow in the wild place I told you about—the territory owned by a lumber company. Besides ginseng there's snakeroot and goldenseal and wild ginger and a host of other medicine roots that haul in big prices."

"It's a nowhere place," said Uncle Jolly. "A nobody world."

"Hit's not altogether uninhabited," defended Pap. He was wound up. "There are scatterings of settlers on the outer boundary, and there's Kilgore post office. When the company lumbered it twenty years ago, they had their sawmill in what's named Tight Hollow. The bunkhouse is still standing, in dandy shape. Aye, I aim to talk to the lawyer in Thacker who has say-so over the property."

"They'll call it Dunce Hollow hereafter, if you move there. But I figure you're talking to hear your head rattle. Or you're dreaming."

"If he's asleep," pronounced Mother, "he'd better wake up."

Pap rushed on. "Stands to reason such a territory is crammed with herbs, the waters jumping with fish, the woods crawling with game. Minks and muskrats who've never smelled a steel trap." He paused, overcome by such prospects. "Have you an idea what a mink skin fetches in the market? A muskrat?"

Uncle Jolly shook his head. He appealed to Mother, "Are you certain your man hasn't been cracked on the noggin?"

Mother answered dolesomely, "He's given to bad judgment sometimes. I can't picture myself stuck in such a wilderness."

Holly said, "I don't aim to move a jillion miles from creation."

"I want to," I cried. "I do."

"Me, too," said Dan.

Uncle Jolly jerked his chin in my direction. "I'd of sworn you favored Sporty where you can plow."

"I do," said I.

"First you want to go crawl with the varmints?"

I thought about it. My mind spun. "I want to live everywhere," I said.

"And what is it that you want to do in the world?"

I weighed that in my head. "Everything," I said. There was no other truth.

Uncle Jolly reached and tapped my head and listened. "Not quite as empty as it used to be. Something in there, a little something."

On the porch of the dwelling across the plank road, a neighbor began to pick a familiar song on his guitar. We could see the guitar player's head bobbing, his arm jerking. The Plunker, Pap had nicknamed him. Presently a girl of six or seven skipped into our yard with a stick of peppermint in her hand. She dropped it into Dan's lap and departed without a word.

"Dadburn!" Uncle Jolly swore. "Six years old and already drawing the women. Never saw the beat."

"The neighbors are ruining him," complained Mother. "He's so spoiled salt wouldn't save him."

"You've done your share," reminded Pap.

I scurried indoors and pulled on my sharp-toed boots. When I returned, Uncle Jolly had the baby in his arms, counting its fingers. He tallied, "Thumbo, Lickpot, Long Man, Ring Man, Little Man." He wagged his chin in mock surprise. "I expected six." Then he glimpsed Dan hiding his crippled hand in a pocket.

"Golly Moses!" Uncle Jolly crowed. He surrendered the baby to Mother and declared, "Dan is in luck. With a pair of fingers short, the picks and shovels won't get him, the army won't capture him. It opens up the world. My belief is he'll amount to a real something, something worth the candy. Aye, he'll be a somebody."

I forgot the boots. They were nothing compared to this. To do something; to be somebody! I was half envious. Mother said quickly, "Yes," and again, "Yes."

"If Dan is to have a chance," Uncle Jolly said, "teachers such as Duncil Hargis and his sort won't help. And with school closed on Sporty, Buffalo Wallow is a far piece to walk. I say send him to the Settlement School at the forks of Troublesome Creek. There the scholars work out their room and board."

Dan pursed his lips. "I hain't a-going."

Uncle Jolly turned solemn. "Listen," said he. "The Settlement's teachers are the knowingest. They will do for you. They'll fit you for living in a hard world. Anyhow, the Buffalo Wallow teacher is a whip-jack. He'll put the bud to you. A bad sign."

Pouting, Dan snuffed, "I don't want to."

A cry raised on my tongue. "I do! I aim to!" Menifee Thomas, a Sporty Creeker, had told me a bushel about the Settlement.

"Send the both," Uncle Jolly said, and spying at me, he added, "When I tapped your head last, I heard more brains than I let on. Didn't want to get you stuck up."

He was staring at my boots as he spoke. He closed an eye, cracked it, and shut the other, acting as if he couldn't credence what he beheld. "I swear to my Never!" he blurted. "If I had a pair as good-looking as that, I could borrow money at the Thacker bank."

Pap explained, "They're his calf boots. Bought them out of his own pocket. First dollars earned." He sighed, feigning envy. "Wears better leather than his own pappy."

Pap's shoes were in sad shape. He bought for himself only when he had to.

From the Morgue

"Where are you speaking from?"

"The morgue—*Gary Independent,* Gary, Indiana. This long distance is costing a bundle."

"Using other people's phone's costing you a lot of money? I wasn't born yesterday."

"The paper pays, naturally. Let me get to the point. You had your one day in the sun. I'll give you another one—the day you die. But I don't want another obituary nobody will read. I want dynamite to go off. I want a bang. Everybody has something in their lives that's so contrary it lights up their world. I want the obit page to sizzle when you cook."

"What about you?"

"Huh? Ever heard of a journalist who's merited a two-inch column in the sheet he worked for? But poets, I have great respect for them. They respect words. Journalists! We throw them around like garbage bags."

"I'll come clean with you. This past year my poetry netted me fifty-two dollars. Twenty-five dollars each for a couple of poems in an anthology. The reviews made no mention of them, lauded others."

"What was the two dollars for?"

"A one-line quote in a magazine."

"It figures. But that's not my lookout. You were somebody once, for a minute. . . . Obit prices have been cut down to seventy-five dollars, but no matter. Money means next to nothing to me."

"But you're managing for others to pay your telephone bills."

"That's their problem."

"How old are you?"

He told me. He was five years my senior. When I remarked on this, he said, "I've already outlined a number of my clients and expect to do so with many another."

I thought I heard a fiendish giggle on the other end of the line. "You are worth seventy-five dollars to me." Again the giggle. "Dead."

"You know my name. May I ask yours?"

He spoke it, but in the manner some scribes affect an unreadable signature at the end of a letter. I was never to know for certain. It was either Vogel or Bogle. Perhaps neither. After then, recognizing his voice, I'd say, "From the morgue?" and he'd say, "About the morgue."

During the first call he explained, "I know all about you—the facts. You're not an alcoholic. That's a switch. You don't hate your mother. You haven't tried suicide. You're too damn normal. Normality is bad for a poet. It doesn't go with the territory."

I had not fully awakened. At that hour my wits were not fully engaged. I couldn't think of a thing out of the ordinary.

"Keep working on it, there's something," he said with assurance.

"How did you get my telephone number? It's unlisted."

"I have my methods."

My telephone number had been changed to unlisted due to its being one digit off the one held by the Water Control Board. At least one call, usually several, came between eight and five to report a broken water main or the curious taste or color of the water that day. They had come in the daylight hours at least. Yet it was a nuisance.

After that first call from Vogel or Bogle, or whomever, his calls were always past midnight—two A.M. was his favorite hour.

Within the year I had this unlisted number changed—not due to Vogel or Bogle, however. I began to receive, day and night, occasional mysterious communications. They were succinct, to the point, no greeting or sign-off. Just "Corner of 8th and Chillocothe, four P.M. sharp," or some other location, never the same. "Bus station, baggage box 67, key's in the lock." "Hogger's Restaurant, first table on the left, eight P.M." This sounded ominous.

Shortly after I had the new number Vogel—or was it Bogle?—called. He had his methods. I recognized his voice.

"You again."

"About the obit."

"This is getting to be a nuisance," I said, and added, "A health hazard. I am not as young as I used to be. Are you aware of the hour? If I'm waked up in the middle of the night I might not be able to sleep another wink."

"Hard on me, too," he said. "I'm growing older than you. It's all in your behalf. What was it T. S. Eliot said? Something about going out with a bang not a whimper. That's what I'm trying to help you with."

"Let me tell you something," I said. "I'll let you in on something that has just happened. A professor at the university has compiled and published an anthology—vanity press, naturally—of seventy-eight poets who were born or have resided in this state. This will tell you my present status. I was not accounted worthy to be included."

"You were somebody once," was the reply. "You may be again. Poets are forever. Take John Donne—was he the king of the hill when he died? The world hadn't heard of him. He's somebody now."

"All I am is a tinkerer—a tinkerer with words. As for recognition, the little I had, that will be all."

"You're not thinking hard enough. There's something you've done or are doing that lifts you above the mundane."

"I tinker, as I said. And garden. Should have been a botanist. I have a primitive desire to dig in the earth and plant seeds. To grow things. Will that do for your purposes?"

"Don't tell me all that stuff. I know it already. Dull, dull. You know what I want. Keep thinking," he advised and hung up.

By the third year, I had still not been able to contribute to his obit on me. Then I had a bit of gratuitous information. The *Gary Independent* had been sold to a Chicago publishing house. They had bought only the subscription list, and the morgue. He was out as a reporter but could still capitalize on the obits he had in process. Obits were always in process until the death of the subject. And the price was up: one hundred dollars per obit.

There were other calls. One from St. Louis. He was retired, living on his retirement benefits, his obits his only employment. He was at a sister's home.

"Who's paying for this call?"

"Goes on the house billing, naturally."

How to get this man off my back? It no longer mattered. It happened almost unintentionally. While I didn't particularly welcome the calls in the night, by this time I had become something of an insomniac, and I began to indulge the old codger. I knew he was old, being five years my elder, and a quaver had developed in his voice. I had never gotten his name for certain, no longer tried. And I'd tease him about who was paying for the long-distance call until he'd reply, "Not me, and that's not the subject." He was always forthright.

During these years I had moved to a small town, then into the country where I could bring my gardening skills into full play. With both moves I acquired new telephone numbers, listed ones. Had they not been listed, he would have acquired them. He had his methods.

One day I had summoned the county agriculturist agent to come test the mineral content of a garden plot where I had fought goat's-foot morning glories for years. I'd cut them down to a stalk, year by year, never allowing them to seed themselves. I told the agent of my victory over the goat's-foot and said, facetiously, "I'm afraid I'm going to lose seed of them." The agent laughed and said, "We can't allow that to happen." I had been to war with this noxious vine. I came to miss it. Given time, my enmity had mellowed.

That night there was a call toward four A.M. Vogel or Bogle hadn't called for more than a year, and I wasn't certain of the caller.

"Is this from the morgue?"

"Right," said the speaker.

I didn't indulge in chitchat. "I think I have something for you."

"Shoot."

"Reckon you know about the government having seed banks at several locations around the country, to keep old varieties of vegetable and crop seed from being lost?"

"Say on."

"Well, I'm afraid the goat's-foot morning glory is going to be lost to the world. I've started my own seed bank to save this unappreciated bane of the agricultural world."

The voice on the other end of the line exploded, "That's it! Not dynamite, but a firecracker. It'll have to do. What I have been waiting for. Good for one hundred bucks! All poets have some eccentricity. This is yours. Now you can die. But take your time."

I fired back, "And your eccentricity is collecting dynamite caps."

The telephone clicked off.

I never heard from him again.

Acknowledgments

A number of people helped to make *The Hills Remember* possible, and I thank them all: Teresa Perry Reynolds, whose support of this and other James Still–related projects is deeply appreciated by all who value Still's writings; the staff at the University Press of Kentucky—Laura Sutton, Ashley Runyon, Steve Wrinn, Allison Webster, Ila McEntire, and Fred "Mack" McCormick—for guiding this project through the publishing process; Jonathan Greene, of Gnomon Press, for permitting republication of the Still stories from *Pattern of a Man*; Ruth Hausman, Steven Solomon, Whitney Mays, and Tiffany WIlliams, for clerical assistance; the staff at the University of Kentucky James Still Collection office, for help in the acquisition of never-before-published Still manuscripts; the staff at East Tennessee State University's Interlibrary Loan Services, for help in the acquisition of previously published Still texts; and Kathy H. Olson, for moral support throughout this project.

Publications

"These Goodly Things." *The Better Home* 1, no. 3 (July-August-September 1935): 15.

"All Their Ways Are Dark." *Atlantic* 157, no. 6 (June 1936): 708–12. Incorporated into *River of Earth*.

"Horse Doctor." *Frontier and Midland* 17, no. 1 (Autumn 1936): 25–28.

"Bare-Bones." *Appalachian Heritage* 38, no. 4 (Fall 2010): 21–24.

"One Leg Gone to Judgment." *Mountain Life and Work* 12, no. 3 (October 1936): 9–10.

"A Bell on Troublesome Creek." *The Better Home* 2, no. 4 (October-November-December 1936): 3.

"On Defeated Creek" [later "The Scrape"]. *Frontier and Midland* 17, no. 2 (Winter 1936–37): 120–24.

"The Quare Day." *Household Magazine* 37, no. 1 (January 1937): 36.

"Job's Tears." *Atlantic* 159, no. 3 (March 1937): 353–58. Reprinted in *The O. Henry Memorial Award Stories of 1937*, ed. by Harry Hansen (Garden City, N.Y.: Doubleday, Doran and Co., 1937): 211–21. Incorporated into *River of Earth*.

"The Egg Tree." *Yale Review* 27, no. 1 (September 1937): 100–109. Reprinted in *The Yale Review Anthology,* ed. by Wilbur Cross and Helen MacAfee (Freeport, N.Y.: Books for Libraries Press, 1942, 1970): 354–63. Incorporated into *River of Earth*.

"Lost Brother." *Frontier and Midland* 18, no. 1 (Autumn 1937): 13–16.

"Brother to Methuselum." *Story* 11, no. 64 (November 1937): 45–52. Reprinted in *Kentucky Monthly* 2, no. 7 (July 1999): 48–52.

"So Large a Thing as Seven." *Virginia Quarterly Review* 14, no. 1 (Winter 1938): 17–25. Reprinted in *The O. Henry Memorial Award Stories of 1938,* ed. by Harry Hansen (Garden City, N.Y.: Doubleday, Doran and Co., 1938): 267–76. Incorporated into *River of Earth*.

"Mole-Bane." *Atlantic* 161, no. 3 (March 1938): 372–74. Incorporated into *River of Earth*.

"Journey to the Settlement" [later "Journey to the Forks"]. *Mountain Life and Work* 14, no. 1 (April 1938): 11–13. Reprinted in a pamphlet published by the Hindman Settlement School, Fall 1938; in *Read* 1, no. 2 (April 1941): 5–6; and in *Short Short Stories*, ed. by William Ransom Wood (New York: Harcourt, 1951): 57–62.

"Uncle Jolly." *Atlantic* 162, no. 1 (July 1938): 68–71. Incorporated into *River of Earth*.

"Bat Flight." *Saturday Evening Post* 211, no. 10 (3 September 1938): 12–13, 50–51. Reprinted in *The O. Henry Memorial Award Stories of 1939*, ed. by Harry Hansen (Garden City, N.Y.: Doubleday, Doran and Co., 1939): 31–48. Incorporated into *River of Earth*.

"Pigeon Pie." *Frontier and Midland* 19, no. 1 (Autumn 1938): 44–45. Incorporated into *River of Earth*.

"Twelve Pears Hanging High." *Mountain Life and Work* 15, no. 1 (April 1939): 14–18. Incorporated into *River of Earth*.

"Two Eyes, Two Pennies." *Saturday Evening Post* 211, no. 40 (1 April 1939): 12–13, 94–95, 97. Incorporated into *River of Earth*.

"Sugar in the Gourd" [later "On Quicksand Creek" and "The Dumb-Bull"]. *Prairie Schooner* 13, no. 2 (Summer 1939): 99–104.

"The Ploughing" [later "Simon Brawl"]. *Atlantic* 164, no. 6 (December 1939): 776–78. Reprinted in *Read* 42, no. 16 (15 April 1959): 21–23. Incorporated into *River of Earth*.

"The Force Put." Excerpt from *River of Earth* (1940). Published under current title in *Sporty Creek: A Novel about an Appalachian Boyhood* (1977).

"I Love My Rooster" [later "Low Glory"]. *Saturday Evening Post* 212, no. 40 (13 April 1940): 16–17, 62, 64, 70–71.

"Snail Pie." *American Mercury* 50 (June 1940): 209–14.

"The Moving." *North Georgia Review* 5, nos. 3–4 (Winter 1940–41): 18–20. Reprinted in *Wind* (1974–1976): 87.

"The Proud Walkers." *Saturday Evening Post* 213, no. 45 (10 May 1941): 111–14. Reprinted in *The O. Henry Memorial Award Stories of 1941*, ed. by Herschel Brickell (New York: Book League of America, 1941): 289–304.

"The Stir-Off." *Mountain Life and Work* 17, no. 3 (Fall 1941): 1–7.

On Troublesome Creek. New York: Viking Press, 1941. 190 pp. Contents include "I Love My Rooster," "The Proud Walkers," "Locust Summer," "The Stir-Off," "On Quicksand Creek" [originally "Sugar in the Gourd"], "Journey to the Forks" [originally "Journey to the Settlement"], "Brother to Methuselum," "Snail Pie," "The Moving," and "The Scrape" [originally "On Defeated Creek"].

"Hit Like to 'a' Killed Me." *Louisville Courier-Journal* (19 April 1942): 22.

"Mrs. Razor." *Atlantic* 176, no. 1 (July 1945): 52–53. Reprinted in *The Best American Short Stories,* ed. by Martha Foley (Boston: Houghton Mifflin, 1946): 419–24; in *The Pocket Atlantic,* ed. by Edward Weeks (New York: Pocket Books, 1946): 68–72; in *Mountain Life and Work* 30, no. 3 (Summer 1954): 34–37; in *Deep Summer: A Collection of New Writing,* ed. by Albert Stewart (Morehead, Ky.: Morehead State College Press, 1963): 30–33; in *23 Modern Stories,* ed. by Barbara Howes (New York: Vintage Books, 1963): 87–91; in *The World of Psychoanalysis,* Vol. 1, ed. by Gloria B. Levitas (New York: George Braziller, 1965): 1084–87; in *Statement* (Spring 1967): 25–26; and in *Appalachian Heritage* 8, no. 2 (Spring 1980): 47–49.

"Cedar of Lebanon" [later "The Sharp Tack"]. *American Mercury* 62 (March 1946): 292–95.

"Maybird Upshaw." *American Mercury* 63 (August 1946): 61–66.

"Pattern of a Man." *Yale Review* 36 (Autumn 1946): 93–100. Reprinted in *Troublesome Creek Times* (13 May 1981).

"School Butter." *Virginia Quarterly Review* 22, no. 4 (Autumn 1946): 561–69.

"The Nest." *Prairie Schooner* 22, no. 1 (Spring 1948): 53–56. Reprinted in *Mountain Life and Work* 44, no. 1 (November 1968): 13–16; and in *Home and Beyond: An Anthology of Kentucky Short Stories,* ed. by Morris A. Grubbs (Lexington: University Press of Kentucky, 2001): 31–36.

"A Master Time." *Atlantic* 183, no. 1 (January 1949): 43–46. Reprinted in *The Best American Short Stories,* ed. by Martha Foley (Boston: Houghton Mifflin, 1950): 390–98; and in *Voices from the Hills: Selected Readings of Southern Appalachia,* ed. by Robert J. Higgs and Ambrose N. Manning (New York: Frederick Ungar Publishing Company, 1975): 253–62.

"A Ride on the Short Dog." *Atlantic* 188, no. 1 (July 1951): 55–58. Reprinted in

The Best American Short Stories, ed. by Martha Foley (Boston: Houghton Mifflin, 1952): 298–304; in *American Accent,* ed. by Elizabeth Abell (New York: Ballantine Books, 1954): 101–9; and in *Appalachian Heritage* 2, no. 4, and 3, no. 1 (Fall-Winter 1974–75): 136–40.

"The Fun Fox." *Woman's Day* 16, no. 12 (September 1953): 101, 137–41. Reprinted in *Mountain Life and Work,* 44, no. 4 (May 1968): 12–15.

"The Burning of the Waters" [later "Tight Hollow"]. *Atlantic* 198, no. 4 (October 1956): 55–60. Reprinted in *Mountain Life and Work* 45, no. 7 (July 1969): 11–17.

"The Run for the Elbertas." *Atlantic* 204, no. 1 (July 1959): 46–53. Reprinted in *The Landrum Leader* [Landrum, S.C.] 6, no. 12 (21 April 1960): 6; and in *Appalachian Journal* 6, no. 2 (Winter 1979): 142–55.

"Encounter on Keg Branch." *Mountain Life and Work* 45, no. 2 (February 1969): 15.

Pattern of a Man and Other Stories. Lexington, Ky.: Gnomon Press, 1976. 122 pp. Contents include "Mrs. Razor," "A Master Time," "Snail Pie," "A Ride on the Short Dog," "The Nest," "Pattern of a Man," "Maybird Upshaw," "The Sharp Tack" [originally "Cedar of Lebanon"], "Brother to Methuselum," "The Scrape" [originally "On Defeated Creek"], and "Encounter on Keg Branch."

Sporty Creek: A Novel about an Appalachian Boyhood. New York: G. P. Putnam's Sons, 1977. 125 pp. Illustrated by Janet McCaffrey. Short stories arranged as a novel; contents include "Simon Brawl" [originally "The Ploughing"], "School Butter," "Low Glory" [originally "I Love My Rooster"], "The Moving," "The Force Put" [excerpt from *River of Earth*], "Locust Summer," "The Dumb-Bull" [originally "Sugar in the Gourd" and "On Quicksand Creek"], "Plank Town," "Tight Hollow" [originally "Burning of the Waters"], and "Journey to the Forks" [originally "Journey to the Settlement"].

The Run for the Elbertas. Lexington: University Press of Kentucky, 1980. 144 pp. Foreword by Cleanth Brooks. Collection of short stories; contents include "I Love My Rooster," "The Proud Walkers," "Locust Summer," "Journey to the Forks" [originally "Journey to the Settlement"], "On Quicksand Creek" [originally "Sugar in the Gourd"], "The Stir-Off," "The Burning of the Waters," "School Butter," "The Moving," "One Leg Gone to Judgment," "The Quare Day," "The Fun Fox," and "The Run for the Elbertas."